Praise for R̶̶̶̶̶̶̶̶̶̶̶̶̶̶̶̶̶̶ vels

"The caring nat
is well demonst

—*RT Book Reviews* on *Noah's Sweetheart*

"*A Wife for Jacob* is sweet and reminds readers
that love is a gift."

—*RT Book Reviews*

"*Jedidiah's Bride* reminds readers to
count their blessings despite life's hurdles."

—*RT Book Reviews*

Praise for Alison Stone and her novels

"[A] well-researched tale with an engaging pace…
it contains sweet romance, palpable suspense."

—*RT Book Reviews* on *Plain Peril*

"Stone is off to a strong start with this Love Inspired
Suspense debut."

—*RT Book Reviews* on *Plain Pursuit*

"Stone creates a great balance of action and
romance, coupled with some interesting twists."

—*RT Book Reviews* on *Silver Lake Secrets*

Rebecca Kertz was first introduced to the Amish when her husband took a job with an Amish construction crew. She enjoyed watching the Amish foreman's children at play and swapping recipes with his wife. Rebecca resides in Delaware with her husband and dog. She has strong faith in God and feels blessed to have family nearby. Besides writing, she enjoys reading, doing crafts and visiting Lancaster County.

Alison Stone lives with her husband of more than twenty years and their four children in western New York. Besides writing, Alison keeps busy volunteering at her children's schools, driving her girls to dance and watching her boys race motocross. Alison loves to hear from her readers at Alison@AlisonStone.com. For more information please visit her website, alisonstone.com. She's also chatty on Twitter, @Alison_Stone. Find her on Facebook at facebook.com/alisonstoneauthor.

Noah's Sweetheart

Rebecca Kertz

and

Plain Peril

Alison Stone

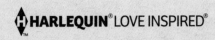

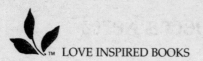

™ LOVE INSPIRED BOOKS

PLEASE RECYCLE · THIS PRODUCT IS RECYCLABLE ·

Recycling programs for this product may not exist in your area.

ISBN-13: 978-0-373-83815-8

Noah's Sweetheart and Plain Peril

Copyright © 2016 by Harlequin Books S.A.

The publisher acknowledges the copyright holders of the individual works as follows:

Noah's Sweetheart
Copyright © 2013 by Rebecca Kertz

Plain Peril
Copyright © 2015 by Alison Stone

www.Harlequin.com

Printed in U.S.A.

CONTENTS

NOAH'S SWEETHEART

Rebecca Kertz

For Judith, with love

And now, Lord, what wait I for?
My hope is in thee.
—*Psalms* 39:7

Chapter One

Spring... Lancaster County, Pennsylvania

Rachel Hostetler watched as Aaron Troyer took her small black valise and loaded it into the carriage.

"If you'll wait in the buggy, Rachel, my sister Martha will soon join you."

"*Danki,* Aaron." Securing the ties of her Sunday-best black bonnet, Rachel nervously chewed on her lower lip.

"Don't worry," he said. "Martha don't take up much room."

"I'm sure she doesn't." Rachel felt her stomach tighten with trepidation. It wasn't the size of Martha that concerned her. It was the type of carriage. The only vehicle available to take her from Lancaster to Happiness was this small single bench-seat buggy, the same type used for courting by the Old Order Amish. Back in Ohio, she'd ridden frequently with Abraham Beiler in a similar buggy when he was walking out with her...until the accident over a year ago that had changed her life forever.

She hadn't ridden in an open courting buggy since, preferring the safety of her family's enclosed carriage.

She didn't want to ride in one now, but it seemed that she had no choice. It was the only way for her to get to the village of Happiness and her new position as schoolteacher there.

Without thought, she slipped her hand inside her black traveling cape to touch a protective hand to her midsection. Some things just couldn't be forgotten, no matter how hard she tried. But scared or not, she'd just have to do it. It wouldn't do to start off here in this new place being a coward.

The horse shifted restlessly; Rachel gasped and retreated a few steps. *Don't be a goose,* she told herself. The bay looked like a perfectly sensible animal. But she couldn't help offering a silent prayer.

"Please, Lord, protect me from all evil," she whispered. *No matter what form evil takes.*

She stared at the buggy, took a deep breath, grabbed hold of the side and climbed on board.

"It's nice of you to drive us to town, Noah." Charlotte King smiled at her neighbor and childhood friend. "*Mam* needs more flour and cinnamon for tomorrow's baking, and *Dat* is too busy repairing the windmill to take me."

Noah nodded. "I know your *dat* is busy, Charlotte. I enjoy going to town. 'Tis no inconvenience to take you."

"And me?" Charlotte's little brother piped up.

"*Ja,* Joshua. Nice to have you along as well." He reached back and tugged the boy's straw hat down over his eyes, and Joshua giggled.

The spring sunshine felt warm against Noah's face as he steered the wagon along the blacktop road toward Bird-in-Hand. The surrounding farmland was beautiful, with spring growth in various stages. Songbirds filled the air with nature's music, and the scent of the earth permeated from the surrounding farms. Only once did the roar of a big truck that passed the buggy, blowing black from its exhaust pipes, drown out the quiet of the fields.

It was a good day for a drive; the fact that the day was to be spent in Charlotte's company only made it better. They'd be running errands for his father as well as Charlotte's mother. When Samuel Lapp had heard that Noah would be taking Charlotte to Miller's Store, he'd provided his son with his own list. He would have made the trip in a day or two himself, Samuel Lapp had told Noah, but since Noah was going now…

The three young people chatted easily as they enjoyed the ride. Spying a familiar face behind a plow, Noah lifted a hand in greeting to Abram Peachy, a member of their church.

"Nice morning for plowing, Abram. See you got an early start."

The man nodded. "Hope the weather holds out until we're done planting." His eyes focused briefly on Charlotte before shifting back to Noah beside her. "Morning, Charlotte," he said.

"Morning, Abram," Charlotte called. "How are the children?"

The widower's gaze softened. "They are doing well. 'Tis nice of you to ask."

"We're going to town!" Joshua said. "We're going to get ice cream!"

"Joshua!" Charlotte scolded with a quick look at Noah.

"I like ice cream," the boy insisted.

"You're not to pester Noah for ice cream every time

we ride into town with him," Charlotte warned. "Last time was a special treat." And to Noah, she said, "You'll spoil him rotten."

Noah winked at Joshua. "We men have to stick together, *ja?*"

Joshua giggled again and slid back on the bench seat. *"Ja."* With an impish grin at his sister, he began tapping his shoes against the floor.

"Sometimes I think you're no older than he is," Charlotte teased.

"But you like me anyway." Noah grinned at Charlotte, who couldn't help grinning back. "We're going for ice cream," he told Abram. "You have a *gut* day now."

The older man waved and then slapped the reins over the horse's back. The big Belgian walked on, and the plow cut a deep furrow in the rich, dark earth.

"A good farm, he has," Charlotte said.

"And a good farmer. A pity Abram lost his wife so young."

"God's will is sometimes hard to understand," Charlotte agreed.

It was easy to drive the wagon through the countryside. As they approached town, the number of cars on the road increased, and Noah had to handle the wagon more carefully. This area of Lancaster County invited tourists, who often didn't realize the danger of passing a horse and carriage at a great rate of speed. Fortunately, on this day, the cars they encountered slowed down appropriately. Perhaps it was the warmth of the spring day that had captured everyone's fancy on this Tuesday. Whatever the reason, Noah was able to relax and enjoy the ride and Charlotte and Joshua's company.

They bought their supplies in several small shops

and then drove along the stretch of road from Miller's Store toward the village of Intercourse, where they would enjoy their ice cream. Joshua could barely contain himself; he was so excited to eat his favorite treat. Charlotte gently reprimanded her younger brother, instructing him to be still.

A dog barked ahead. A horse whinnied and then snorted. Noah heard a high-pitched scream as he saw a spooked horse rear back before bolting at a dead run in their direction. He caught sight of a woman's pale face under a bonnet as the open four-wheeled buggy came barreling down the road. He felt a thundering in his chest as he immediately saw the danger she was in.

"Charlotte, take the reins!" he said as he pulled his wagon off the road.

"Noah!" Charlotte exclaimed with alarm as Noah bounded from the wagon. "Be careful!"

But he was already running out to try and stop the panicked horse before the buggy overturned. Fear lodged in his throat at the glimpse of the terrified young Amish woman who sat in the buggy, clutching one side with white-knuckled fingers.

The horse raced closer, its ironclad hooves pounding the road. Noah shifted right, out of its path, at the last moment and then jumped to grab the animal's harness. He cried out with triumph as he got a firm handhold. *Please, Lord, give me strength!* He fought to hold on as the horse continued its runaway pace. Struggling not to become entangled in the gear, he levered himself onto the horse, gripping its sides with his legs to hold on to his seat.

The animal neighed in angry protest. Heart pounding, Noah leaned low against the horse's neck to grab hold of the reins. Successful, he straightened, pulling back on the leather straps.

"Whoa!" he called. *"Schtupp!"* He applied pressure slowly but firmly. The horse jerked and fought before breaking into a trot and finally a walk as he continued to murmur soothingly. "Gently. Take it slow, now. *Gut* boy!"

At last, the carriage rolled to a stop, still upright, as the animal finally obeyed the command, and Noah felt a sudden rush of relief. Once the horse was calm, he turned to check on the buggy's terrified passenger.

"Are you hurt?" he asked.

She gasped for breath, unable to answer. He saw only the top of her black bonnet as she bent forward, hugging herself with her arms.

He climbed down from the horse carefully, patting the animal's neck, speaking to it softly, reassuringly.

"Noah, you could have been killed." A man ran up to help Noah. He took hold of the horse's bridle, freeing Noah from the task.

"Danki, William," Noah said, recognizing a neighbor and fellow church member, William Mast. He didn't want to think about what could have happened if things hadn't gone his way.

With growing concern, he approached the occupant in the buggy, stopping at her side. "Are you hurt?" he repeated softly.

Sitting back, she shook her head. *"Nay."*

"What happened to spook your horse?"

He watched her pull herself together enough to stiffen. "Not my horse," she replied. "Not my buggy."

She met his gaze head-on, and he felt a jolt. She had lovely dark eyes, but her pallor was sickly, and he saw that she trembled. "I'm sorry," he said, not really knowing for what. "Are you cold?" He stood back and took off his coat, placing it over her shoulders and around her. "You are shaking."

She released a solid breath. "I could have been killed. You saved me. *Danki*." A shy smile lit up her face, and in that moment he felt his pulse quicken as he noticed every little detail about her…the warmth of her chocolate-brown gaze, the whiteness of her smooth skin, her small nose… the rosy pink of her lips…the glimpse of her white *kapp* beneath her black traveling bonnet. The sweep of hair from a center part across her forehead was dark. She wore a black cape over a dress of spring green.

"I was happy to help." He offered his hand to help the woman alight from the buggy. He sensed her hesitation for only a moment, and then he felt the warmth of her fingertips as she accepted his assistance.

"Rachel!" Aaron Troyer approached at a run. He nodded at William, who gave possession of the horse's bridle to its owner. The animal's sides were caked with sweat, and it was trembling all over.

"Are you all right?" Aaron asked Rachel as he ran his hand over the horse's neck and murmured soothingly to it.

"I am fine, Aaron. Thanks to—"

"Noah," Noah supplied. "Noah Lapp."

"Noah," Aaron said, out of breath. "I'm grateful." Then to the woman he said, "I didn't realize that Josef would be so easily scared. My brother meant for you and Martha to take Daisy."

"Is Josef all right?" She appeared concerned.

"*Ja,* with some care, he will be fine."

"Noah! Noah! Are you hurt?" Charlotte called out

from the wagon seat. "*You could have been killed!* When I saw you jump onto that horse, I was afraid you'd fall and be crushed—" She had steered the wagon to within yards from where the buggy had come to a full stop.

"You doubt my ability with horses?" he teased. Upon seeing her expression, he sobered. "I'm fine, Charlotte."

Charlotte's gaze settled on the woman standing next to the buggy and her eyes widened. "*Rachel?* Rachel Hostetler?"

The woman seemed to search her memory before her features brightened. "Charlotte!" she exclaimed. "I am surprised that you got my message so quickly."

"We didn't." Charlotte climbed down from the wagon. "We were in town to pick up supplies for *Mam* and Noah's *vadder*. We didn't expect you to arrive until tomorrow."

"The English driver my family hired had to leave a day earlier. He had a family emergency and apologized that he couldn't drive me directly to Happiness. He left me at Troyers' Buggy Excursions. I called the number your *mam* sent me from a payphone while I waited for a ride."

"*Ja.*" Charlotte nodded. "Whittier's Store. They take messages for us."

Surprised, Noah watched and listened to the exchange with growing interest. The two women talked as if there was no one else around. "Charlotte?"

Charlotte looked startled as if she suddenly remembered there were others nearby, waiting for an introduction.

"Noah, this is Rachel Hostetler. She is our new *schuul* teacher—" Charlotte smiled "—and my cousin. Aaron—it seems that you have already met."

"You're Charlotte's kin?" Noah asked, pleased to learn that he'd be seeing more of her. Rachel nodded. "And you are a schoolteacher," he said. "At our Happiness school?"

Rachel studied him and nodded. *"Ja."*

"Welcome to Lancaster County," he said. "Come. We'll take you home."

The intensity of Noah's regard captured her gaze. Feeling her cheeks heat, Rachel quickly looked away. She felt the warmth of his coat and, embarrassed, she removed it and handed it back to him.

"Rachel, let's go," Charlotte urged, drawing Rachel's attention and saving her from acting foolish. "You will come with us—*ja?*"

"We're going for ice cream," Joshua said.

"I don't know now, Joshua," his sister said. "Rachel has had a terrible fright. She may want to go straight home."

Rachel studied the young boy seated in the back of the wagon. "You're Joshua—and such a big boy! I'm your cousin Rachel. We've never met. The last time I saw your sister was years ago, when we were eleven and twelve, I think." She looked to Charlotte, who nodded.

"We're not going for ice cream?" Young Joshua looked crestfallen.

"No, I think I'd like to have ice cream," Rachel said, and then asked Joshua, "What kinds can we choose from?"

She did feel a bit shaky, she realized, as Joshua began to list the many flavors of ice cream available, but she didn't mind stopping for the treat first. It might help to put away the thought of what could have happened if not for the sudden appearance of Noah Lapp.

Rachel sensed the intensity of her rescuer's look, but refused to meet his gaze. She felt as though she was still wrapped in the warmth of his coat.

"Let's go, then," Noah said quietly. "I'll get your bag."

Only then did she glance his way. His soft, quick smile in her direction did odd things to her insides.

"Are you certain, Rachel?" Charlotte asked.

She nodded at her cousin. "I have the Lord to thank for my safety. The Lord and your friend Noah Lapp."

"I'm so glad that *Mam* needed some things in town or we may not have been here when…"

Rachel shuddered.

"I'm sorry, Rachel," Aaron Troyer said.

"No harm done," Rachel assured him with a half smile. "I'm fine."

"Here's your money. Next time you need a ride, there will be no charge." After Rachel thanked him properly, Aaron left, leaving her alone with her cousins. With Rachel's bag in hand, Noah stopped to speak with Aaron.

"Are you truly all right, Rachel?" Charlotte asked. "I can't believe this happened to you. I can only imagine how you must have felt with the memory of that awful accident last year."

Rachel still felt shaken. "It was a terrible time."

"Ja," Charlotte agreed as they made their way toward the wagon on the side of the road. *"Mam* and *Dat* will be happy to see you. You'll be staying at the house until the cottage near the *schuulhaus* is finished."

"I will like that." Rachel breathed deeply in an attempt to calm her fear as she climbed onto the wagon.

"You have nothing to be afraid of, Rachel," Charlotte told her. "Noah is a *gut* driver."

Rachel nodded. "I know." She glanced in his direction.

The Lord was watching over her. He hadn't abandoned her so far from home. He'd sent her help in the form of Noah Lapp…from Happiness, Pennsylvania. What more could she ask for?

Chapter Two

The aroma of baking bread drew Rachel from the bedroom, which she shared with her cousins Charlotte and Nancy. She had overslept. Last night her sleep had been fraught with memories of the buggy accident that she'd been involved in a year ago, the near accident yesterday…and her unforgettable first encounter with Noah Lapp.

She felt terrible that she hadn't awakened earlier to help with the chores. Her relatives had been kind enough to provide a place for her; earning her keep was the least she could do.

The delicious smell grew stronger and mingled with the tantalizing scents of pies and biscuits as she descended the stairs and neared the kitchen. The warmth from the oven filled the room, surrounding her as she entered, making her feel instantly at ease, taking away some of the feeling of being far from home.

Charlotte, Nancy and Aunt Mae were gathered around the flour-dusted kitchen table, kneading dough and assembling pies. There was a streak of flour across Nancy's cheek and a dusting down the front of Charlotte's apron. Tendrils of hair had escaped from beneath their black *kapps* and their cheeks were flushed from the heat of the oven, but they didn't seem to notice or care, so intent were they on the tasks at hand. Nancy looked a lot like her older sister, but her hair was brown whereas Charlotte's was golden. Both had pretty blue eyes and ready grins.

Aunt Mae looked spotless. She wore a white *kapp* and her light brown hair in a bun from a center part that was drawn back more severely than Nancy's and Charlotte's. But there was a softness about Mae's expression that told Rachel how much her aunt enjoyed working with her daughters. As the King women worked, they chatted happily, giggling at something Nancy and then Charlotte said.

Rachel felt her heart lighten at their laughter as she approached.

After setting a layer of crust on the bottom of a pie pan, Charlotte looked up and saw her. "Rachel. *Gut* morning."

Rachel smiled. "*Gut* morning. May I help?" she asked.

"You're up," Aunt Mae said with satisfaction. "*Ja,* you can help."

"You didn't sleep well," Charlotte said, her gaze sharp as she studied her cousin.

"I'm sorry I overslept."

"You needed your rest," her aunt said. "Would you like breakfast?"

"I'd rather help with the baking."

Grinning, Charlotte and Nancy made room at the table for Rachel. "Here, Rachel," Nancy invited. "You can work here."

Rachel slid between her cousins, grabbed a bowl of

dough, and without instruction began to roll and cut out strips to make lattice for a strawberry pie that Charlotte was assembling. Working in the kitchen, she felt instantly at home.

"It's kind of you to have me." She smiled at her cousins. "I appreciate your sharing."

"We don't mind," Charlotte said. "We are family."

"There is plenty of room," Nancy agreed. "You are comfortable?"

"*Ja.* The bed is *gut.* Yesterday it was a long journey from Millersburg to Lancaster."

"It is a long way. It has been many years since I have visited my brother's family," Aunt Mae agreed. "Your driver? He is a *gut* man?"

"*Ja,* Aunt Mae, he is from Ohio, too, and has family in Lancaster County. We had to leave early, as his brother-in-law is ill and his sister needed help."

"Family is important. I am glad you had a driver who understands that." She glanced at Rachel's handiwork as she kneaded and rolled out pie dough. "Nice work. Your *mudder,* if I recall correctly, was a *gut* cook, but she does not enjoy it in the kitchen much. Who taught you to cook?"

"*Grossmudder.* She loved to bake and insisted I help whenever it was baking day." Rachel had enjoyed cooking and baking with her grandmother. *Grossmudder* had been a perfectionist when it came to her cakes, biscuits and pies, and she had instilled that trait in her eldest granddaughter. And Aunt Mae was right: her *mudder* did not like to cook, but she took care of her family, as a good wife should. Rachel and her siblings always ate well. But it was *Grossmudder* who shared her love of cooking and baking with her granddaughter, imparting a sense of understanding that family and good food went hand in hand.

Rachel began to assemble the pie lattice, placing each dough strip carefully over the filling, spacing each evenly in a lovely woven pattern. When she was done, she stood back to eye her handiwork. "Bread, biscuits and pies," she said with a smile. "Are we having company? Or are these all for family?"

Nancy spoke up. "*Nay.* We sell baked goods to a new shop in Kitchen Kettle Village. We bring them pies at least once or twice a week. Our pies sell well, and the owner is pleased to have them."

"The bread, too? It smells delicious."

Aunt Mae grinned. "The bread is for dinner this evening."

Rachel grinned with pleasure. "I can almost taste it now."

An hour later, Rachel had rolled out dough enough for three pies, made a filling for one crust, cut out biscuits and stirred the ingredients of an upside-down chocolate cake into a pan. The smell of all this good food made her stomach growl.

Charlotte chuckled. "I think you should take time for breakfast."

Her stomach protesting loudly again, Rachel said, "*Ja.* I think you're right."

"Fresh biscuits out of the oven?" Aunt Mae asked.

Rachel's mouth watered. "*Ja.* A fresh biscuit sounds *gut!*"

She ate her biscuit and sipped from her cup of tea.

"Would you like another, Rachel? Or would you like eggs and bacon?"

"*Danki,* but no, Aunt Mae. It's too late for more than

this." She rose with plate in hand to wash it in the dish basin.

Aunt Mae left the house to take Uncle Amos something to drink. Rachel's uncle was working in the fields. The day was again lovely but a little warmer, and Amos would want something to quench his thirst.

As she dried her clean plate, Rachel heard a knock resound loudly on the outside door. She couldn't see who it was as she put away the dish and hung the dish towel over the drying rack.

"Noah!" she heard Nancy exclaim, and Rachel felt her stomach flutter.

"It's nice to see you, Noah," Charlotte said cheerfully. "Would you like a biscuit or piece of pie?"

"I appreciate the offer, but no, Charlotte. After helping *Dat* early in the fields, I ate a huge breakfast."

Rachel heard every word spoken between her cousins and Noah Lapp, but she didn't turn around. With the warmth she felt since Noah's arrival, she knew her cheeks would be blazing red. Besides, he had come to visit with Charlotte, surely. Although both had behaved in the most appropriate manner in town, it seemed clear to Rachel that Charlotte and Noah were sweet on each other.

"*Gut* morning, Rachel." Suddenly Noah was next to her, overwhelming her with his presence. "Are you settling in nicely?"

Forced to meet his regard, she nodded. "*Ja*. My uncle and his family have made me most welcome." He smelled and looked nice, she thought as he turned to speak with Nancy. He must have bathed after working in the fields, for his shirt was clean, as were the dark triblend denim pants that he wore. She tried not to notice the way his suspenders fit over his shoulders. He had a firm jaw and a ready smile. His golden-brown eyes sparkled. His sandy-brown hair looked neatly combed beneath his banded straw hat.

She recalled suddenly how he'd looked yesterday after he'd rescued her: tall, thin but strong enough to leap onto the back of a galloping horse and hold on. He had lost his hat during his wild ride when he'd leaned low for the reins. His hair had become tousled and windswept during his efforts to take control of the runaway horse and buggy. She recalled how her heart had hammered and the relief she'd felt when he'd straightened, triumphant.

Watching him now, she felt the back of her neck tingle. What was wrong with her? *Abraham Beiler. Noah Lapp.* She frowned. Was one man any different from another? She was here as a schoolteacher. She would be content with teaching children other than her own.

Startled by her own thoughts, she glanced to see if anyone was watching her. Her gaze encountered her cousin Nancy, who rewarded her with a little smile.

"Rachel?" Noah's voice brought her attention back to him.

"I can't thank you enough for coming to my rescue."

"It was my pleasure." Noah smiled. Rachel looked well and content…and extremely appealing with flour on her nose and a dusting across the front of her apron. It was good to see that she suffered no lasting effects of her frightening experience the previous day.

"Noah!" Aunt Mae exclaimed as she came in from outside. "I thought I saw you from across the yard."

He reluctantly drew his attention away from Rachel to grin at her aunt. "*Gut* morning, Aunt Mae. I thought to take Rachel over to see the new *schuulhaus*."

"That is a wonderful idea, Noah." Aunt Mae appeared delighted.

"What do you think, Rachel?" Noah asked. "Would you like to see your new *schuul?*"

"Noah and his brothers have worked hard to fix it up for you," Charlotte said.

"That was nice of you, Noah," Rachel said. "*Ja,* I would like to see the *schuulhaus.*"

"It is not far," Nancy said. "It's just off our property and down the road a little ways between our land and the farm belonging to Noah's family."

"Charlotte," Aunt Mae said, "you can go with them. Nancy can finish these pies on her own."

"Are you sure you do not want us to stay and finish?" Rachel asked.

Aunt Mae smiled. "We will be fine. Go and see where you'll be spending a lot of your time soon."

Rachel grinned. "I will enjoy this." To Noah, she said, "I will be with you in a minute. Just let me get cleaned up."

The relief he felt when she agreed to come made Noah realize just how eager he was to show her the *schuul.*

Charlotte and Rachel went upstairs to change their aprons and wash their hands and faces of baking dust. Rachel was the first one downstairs and out the door.

When she stepped outside, she noticed the buggy parked in the yard. It was an enclosed family buggy with a gray roof. Seeing it, she sighed with relief. Two mishaps in small open buggies had made her leery of riding in one again. She and Noah were alone, waiting for Charlotte to join them.

She grinned at Noah. "Nice carriage."

Noah grinned back, pleased by her response. "I

thought after that little accident yesterday that you'd prefer riding in this." Her smile made him feel good inside.

"Danki," she said.

Charlotte soon appeared, and she climbed into the front seat next to Noah, while Rachel climbed into the back.

"And I hitched old Janey. She's twenty-five years old and you couldn't get her out of a trot if you tried." Noah clicked his tongue, slapped the reins, and the carriage took off down the dirt lane toward the main road.

Rachel sat behind Noah, aware of his straw-brimmed hat, his sandy-brown hair cut in the bowl-cap style that all the Old Order Amish men wore.

Charlotte turned around to smile at her. "I think you will like the schoolhouse. Samuel Lapp and his sons built a new one, large enough for all of the school-aged children in our church district. The Lapp men are good carpenters. Noah is the best, after his *vadder.*"

"How many brothers do you have, Noah?" Rachel asked.

"Six," he said with his eyes still on the road. They had come to the end of the lane and he steered the buggy left onto the paved street. "Jedidiah is the eldest, then I am next." He turned his head to flash her a quick smile before his gaze returned to the road.

"The Samuel Lapps include Samuel's seven sons and one daughter," Charlotte said. "Hannah is only six months old."

"You will meet them all on Sunday," Noah said. "It's visiting Sunday, and some of our friends will meet at our family farm."

The clip-clop of the horse's hooves was the only sound in the buggy for a time, allowing Rachel to digest what she had learned. Noah pulled the carriage off the blacktop and onto a dirt drive that ran next to a white building with a front porch.

"The *schuulhaus*," Charlotte announced.

Charlotte got out on the right side of the vehicle. Noah climbed down and offered his hand to Rachel. "Welcome to your new *schuul*."

Conscious of Noah's relationship with Charlotte, Rachel smiled as she ignored his hand and stepped out of the buggy on her own. She studied the building with excitement. This was her school! Soon, it would be filled with her students!

"It is very nice," she said sincerely. "The nicest *schuulhaus* I've ever seen."

Noah looked pleased. "Let's go inside."

They heard hammering as they approached. "Jedidiah or *Dat* is finishing up," Noah said.

The door swung in easily, and Rachel and Charlotte followed Noah inside. An older man with hammer in hand was bent low over a floorboard. *"Dat,"* Noah greeted.

"Noah, you have brought our new schoolteacher."

"Ja, this is Rachel Hostetler," Noah introduced. "Rachel, my *vadder*—Samuel Lapp."

Rachel nodded. "It is nice to meet you. You have done a *gut* job with this school. I am happy to see it."

Samuel's eyes sparkled in a face that was an older version of his son Noah's, except for the beard that edged his chin. As in Rachel's Ohio Amish community, married men wore beards along their chins, but not on their upper lips. "Come in. Come in and look about. There is much for you to see."

The interior of the one-room schoolhouse was white

and smelled of fresh paint and newly varnished wood. Someone had been thoughtful enough to hang posters of the alphabet printed on lines like those on primary writing paper. There were also numbers from one to ten. Beside the schoolroom door, there were built-in glass-fronted cabinets. The community or school board had been kind enough to fill the shelves with books.

Noah and Charlotte talked with Samuel while Rachel wandered about, studying her surroundings.

What captured her heart the most were the rows of student desks—five rows of eight, all newly crafted, stained and varnished and ready for use. Her heart gave a little leap as Rachel saw the teacher's desk at the front of the class. It was a beautiful piece of furniture, made with care. She approached the desk and ran her fingers over the smooth, varnished surface.

"You like the desk?" Noah asked, suddenly beside her.

Rachel had sensed him instantly. She glanced over at him and nodded. "It is a wonderful desk." Her gaze flashed briefly to the other side of the room and Charlotte, who was grinning at something Noah's father had said. Her attention returned to Noah standing next to her. "It is beautiful."

"I'm glad you like it. I made it."

"You did?" She was impressed. "You are not only a carpenter but a cabinetmaker as well?"

Noah shrugged, downplaying his enjoyment of creating something wonderful from a few blocks of wood, of running his fingers over the smooth, polished surface as he eyed the finished product. "I like making furniture. My *grossdaddi* makes wonderful furniture. Many come from miles around to buy his chairs and tables."

"A fine craft he has—as do you." She awarded him a smile. "I will enjoy the desk."

Noah felt a rush of pleasure. He didn't know what it was about Rachel, but he was feeling things he'd never felt before. He became aware of a sudden desire to confide in her, to tell her about his dream of opening his own furniture shop someday. "Rachel—" he began, but stopped at Charlotte's approach.

"Do you like the new school?" Charlotte asked.

"*Ja.* It will be a good place to teach the children." She eyed the number of desks. "Are there that many children who will attend school?"

Charlotte chuckled. "Not yet, but the bishop wanted to make sure that there would be room for more in the future."

Rachel felt a sigh of relief. "There are forty desks."

"*Ja,* but only thirty-one children," Charlotte said and then laughed when she saw her cousin's astonished expression.

"It is a good thing we have the room, then," Rachel agreed. *Thirty-one children!* It was going to be an interesting school year, she thought.

"Rachel," Noah said. "Let us show you where your house will be."

She turned to Noah's father. "It is a wonderful *schuulhaus,* Samuel. I appreciate all that you and your sons have done."

Samuel graciously accepted Rachel's thanks. "I will see you on Sunday, Rachel, if not before."

"*Ja,*" she said with a nod. "I will see you on Sunday."

Then she followed Noah and Charlotte outside and they headed farther down the dirt lane in the opposite direction from where they had parked the buggy.

Chapter Three

They walked in silence; the only sounds were the crunch of their shoes against dirt and gravel, the distant tapping of a hammer coming from inside the school, and the sweet chirping of a robin redbreast.

Rachel, pleased with the schoolhouse, could hardly wait to see where she would live as the teacher. She wasn't expecting anything fancy. She needed only the basics to make a home. Whatever her family district provided, she'd be grateful for.

They'd not gone far when she'd spied the building. She gasped in wonder. It was a small cottage, slightly bigger than the schoolhouse with white siding, working dark blue window shutters and a matching blue door. She couldn't help the silly grin that spread to her lips. "This is the teacher's house?"

"Ja." Noah gazed at her with a smile. "Do you like it?"

Rachel nodded, still grinning. "It is lovely." It was unusual for the school board to build a house for the teacher. Usually the teacher was selected from among the members of the community, but Rachel was from

Millersburg, Ohio, far away. Was that why she would have her own house as long as she continued to teach here? *Lord, thank You for Your blessings.*

"It will be the right size for you, *ja?*" Charlotte said. Rachel saw that her cousin looked happy for her.

"It is perfect," Rachel agreed. She was eager to get a closer look. "Is it safe to go inside?"

"*Ja,* we can go in and look around," Noah said, "but I don't want you to be disappointed. The outside is finished, but the inside is not."

As she stepped into the interior of the house, Rachel felt a sense of home. There were only wooden studs where the walls would be, but she could see the size of each room and the opening of each doorway. Her imagination finished the rest for her.

"I'm sorry it is not done yet," Noah apologized.

Rachel met his gaze. "I'm not," she said sincerely. "I will enjoy watching each stage of construction." And she could help. She wasn't afraid of hard work.

"*Dat* thought it would be best to get the *schuulhaus* finished first," Noah said as he led the way to the back of the house and into a room that, Rachel decided after judging its size, must be the kitchen. "The old *schuulhaus* burned to the ground last summer." He waited for Charlotte, who had stopped to gaze out a window, to catch up. Once she joined them, he continued on. "We will work on the house next. We have been busy planting, but we will do our best to get it done for you soon."

"I'm grateful." Rachel rewarded her cousin with a smile. "As long as Charlotte doesn't mind sharing, I don't mind waiting for the house. It is fun to spend time with my Lancaster County family."

Charlotte grinned back. "And we like having our cousin stay with us."

Noah gave the two cousins a guided tour and then showed them the yard out back. "You will be able to plant a vegetable garden here. There is plenty of room. I'll be glad to come over and plow an area for you. And look—" He pointed to two spreading, flowering trees with white blossoms, not far from the back door. "You will have your own apple trees. They are Braeburn."

"A *gut* all-around apple." Rachel went to examine them more closely. "I will enjoy having apple trees. I can share fresh, crisp apples with the *kinner*. They can eat them during recess."

"And you can make apple pies," Charlotte said. "You make delicious pies."

"I would like a piece of Rachel's apple pie," Noah told Charlotte in a low, teasing undertone.

"I heard that!" Rachel's voice held a hint of laughter.

"You would keep pie from one of the builders of your new house?" Noah said, feigning sadness.

Rachel sighed...loudly. "All right. You can have a piece of my apple pie." Noah's face lit up with eagerness, and Rachel caught her breath at how handsome he looked. Fighting the feeling, she added, "As long as you get my house done before apple season."

"It will be done in a month," Noah promised.

"If he says it will be done, it will be done," Charlotte said when Rachel was skeptical. "The Lapp men are good carpenters."

"Men of many talents," Rachel said softly, thinking of Noah, recalling his skill with her rescue and the desk he'd made for the teacher.

"It is getting late," Noah said. "Aunt Mae will be wondering why I kept you so long."

"Ja," Charlotte said. "There is cooking to be done before we come on Sunday."

Rachel had almost forgotten. They would be spending time at the Lapp farm on Sunday. She would meet not only Noah's mother, but also all of his other kin. She was both terrified and excited by the prospect. Were all of the Lapp brothers as handsome as Noah?

They left the cottage, and it seemed a much shorter walk back to the buggy, where the old mare Janey waited patiently for their return. Rachel climbed into the back of the buggy, conscious of Noah waiting for her and Charlotte to be seated.

"I will be right back," Noah said and he disappeared around to the rear of the schoolhouse. He was back within minutes with two handfuls of wildflowers. Without a word, he gave Charlotte and Rachel each a small bouquet of colorful, delicate blooms.

Rachel remained silent as Charlotte thanked him profusely. The gesture was sweet and thoughtful, and she didn't know what to make of it. No doubt he'd wanted to give flowers to Charlotte but felt it'd be awkward not to give any to Rachel.

Whatever his reasons, Noah had pleased her, and Rachel tried to shut down her feelings. It wouldn't do to like Noah, who was the man in her cousin's life. It wouldn't do to get involved with any man. She had learned a hard lesson from Abraham Beiler, and she should never, ever—could never, ever—forget how awful she'd felt.

Rachel went with the Amos King women to the Lapp farm on Friday. She hadn't expected to visit so soon, but

Katie Lapp had seven sons and only a baby daughter. Katie needed help getting ready for the five families who would come to visit on Sunday.

They had delivered pies to Kitchen Kettle Village on Thursday morning. On Thursday afternoon they had baked two more cakes and four more pies. These treats were for the social.

Rachel had a pie on her lap as Aunt Mae drove the family buggy over to the Lapp farm. It didn't take long to get there. As her aunt pulled the carriage into the Lapps' barnyard, Rachel stared at the house. It was a big house, bigger than the Amos Kings' and bigger than her home back in Ohio. White with a large front porch and many windows across the second and first floors, it was a plain but beautiful structure that displayed signs of a contented life.

Her aunt and cousins alighted, and as she climbed out, Rachel was conscious of chickens clucking and running about the yard. A low mooing from the barn could only have come from the family cow. Two young Amish boys of about six or seven ran about, chasing each other, while an older boy, who looked to be eleven or twelve, carried wood from the shed with his gaze on his two younger brothers. Noah's brothers? Rachel wondered.

"John! Jacob!" Aunt Mae called. "Come say hello to your new schoolteacher." She turned to Rachel. "John is *mei kinskind.* He is your cousin Sarah's son. He is five."

Rachel blinked. "Sarah? Sarah is here?"

Aunt Mae nodded. "She and Eli live on the other side of Bird-in-Hand. They have been away to Delaware. They were due back late yesterday." She smiled as the boys approached slowly, eyeing Rachel with cautious curiosity.

Rachel hadn't realized that Sarah had had children. Sarah was the eldest of the Amos Kings. She had married when Rachel and Charlotte were young children, so it was natural that she now had one or more daughters or sons. She studied John, Sarah's son. He was a handsome boy with blond hair and brown eyes. Did he look like his *vadder* or Sarah? Rachel could barely remember what her cousin Sarah looked like.

"Rachel," her aunt said, "these boys will be your students. John, Jacob, this is your new schoolteacher. John, Rachel is also your cousin. Jacob belongs to Abram Peachy. Abram is deacon." And then to Rachel, she whispered, "and a widower." The boys had started to turn away, ready to play again.

She called after them. "Boys! What do you say to your new schoolteacher?"

"*Gut* day to you, Rachel. We are pleased to meet you." It was Jacob Peachy who spoke.

John stared at her. "What do I need school for? I like working on the farm."

"You must learn English," Rachel said, "so that you can do farm business in town."

Jacob was nodding as if he understood. "*Ja,* John. You don't want to be a bad farmer, do you?"

"I will be a *gut* farmer! I know a lot about plowing and planting…and harvesting!"

"I'm sure you do, John," his grandmother said. "But Rachel is right, it is important for you to learn things to help you someday when you are big and can take over your father's farm."

"We will both come," Jacob added.

Rachel gazed at his sweet face and thought how unfortunate it was that this poor boy had lost his mother. "I will see you in class in two months."

The boys nodded before they ran off to finish their barnyard play.

Rachel became aware of several things at once as she entered the Lapp family home. First was that the house was filled with women she didn't know. Then she saw Charlotte greet another woman warmly with a hug. She heard "Sarah" and she realized that this was the cousin she had met only once when she was barely old enough to remember.

Charlotte came back and grabbed Rachel's hand, leading her toward her older sister. "Sarah, this is cousin Rachel."

Sarah smiled. She looked so much like Aunt Mae that Rachel had to keep herself from staring. "You were young when we met."

Rachel nodded. "*Ja.* You took me for a walk to see the barn animals."

"That's right." Her eldest cousin looked surprised. "You were three."

Rachel studied her cousin's face carefully. "You have the look of your *mudder.*"

"We all do," Sarah said, referring to her sisters. She turned to softly scold a little girl who was trying to put her fingers into a freshly baked chocolate-cream pie. It was one of Rachel's pies brought from Aunt Mae's, which hadn't been put in a cool place yet. "Rose Ann!" she exclaimed. "You must not touch that pie." Seeing the little girl's face begin to crumple, Sarah bent to scoop up the child into her arms. "You can have a piece of pie when we get home." She kissed her daughter's forehead and turned back to Rachel. "This is my youngest—Rose Ann. She is three and she likes chocolate."

Little Rose Ann nodded vigorously. "Chocolate."

Rachel felt her heart melting as she stared into her little cousin's hazel eyes. Rose Ann's hair had a hint of red highlights. She was a beautiful child with an inner glow.

"Ah, pie!" Noah was suddenly near the pie, ready to do what little Rose Ann was forbidden to.

"Nay!" Rachel exclaimed. She had sensed immediately when he'd come in. "That is for Sunday. You must not touch it now—"

"Just a taste?" he asked with a look of boyish innocence, but Rachel could see the mischievous twinkle that spoiled his whole act.

"Ows!" Charlotte exclaimed. "Rachel is right. You should not be here. We are here to do women's work. You don't look like a woman to me."

Noah's face beamed. "I'm glad you noticed."

"No-ah!" Katie Lapp's sharp tone was like a shout across the room.

"Mam?" he said as his mother approached. Katie was a strikingly plain woman who would stand out no matter if she wore Amish clothing or a potato sack. Her white prayer *kapp* sat properly on her head, revealing a glimpse of sandy-brown hair, the same color as her son's.

"Doesn't Jedidiah need help moving the furniture?"

"We finished in the house, *Mam*."

"Then go check with your *vadder*. I'm sure he has something for his wild son to do." But Katie's tone had become soft, affectionate. It was clear that she loved him.

"I only wanted a piece of pie."

"Pie for Sunday," little Rose Ann said firmly.

Noah flashed the little girl a bright smile. "Right you

are, then, Rosie." He lowered his voice. "We just wanted one little piece, didn't we?"

Rose Ann grinned and nodded. "Just one piece."

"I guess I had better find something to do before the pie begs me to grab a bite of it." And Noah left, taking some of the fresh air that had come in with him.

"Charlotte, he will be a handful, that one," Sarah said.

Charlotte nodded, but her eyes held warmth and something like affection...or more. "Noah Lapp is a man all to his own."

Rachel, listening to the exchange, felt a little knot form in her stomach. She had to avoid him. He was Charlotte's special friend—not hers. Something she couldn't—mustn't—forget.

She'd been amazed by Noah's ability to make a small child feel special. She had seen him come in and pour himself a glass of water from a pitcher. The last thing he'd seemed to want was a piece of chocolate-cream pie, but he had heard the exchange between little Rose Ann and her mother.

He was a special man. *No, I mustn't think about him!* She felt a twinge of guilt. There were reasons for her to forget Noah Lapp, and it was more than just his being her cousin Charlotte's friend. They might not be courting yet, but no doubt they would be soon. And wasn't that reason enough itself? The two were more than comfortable with each other. Just the way she and Abraham had been when they'd begun courting. She fought back mixed emotions. There were other reasons not to become involved with a man again—reasons she wasn't ready to ponder too deeply.

The women began to disperse to different areas of the house, where they would work to give the rooms a thorough cleaning. Katie accepted their help with silent gratitude. Rachel approached to introduce herself, and Katie placed her arm around Rachel's shoulder as she led her into the large front room.

"I have heard much about you, Rachel," Noah's mother said pleasantly. "You like the new school?"

Rachel beamed. "*Ja.* Samuel and your sons have done a *gut* job."

"You will have a lot of children in class." Katie walked through the room, checking that all was in order.

"Will I have some of your sons?"

"*Ja.* You will have Daniel and Joseph, my two youngest sons."

"I look forward to having them in school."

A baby cried from above, but was instantly silent. Katie's expression was soft. "That is Hannah, my baby daughter. She has been napping. Someone must have picked her up." She seemed unconcerned about who had seen to her daughter. Unlike the Englishers, the Amish cared for their neighbors and their community and were always willing to lend a hand.

Katie straightened a framed embroidered wall-hanging. On it, the Lapp family tree was depicted. Rachel saw Katie and Samuel and all their children: Jedidiah, Noah, Jacob, Elijah, Isaac, Daniel, Joseph, and little Hannah. It was a lovely piece of stitchery.

Noah's mother studied the family tree for a moment before turning slowly to capture Rachel's gaze. "Mae and I are close, almost as close as sisters."

Rachel waited, sensing the woman had something to say.

"Rachel, I hope you can begin a new life in Happiness." She glanced back at the frame on the wall. "It is sometimes difficult to start over," she said. "Are you doing well?" Her brown eyes found and steadily held Rachel's attention.

"*Ja.* Everyone has been welcoming."

Katie smiled. "*Gut.* That is how it should be." She seemed to hesitate a moment. "You are feeling well?"

Rachel frowned, uncertain of what Katie meant. "I am fine."

"Your accident. I read about it in *The Budget.*"

She must have looked upset, because Katie patted her arm. "No one knows but you, me and your aunt Mae. It is my relationship with Mae that made me understand what happened."

How much did she know? Rachel wondered fearfully.

"You spent weeks in the hospital."

Rachel nodded. "I was walking out with Abraham Beiler. We were in his courting buggy with my brother Moses as chaperone. It was winter and the road was icy. We were managing fine until a car came speeding around the bend and forced us off the road. I was on the right side and I fell into an ice-water-filled ditch. The buggy fell on top of me. Abraham and Moses were injured only slightly. I was hurt the worst."

Katie's eyes softened with sympathy. "It must have been terrible."

"*Ja.* It was a dark time, but I had the Lord to guide me until the darkness lifted." If it hadn't been for her faith in God, she would never have survived her injuries and the time that followed.

"And Abraham?" Katie waited as if she already knew but wanted to hear Rachel's version.

"He decided that I was not the girl for him. He began courting Emma Mast, my best friend, before I even got

out of the hospital. They were married in September."
Only six months after he'd asked to court her…and not
Emma. They hadn't even waited until the time most cou-
ples married in their Ohio Amish community.

"It must have been awful for you," Katie said. "But
I can see that you are well and doing fine. You are a
schoolteacher and in our village of Happiness! I think
you will like it here, Rachel. The Lord works in ways
we can't always understand, but I have a feeling that you
were meant to come here…that Happiness was God's
plan for you all along."

Rachel could only nod. "Katie—"

"I will tell no one of what happened to you in Millersburg, Rachel. Your secret is safe with me." She gestured toward the door to the kitchen. "Let's have a cup
of tea. If we don't stand watch, there may be no pies and
cakes for Sunday. My sons are big eaters."

Relieved at the change of subject, Rachel gladly
accompanied Katie Lapp into the kitchen, where two
neighbor women were rearranging Sunday's desserts.

"Shall we put this in the refrigerator?" Agnes Troyer
asked of Rachel's chocolate-cream pie.

"*Ja,* it will keep better," Katie said.

"I'll take it," Rachel offered, eager for a few moments
alone after her heart-to-heart talk with her aunt's friend
Katie. She picked up the pie and went into the other
room, where a gas refrigerator and separate gas freezer
were located. She opened the refrigerator door, her hands
shaking slightly as she rearranged a few items to make
room for the pie. When the pie had its own place, she
shut the refrigerator door and leaned against it. Her heart
was beating rapidly. There was a sick feeling in the pit

of her stomach. She didn't like to remember the accident that had changed her life and taken away her sweetheart.

Thank You, Lord. I praise You, Lord, for all Your goodness and grace. Thank You for not allowing anyone to realize just how much the accident changed me. Thank You for being there whenever I need You.

She stood for a moment, fighting tears, reining in her emotions. Upon hearing laughter from within the kitchen, Rachel straightened. She wiped her eyes, pulled herself together and went back to rejoin the others to ask what she could do to help.

Chapter Four

Noah stood on the front porch of the Lapp family farm-house, watching as neighbors and friends drove their horses into the yard and parked in line with the other gray family buggies. All of the male Samuel Lapps—from their father Samuel to his youngest son, Joseph—were dressed in their black Sunday best. They stood, offering greetings and handshakes as the Amish men from other households joined them on the porch, while the women bustled into the house to join Katie in the kitchen.

The Kings' gelding trotted down the lane and turned into the yard. Noah felt an odd sensation in the pit of his stomach as the family alighted from the buggy and crossed toward the house.

He nodded to Charlotte's father as Amos climbed the porch steps and joined them. "Fair weather this day," he said, and the man agreed. Conscious of the women, especially Rachel, who got out of the buggy last, he turned his attention first to little Joshua, who had run up to the house. "Have any ice cream lately?"

"Nay." Joshua scowled. His eyes suddenly lit up. "Can we go this week?"

"If there is time for a trip into town."

"Joshua!" Charlotte scolded as she climbed up the stairs. "What did I tell you about bothering Noah?"

"I wasn't bothering him." He looked up at Noah with big eyes. "Was I?"

"Nay, Joshua," Noah replied and then grinned at Charlotte. "What's that you're carrying?" he asked her. "Could it be chocolate cake?"

Charlotte's eyes twinkled. "Shoofly pie."

Noah knew the exact moment when Rachel climbed the first step of his family home. She was wearing a blue dress with black apron and cape. This day her bonnet and the prayer *kapp* covering her dark hair were both black. She was lovely, and he couldn't take his eyes off her sweet face. "And what do you have there?" he asked, casually, forcing himself to study the pie in her arms. "Another chocolate-cream pie?"

"Ja." She met his gaze but then quickly glanced away.

"I think I'd like some of that pie," he murmured softly for her ears only as she hurried past, following in her cousin's footsteps.

"That was the new schoolteacher?" Jedidiah said.

Noah narrowed his gaze on his older brother. "I thought you saw her when she came to help *Mam.*"

Jedidiah, watching the arrival of another buggy, shook his head. *"Dat* and I were finishing up at the *schuulhaus."* His attention fixed on Abram Peachy as he climbed out of his buggy and helped his five children to alight. "I heard you got your fields planted," he called to Abram.

Abram waved his children into the house. "The weather held, thanks be to God."

"You meet the new schoolteacher yet?" Jedidiah asked, and Noah glanced at his brother sharply before turning to gauge Abram's response.

"Nay," Abram said. "I hear she's a King cousin from Ohio." He seemed to exhibit only polite interest.

Noah felt himself relax. *"Ja.* Rachel Hostetler."

"Nice girl," Noah's father said.

Jedidiah elbowed his brother. "I hear you were the great rescuer the other day."

Noah shrugged. "'Twas nothing."

"Not from what my daughter tells me," Amos King said.

Abram suddenly looked interested. "Something happen in town?"

"Ja," little Joshua piped up, as he returned from inside to stand with the men. "Aaron Troyer's horse spooked, and Noah saved cousin Rachel from crashing."

Abram smiled. "From crashing what?"

Joshua pulled himself up and tugged on the bottom of his small black coat. At seven, he was a miniature version of his father. "The buggy! The horse was galloping right down the middle of the road, and he took Rachel and the buggy with him. Noah had to jump onto the horse's back while he was still running to stop him. The horse's eyes were rolled back in his head, all big and white, and he was sweaty. Aaron Troyer came running up to take care of his horse Josef and to see if Rachel hurt herself!"

Noah felt himself the object of several male gazes. He was uncomfortable with this particular discussion and being the center of attention. "It wasn't anything one of you wouldn't do."

"That's not what cousin Rachel said," Joshua replied. "She said she could have been killed if Noah hadn't come to save her."

"Ja." Abram removed his hat, pushed his hair back, and then settled his wide-brimmed black-felt hat back on his head. "Could have been. One of Obadiah Fisher's daughters out in Missouri—she got killed last summer when her horse ran away. Terrible thing for the family, and her just fifteen. Lucky for the new teacher you were there."

The Zook family arrived at that moment, putting a temporary end to the topic of conversation. As he greeted "Horseshoe Joe" Zook's wife, Miriam, Noah could feel Jedidiah watching him. He pretended not to notice, and soon Jedidiah's attention turned to the middle Zook daughter, Annie.

Five families had come to visit. The men stayed outside while the women inside readied the midday meal. Moments of the men's conversation intermingled with periods of silence, as the weather was good and there wasn't a need for talking.

"The cousin was grateful," Jedidiah said to Noah. "What does Charlotte think? Must have put a fright into her, seeing it."

"Rachel is Charlotte's first cousin. She's glad I was there to help."

Noah wondered how Rachel was getting along. She'd been here less than a week, and she must have feelings about their Happiness community.

"Charlotte is an understanding girl," his brother persisted. "Good head on her shoulders. Make some man a mighty good wife."

Noah glared at him, wondering where Jedidiah was headed with this conversation. "And why are you telling me? Charlotte and I have known each other a long time."

"Ja," Jedidiah said, "and well you should remember this."

His older brother could be annoying at times, Noah thought. They were close in age—Jedidiah was only a year and a half older than he was. What was Jedidiah implying? That Charlotte was jealous? That he shouldn't have saved Rachel because he and Charlotte were friends?

Noah shook his head. Sometimes Jedidiah made no sense.

"He did save her!" He suddenly heard Joshua shout from across the yard. "Ask him. Better you should ask cousin Rachel! Cousin Rachel!" the little boy called as he ran from the barn toward the house, followed closely by Jacob Peachy.

The boys rushed inside before Noah could stop either one of them. The last thing he needed was for Rachel to become embarrassed by all the attention—no matter how innocently it began.

"Cousin Rachel!" Joshua cried.

Noah cringed. All he did was stop a runaway buggy. Why couldn't everyone just leave things be?

"… And the little Englisher was caught stealing a brownie from a pan cooling on Elisabeth Schrock's windowsill," Alta Hershberger was saying.

Miriam Zook's eyes widened. "What did she do?"

Alta grinned. "She gave him a piece of her mind and then handed him another brownie."

The women chuckled in response as they unwrapped the food they'd prepared previously.

"Abram's children are growing fast, like weeds," Mae commented as she sliced bread and arranged muffins. "Such a shame that those precious children have no *mudder* to guide them."

"Abram's doing the best he can, *Mam,*" Charlotte said.

"*Ja,* daughter. But the deacon can't be all things to everyone. It's hard when there are children to raise alone and a farm to run. It's time he thought about marrying again."

"I'm sure he will when he is ready," Katie said gently. She unwrapped a plate and set it on the table. "A shame Sarah couldn't come."

"*Ja,*" Aunt Mae said. "I was sorry to hear David came down sick—"

Two young boys burst into the kitchen and stopped, the door slamming shut behind them. "Rachel! Cousin Rachel!"

"Son!" Aunt Mae scolded. "We walk, not run, into a room!"

Rachel grinned as Joshua searched the room and found her. "Little cousin, what's wrong?" She tossed each boy an apple from a bowl on the counter.

"Jacob doesn't believe that Noah saved you!" Joshua exclaimed before he took a big bite.

"Noah did save me, Jacob," Rachel said, her breath catching at the mention of Noah's name. "If he hadn't stopped the horse, the buggy could have hit someone or something, and I could have been hurt or even killed."

Jacob's eyes went big as he listened to Rachel. "Noah

saved her," he said to Joshua. "And he kept Aaron Troyer's horse from maybe breaking a leg and having to be shot."

Joshua nodded vigorously, glad that his friend finally understood. "When are we going to eat?" he asked his sister, who'd been listening with amusement.

"Soon," Charlotte said, handing each boy an apple-walnut muffin. "Go outside and be *gut* boys. We will call you when it is your time to eat."

"Would you take this to the table?" Miriam asked.

Rachel nodded. She accepted the large bowl of potato salad and carried it into the front room, where she set it down on one of several makeshift tables that had been constructed for today's visit. Her thoughts on Noah, she went to the window and peered outside. She couldn't see him at first, and she started to turn away. Then his father moved and there he was, speaking with two men she hadn't met. Noah nodded and then smiled at someone's answer. He turned toward the house as he chatted, and his gaze locked with hers briefly through the glass. Rachel quickly retreated, embarrassed at being caught staring. She hurried back to the kitchen.

"The meal is ready," Katie Lapp announced to the men outside.

The oldest men entered the house first. They sat down at a table, and then the younger men took their seats. The women had prepared the food earlier in the week. There was cold roast beef and chicken, potato salad, sweetened-and-vinegared green beans with bacon, frosted raisin bread, sweet-and-sour chow-chow, muffins, yeast rolls and coleslaw. There was an assortment of cakes and pies for dessert, including Charlotte's shoofly pie and Rachel's chocolate-cream pie.

The men ate without conversation, and when they were done, the women and children sat down to eat. Rachel enjoyed the meal, especially the sliced roast beef and potato salad with peas. Aunt Mae had made the green beans, and they were delicious.

Nancy took a second helping of her mother's dish before tasting other foods. "*Mam* makes the best sauce for her beans," she said.

Rachel smiled. "Everything is wonderful. Did you have some of Miriam's chow-chow? Sweet and sour is my favorite."

"Mine, too," Charlotte replied as she lifted a forkful of the vegetables to her mouth. "Did you see Alta Hershberger's vanilla pudding? Before the day is done, I'm going to have me a cup."

"May I have some pudding with you?" A little girl stood at Charlotte's side.

Charlotte's expression softened. "I'll call you when I'm ready to get some. I'll scoop you a cup so we can eat it together." The child looked pleased as she turned and ran back to sit with her sister and brothers. "That's Ruth Peachy," she told Rachel. "Abram's youngest."

Rachel eyed the youngest Peachy child as the little girl ate carefully, mimicking her older sister. "She's too young for my classroom."

Charlotte agreed. "She's not yet four. She's a pleasant girl. For some reason, she's taken a liking to me."

"The reason is simple," Rachel said. "You're as purehearted as she is, and you treat her nicely."

"I like her."

Rachel smiled. "I can tell you do."

Suddenly, Rachel felt the back of her neck prickle. She turned, only to encounter Noah's gaze.

Charlotte stood and approached him. "Can I get you something?"

Noah withdrew his gaze, turning his smiling attention to Charlotte. "Not unless you're cutting the pies."

Charlotte chuckled. "We'll be serving them soon, Noah." Her eyes twinkled. "You're still hungry?" she teased.

"Only for pie or cake."

"I'll bring you a piece after we cut it," she offered.

Noah shook his head. "I'll be back to get it myself." His eyes met Rachel's briefly as he left as quickly as he'd come.

Everyone enjoyed the cakes, pies and other sweets provided by the women. Noah had come for his piece of Rachel's chocolate-cream pie, as promised. He appeared to relish every bite before he was back for more. Rachel couldn't help feeling pleased that he took so much pleasure from it. Charlotte and Ruth Peachy sat side by side with their bowls of vanilla pudding. It seemed the most natural thing when Charlotte reached over to wipe pudding off the little girl's mouth when Ruth was done. Rachel ate a tiny slice of shoofly pie and then enjoyed a small taste of Miriam Zook's butter coffee cake. Soon, with bellies full and the time growing late, families began to gather their leftovers and their youngsters to leave.

Later, only the Amos Kings and Rachel stayed behind to visit a little longer with the Samuel Lapps and to help Katie with the cleanup. As she collected dishes to bring to the kitchen, Rachel saw the older Lapp brothers begin to take apart the front-room tables. She had met all of Noah's brothers this day. They were a fine bunch of young men and boys who teased each other while they worked together as a team. Hearing them reminded her of her own three brothers back home in Millersburg, and she got misty-eyed for a few seconds. There was at least one Lapp brother close in age to each of her brothers, Moses, David and Thomas, who were all younger than she. Today would be their day for Sunday visiting, too, and it did make her feel a little better to know that, in a way, things were the same here as back in Millersburg.

The kitchen was clean, and the food was put away in Katie's refrigerator and pantry or in dishes ready for the Kings to take home. The men had gone outside to look at Samuel's new milk cow. Katie, Aunt Mae, Rachel and her cousins sat on the front porch. Katie bounced her baby daughter on her knee. Little Hannah had been happy and smiling since she'd woken from her nap and eaten. She seemed content to sit on her mother's lap and gaze at the other women.

Rachel studied the little girl and had the strongest urge to hold her. "May I?" she asked Hannah's mother.

"*Ja.* Don't be alarmed if she fusses," Katie warned as she surrendered her baby into Rachel's outstretched arms.

Baby Hannah cuddled against her without complaint. Rachel felt an overwhelming contentment as she rocked to and fro in the front-porch rocking chair, enjoying the warmth of the spring afternoon in the companionship of women she liked and respected.

Soon it was time for the Kings to return home. They didn't have far to go, but it was getting late and there would be time for the family to enjoy the rest of the day reading, playing games or just resting in the comfort of their own home. Rachel stood and handed Hannah back to her mother. To everyone's surprise, Hannah fussed a little before she settled down as Katie stood, rocking her against her shoulder.

"Good food and fine company," Aunt Mae said. "A perfect Sunday visiting."

Rachel and her cousins agreed. "*Ja,* and the weather is fine," Nancy added. They went inside to gather their dishes and the leftovers given to them by their hostess.

"It's been a *gut* day," Rachel said as she prepared to descend the porch steps. There was no sign of the men yet, but she expected them to appear at any moment.

Katie smiled as she continued to pat her daughter's back. "I enjoyed your company." Her gaze shot past Rachel toward the barnyard. "You'll come again soon. Don't wait until next Sunday's church services to see us."

Rachel murmured agreement as she glanced back to see Samuel, her uncle Amos, Noah and three of his brothers as they stepped from the barn and started toward the house. She watched the men's approach, trying not to look too much at Noah, but it was Noah who drew her attention. When she realized that he watched her, she felt her face warm and quickly glanced away.

With a dish in hand, she followed Charlotte as her cousin crossed the yard toward their buggy. Suddenly, Charlotte stopped and Rachel nearly bumped into her.

"Noah, would you like any of these cookies?" Charlotte asked. "Annie Zook made them."

Rachel didn't hear his response. She was trying desperately to move away, to give them time to visit alone. But as she hurried to turn, she tripped, and it was Noah who was suddenly there to steady her, his hand warm through her long dress sleeve.

Blushing, Rachel was saved from having a conversation with him when Aunt Mae appeared to urge them into the buggy. She could feel Noah's gaze as she climbed inside. She didn't glance back, but kept her eyes trained ahead.

Rachel hated that he had this strange effect on her. She had to avoid him as best she could without things appearing odd to anyone. Earlier in the day, several of the neighbor women had wondered aloud why Noah and Charlotte had not begun to court openly yet, but even if they were not official sweethearts, Rachel would not interfere. "It's only a matter of time," Miriam Zook had assured a small group of women when neither Katie nor Aunt Mae was present.

Since then, every time Rachel was affected by Noah's presence, she felt a sense of betrayal toward her cousin, guilty about the way Noah made her feel. She knew what it felt like to be betrayed…and it was the worst thing she'd ever experienced.

Chapter Five

The day was warm, with a stiff breeze that tore at the garments Rachel and Charlotte were hanging to dry. Rachel secured cousin John's overalls on the clothesline. Satisfied that the wooden clothespins would hold, she bent and lifted a wet mint-green shirt, enjoying the warmth of the sun on her face as she pinned it into place next to the overalls. The linen scent of detergent mingled with the aromas about the farm...the bright-red roses planted in the yard near the house...the smell of the family cow in a nearby pasture...the freshly tilled earth in the vegetable garden.

The wind tugged a dress from Charlotte's hands and sent it flying across the yard toward her cousin. "Rachel!" she cried. "Get it!"

Rachel laughed as she quickly caught the damp garment before it hit the ground. "I almost missed it."

"*Gut* catch," her cousin said with a grin. She looked carefree and happy in a pale blue dress, white apron, and white prayer *kapp*.

Rachel returned her grin as she hung the dress. "These clothes won't take long to dry in this weather."

"*Ja.* It's the perfect day for laundry," Charlotte agreed as she reached into the basket for her sister's black apron. "*Dat* and BJ are going to clean out the side room in the barn for this Sunday's singing," she continued, referring to her brother John, often called BJ, for Big John, when the family gathered. Little John was Sarah and Eli's son—Charlotte's nephew. "I think *Dat* is afraid if we stay in the house we'll keep him up at night with our songs and fun."

"It's a *gut* space," Rachel said. She grabbed a black prayer *kapp* and pinned it on the line. "How many will come?" The young people's singing was an event held the evening of each church Sunday, usually at the same farm or home as the church services that morning. It was a time for young men and women of the community to intermingle for song and fun. Rachel had always enjoyed singings in her Millersburg community in Ohio.

Charlotte looked thoughtful as she continued to hang clothes. "There will be four of us—you, Nancy, BJ and me...the four oldest Lapp boys. The Zooks and Mary Hershberger..."

Noah will be coming, Rachel thought, a little disturbed to realize that she was pleased.

"And then there will be some young people from the next church district... I'm not certain how many." Charlotte bent for a shirt and nearly collided with Rachel, whose thoughts had drifted. She laughed as she drew back quickly. "I don't know. Fifteen or twenty?"

It would be a large gathering. "We'll have a wonderful time," Rachel said.

Charlotte grinned. "*Ja.* Lots of *gut* food, fine singing and wonderful company."

The young women finished the chore and headed toward the house, their spirits high and their appearance disheveled from the wind that had loosed fine strands of hair from their pins.

"We've finished, Aunt Mae," Rachel said as she entered the house. She reached up to attempt to fix her hair and then gave up, unsuccessful. "What else can I do to help?"

"You've done enough, Rachel. Why don't you head toward the *schuul* to see how the construction is coming on the teacher's cottage?"

"Ja," Charlotte urged her. "You said you'd enjoy watching the work take place."

Rachel nodded. "But surely there is more you'd like me to do first."

"Nay," Aunt Mae said. "Horseshoe Joe came by for Uncle Amos early this morning. They went over to Abram Peachy's house. I told Amos that we'd come for him before supper.

"Your new *haus* is not far, and it's a nice day for a walk. Just head up the lane and turn right. Be careful," she warned, "of speeding cars along the narrow road." She rolled her eyes. "Some of these Englishers drive like…"

Rachel nodded, pleased with the idea of visiting the cottage. "I will." She knew her hair must look a sight. Should she head upstairs to put herself to rights first? The breeze would only pull her hair free…unless she put in extra pins.

She debated whether to fix her hair when Aunt Mae approached. "You can take these muffins for the workers. I'm sure they would enjoy something to eat about now."

Charlotte came up from behind her mother and handed

Rachel cups and a water jug. "The Lapp men will be thirsty as well."

"Go along now, Rachel." Aunt Mae didn't see anything wrong with the way she looked, Rachel realized, so it must be all right for her to go just as she was. Besides it was wrong to worry about one's looks. Vanity was a sin that she wouldn't give in to.

With a brown paper bag filled with sweet muffins and cups in one hand and the jug of water in the other, Rachel started down the dirt lane that led through the King property toward the main road.

The sun felt wonderful, and Rachel tilted up her face to enjoy its warmth. A fly buzzed about her ear and, laughing, she swatted it away. The warm breeze held the scent of fresh-tilled earth and the honeysuckle that grew along one side of the lane. Rachel felt a deep sense of peace and contentment as she walked.

Would she see Noah at the house? Her heart gave a little thump. She hadn't seen him since Sunday. While she fought hard to get him out of her mind, she couldn't forget his face, his endearing smile and the many kindnesses he had shown her.

She reached the end of the dirt lane and waited at the edge of the paved road until a car sped past before she ventured to cross the street. She turned right and continued along the roadway, facing traffic. She smiled as she caught a glimpse of the schoolhouse and hurried on. With her heart buoyed by lightness, she approached a window and peered inside.

She grinned. She loved the rows of desks and the larger one in the front of the room. The schoolhouse was empty. Would it be unlocked?

She tried the door and realized that it was necessary

to lock it when no one was about. *Such a shame.* She would have liked to wander around inside again.

Soon, she thought. Soon she would be standing before her class of eager students.

Rachel rounded the building and headed along the dirt drive toward the teacher's cottage. The day was quiet. The only sounds she could hear were an occasional insect or a passing car on the main road and the breeze stirring the nearby trees and her dress hem and apron. Perhaps the Lapps couldn't find time to work on the house today, she mused, disappointed.

Unlike the school, the cottage door stood partially open. With a frown, she hesitated only a few seconds before pushing the door in and entering.

"Samuel? Jedidiah? Noah?" she called out. "Is anyone here?"

"In the back of the *haus,* Rachel!" Noah appeared within seconds. "You've come to see the construction," he said, sounding pleased.

Her senses humming at the sight of him, Rachel nodded. "I brought muffins and a jug of water."

His eyes were warm as he smiled. "I am hungry and could use a drink." He waved her to follow him. "Come and see what we've done."

Eagerly Rachel followed Noah toward the rear of the house, her neck tingling as she studied his back. He wore a royal-blue shirt under his denim overalls. She watched as he lifted his wide-brimmed straw hat, ran his fingers through his silky, sandy-brown hair before settling the hat back onto his head. There was a fine sheen of moisture across his nape. She tried not to look at his neck, glancing instead at the house as they walked through.

"Is Samuel here?" she asked.

"Nay," Noah said without turning. "I am the only one working." Suddenly, he spun to smile at her, and the impact of his twinkling, warm brown eyes made her head spin and her heart leap within her chest. "I told you that the house would be done in a month. It may take a little longer."

He nodded toward the kitchen area. A brick hearth had been built since her last visit. The walls had been insulated and the drywall hung. The room was large, bright and inviting. She could picture those walls whitewashed and a table with chairs in the center of the room.

"A fine *kiche,*" she said. She imagined the kitchen as it would one day be, filled with the smells of good food cooking and company gathered around the table.

"My *grossdaddi* is making the kitchen cabinets," Noah told her, helping to paint a better picture for her. "I think you will like them. He does *gut* work."

Both the school and the house seemed to solely be the work of the Lapp men, and she mentioned this to Noah.

"We've had help from all," he said. "We had a house-raising for the initial framework. But this land once belonged to *mein grosselders* and there was time before the house needed to be completed. With the spring planting, we worked when we were able…to make sure everything was right for the teacher in our community." His voice softened. "*You. Grossdaddi* is a kind man."

Like *grossdaddi,* like *kinskind,* she thought. The man's grandson Noah, too, was kind. "Noah, everything is very nice. I know I will be happy here."

Her words trailed off as their gazes met and something warm passed between them. Flushing, Rachel glanced away.

"I am glad, Rachel." Noah studied the young woman

before him, noticing how appealing she looked with soft
tendrils of hair about her face and neck. She wore a
lavender dress with a white cape that tucked into the
waistband of her white apron. A matching white prayer
kapp covered her shining dark hair. She had the pret-
tiest eyes…large and glistening. He could feel himself
drowning in her gaze, felt the pull of her nearness. He
drew a sharp breath and looked quickly away. He hadn't
expected to see her today, and the pleasure he felt seeing her, hearing her voice, was beyond anything he'd
ever experienced.

There was a brief but potent moment of silence. Noah
felt impelled to break it. "Would you like to see more of
the construction?"

She seemed relieved as she nodded. "You have done
a lot in one week's time."

"There is still much to do, but we will be finished
before school starts."

"May I look around?" Rachel asked.

"Ja," Noah said with a grin. "Come. I'll show you
more and explain what we will be doing next."

Rachel enjoyed the tour of the house with Noah as her
guide. He showed her where the bedroom would be, the
parlor or front room and the pantry, where she would be
able to stock her canned and baked goods.

Every step of the way, Noah was conscious of Rachel
beside him. He could hear every tiny exhalation of her
breath, detect the clean scent of her skin. He could feel
the warmth that radiated from her to him. She smelled
like sunshine and rose-petal soap.

"You will have all that you need to be comfortable,"
he said.

She followed him as he stepped outside the house.

"Preacher Stoltzfus and his family are donating the stove and freezer," he said, "and the Zooks have given money toward a new gas refrigerator." Before Rachel could comment, Noah continued. "We will put a clothesline here." He gestured to a grassy area in full sun. "I will make the wooden T-bars for the line myself—"

"Rachel!" Samuel, Noah's father, came up the dirt driveway. He carried a handsaw and a carpenter's tool belt. "You like the house," he said knowingly.

Rachel glanced over in surprise that he could read her thoughts. "It is wonderful."

Samuel looked pleased. "Abram Peachy and your uncle Amos will be helping us to finish the floors."

"Rachel brought muffins and water, *Dat.*"

"Aunt Mae's muffins," Rachel said. She liked Noah's *dat.* He was a gentle man with a ready smile. *Noah is like him,* she thought, but then was embarrassed by her own thoughts.

"Tell Mae we appreciate the muffins."

Rachel nodded. "May I see inside the *schuulhaus* again?" she asked.

"Ja." Samuel grinned. "You will enjoy teaching?"

Rachel grinned back as she inclined her head. "I am glad I was asked to come. Everyone in Happiness has been kind to me."

"We are glad that you came to us," Samuel replied. "You will be good for our children. Come and I'll open the school for you."

"You are easy to be kind to," Noah said softly as they trailed behind Samuel.

Surprised by the intensity of his tone, Rachel flashed him a look and was stunned by his expression. It was almost as if he liked her, felt the same little thrill that she experienced whenever they were together. But that couldn't be… It was Charlotte who had stolen his heart and affections.

Samuel unlocked the schoolhouse door and then handed Rachel the key. "For you. So you…can come and visit whenever you wish. I'm sure there is much to be done before a new session of school starts."

Rachel was touched by Samuel's thoughtfulness. She saw Noah in his father's face. *Is this what Noah will look like in the years to come? Cousin Charlotte is lucky to have a good and kind man,* she thought.

Samuel and Noah accompanied Rachel inside the schoolhouse and reported on the progress made since her last visit.

"You now have writing paper and pencils," Samuel said.

"We have installed a pencil sharpener," Noah added.

Eyeing the metal crank sharpener, Rachel beamed. "I'm eager to begin."

"The first day of class will be here in no time," Samuel said.

Rachel noted that the *schuul* room still smelled like newly varnished wood but she could detect additional scents…of paper and chalk, pencil shavings—someone must have tried out the pencil sharper, she thought— along with the roses that someone had left in a vase on the teacher's desk. The combined scents reminded her of her own *schuul* days and the joy she'd gained from learning English and math and other important lessons for life.

Shortly afterward, they returned outside.

"We'll be putting in two swing sets for your students

to use at recess." Samuel showed her where they planned to construct the swings.

"Two! How wonderful," Rachel said. The nearest *schuul* to her parent's home had an old swing set in the yard, and she had often watched how much the children enjoyed it. With the number of students she expected in her classroom, she realized that they would need more than one set.

"There will be a bench for you there," Noah said. "I should be done with it soon."

Rachel felt her throat tighten with emotion. The Lord had brought her to this new home, and now she was beginning to see that He had decided that she and Abraham were not meant to be together. Some of her burden of pain began to ease. There were feelings, though, that would take longer to resolve, but with the Lord's help, she would settle them.

"I'd best get back to work." Samuel's sincere gaze warmed her. "You come here whenever you'd like." He nodded at his son. "You will help with the floors?"

"Ja."

Samuel smiled. *"Gut."*

"I will see you Sunday, Rachel," Samuel said.

"Ja, Samuel," Rachel said. "Thank you for building me such a *gut* house. I am grateful for your hard work."

"Sunday service is at your aunt's," Noah said quietly after his father had gone back inside the cottage.

"We have been baking cakes and pies." She felt tingling along her spine whenever she was in Noah's presence.

Noah's eyes lit up. "What flavor did you bake?"

"Strawberry," she said, thrilled by his reaction. "And chocolate."

He grinned. "I will enjoy having more of your pies."

Her reaction to his grin made her glance away. She should have come with her cousin. Noah was Charlotte's friend; she should not be feeling anything but friendship whenever she was with him. The closest thing she'd ever felt to this was when she and Abraham Beiler first started to walk out together. Only this feeling with Noah seemed more…intense.

Guilt made her stomach churn. She sent up a silent prayer that God would help her to control her feelings, to remember that she and Noah were meant only to be friends. The sound of a buggy's wheels and the clip-clop of horses' hooves on macadam made Rachel glance to the road, where she caught sight of Charlotte behind the reins of the Kings' gray family buggy.

"Rachel!" she cried. "I'm headed over to Abram Peachy's for *Dat*. Care to go with me?"

Noah stepped out and waved to her. "Charlotte," he greeted with a grin.

"How's the construction coming, Noah?" she asked, grinning back.

"Comin' along." He gestured toward the cottage. "Do ya have time to take a look?"

"Nay." She appeared disappointed. "But I'll stop by to see it the next time Rachel wants a look."

Rachel smiled at Noah before hurrying toward the King buggy. "I enjoyed the tour, Noah. The teacher's house is looking fine."

"A few more weeks, and it will be done." He nodded toward the school. "We'll have the swing sets finished as well."

"A swing set," Charlotte said, looking pleased. "The children will enjoy that."

"Ja," Rachel said as she climbed into the buggy to sit beside her cousin. She could envision the *kinner* at play.

"We will see ya at Sunday church service," Charlotte said to Noah.

He nodded, and with a last quick look in Noah's direction, Rachel settled in to enjoy the ride with her cousin and remind herself that Noah had just been nice to the new schoolteacher when he took her on a tour of the house and school. It was Charlotte who was his friend, Charlotte who had his interest.

"I promised to watch Abram's younger children whenever he and *Dat* head over to work on your new floors."

"That is thoughtful of him to help," Rachel said.

Charlotte nodded. "Abram Peachy is a fine man."

Rachel looked at her, surprised by her cousin's tone, but nothing about Charlotte's expression gave away her thoughts.

"Noah showed you the progress?" Charlotte said.

"Ja, as he said, the house is coming along." Rachel sat back to enjoy the weather and the day. "Did you see the kitchen fireplace? *Gut* craftsmanship. I will enjoy using that."

"And you will have a gas stove as well."

"I learned to cook on a fireplace," Rachel said. "I will use both." She leaned closer to the side window to watch two Amish children at play. It jogged her memory. "Noah said that there will be two swing sets in the school yard."

"Two?" Charlotte said as she steered the buggy onto a dirt road that led to a farmhouse surrounded by newly planted fields. "You will need both sets for thirty-one students."

Rachel beamed. "I am eager to see them."

The buggy's wheels kicked up a small cloud of dust as Charlotte steered the vehicle into Abram Peachy's barnyard. Driving the buggy close to the house, she pulled back on the reins and the old family mare settled to a stop.

Abram immediately came out of the house as if he'd been watching and waiting for them. His gaze went first to Charlotte.

"Charlotte." Abram nodded shyly. "Rachel."

"Abram," Charlotte greeted. "*Dat* ready to come home?"

"*Nay.* In fact, he thought this afternoon would be a *gut* time to head over to the *schuul* yard to build the swing sets. Can you stay and watch Ruthie and Jacob? Nathaniel and Jonas are at the Masts', helping William. Mary Elizabeth will be leaving for town soon with Alta and Sally Hershberger. Rachel, I didn't know you'd be coming—do you mind if Charlotte stays? We could give you ride back home if you'd rather not."

"I don't mind staying," Rachel said with a smile. "I am happy that you are helping with the schoolyard swings." She saw the man redden slightly. There was kindness in the man's features, a trait her cousin seemed to appreciate, if Rachel could read Charlotte's expression accurately. She understood why Abram had been made deacon in the church.

Charlotte had remained quiet at first. She got out of the buggy and rounded to where Abram stood waiting.

"How is Ruthie today?" Charlotte asked.

Abram's smile told of his affection for his youngest. "She is eager for you to stay with her."

"I brought a pie and a few other things for the children's lunch."

"I'd appreciate it if you'd save me a piece of the pie," Abram said.

"Nay," Charlotte replied and Rachel saw the man's face fall. Her cousin must have noted his expression, too, for she grinned and reached into the buggy to show that she had brought another dessert. "For you, I brought some peach cobbler."

Abram's eyes crinkled with delight. "Peach cobbler. You made it?"

"Ja," Charlotte said. "From peaches we canned last summer. They are the sweetest we've ever tasted. I don't know what we'll do if this year's fruit isn't as tasty."

He beamed at her. *"Danki."*

Abram's three youngest came out of the house—Ruth, Jacob and Mary Elizabeth. Spying Charlotte, little Ruth ran to throw her arms about the young woman's waist.

"Charlotte!" The little girl wore no bonnet, and her hair was coming loose from its back roll. "Mary Elizabeth tried to do my hair, but it keeps falling." She looked up at Rachel's cousin with big blue eyes. "Will you fix it for me?"

"Ja, Ruthie. Go back inside, and we will join you." Charlotte placed a hand on the girl's shoulder. "You remember Rachel?" Ruthie nodded. "No need to worry, Abram. All will be well here. I'm going to start by repinning Ruth's hair."

Abram nodded, appearing grateful. *"Danki,* Charlotte—Rachel."

"We are here to help, Abram," Rachel said. "Go assured that we shall take *gut* care of your children."

"I know you will," he told Rachel.

Amos King, Rachel's uncle, came out of the barn and approached. "You came with Charlotte."

"*Ja,* Uncle Amos." She had climbed out of the buggy, and now she waited before securing the horse to the hitching post. "Will you take the family buggy?"

"We'll take my wagon," Abram said.

"We'll stop by the house to tell Mae that you'll be staying at Abram's," Amos said as he climbed into Abram's wagon and took his seat beside the kind widower.

Rachel watched as the men waved and Abram steered his mare Mattie in the direction of the school yard. "Abram, we will have supper ready when you get back!" she called out.

Abram acknowledged her comment with a wave and a grin. Rachel turned and headed into the house to help her cousin watch the Peachy children and clean the house.

Within moments, Alta Hershberger came in her open market wagon for Mary Elizabeth, and Charlotte and Rachel were left to mind the two youngest Peachy *kinner* and enjoy the afternoon.

On Friday of church-Sunday weekend, Rachel heard the wheels of the bench wagon as it pulled into her uncle's barnyard. From the house, she watched as Noah and two of his brothers jumped off the back of the wagon and began to unload. The wooden benches were long and backless and used for every Sunday church service. The day before, Uncle Amos, with Sarah's husband, Eli, their son David and cousin John had cleared the great room of furniture to make room for the bench seats.

Rachel, Charlotte and Nancy had spent the latter part

of the week cooking, baking and preparing for Sunday services and the shared meal afterward.

Soon, Sunday morning arrived and at eight o'clock came members of their church district. Noah climbed down from his family wagon and headed straight for Rachel, his gaze focused only on her. Rachel felt a rush of joy, which she quickly checked as she glanced toward her cousin and others around to see if anyone had noticed. No one seemed to note anything untoward in Noah's behavior. Rachel closed her eyes with relief, and when she opened them again, Noah stood directly before her. He held his hand outstretched toward her with something on his palm. "Here is your key."

Rachel blinked. "To the house?"

"Ja." Noah grinned at her reaction, enjoying her surprise mixed with stunned pleasure.

"It cannot be finished."

"Nay," he agreed. "But we would like you to come and go as you please to see the progress."

She was touched by his—and no doubt his father's—thoughtfulness. She smiled her thanks as she accepted the key. She stared down at the brass object, feeling the weight of it in her hand, knowing that with it came the responsibility of educating their Amish community's children.

"Noah." Charlotte approached and saw what Rachel was holding. "How wonderful!" If she sensed attraction of any kind between her cousin and Noah, she didn't show it. She seemed genuinely glad for Rachel. "Will you take us through the house tomorrow?"

Noah nodded.

"Noah! Charlotte!" Aunt Mae called.

It was time for Sunday services. Obediently they filed

into the King house and took their seats on the benches
set out for them. The men were on one side, the women
on the other. The benches filled three sides of the room,
with the fourth side for the preacher who would conduct
the service.

Noah's gaze met Rachel's from across the room. Feeling her face heat, she quickly glanced downward before
focusing on the minister. She could feel the intensity of
Noah's attention, but she refused to glance his way, focusing instead on the word of God. The congregation
began to sing from the *Ausbund,* the book of hymns.

Rachel thought she heard Noah's voice above the rest,
but realized that with her continued thoughts of him, she
had probably just imagined it.

As they moved from the *Loblied,* the second hymn
always sung at every church service as well as at weddings and other sacred events, Rachel listened intently
as Preacher Levi Stoltzfus spoke about God's word. He
talked with great emotion, and Rachel could feel the
depth of his passion for the *Ordnung,* his deep belief in
the Amish faith. She felt the love of God and the warmth
of His people as she sat in church in her aunt's home.

Soon, they were singing a third hymn from the *Ausbund.* Rachel glanced in Noah's direction, but then hur-
riedly looked away when she realized that Noah had
continued to study her throughout the entire Sunday
service.

Chapter Six

After the congregation sang the last hymn, Preacher Levi closed the service, and the church members dispersed for food and fellowship. The house instantly became a hive of noise and activity. The worship service had taken a little over three hours, and the children who had been good and obedient during church were ready to run about and burn off energy.

With purpose evident in her steps, Aunt Mae went straight to the kitchen, followed by her daughters and niece. The young men of their church district worked to move benches and set up tables in preparation to dine. The older men went outside to load any unused benches into the cart.

"Rachel," Aunt Mae said, appearing every inch the one in charge, "will you get the potato salad and coleslaw out of the refrigerator? Charlotte, see if any of the tables are ready and work with Nancy to get out the plates and utensils."

"Yes, *Mam*." Charlotte grinned at Rachel as they passed each other on the way to do Mae's bidding.

Rachel smiled as she heard her aunt address her eldest, married daughter. "Sarah, please check on the children and make sure they don't get into the desserts before dinner."

Conscious of the way Noah had watched her during Sunday service, Rachel headed toward the back room, where the gas-powered refrigerator and chest freezer were situated.

She opened the refrigerator. The appliance was full. The women of their church district had brought enough to feed the entire community. Rachel bent inside, searching first for the potato salad. She found the large bowl on the back of a shelf. Rachel rearranged and lifted several other food items so that she could reach the glass bowl of Aunt Mae's potato salad.

Rachel had trouble balancing what she held in her arms as she shifted another platter on the shelf to better reach the coleslaw.

"Here, let me take that," a familiar voice said.

Rachel gasped and nearly hit her head on the inside of the refrigerator. "What are you doing back here?"

"Offering to help you." Noah grinned at her as he relieved her of her armful.

Rachel stared at him, unable to respond or look away.

"Aren't ya going to find what you've come for?" he asked softly.

"Ja." Rachel quickly bent inside to retrieve the potato salad and coleslaw bowls. She stood carefully, only to find that he continued to study her. Blushing, she found a place to set down the bowls and then tried to gather the dishes Noah was holding.

He released them and Rachel set them back in the refrigerator. Noah was holding the potato salad and coleslaw when Rachel turned around.

"I can take them now," she murmured as she reached for the bowls while unwilling to meet his gaze.

"I'll carry them for you." Noah felt a spark of delight as he watched pink stain Rachel's cheeks.

"It's not necessary," she insisted. "Shouldn't ya be helping the men set up tables?"

"Nay." Noah studied her intently, making her face warm.

She arched her eyebrows as her eyes finally met his. "And why not?"

The corners of his lips tilted upward. "The tables are done, and the men are outside waiting to be called to supper." He held up his filled arms. "I prefer to help with the food." His voice softened. "To help *you*." He grinned. "A much better pursuit than talking about today's weather or the growth of one's field crops. Besides, the potato salad may be Aunt Mae's, but the coleslaw my *mam* made."

Noah watched Rachel's changing expression as he spoke. Truth be known and admitted only to himself, he would rather spend the day in her company than do any other thing on the good Lord's earth.

He had enjoyed watching her during church service. He could tell she was as aware of him as he was of her. She met his gaze and then averted her glance. He saw her look about to see if anyone had noticed the silent interaction.

He liked Rachel Hostetler. He liked her a lot.

"What about Charlotte?" Rachel asked, interrupting his thoughts.

"What about Charlotte?" he echoed. Had he spoken his musings aloud? No, he realized. She would have looked mortified or pleased—whichever reaction she might have had if he had spoken how he felt about her.

"She will be looking for you."

"*Nay.* Charlotte has enough to keep her busy with Mae's directions."

At the mention of her aunt, Rachel stiffened. "Please," she said, "she asked me to bring the salads to the table. If I take too long, she will wonder—"

"Wonder what?" Noah teased.

"Noah!" Charlotte said as she entered the room. "Are you helping or hindering cousin Rachel?"

Rachel met her cousin's gaze with gratitude. "He's offering to help me, but I think he should be helping the men."

Charlotte laughed. "Rather than you?"

Rachel was surprised by Charlotte's reasoning. "He's like a younger brother. I think he enjoys teasing as much as helping."

"*Ja,* Rachel," her cousin answered. "You are most probably correct." And she didn't seem in the least concerned at finding her and Noah together in the back room.

Her cousin did not seem upset by Noah's attention to her. Were the women of the church district mistaken? Were Charlotte and Noah destined to be man and wife— or was it just wishful thinking on the part of the elders?

Noah had his way. He carried the potato salad and coleslaw to the main table where the men would be invited to dine. Rachel, in the meantime, had found Aunt Mae and pitched in to help carry in the meats and breads and vegetables.

"Rachel," her cousin Sarah said as she arranged cookies and muffins on a plate on the kitchen worktable, "you are enjoying our community?"

Rachel smiled, for she easily could admit the truth. "*Ja.* I like Happiness and I'm eager to work with the students here."

"The teacher's cottage," she said, "it looks *gut?*"

Rachel nodded, noting again how much Sarah resembled Aunt Mae. "It will be done soon. The *schuulhaus* is ready, too. There will be swing sets for the *kinner*. The men have been working hard to ensure that all will be ready."

"Noah has been working there often," Sarah said.

Rachel's heart skipped a beat. "Noah and Samuel and Noah's brothers."

Her older cousin nodded. "You will have my John in your class."

Rachel smiled. Little John was Sarah's youngest son; David, her cousin's eldest, had finished the eighth grade over a year ago. "I will. John is a *gut* boy and smart. He does not think he needs to go, but I will show him differently. He will make a fine farmer, but he should know how to deal with the English."

Sarah agreed, but soon Eli approached to speak with his wife, taking her attention. Eli Schrock was a man of short stature, even shorter than his wife. His hair and chin-beard were dark, his build strong. Sarah made introductions between Rachel and Eli.

Dressed like the other Amish men of the community in his black Sunday best, Eli was polite and pleasant, his gaze recognizing her as a family member. He wore a black vest over a white shirt. His trousers matched his vest and wide-brimmed felt hat, which he wore low and that shaded his serious blue eyes. "'Tis *gut* to meet ya, cousin Rachel."

Rachel nodded and murmured an appropriate response. "And you, Eli."

Watching the interaction between husband and wife, Rachel saw how suited Sarah and Eli seemed for each other. Their two youngest offspring, John and Rose Ann, were enjoying a game of tag nearby. Rachel caught the look of affection that glistened in Eli's eyes as he watched them at play.

This is what God intended, she thought. *A* gut *man loving and caring for his family.*

Would she ever find happiness with a family of her own? Rachel experienced a flash of pain as she recalled her courtship with Abraham Beiler and the plans they had made to have a family together. She no longer knew if a husband and children were in her future. In the Amish community, it was important for a woman to have a family, but it could be that the Lord had other plans for her.

Unbidden, an image of Noah's smiling face came to mind. Was it possible that the tiny spark she felt when she was in Noah's company was a sign sent by God to give her hope that she could someday have a husband? Not Noah, she assured herself quickly, but some other fine man? She sighed. She was afraid to care for a man. She'd felt betrayed by Abraham. Could she ever recover from his betrayal?

The men, including the church elders, came to the table to eat. The women served them, and then while the men enjoyed their food, the women and children ate in the kitchen. The King house wasn't as large as the Lapp residence, but all of the church members still fit nicely.

"It was a fine church service," Miriam Zook said as the women cleaned up afterward.

"Ja," Agnes Troyer said, "Preacher Levi is a blessing to us all."

"So is our deacon, Abram Peachy," Alta Hershberger commented as she wrapped up the leftover loaves of bread and set them on the table for others to take home afterward. "He is a man with a kind heart."

"She thinks every available man has a kind heart," Emma King whispered to Rachel. "Always looking for a husband for her Mary, poor thing. Mary can find a husband without her dear *mudder*'s help."

Rachel had to control a grin. Emma King was her cousins' *grossmudder.* She and *Grossdaddi* Harley had returned recently from a trip to North Carolina, where they'd been visiting relatives of Emma's. Charlotte's grandparents were outspoken and full of common sense. Meeting them for the first time, Rachel had liked them immediately.

Unaware of Emma's comments, Alta, Agnes and Miriam continued their conversation about Deacon Abram and his children.

Rachel couldn't help listening with interest. She looked at her cousin, who met her gaze with a barely perceptible smile curving her lips. Charlotte had seen Rachel listening to *Grossmudder* Emma.

"Do you think he will ever marry again?" Miriam put the lid on a bowl of pickled beets.

"Abram?" Alta arranged leftover muffins from different sources on one plate.

"Ja."

"'Twould be a shame if he didn't," Alta said. "Those

five *kinner* of his need a *mudder,* and there are some girls in our community who need a husband."

The women finished cleaning up the table and moved outside to sit in chairs arranged in the front yard under a shade tree. The sun was warm and the sky was clear. Rachel thought they couldn't have asked for a nicer day.

Alta settled her attention on the two cousins who stood near their seats, waiting for Aunt Mae and some of the other women to come out into the yard. "Charlotte, Rachel, you would like to marry someday, *ja?*"

Rachel and Charlotte could only nod. It would have been a terrible thing to do any differently.

"Now, Alta and Miriam, don't you be planning any of my girls' weddings," Aunt Mae said as she joined the group. "There will be time enough when God wills it."

Rachel sat down, while Charlotte returned to the house. Katie Lapp joined the group, carrying baby Hannah. "May I hold her?" Rachel asked, loving the way the child had curled into her the last time she'd held her.

Katie smiled and handed over the sleepy little girl. "She feels comfortable with you," Noah's mother said. "You have a gift with children. You will be a wonderful teacher."

Rachel stood to settle the baby comfortably against her and then sat, ready to enjoy the afternoon. As the women chatted about the service, the meal and their children, she listened, content as she rubbed her hand over a dozing Hannah, who lay against her chest. She was conscious of the warmth of the baby against her and tears threatened. She closed her eyes so that no one would notice and willed the memory, the pain and fear, away.

A young boy's shout, followed by a woman's scolding, drew Rachel's attention. Opening her eyes, she couldn't help but laugh at what she saw. The second-eldest Peachy boy, eleven-year-old Nathaniel, had grabbed his sister's head-covering and was parading about the yard wearing Ruthie's Sunday black bonnet.

"Nate!" Charlotte King reprimanded, trying to look stern, but Rachel could see that her cousin worked hard to stifle her own amusement. "See how upset you've made your sister. Where is *your* hat?"

"Over there, Charlotte." He gazed up at her with wide eyes.

"Why don't you give Ruthie back her bonnet and put on your hat."

"*Ja,* Charlotte."

Charlotte nodded, approving his choice. As Nathaniel ran to do her bidding, she caught Rachel's gaze. Her eyes twinkled and Charlotte's lips broke into a grin. Rachel nodded and grinned back at her.

"Charlotte?" Ruthie Peachy drew Charlotte's attention. Rachel felt a little catch as the grateful little girl offered her hand to Rachel's cousin, and the two set off to enjoy a walk together.

Rachel closed her eyes again, but this time her thoughts were amused with visions of a little boy in his sister's bonnet.

"She'll make a *gut mudder,*" Alta Hershberger said, her eyes narrowing as she watched Charlotte and Ruthie walk away, hand in hand.

"*Ja,*" Aunt Mae agreed. "Charlotte, like my niece Rachel, has a way with children."

Hearing her name, Rachel opened her eyes. "Charlotte had a good teacher in her *mudder,*" she said lazily. Hannah stirred, and Rachel calmed her with a gentle hand on the back of her head. Katie Lapp had removed her daughter's *kapp,* as it was too warm for the child to be wearing it, especially when she had no need to wear one at her age.

"Alta, how is your *mudder?*" Katie Lapp asked.

The two women got into a conversation about Alta's ailing mother, who had problems with diabetes and arthritis, and Rachel listened, only partly hearing.

"Joshua!" Katie called a while later. "Will you find Amos or one of my sons for me?"

"Mam?" Noah appeared suddenly. "Were ya looking for one of us?"

"Ja, Noah. Joshua! No need to go looking for Amos." And Aunt Mae's youngest was only too happy to scamper away and play. "Once again, you are about when I need you," Katie said with a smile.

He had been near but out of sight for some time, watching Rachel as she held his baby sister. She'd looked relaxed and peaceful. *She'll make a* gut mudder. He could easily see her married and with children. As he'd watched, he'd realized suddenly that he wanted to be her husband. He wanted to be the father of her children. He saw her eyes pop open when she heard his voice, saw her stiffen and sit up straighter. Hannah started to cry but Rachel immediately soothed her.

"Noah?"

He quickly recovered himself. *"Mam?"*

"Would you tell your *vadder* that the cleanup is done here and we can go whenever he is ready?"

He focused his attention on his mother. *"Ja.* He is in the north field with Amos."

As he went to find his father, Noah couldn't dispel the mental image of Rachel holding Hannah, of the loving way she patted the baby's back and cradled the child's head. His feelings for Rachel reminded him of a conversation he'd overheard earlier between Miriam Zook and Alta Hershberger regarding his friendship with Charlotte. Many of the church district women believed that he and Charlotte would court, marry one day and then have a family. He might have entertained the idea a year or two ago…long before Rachel had arrived in Happiness.

But what of Charlotte? Did she expect them to wed? She was a dear friend; he certainly did not want to hurt her. Nothing had changed in their relationship to suggest that she had any intentions to have him for her husband.

He needed to speak with Charlotte and soon. He had to gauge her reaction and be honest with her. He owed her that.

She will make a great mudder *as well,* he thought as he recalled how she had scolded the youngest Peachy boy. He grinned. She had a strong sense of character and of right and wrong. He knew that Abram would have been distraught to see Nate teasing his little sister. Charlotte knew it as well. She had to be hard on the boy for Nathaniel's own good. And truth be told, Nate had obeyed without question. He hadn't seemed to mind at all.

Noah found his father in the north field, where he had seen him last. *"Dat!"*

The sun was bright as he approached, and he tugged down the brim of his black felt hat.

"Noah." His father waited patiently for him to join the men who had gathered to admire the field.

"*Mam* said that the cleanup is done and she is ready to leave when you are."

Samuel Lapp nodded and then turned to Amos. "You'll be getting ready for the singing."

Amos King agreed. "Jedidiah and the twins are helping BJ prepare the barn."

The singing held on the same Sunday as church service was a gathering of young people for the purpose of singing hymns from the *Ausbund* and for girls and boys to spend time together in an appropriate manner. A large table would be set up with seats prepared for the boys to sit on one side and the girls across from them. The singing would begin early evening and end about 10:00 p.m., but the young people would often stay longer to visit. The young men would take their sisters, but not the girls they were sweet on…although looks would definitely be exchanged between a young man and the girl he liked. Sometimes, the young man would ask to take his prospective girlfriend home. "You'll be attending the singing, Noah?" Amos King asked.

He had an immediate image of Rachel sitting at the table, her voice raised in song. "*Ja,* I will be there."

"Then I'd better see how the barn is coming," Amos said with a smile.

Samuel nodded. "And I'd better gather up my family and take them home."

Noah would attend the singing and gladly. He wanted the chance to spend time in Rachel's company. He couldn't take her home this night, as this was her home and she would not need a ride. Still, he would enjoy the opportunity to be near her.

Chapter Seven

❧

That evening, Rachel stood outside the Kings' barn with her cousin Nancy, greeting the young people as they arrived for the singing. Amish teens from another church district would be joining them. There would be sixteen attendees in all, but it was Noah and his brothers who drew her attention as the Lapp buggy pulled into the yard and stopped. Rachel felt her insides begin to thrum as Jedidiah, Elijah, Jacob and finally Noah alighted and then approached. She tried to look away, but she couldn't keep her eyes off Noah.

"You have brought your singing voices?" Nancy teased with a smile.

"Ja," Elijah Lapp said shyly.

"What singing voices?" Jacob eyed the cousins with a grin. "Who said anything about singing voices? I thought we were here to—"

"Jacob!" Jedidiah scolded. "Mind what you say to Nancy and Rachel."

Unembarrassed by the exchange, Rachel grinned at Jacob and then Jedidiah before she greeted Elijah. Lastly, she felt a little thrill as she spoke with Noah.

"Did you bring your appetite?" she teased Noah. "There are chocolate brownies and fudge candy."

Noah grinned. "*Ja,* I'm always hungry for chocolate."

Several other buggies pulled into the yard, drawing their attention. Rachel remained conscious of Noah beside her as Annie Zook, her brother Josiah, her sister Barbara and Mary Hershberger got out of a carriage and approached.

"Annie," Jedidiah greeted, "I heard you have a new dog. How is she doing?"

Annie regarded him with bright eyes as she nodded. "Millie is doing fine. She follows me all about the yard and house." She lowered her voice. "*Dat* lets me keep her inside."

The Miller sisters, Rebekka and Mary Anne, and their brother Reuben joined the gathering, and Nancy introduced them. Rachel stood and greeted the Millers and then each person she met: the Troyer brothers—Ron and Wayne, along with the Mast twins—Mark and Martha. She tried to remember their names, but her thoughts were filled with Noah, who had chosen to stand next to her.

"The Mast twins love M&M candy." Noah leaned close to whisper in her ear, and Rachel could detect his lemon-scented shaving soap. "Martha and Mark—M and M. Remember that and you'll know their names. They've probably brought some of the candy with them."

She chuckled. "Any other helpful hints?" she asked him.

Noah looked thoughtful. "RW for the Troyer brothers? Ronald and Wayne."

"RW? How am I to remember that?" Rachel stuck a hand in her apron pocket.

He shrugged but looked amused. "It was the only thing that came to mind."

The young people stood outside talking and teasing one another. The younger Lapp brothers, Elijah and Jacob, moved away from the group to speak privately. Rachel saw Elijah nudge Jacob as he gestured toward someone—Nancy, she thought—in the gathering of young women. Jacob scowled as he listened to his brother before he and Elijah headed back toward the barn. They stopped to let the girls go first, and then crowded each other in the doorway as Elijah tried to beat his brother inside, probably to find a seat at the table nearest to the particular girl he had his eyes on.

Noah waited outside when Rachel hesitated about entering the barn. "Would you like to go in?" he asked.

She nodded. *"Ja."* She was overly aware of the fact that they were the only ones in the group remaining outside. She felt a fluttering in her stomach. Noah looked wonderful in his white shirt and black vest. She glanced away from his intense regard, her gaze dropping to his black shoes, traveling up his black trousers to stare at his neck.

"A *gut* night for a singing," he said softly.

"Ja." Was that all she could think of to say? She could sense his amusement, which bothered her, so she pretended to be indifferent. "We should go inside."

Charlotte came out of the King house and waved as she crossed the yard. Spying her, Noah immediately excused himself. "I need to speak with Charlotte," he told Rachel. "Go ahead inside and we'll join you in a few minutes." He hurried from Rachel's side to meet Charlotte halfway across the yard.

Rachel felt her heart grow heavy to realize that he

hadn't even waited for her answer. Unable to watch the two deep in conversation, she turned and slowly entered the barn.

Noah hurried toward Charlotte. "May I talk with you?" This was the first opportunity he'd had to discuss privately the community's expectation of their courtship and marriage.

Charlotte frowned. "Is something wrong?"

Waving her to follow, he moved away from the barn so that their conversation couldn't be overheard. "We have been friends a long time, *ja?*"

"*Ja,* Noah. Since we were children."

"The community expects us to marry." He pushed back his hat and locked eyes with her.

She scowled. "Noah, you're not going to ask to court me, are ya?"

He waited a heartbeat to search for the right answer. "Have you been waiting for me to ask you?" This was Charlotte, his closest friend for many years. He didn't want to offend her.

"*Nay.*" She shook her head, her expression concerned as she gazed up at him. "Noah, may I tell you what is in my heart?"

"*Ja,* you can tell me anything." He stood leisurely with his hands in his pockets, waiting for her to respond, but he felt anything but calm.

"I care for another. At one time, I thought we might one day court and wed, but not now—"

Relieved, Noah grinned. "I too care for another," he confessed. He glanced toward the barn, at where Rachel had been standing earlier.

"My cousin Rachel."

He was surprised by her perception. *"Ja."*

"Gut." She glanced briefly toward the barn, as if she was eager to join the others.

"You don't mind?" he asked, wondering if it was true. Was she glad that he liked Rachel?

She regarded him with twinkling blue eyes. *"Nay.* How can I mind when my heart wants Abram?"

Noah chuckled, happy with her revelation. "Abram Peachy." He raised his eyebrows. "And his five children. The little ones do love you. Has Abram shown an interest?"

"Not yet."

"Maybe I can help you—" He grew thoughtful. "What if I arrange it so that you get to spend time in Abram's company?"

She nodded, pleased. "And I tell Rachel about all your good qualities. I've seen the way she looks at you. She may like you but is too shy to show it."

He shrugged. "She doesn't seem shy to me."

"She doesn't know you as well as I do," Charlotte said as the two headed toward the barn. "But she will after she spends more time with you. What if we plan a trip into town? She'll feel comfortable with me there and it will give you a chance to talk with her. *Mam*'s been wanting me to shop for her. Are you busy tomorrow?"

"Tomorrow will work. Do you want to ask her or should I?"

"Let's see who has the first opportunity. If you get a chance first, you ask her. If the opportunity comes my way, then I will."

"All right. Let's hurry. I'd like to sit across from Rachel if the seat isn't already taken."

"Noah?" Charlotte said, and he halted, faced her. "Be yourself…and you'll win her heart."

He grinned at her as they continued toward the barn. "I can say the same about you and Abram. Abram is a shy man. He will open up more if he is comfortable. You've done a wonderful job with his children. They already love you. I think that Abram may care for you, but he is not yet ready to admit it to himself…or you. Let me think about it, and I'll see what I can do to help you to spend more time with him, and *not* cleaning his house or watching his children. Something more enjoyable for the two of you."

Jedidiah Lapp led the singing, his strong voice clear and vibrant. His brothers Jacob and Elijah and Mary Hershberger quickly joined in, and the others followed, their voices raised in Jedidiah's choice of song. Noah took a seat next to his brother and across from Rachel.

Rachel met his gaze as Noah sat and smiled at her. She attempted to smile back, but she knew that she'd failed miserably. She had no reason to be upset. She knew that Charlotte and Noah were friends, and she shouldn't be surprised that Noah wanted to talk with her cousin alone. But it was hard to watch him walk away from her and go to Charlotte. She wasn't jealous or envious—it was a sin to be either one. She felt sad.

Jedidiah sat across from Annie Zook, and Annie gazed at him as she sang his choice of hymn from the *Ausbund.* After everyone finished the hymn, it was Annie's turn to choose. Each teen would get a chance to select a favorite hymn. In between songs, there would be refreshments and other little games to make the evening fun.

The evening passed quickly. Rachel relaxed and began to enjoy herself. She was no longer upset. It was hard to be upset when she remained the focus of Noah's gaze and smile as she sang along with the others.

Soon it was time for all to head home.

"May I walk you to the house?" Noah asked Rachel as he came up from behind her.

"It's just across the yard." Rachel searched for Charlotte, but her cousin had disappeared, perhaps in the company of Nancy as she headed home.

He tugged on the bottom of his black vest. "I'd like to walk you across the yard," he said.

Uncertain what to think, she could only nod. Truth was…she liked spending time with him.

A full moon lit the night, making it easy for them to see. "Nice evening for a walk," he commented conversationally. He seemed reluctant to move.

Rachel glanced at him and caught him staring at her. "*Ja*. There is a cool breeze." She quickly averted her gaze. "A *gut* time to leave the windows open."

There was a long moment of silence, or so it seemed to Rachel.

"Charlotte asked me to take her to town tomorrow," Noah said. He leaned a shoulder against the barn and crossed his legs. "Will you come?" His stance seemed waiting…expectant.

Suddenly nervous, Rachel fiddled with her *kapp* strings. "Charlotte didn't mention going into town."

A mosquito buzzed in her ear. Noah straightened, raised his fingers as if to swat the insect away. He quickly dropped his hand to his side, as if he'd thought better of it. "She asked before the singing this evening."

Was that what they were discussing earlier? Rachel wondered.

"Charlotte may not want me to go." She began to walk toward the house, and Noah followed her lead. "Aunt Mae may have chores for me."

"Charlotte wants you to come." He stopped and caught her arm before quickly releasing it, but not before Rachel saw something flash in his eyes. He continued across the yard. "I'm sure she'll ask you."

Did she dare go into town with Charlotte and Noah? Rachel wondered. She shouldn't; she liked being near Noah too much. Still, if they both wanted her to come, why shouldn't she?

She paused and turned toward him. "Will Joshua be coming for ice cream?"

Noah grinned. "*Ja.* I'm sure he'll want some."

"It was delicious ice cream." Smiling, she walked on, and he fell into step beside her.

"Then you will come?" he asked, sounding hopeful, his soft voice close to her ear.

Rachel inhaled sharply and fought the temptation to lean into him. "If Charlotte asks me and Aunt Mae does not mind."

"Charlotte will be shopping for Aunt Mae."

Another mosquito buzzed in Rachel's ear, and she stopped to swat it away. Noah's hand was there first, brushing the insect from her *kapp.* Their fingers touched briefly and withdrew.

His nearness in the semidarkness had a strange effect on her. "I'm here," she announced unnecessarily as she climbed the porch steps. She turned, placed a hand on the railing. "It was nice of you to walk me across the yard." Her voice sounded shaky to her own ears.

"The pleasure was mine," he said huskily as he leaned in closer to her. He withdrew but seemed reluctant to leave.

Rachel thought she heard him sigh. "I will see you tomorrow morning, Rachel."

She nodded, silent, and then she opened the door, stepped inside, and quietly closed the door.

"Rachel!" Charlotte came out of the kitchen, holding up an oil lamp. "Would you like some cake?" The light cast shadows on her features, making her eyes shine.

Rachel grinned as she trailed behind her cousin into the kitchen. "Chocolate?"

"Ja." Charlotte waved her toward a chair.

Rachel sat down at the table and accepted the plate of chocolate cake that Charlotte handed her.

"Would you like to go to town tomorrow?" Charlotte sliced a second piece of cake and took the seat across from Rachel. "Noah is going to take us. *Mam* gave me a shopping list."

Rachel paused with her fork midway to her mouth. "You want me to come?"

Charlotte frowned. *"Ja.* Why wouldn't I? We'll have a nice day."

"It would be fun to go." Rachel ate a bite of cake. "I haven't been into town since I first came. Will Noah bring Samuel's market wagon?"

Charlotte nodded as she finished swallowing a spoonful of icing. "He is a *gut* driver. You won't have to worry," she assured her cousin as if she'd suddenly recalled what had happened in town with the runaway hired buggy.

"I know he is." Rachel got up and went to a cabinet. She opened a door and took out two drinking glasses.

"Noah is a *gut* man, isn't he?" Charlotte said.

Rachel filled the glasses with water and returned to hand her cousin a glass before she sat down again. "He has been kind to me. His family has done a lot for the school and the teacher's house."

"He will make a wonderful husband someday."

Rachel shot her a glance and found Charlotte grinning at her.

"Noah makes quality furniture." Charlotte spooned up a taste of cake.

"I like the desks he made for the *schuulhaus*." Rachel tugged off her *kapp* and set it on the chair next to her.

"He makes chairs and house furniture, too. And he can make cabinets. His *grossdaddi* taught him well."

Rachel felt a little pang. It was obvious that Charlotte was in love with Noah. Her cousin couldn't stop talking about him…how kind and good he was…his ability to make quality furniture…

Charlotte must be thinking about marrying Noah and perhaps soon….

The conversation about Noah dwindled, for which Rachel was grateful. She had known that Charlotte and Noah had a special relationship. She forgot that fact every time Noah did something nice for her.

They finished their cake in silence and then decided to head to bed. Charlotte picked up the oil lamp and led the way. The house was quiet. Their footsteps echoed on the wooden stairs as they climbed to the second floor. The air held the scent of burning lamp oil and the lingering aroma of their evening meal of cold fried chicken and sweet-and-sour chow-chow.

"Charlotte," Rachel whispered as they reached the

top landing, "are you certain you want me to come tomorrow?"

"*Ja,* why wouldn't I be?" Charlotte answered. "The day wouldn't be the same without you."

"I will come, then." No matter how difficult it might be to see Charlotte and Noah together, she would go and try to enjoy the day.

They slipped into the bedroom with barely a sound. The windows had been open and the room had the fresh smell of the day's sunshine mingling with the rich floral scents of the night from outside.

"Nancy?" Charlotte whispered.

Rachel leaned toward the bed. "I don't think she's here."

"Who?" Nancy entered the room with a pleased look on her face.

"Where have ya been?" her sister asked, studying Nancy from beneath lowered eyelids.

"Jacob and I were talking. He walked me home."

Charlotte grinned. "Jacob Lapp?"

Nancy scowled at her. *"Ja."* She dropped down on the end of her bed, which squeaked softly under protest.

"You had a nice time," Rachel said quietly.

"I did." Nancy removed her black prayer *kapp* and reached over to hang it on a wall peg. She began to remove her hairpins. "Jacob is nice. I like him, and I think he likes me."

Rachel wasn't surprised. From what she'd seen, Jacob was interested in someone, and Elijah probably had been teasing his brother about Nancy.

"All the Lapp men are nice," Charlotte said. "But if you like him, I hope he likes you the same way."

With the pins out of her hair, Nancy donned her nightgown. When Rachel and her sister had done the same, Nancy turned out the oil lamp while Charlotte and Rachel climbed into bed.

"It was a great night," Charlotte said.

Rachel could hear the rustling of the bedsheets as Charlotte and Nancy got comfortable. Thoughtful, she was silent for a long moment. "A great night but a long day. I'm suddenly tired."

"Me, too," Charlotte said softly.

"*Gut* night," Rachel murmured.

"*Gut* night," her cousins echoed sleepily.

The two weeks that followed passed by quickly with several days of rain. The trip to town with Noah had been canceled due to the wet weather. Since the rain cleared, everyone had been too busy to take the buggy to Miller's. Aunt Mae had garnered some of the supplies she'd needed from Katie Lapp. The rest could wait until there was time to visit Miller's Store.

Rachel had kept occupied helping her aunt with chores, and when she was done at the King residence, working with Charlotte at Abram Peachy's house. The next Sunday church service was to be held at Abram's. With no wife to ready the house for him, he was happy to see Charlotte, Nancy and Rachel arrive to clean and cook and keep an eye on the children while Abram went about his chores.

"Mary Elizabeth, would you like to make a cake with me?" Charlotte asked as she tied on a patched but clean work apron.

"*Ja,* that would wonderful," the little girl said, looking pleased.

"What about me?" little Ruthie piped up as she entered the kitchen.

Charlotte smiled. "I have something special for you to do as well. Have ya ever made pudding?"

Ruthie shook her head. "We ate pudding together."

"*Ja,* we did. What kind of pudding would you like to eat on Sunday? Chocolate?" She opened a cabinet and pulled out a large porcelain bowl.

Ruthie nodded vigorously. "And I can help?"

"You can help," Charlotte agreed. She tied her *kapp* strings to keep them from swinging too close to the stove while she cooked. She then reached to remove Ruthie's *kapp* and set it on the table, out of harm's way.

Nancy came out of a back room. "Charlotte, I think we need to clean out Abram's refrigerator. I'm not sure everything is safe to eat."

"He receives a lot of food from our friends and neighbors," Charlotte told her. "Probably more than he and the children can eat."

Nancy wrinkled her nose. "Some of it is not something a child would want to eat, and I'm sure Abram is too nice to turn someone's generous offering away."

Rachel checked through the cabinets for baking supplies. "We may have to go to Miller's Store for a few things. I don't see any vanilla or cocoa powder."

"*Mam* has extra," Charlotte said as she pulled a bowl out of a cabinet. She hunted through a drawer for some utensils. "Would one of you mind taking Abram's buggy back home for what we need?"

"I could go," Nancy said after a quick look at Rachel.

"I can drive the buggy," Rachel offered, but a knot of fear became lodged in her throat.

Chapter Eight

Rachel realized that she was right; Nancy didn't want to go after the baking supplies. *I can do it,* she told herself, *and I'll be fine.* She hadn't driven a buggy in over a year, but she would drive one today. "What else will we need?"

"I'll make a list," Charlotte said, searching through a drawer for paper and pencil. "While you're gone, we'll finish cleaning the bedrooms upstairs. Mary Elizabeth, Ruthie, would ya like to help us?"

"May we?" Mary Elizabeth asked just as Ruthie exclaimed, "*I* would!"

With list in hand, Rachel went outside and unhitched the horse. Telling herself to remain calm, she settled herself into the King family buggy and picked up the reins with shaking hands. She took several deep breaths, then, with a click of her tongue and a light flick of the leather straps, she guided the horse in the direction of her aunt and uncle's farm.

She was more than a little nervous at first. She hadn't driven since before the buggy accident that had hospitalized her for nearly two months, but soon the tension lifted and she started to feel at ease. It was a lovely warm June day, and she encountered little traffic on the roadway. She enjoyed the gentle roll of the carriage and the clip-clop sound of Mattie's hooves on the macadam.

A car came around a bend, startling her, and she held her breath and waited as the vehicle slowed as it passed.

How fast the Englishers go! They have little time to enjoy the simple things in their racing cars...the sights and sounds of early summer...the bright colors of rudbeckia or black-eyed Susans that grow profusely along the roadway and in folks' yards...the scent of clean, damp laundry drying on the clothesline.

As she drove along the road, she spied a familiar face—Thomas Schrock, a young boy in their Amish community. Thomas was riding his Amish scooter bike, a two-wheeled bicycle without pedals that was propelled with one's foot.

"Rachel!" Thomas greeted with a wave. The young towheaded child was Sarah and Eli's ten-year-old nephew, son of Eli's brother Matthew and sister-in-law Jane.

"Where are you riding today?" Rachel asked.

"Going to visit my cousin John."

"Tell your aunt Sarah that I will be by to see her soon."

"I will." With a push of one bare foot, Thomas was off, riding down the road toward Rachel's cousin Sarah's house.

As Rachel drove by the schoolhouse on her way to the King farm, she saw Noah and Jedidiah outside the teacher's cottage working to trim the bottoms off several wooden interior doors lined up on sawhorses. She waved as they looked up.

"Rachel!" Noah greeted, and Rachel could see his surprise in finding her alone in the buggy. With saw in hand, he approached. "It's nice to see you out and about."

"Your house is almost finished," Jedidiah said with a smile as he joined Noah. "Would you like to come see?"

"I would," Rachel said, "but I have to pick up a few baking supplies and get back to Abram Peachy's."

Noah nodded. "This Sunday's church services are at Abram's."

"*Ja,* which is why Charlotte is waiting for me to bring her unsweetened cocoa powder and vanilla."

"Will you stop by later?" Noah asked.

"Tomorrow if not today," Rachel said.

"You'll be able to move in the week after next," Jedidiah informed her.

"I'll try to come after I'm finished at Abram's. I'd like to see the house. It's been some time since I've visited. Charlotte and Nancy will want to see it, too."

Noah pushed back his hat with his free hand. "*Mam* is making you window curtains."

They would be plain white window coverings, nothing fancy, as was the Amish way, but useful for privacy. "That is kind of Katie." The mare danced lightly, and Rachel calmed her.

"She wants to know when you'll stop by to visit."

"Tell her I'll be by as soon as I can. We've kept busy in Aunt Mae's vegetable garden. It's coming along nicely. We've been picking weeds brought on by last week's rain." She wanted to stay and chat, especially with Noah, but she had to go. "I will try to come back, but if I don't make it, I will see you on Sunday."

"Be mindful of the traffic on this road, Rachel Hostetler," Noah said softly.

"I will." Then she was off again with a light toss of the leathers until the vehicle reached the dirt lane that ran to the King home. Swallowing the nervous lump in her throat, she gently tugged on the reins, guiding the horse toward the farmhouse. The gentle animal responded and Rachel found herself even enjoying her return to independence. But as her fears receded, thoughts of Noah lingered, and she tried to force them away.

There was no time for Rachel or either King cousin to see the teacher's cottage that day. The next afternoon the three young women decided to walk to the schoolyard and cottage.

"Jedidiah said I can move in the week after next," Rachel said as they walked.

"I don't think I like you leaving us," Nancy replied.

"I'll miss you, too, but I won't be far, and you can come visit, and even stay the night when you can."

That seemed to cheer Nancy. "Charlotte, was Abram happy with how the house looked?"

Charlotte had been the last one to leave the Peachy farm. Abram and the children had brought her home after she'd made their supper. "He seemed pleased. The girls enjoyed helping us."

"Ruthie likes chocolate pudding as much as vanilla," Rachel said with a smile.

Charlotte's gaze held a look of fondness for the child. "She had chocolate all around her mouth before she was finished helping."

"Mary Elizabeth had fudge icing around hers. She did well with cake baking. She'll be a good cook someday."

"As long as she has someone to teach her," Rachel said. "Such a shame that the children have no mother."

"I imagine he'll marry one day soon," Nancy commented.

A strange look passed over Charlotte's face. "What makes you think that?"

"It's what Alta Hershberger believes. She said Abram suffered the death of his wife hard, but he seems to be less burdened now. Once a man is less burdened, then it's only a matter of time before he can open his heart and home to a new wife."

"Alta Hershberger thinks a lot of things, but that doesn't make them true," Charlotte pointed out.

"Ja," Nancy agreed as she ran fingers over a honeysuckle bush as she walked.

"Has she decided who this new wife will be?" Charlotte stopped to pick a wildflower.

"Nay. She said Abram will decide when the time is right and he has made his choice."

Sunday came and went with church services at Abram's, but with the singing back at the Kings'. As he had the last time, Noah asked to walk Rachel to the house, and she accepted.

During the week that followed, members of the Amish community in Happiness came to furnish and finish the teacher's house. Rachel was pleased with the way the cottage looked and felt. It would be another week or so until her bed, table and chairs were finished.

Rachel joined the others in whitewashing the interior walls and sweeping the construction dust from the floors and counters.

"You should do well here," Aunt Mae said as she picked up a dust cloth.

"I will. I will miss living with you and Uncle Amos,"

Rachel said as she swept the kitchen floor. "I will miss my cousins."

"You're welcome to stay with us as long as you like and to come back anytime. You may not want to move in until right before school starts. I don't know if I like the idea of you living here alone." Mae dusted the kitchen-cabinet doors.

"I'm not far from the farm," Rachel reminded her, "and the Lapps are just a few acres away."

"*Ja,* I suppose so." But Aunt Mae looked unconvinced. "You will let Charlotte or Nancy come and stay for a time?"

"Of course." Rachel paused in the act of sweeping an area near the base of a cabinet. "We're all family."

Aunt Mae's expression softened with a smile as the woman patted her niece's cheek. "You are a *gut* girl, Rachel Hostetler."

"It must be the blood we share," Rachel teased as she raised the broom again, and her aunt chuckled.

Charlotte appeared at the open back door. "Look what he's brought!" she cried excitedly before she hurried back outside.

Noah entered the kitchen carrying one end of a trestle table, his brother Jedidiah holding the other end. Behind him, brothers Elijah, Jacob and Daniel each brought in a matching chair.

"Thought you might like this now," Noah said as he set his end of the table down.

"I bet you didn't expect this today," Jedidiah added with a grin. He had the handsome Lapp male face, much like Samuel's and Noah's, but his hair was dark, and his chin had a slightly different set than Noah's. His eyes twinkled as he met her gaze before he turned to instruct his younger brothers on where to put the chairs. Elijah, Jacob and Daniel resembled both Katie and Samuel to varying degrees.

"There are more chairs in the wagon," Noah said, and Rachel followed him outside with broom in hand. There were three more chairs, six in all.

"You made these?" Rachel asked Noah as she watched him hand down another chair to each brother.

"*Ja.* I would have had them done sooner, but I thought it important to finish the house first," he said.

Rachel nodded as she leaned against the broom handle. "You do fine work."

"The furniture is serviceable." He grabbed a step stool and carried it inside the house. He set it beside a cabinet. "For reaching the top shelf."

Smiling, she'd followed him back inside and set the broom against the wall. She was surprised to see Abram inside the house talking with Charlotte.

"Rachel, Abram brought you a rocking chair and a sewing box," Charlotte said, looking pleased.

"They are not new. The chair and box belonged to Elizabeth."

"I will need these, Abram." Elizabeth was Abram's late wife. Rachel realized how difficult it must have been for the deacon to lose someone so young. She caught a look between him and Charlotte, and her eyes widened.

She turned, her gaze settling on Noah, who was setting all the chairs in place around the table. Did it bother him to see Charlotte with Abram? Or was she seeing something that simply wasn't there?

She had thought that Charlotte's excitement had been in seeing Noah arrive with the furniture he'd made for the teacher's cottage. Had it been Abram who had drawn her attention and excitement and not Noah?

Studying Noah, she couldn't help but notice the difference between the two men. Noah was younger, with twinkling eyes and a ready smile. Abram was older, solid, and with kind eyes and a steady yet shy gaze.

Rachel watched her cousin. Charlotte stared at Abram, gazing at him particularly when he wasn't looking. Rachel frowned. What of Charlotte's relationship with Noah? Should she ask Charlotte? *The Lord will want me to mind my own business.*

The teacher's house was coming together. It wasn't ready for her to move in yet. She needed a bed, a stove and linens, as well as other essentials.

"You have all been kind," she told everyone who had come to help.

As they left, one by one, to return home for supper, Noah stopped before her and said, "It is easy to be kind to you, Rachel Hostetler."

His words gave her a lot to ponder on the way home.

That night Rachel thought of Noah as she lay, staring at the ceiling. The house was still. All was dark and quiet. Suddenly, she heard a double rumble of thunder.

"What was that?" Nancy said, sitting upright.

"I don't know," Charlotte replied. "I don't think it's a storm."

The rumble started again.

"I think it's the front door," Rachel whispered.

Charlotte sprang out of bed and into the hall. Mae stood on the landing with a flashlight.

"*Mam,* what is it?"

"Someone is at our door," Mae said. "Your *dat* went down to see."

"I hope no one is in trouble," Rachel said as she joined the other two at the top of the stairs.

Nancy padded out afterward. "What—"

"Shh!" her mother scolded. "I think it's Abram Peachy."

"Oh, no! I wonder what he wants."

"Amos." Abram stood at his friend's front door, looking distraught. "Jacob is missing."

Amos frowned as he stood back and gestured his friend inside. "How long?"

"I don't know. I thought he had gone to spend the night at your daughter Sarah's."

"Dat." Amos's son-in-law, Eli, followed Abram inside.

"Eli," Amos greeted. "You've not seen Jacob?"

"Nay. He was to spend the night with us, but the Zooks treated a group of youngsters to ice cream. I thought Jacob went, too, but then John came home alone. We've searched everywhere on Abram's farm, but not here."

"We should check here, then—and the Zooks'." Amos turned toward his wife, who was descending the stairs. "Jacob Peachy is missing."

"We will find him," Mae said firmly. She addressed her son-in-law. "Sarah and the children?"

"They are at home." Eli fidgeted as if he was eager to get on with the search. "They are upset and still looking, but she will stay home in case Jacob shows. Abram's other four are with them. We think it's best if they remain with Sarah while we look. We searched our property before we came here."

The cousins and Rachel, overhearing from upstairs, rushed to dress and join the others.

"We'll help," Charlotte said.

Rachel nodded. "I'll check Joshua's room," she offered.

Aunt Mae's eyes lit up. "*Ja,* do that."

Nancy said, "I'll go with Eli to the barnyard."

"I'll take Abram about the property. There are many places a little boy might hide, and I know them," Charlotte said.

"I'll head over to the Lapps'." Amos hurried upstairs and returned in less than a minute, dressed. He grabbed his hat and settled it on his head. "Abram, Samuel and his sons will help us find him."

"*Danki,*" Abram whispered to Charlotte as they headed out into the night, their path lit by the flashlight Abram carried.

"He'll be found alive and well soon, Abram." Charlotte caught and squeezed his hand before releasing it quickly. "Jacob is a *gut* boy, but he is easily distracted."

"*Ja.* The last time he disappeared, I found him in the barn, sleeping in the hayloft." He hesitated. "But not this time."

"Let's check the north field." She gestured in that direction. "There is an old lean-to there. Maybe he ran after an animal and took shelter there because he didn't know how to get home."

"I hope you are right, Charlotte." Abram trained the beam of the flashlight across the path before them. "I pray to the dear Lord that he isn't injured or hurt."

"I pray, too," Charlotte whispered as she stepped carefully over a rock.

Back at the house, Rachel waited with Aunt Mae. Jacob wasn't with Joshua, nor had Joshua seen his friend.

Nancy had decided to search with Eli. Amos would return shortly with the Lapp men.

Rachel stood at the window, her heart filled with fear for a frightened little boy. He had been a joy to spend time with when she and Charlotte had watched Jacob and little Ruth earlier in the week. The boy had a lively sense of humor, and she looked forward to having him in her class. He was bright far beyond his young years.

She spied Amos's buggy and another that followed. "Uncle Amos and the Lapps are here." She went out onto the porch to meet them.

Amos climbed down from the buggy and approached. "Did ya find him?" he asked. He held his hat in his hands, and his hair looked as if he'd run his hands through it many times.

"*Nay*. Nancy and Eli are checking the barnyard and barn. Charlotte and Abram have gone looking over to the north field."

Amos looked worried. "We'll search all of our property before heading back over to the Lapps'. Samuel's boys are searching there.

"Samuel, you can come with me." He headed back to his buggy with Samuel following.

"I'll look with Rachel," someone said.

Rachel's breath caught as Noah stepped out of the darkness and onto the porch, his eyes glistening.

"Rachel," he greeted softly.

Chapter Nine

She stared at Noah in fascination. In straw hat, maroon shirt and denim trousers held up by suspenders, he looked wonderful…just as she'd thought of him only moments before.

"Aunt Mae?" she asked, her heart beating wildly. Would her aunt forbid her to join in the search…and with Noah?

"Go, girl. Find Jacob and bring him home." She had given three LED flashlights to the others. She rummaged in a drawer and discovered a fourth flashlight with an incandescent bulb.

Noah accepted the flashlight and waited for Rachel to join him. "Do ya have an idea where to look for him?"

Rachel frowned. "When I went into Joshua's room earlier to see if he knew where Jacob could have gone, my cousin said that Jacob was fascinated with a puppy he'd seen a couple of days ago. If the boy saw a stray or some kind of animal, it's possible he followed it."

Noah looked concerned as he gazed into the night. He clicked on the flashlight, which wasn't bright like an

LED light, but it allowed them to see. "It's so dark. If he is anything like my younger brothers, he'll be terrified."

"We have to find him," she said urgently.

"We will." Noah touched her shoulder, then as quickly pulled his hand away.

That light touch was enough to send her heart careening wildly. She inhaled sharply and tried to maintain her balance.

"Maybe we should check the schoolhouse and cottage," Noah suggested. "Jacob visited both the other day when Abram stopped by to find out when we planned to finish the floors. He seemed fascinated by the school… and the swing sets. He may have wandered down to play on the swings. When he realized that he had missed ice cream with the Zooks, he probably stayed to play. Later, after realizing how late it was, he may have found a way into one of the buildings to wait until morning before seeking help to get home."

"Shall we take the buggy?" Rachel asked, thinking it worth checking the school and cottage.

"*Nay.* It's not too far. Unless you're afraid of the dark?" he teased.

Most definitely not with him beside her, Rachel realized. "I'm not afraid. Let's go. We should tell someone where we are going."

"We'll probably pass Amos along the way. If not, we can get there and back before anyone worries." He looked concerned as they continued along the lane.

Was it wise? she wondered. He was probably right, but whether or not it was wise to walk alone with him was another thing.

The night held the sound of crickets and an occasional car on the main road ahead as she and Noah made their way toward the schoolyard. Rachel was quiet. She could hear the crunch of their feet on the dirt lane and the thunder of her own heartbeat.

Would Charlotte have chosen to search with Noah if she'd known he'd be arriving after she'd left with Abram?

Jacob, she thought. *If anything happens to him...*

"He'll be fine, Rachel," Noah said softly, as if reading her mind.

"I pray that it is so."

She could feel his gaze studying her and she turned to face him. "Do you think we can hurry?" She swallowed.

He nodded solemnly. *"Ja.* That is a *gut* idea."

They picked up their pace in unison, hurrying toward the road, running across to the other side. The buildings looked dark as they approached, which was no surprise, since the school and house weren't in use yet.

"Do ya have your key?" Noah asked as he dug a hand into a pocket of his trousers.

"Nay," Rachel said, upset. "I didn't think to bring it."

Noah grinned, his teeth a flash of white in the semi-darkness, lit only by their flashlight. "I did." He held up a key, which glinted in the light.

She laughed. "You are a smart man, Noah Lapp."

He crinkled his nose and said simply, *"Ja,"* which only made her chuckle more.

The truth was Rachel felt nervous and scared, and at times, she laughed when all she wanted to do was to cry out or scream. Laughter was her way of coping. Did Noah think her awful for chuckling when the situation was worrisome?

They checked the schoolyard first, especially the area of the new swing sets, since Jacob had shown an interest in them. But there was no sign of him. Rachel looked closer and saw what could be scuffmarks in the dirt below one swing, but she couldn't be sure.

"Noah," she said, "would you bring the light closer?"

He quickly obliged, holding the light so they could carefully inspect the dirt. "It's possible he was here earlier...or someone else was. But it could have been any one of the *kinner* in our community."

"But no one knew that the swings were finished, except those families whose fathers constructed them. Jacob!" Rachel called.

Noah joined in with her. "Jacob!" they called together. They listened in silence for a response, but there was none.

"Do you think he may have somehow entered the school?" Rachel asked as she walked along the outer wall of the building.

Noah shook his head. "Not if it's locked." He had taken off his straw hat before he'd left the King farm, and she couldn't take her gaze off his glistening eyes, straight nose and clean-shaven jaw.

"May we check?" she started to say, but Noah was already rushing to unlock the schoolhouse door.

"Jacob?" Noah called. "Jacob Peachy? It's all right. You won't get in trouble, but your *dat* is worried about you. Come out and we'll take ya home. It's me, Noah, and I'm with Rachel Hostetler."

But the schoolroom remained silent.

Rachel felt tears fill her eyes. "It's so late. With each passing minute, I get more frightened for him."

"Let's check the cottage," Noah suggested, and they hurried down the drive toward the new teacher's house.

They had just reached the door when they heard a shout.

"Noah! Rachel! Any luck?" Charlotte said. She and Abram Peachy joined them as they were about to enter the house.

"We checked the school, but he isn't there. We were about to see if he could have hidden inside when it got too late for him to find his way home again."

Rachel's gaze went to Abram Peachy, who looked ashen. "Abram—"

"We have to find him," the widower said.

"We will," Charlotte assured him and touched his arm briefly.

Noah went to insert the key into the lock, and the door pushed open at his touch. The four searchers looked at each other.

"Go ahead," Noah urged Abram.

The kindly older man nodded and entered with Charlotte close behind him. Noah and Rachel hung back.

"Shall we search the yard in the back of the house?" Rachel suggested, feeling helpless while waiting.

"Jacob?" she heard Abram call. "Jacob, son, if you're here, come to *Dat*. I won't be angry. I just want you safe at home."

Rachel heard Charlotte's voice. "Jacob, listen to your *dat*. He loves you. Please come out if you're here."

Noah and Rachel were rounding the house back toward the door when they heard a sudden jubilant cry.

"He's here!" Charlotte cried out to the two of them. "He was hiding in the bedroom. He's well." She went back inside to check on father and son.

"Praise the Lord," Rachel whispered.

"Amen," Noah whispered. He looked at her, and she saw him blink away tears.

"It was a *gut* idea to search here."

"And we weren't the only ones who thought of it," Rachel replied. She closed her eyes, listening to the sounds of the night, happy that a little boy was reunited with his father.

"We should get back," Rachel murmured, although she wasn't in any hurry to move.

"I'd like to see Jacob when he comes out," Noah said.

Rachel agreed. "Will Abram keep his word and not be angry with Jacob?"

"*Ja.* Abram is a man of his word, a *gut* man. And he is a father who just wanted his youngest son out of danger."

Charlotte came out of the cottage first. She beamed at them. "Now we will be able to sleep well tonight."

Abram followed her, carrying his son in his big, strong arms. He had tears of joy as he approached. *"Danki,"* he said in a choked voice.

Noah smiled in acknowledgment. "Jacob, boy, next time you want to play on the swings, ask one of us to take you."

"*Ja,* Noah," the little boy whispered. He looked as if he'd been through a lot. He still wore a frightened look until Abram tightened his hold on him.

"We'd best get back. Did ya walk?" Noah asked Charlotte.

"*Nay,* we went back to the house and got the carriage," Charlotte said.

Rachel saw then the small open buggy that Charlotte and Abram had taken from the Kings' barnyard.

"Ya can ride with Charlotte," Abram told Rachel.

"We'll enjoy the walk back to the Kings'," Noah said

with a glance at Rachel, who nodded. "It's a nice night and it didn't take us long to get here."

Charlotte eyed her cousin in understanding. She said something softly to Abram, and then she, Abram and Jacob climbed into the courting buggy and with Jacob on Charlotte's lap, they headed out onto the road toward the dirt lane that would take them back to Aunt Mae and the others who would be waiting.

Rachel and Noah began to walk back. The night seemed alive with summer scents. The cricket chirps joined the croaking of frogs along a ditch by the roadway.

Rachel felt Noah's presence more keenly. She tried not to think of anything but returning to the house, but she couldn't help but be aware of Noah, who made her feel alive…and tingly…and afraid to put a name to her feelings.

Noah walked silently beside Rachel, keenly aware of her nearness. She looked appealing with the *kapp* upon her hair slightly askew. She had been disturbed from her sleep and no doubt dressed quickly. She appeared vulnerable and he couldn't keep his eyes off her.

She cut him a glance, and he averted his gaze. "It's so quiet," she said softly.

"Ja," he answered. "You can hear the frogs and crickets."

Distant cries of happiness interrupted the night. Rachel and Noah exchanged grins. Abram and Charlotte must have arrived with Jacob.

"I imagine you'd rather have ridden with Charlotte," Rachel murmured.

"Nay, I'm content enough to walk back. It's a nice night."

Rachel's stomach fluttered. "It was thoughtful of you to walk back with me."

Noah stopped to stare at her. "There was nothing thoughtful about it, Rachel. I wanted to walk back with you."

And her heart started to thump hard. She didn't know what to say, didn't know how to answer. She remained silent as she accompanied him back to her aunt and uncle's farm.

As they approached the farm, Rachel began to hurry. It wasn't that she didn't want to spend time in Noah's company, but she was more confused than ever about her feelings for him.

She tripped and Noah caught her before she fell. He held her a few seconds, and Rachel stared up at him, breathing hard.

"Danki," she whispered.

He seemed to struggle with something. "We should go," he said huskily.

Rachel nodded as they continued through the night back to the King farm.

Aunt Mae, Charlotte and Nancy were fussing over Jacob as Rachel and Noah approached.

The child looked grateful to be back within sight of his father.

"I should get home," Abram said.

"Nay," Aunt Mae insisted, "you must stay the night with us. Mary Elizabeth, David, John and Ruthie are at Sarah's, *ja?"* The widower nodded. "No sense going there to wake up the children," she continued. "Eli will head home to let Sarah know that Jacob is all right. Jacob

can sleep with Joshua and John. I can make a bed for ya down in the parlor."

"*Ja,* stay," Charlotte urged.

Abram nodded. "I am tired, and it is late. As long as the others know that Jacob is fine and we'll be spending the night here."

"Jacob." Charlotte held out her hand, and the little boy took it. "Come with me."

"*Dat?*"

Abram reached down to pick up his son, gave him a hug before setting him down. "Go along with Charlotte, now."

Charlotte's gaze met Abram's over Jacob's head as the boy took the young woman's hand.

"I'll get bedding for Abram," Rachel offered, noting the look of warmth between her cousin and the widower. She shot Noah a glance. Did he notice that something was happening between Charlotte and Abram? Or was she mistaken?

Noah didn't seem in the least concerned.

"Is there anything I can do to help?" Noah asked as he followed everyone inside.

"You have done more than enough, Noah," she heard Abram answer as she entered the house to find the linen cabinet.

Noah allowed his gaze to linger on Rachel as she hurried upstairs. If not for the worrisome circumstances of the evening's search, it would have been a wonderful night spent in Rachel's company. He had been focused on finding Jacob, but he had also enjoyed the closeness brought on by the dark night during the walk back. Something was happening between them. He sensed that she felt it, too.

"I guess we should head home, son," Samuel said, interrupting Noah's thoughts. "We need to tell your *mam* and brothers that Jacob is found and they can stop looking."

Rachel returned with a pillow and a quilt. Her gaze caught Noah's briefly as she left the room to make up Abram's bed.

"Is anyone hungry?" Amos asked. "Noah? Samuel?"

"*Nay,* Amos," Samuel said.

Samuel, Amos and Abram talked about the fright they'd suffered and the blessings of the good Lord in finding Jacob so quickly.

"But I wouldn't mind a muffin or piece of cake," Noah said to Rachel as she entered the room.

"I'll find something for ya in the *kiche,*" she said.

He trailed behind her toward the kitchen pantry. "Got any chocolate cake or pie left?"

Rachel chuckled. "I'm sure there is some of each."

Noah waited while Rachel cut him two pieces of cake and set them along with two blueberry muffins on a plate for him to take home.

She smiled. "In case Samuel is hungry when you get home." She stopped as if to listen, and he heard the sound of horse hooves and turning wheels on dirt in the yard near the house. "Your *dat* has brought the wagon around," Rachel said.

Noah nodded. Using two fingers, he sneaked a piece of cake and placed it between his lips. "I like chocolate."

"I couldn't tell," Rachel replied, her eyes twinkling.

"Noah!" Samuel called.

"Coming, *Dat.*" His brown eyes warmed as they settled on Rachel. "I will enjoy the cake and muffin."

Rachel nodded as she followed Noah through the

house and front door. "Enjoy the desserts, but offer some to your *dat*." She stood on the porch, watching as Noah descended the steps.

Suddenly, he turned to capture her gaze. "I'll see you soon," he promised.

Her heart fluttered within her chest. "You'd better go. Your *dat* is waiting."

"Some things are worth making one wait," Noah returned with a smile, which sent Rachel's pulse racing. He left then to join his father on the wagon.

Amos and Mae saw them off with Rachel watching from a distance. It had been an unusual evening, she thought. Who could have imagined that they would be out looking for a child so late at night?

No blame would be given this night. Jacob had disappeared and was found, that was all that mattered to anyone, including the boy's father.

"Sleep in for a while in the morning," Aunt Mae told Rachel as they returned to the house and prepared to ascend the stairs.

Rachel nodded. She looked up as her cousin appeared at the top of the stairs. "Jacob is sleeping," Charlotte said. She looked concerned as she continued, "How is Abram?"

"He is glad now that he has his boy again. He has just gone to bed," Aunt Mae answered from behind Rachel. "You should all sleep in tomorrow. There will be plenty of time to get our chores done. Nancy?"

"Mam?" Nancy came in from outside and went to the bottom of the stairs.

Mae smiled at her daughter. "Head on up to sleep, now."

Nancy nodded. "*Gut* night, *Mam—Dat*," she added as Amos joined Mae.

Then she headed up to bed, with Rachel following closely.

"*Mam.*" Charlotte paused on the stairs and faced her mother. "Abram need anything?"

Mae smiled. "Abram has everything he needs for now."

Satisfied, Charlotte continued upstairs. Rachel and Nancy were ready for bed when she joined them in their room.

"What a frightening night," Rachel said softly as she climbed into bed.

"*Ja,*" Charlotte replied. "Terrifying. Thank the Lord that Jacob was found."

"Amen," Nancy murmured sleepily, and then a couple of seconds later, she said, "I'm tired."

"We should get to sleep," Charlotte said, snuggling down under the covers. "I think *Mam* forgot that we'll have two extra mouths to feed in the morning."

Chapter Ten

Despite her aunt's urging to sleep in, Rachel was up at the crack of dawn. Nancy, she saw, slept on. Charlotte was already out of bed and downstairs.

Rachel dressed and went down to find Aunt Mae and Charlotte fixing breakfast for Uncle Amos, Abram and little Jacob.

"Looks to be a fine day," Rachel greeted as she entered the kitchen.

"Ja." Amos flashed her a smile. "Ya look well rested."

"I am." She pitched in to bring food to the table.

Little Jacob waited while Charlotte fixed him a plate of eggs, bacon and a freshly baked biscuit. He grabbed a fork and started to dig in.

"Jacob," his father scolded softly, "we need to thank the good Lord."

The boy looked at Abram, nodded and put down the fork.

When all of the breakfast food had been placed on the table, Aunt Mae, Charlotte, Rachel and Nancy, who had just joined them, stood and bowed their heads. Amos, Jacob and Rachel's cousins John and Joshua bowed their heads and waited patiently while Abram led them in a prayer of thanks to the Lord God.

"Lord, You have blessed us with many things…this fine food Mae has placed before us…the love of family and friends…and helping us to find my Jacob." He was silent a moment as if overcome with emotion. Rachel chanced a look and saw that he was.

"You have given us much and we thank You for it. Help us to continue to do Your will. In this, we pray."

"Amen," everyone said.

Abram gave his son an approving look. "Eat, Jacob." And the boy was only too happy to oblige as he ate with a gusto that made his elders chuckle even while Charlotte urged him to slow down so that he didn't get a bellyache.

Rachel helped to clean up after the meal, and then she accompanied Charlotte, Abram and Jacob to the Peachy farm. They arrived to find Sarah with Jacob's brothers and sisters. The children ran toward Jacob when they saw him, firing several questions at once.

Jacob answered one or two while Abram watched silently until finally he spoke up. "Mary Elizabeth, did you feed the chickens?"

"*Nay, Dat.* We only just arrived."

His expression soft, he said, "Go feed them, then." His daughter nodded and then scurried away. He turned toward his son. "Nathaniel—"

"Going to let out the horses now, *Dat.*"

Abram nodded approvingly.

"Rachel and I will milk the cows," Charlotte said, and without waiting for an answer, she waved her cousin toward the barn to get the job done.

Rachel didn't mind doing the milking. It was a chore

she did happily. There was something calming about the simple task…the scent of the barn…the warmth of the cow's teats as she gently squeezed and pulled rhythmically…the heifer's low, pleasurable mooing as her milk supply was relieved.

Abram had four milk cows. Rachel and Charlotte each milked two and transported the milk from their stainless steel buckets into a large gas-refrigerated storage can. They would bring enough into the house for the family's use. The rest would stay cold and ready for sale for the community residents and the occasional English dairy farm looking for any extra fresh milk to pasteurize.

As the young women picked up their stools, Charlotte said, "We can stop at the house to see if anything needs doing before we head home."

Everything was being taken care of back at the house. Cousin Sarah had stayed to help, and the kitchen was spotless as the young women entered.

"Where is Abram?" Charlotte brushed stray strands of blond hair from her face, tucking them under her *kapp,* as she entered the house.

"He has gone out into the fields." Sarah smiled. "He took Jacob with him."

"Afraid to let him out of his sight," Rachel suggested.

Charlotte nodded. "Are you going to stay awhile?" she asked her older sister.

"I told Abram I'd stay until he got back. You can go home. I'm sure *Mam* has things for you to do."

"She does. Where are the girls?" Charlotte approached the stove where her sister stirred a pot of simmering chicken stock.

"Upstairs in their room." Sarah briefly gestured over

her shoulder toward the front of the house before she added a bowl of cut carrots to the stock.

"I'll just say goodbye," she told Rachel, "and then we'll leave."

Rachel would have offered to come, but she had the feeling that Charlotte wanted to see the children alone. She turned to find a thoughtful look in Sarah's expression. Perhaps Charlotte's behavior seemed strange even to her sister.

"Rachel! Noah is here to take us to Miller's!"

"Coming, Charlotte!" Rachel hurried to get ready for the trip into town. It had been a long time since she'd been shopping. Today Charlotte, Noah, Joshua and she would be heading to not only Miller's but to other stores before stopping for ice cream. She had looked forward to the trip since they first spoke about it weeks ago.

She wanted to get a few things for the classroom and her new house. Her new church district had given her money to buy what she needed. Perhaps she'd purchase some linens and kitchen utensils....

And she was pleased that it was Noah who would be taking them.

With her *kapp* set neatly on her hair and her apron secured over her royal-blue dress, Rachel hurried downstairs to join the others. She wore black shoes since she would be traveling among the English. If she'd stayed home, she would have gone barefoot because of the warm, sunny day.

Charlotte stood talking with Noah on the front porch when Rachel appeared.

"Rachel, I won't be able to go," she said. "Here—"

She handed her Aunt Mae's list. "You can handle the shopping, can't you?"

"Ja." Rachel frowned as she accepted the sheet of paper. "But I thought you were going, too."

"That was my plan," her cousin said, looking unconcerned, "but I just found that Grandma Emma needs me to help her in the house. She's feeling poorly and wants me to spend the day with her."

Ride into town with Noah but without Charlotte? Rachel felt a bit discomfited. Was it proper?

"Joshua will be going," Charlotte said, as if she'd read Rachel's mind. "He wants his ice cream."

Aunt Mae joined them on the front porch, wiping her hands on her quilted cooking apron. "All set?" she asked.

Joshua burst out of the house, and Charlotte grabbed hold of her brother and ruffled his hair. "I told Rachel that I'll be staying to help Grandma Emma today."

Aunt Mae nodded as if she'd known about the arrangement. "Would you mind taking John? He may want to go. Joshua?"

"Mam?" He squirmed out of his sister's grasp.

"Go find your brother and ask him if he wants to go into town with Noah and Rachel." Mae eyed her youngest son's tousled hair. "And get your hat! You'll not leave the house without your head properly covered."

As if to tease his older sister, Joshua skirted an area far from Charlotte before he ran to do his mother's bidding.

"You want me to stay and help?" Rachel offered, feeling that she should.

"Nay, child. You go into town. I need someone who knows how to cook to do my food shopping. You've

been working hard since you came to Happiness. Go and enjoy your ice cream."

Wearing a straw hat on newly combed hair, Joshua appeared moments later with his older brother.

"We're going for ice cream?" John put on his banded straw hat as he approached.

"Ja." Noah pulled dollar bills out of his pants pocket.

"I'll go!" His excitement waned as he suddenly gave his mother a little-boy look. "You sure *Dat* won't mind?"

"Nay, he'll be fine with it. You go, son, and have a nice time in town."

"I'll be sure to get everything on your list," Rachel promised.

"Don't forget the raised doughnut mix," Aunt Mae urged, "and have a wonderful time."

Noah helped Rachel onto the front seat of the wagon, while the two King boys climbed into the back. Rachel felt the dip and sway of the vehicle as Noah climbed on board and sat next to her.

Aunt Mae came off the porch and shielded her eyes from the sunlight with her right hand. "Noah, mind you bring them home before supper time."

"I will, Aunt Mae." He grinned at her as he picked up the reins. "Want any candy?"

Mae's eyes lit up with delight. "Licorice," she said.

"Licorice it is," Noah replied with a grin, and then they were off on an adventure into town for shopping and fun.

Rachel was silent as Noah guided the horse-drawn wagon down the lane and then left onto the paved road. Behind them, Joshua and John teased and taunted one another.

"I can eat more ice cream than you!" Joshua said.

"I'm bigger. I can eat more." John pushed down the rim of his brother's hat and Joshua tilted back his head to look up at him and said, "Can*not*. I may be little but I've got a bigger hunger than you!"

The exchange between them continued until their claims and excuses had become so funny that they laughed uproariously. Rachel and Noah flashed each other grins before they too succumbed to laughter.

"John, Joshua," Noah said when the hilarity had died down. "I know someone who can eat more than the both of you put together."

"Who?" John asked.

"Rachel!"

Her eyes widening, Rachel looked shocked. "Noah Lapp, you know that's probably true!"

Which was the last thing anyone expected her to say and everyone laughed again merrily as they traveled down the road on the beautiful, sunny day in Happiness, Pennsylvania.

They reached Miller's Store first. Rachel brought in her aunt's list, and with Noah's help, she was able to gather and purchase all the requested supplies quickly.

John and Joshua wandered about the shop, exclaiming about the cookies and candy for sale.

"All done, boys," Rachel announced. "Time to go. You want to try to out-eat me in ice cream, *ja?*"

Noah took some of her purchases, set them in the rear of the wagon, and then helped her to climb up onto the seat.

"Did you get everything you needed?"

"For Aunt Mae, *ja,*" Rachel said. "Among other things, I purchased two bags of doughnut mix for her."

She straightened her skirt over her legs. "I had hoped to find a few things for the house."

"I know where you can get some household items. Shall we head there next?"

"Will they have linens and cookware?"

Noah nodded. "And fabric and many other household goods."

"That would be helpful," she said. "I would like that."

Noah took her to a small Amish shop located on a back road just outside of Happiness. He guided the horse onto the drive that led to a farmhouse and reined in by a small white outbuilding. He climbed down and roped the leathers around a hitching post.

"Yoder's General Store," Noah announced with a sweep of his arm.

Joshua and John scurried down from the back of the wagon. "May we go up to the house to see if Henry is there?"

"Don't be long. We'll have to be on our way soon if we are to finish shopping and eat our ice cream." Noah gestured toward the door of the store. "It may not look like much outside, but Margaret has a lot to offer. She can help you with whatever you need. If you don't see it in the store, she can get it for you." He held open the door for her. "Henry is Margaret and Harry's nine-year-old son."

"Noah, this is a nice surprise," Margaret said.

"I brought our new schoolteacher."

Rachel smiled. "Noah tells me you can help me find what I need for the new teacher's cottage."

Margaret returned her smile as she glanced back and forth between Rachel and Noah.

Rachel had made a list of things she needed before

she could move in. "Sheets, towels…and do you have a good stockpot?" She read off several more items she would need after school started.

Rachel bought several items on her list and then ordered a couple from Margaret. "I appreciate your help."

"Let me know if there is anything else you might need."

The door burst open and Joshua, John and a third towheaded boy ran inside the store.

"Mam!" cried the boy Rachel decided must be Henry. "They're going for ice cream. Can we go, too?"

"Not today, Henry. I'll take you myself tomorrow."

Henry tried to hide his disappointment, but failed.

"Would you like me to take him and then bring him home?" Noah offered.

Margaret opened her mouth as if ready to decline. Rachel saw her study her son's eager expression, and she watched as Margaret relented.

"I'm sure Henry would enjoy that." Margaret reached into a jar behind the counter and came up with a few dollars. "Enjoy the ice cream on me."

Noah held up a hand. "That's not necessary. We're happy to buy Henry's."

Margaret hesitated, but then seemed to read something in Noah's features. "All right. *Danki.*"

"Come on, boys, let's get some ice cream!"

Rachel spoke briefly with Margaret about her order, and then she walked with Noah to join the excited young boys.

They drove toward the ice cream store, but then Noah pulled into the parking area of a local restaurant.

"I think we need to have a meal before ice cream," Noah said.

"*Gut* idea," Rachel agreed.

The boys weren't as enthusiastic. "Dinner," Joshua complained.

"How about a hamburger?" Noah suggested.

John's and Henry's eyes lit up. "*Ja!* Hamburgers!" they chorused, and Joshua joined in.

Noah hitched the horse to a post before he, Rachel and the three now-eager boys entered the restaurant. They were taken immediately to a table.

Noah glanced at each one of them. "All having the same?" The boys nodded. "Five burgers and fries," he said with a grin to the waitress.

"Something to drink?" the Englisher said.

"Three milks and two iced teas," Noah replied and was happy to see Rachel's nod of approval.

Seated across from Rachel, Noah studied her and liked what he saw. She chatted with the three boys, increasing their enthusiasm for the meal to come and the ice cream to follow soon after.

He felt a tightening in his stomach as Rachel flashed him a smile. She seemed relaxed and happy, and he was pleased that the first moments of tension between them, when she'd learned that they'd be going into town without Charlotte, had passed. If she was uncomfortable now, she didn't show it.

It wasn't long before the food arrived. John grabbed a bottle of ketchup and poured it liberally under the top of his hamburger bun and onto his plate for his fries.

The conversation was fun and teasing as Rachel and Noah watched three young boys enjoy their lunch.

Rachel was conscious of Noah's eyes on her whenever she wasn't looking at him. His glance made her feel flushed. She turned quickly to catch him staring and raised her eyebrows. Noah chuckled and handed her one of his fries, which she promptly popped into her mouth.

When they were done eating their burgers, they left the restaurant for the ice cream parlor. Everyone ordered a different flavor of ice cream cone. Rachel loved chocolate-chip-mint ice cream, while Noah liked rocky road. The two older boys tried unusual flavors like strawberry fudge ripple and banana crunch moon pie. Joshua was happy with a chocolate ice cream cone dipped in a chocolate candy shell.

They stood out in the warm sunshine, licking their cones quickly so that the melting ice cream wouldn't make a mess. They had just finished eating and climbed back into the buggy when Noah gestured toward the western sky.

"It looks like it's going to rain."

Rachel studied the darkening sky. "It appears black enough to storm. We'd better get Henry home and then head home ourselves before the rain hits."

Noah turned to the boys in the back of the wagon. "We're going to take Henry home."

"I liked the hamburger and ice cream, Noah," Henry said with a grin. His straw hat was slightly askew and his face was streaked with strawberry and chocolate.

"I'm glad you enjoyed it, Henry." Noah flicked the leathers and guided the horse onto the road.

"We did, too, Noah," Joshua said. "This has been the best day ever."

Rachel turned back to smile at him. "You're easy to please, cousin," she said. She reached out to tug his hat brim down over his eyes. Joshua snickered and pushed it back so that he could see again.

"John," Rachel said, "are you glad you came?"

"*Ja,* it was a *gut* day, all in all. I'm glad *Dat* let me out of my afternoon chores."

It wasn't long until they reached Henry's home. They found Margaret where they last saw her in the little shop. She had customers, William and Josie Mast and their daughter Ellen. The family was leaving as the town adventurers came in. "Afternoon, Noah," William greeted.

"*Gut* to see you, William, Josie." Noah pulled one of their daughter's *kapp* strings. "And how is Ellen today?"

The girl giggled. "Fine, Noah. *Mam* bought me candy."

Candy! Noah thought, recalling his promise to bring licorice to Mae. When the Masts had left, Noah turned to Margaret. "Do you have any licorice?"

"Aunt Mae!" Rachel exclaimed, and Noah nodded.

"Hard licorice or soft?"

"Soft," Noah decided, and Margaret scooped fresh licorice from a jar into a paper bag and handed it to him.

"How much do I owe you?"

"Zero cents."

"Margaret…" Noah narrowed his gaze and tilted his head, and Rachel thought he looked delightful.

"You bought my Henry lunch and ice cream," the shopkeeper said. "The least I can do is pay for the licorice."

Noah relented with a smile. "The candy is for Mae King."

"Please give her my regards," Margaret said.

There was a sudden low rumble of thunder. "We'd better get moving," Rachel said as she went to the door to look outside. "The storm is on its way."

"Let's go. John? Joshua? Back to the buggy! I've got to get you home."

A second distant rumble of thunder convinced the boys to hurry to the wagon, where there would be little protection if the storm hit before they got home.

Old Bess rose to the occasion, taking them quickly to the King farm and into the yard.

John helped Noah to unload the supplies and carry them into the house. Aunt Mae came from around the outside of the house with a basket of air-dried laundry.

"You're home in the nick of time," Aunt Mae said. "Noah, would you like to stay for supper? You can ride out the storm with us."

"I'd better go now, Aunt Mae. *Mam* will be worried, and it looks like the weather may take a while to clear."

The others went inside, and Rachel turned to Noah. "I had a lovely time today."

"I enjoyed our day together, too."

"The food was delicious."

The corners of his mouth tilted upward. "And the company?"

"The boys were entertaining," she admitted.

"And me?" he asked, and Rachel thought she detected a serious note beneath his banter.

"You are a skillful driver and a *gut* sport. I had fun spending the day with you."

His body seemed to sigh with relief. Studying him, Rachel had the strongest urge to touch his face, to trace his eyebrows…his nose…and the shape of his mouth. Shocked, she stepped back and looked away.

"You should go before the storm hits," she urged.

Noah studied her, wondering why she suddenly looked upset. There was already a storm within him. His feelings for her were causing all sorts of sparks and thunder and rain inside.

"I will see you again soon, Rachel Hostetler."

"Be careful, Noah Lapp." To his surprise and hers, it appeared, she touched his arm and drew back quickly.

A third rumble of thunder and old Bess's uneasy neighing had Noah jumping into the wagon. With a wave, he turned the wagon around, and with a loud *yah,* he headed toward home.

Rachel watched the wagon grow smaller as Noah drove away.

Noah Lapp. What was it about him that had her forgetting for not only moments but for an entire day the pain of her broken relationship with Abraham?

She had thought Abraham a kind man, but Noah was kinder. She had been attracted to Abraham, but not as much as she felt drawn to Noah.

Abraham had seemed to enjoy her company; Noah gave her all of his attention and wanted hers. He didn't just enjoy her company; he appeared to revel in it.

Charlotte. She knew she should have waited until Charlotte could come. What was she doing mooning over Charlotte's friend?

She closed her eyes as she stood outside. "Dear Lord, help me to be strong and true to Your word. Protect me from myself, in this I pray. Amen."

She turned and entered the house, and wondered how she was going to face Charlotte when she felt so guilty for liking Noah.

Chapter Eleven

Rachel stood by the window, studying the storm clouds. As it turned out, they had reached home in plenty of time. The thunderstorm was moving slowly. The residents of the King farm had just finished a simple supper of eggs, toast and ham. Now they could hear the wind pick up, rattling against the windowpanes. Lightning streaked the evening sky, followed by a deep rolling rumble of thunder.

A lightning bolt zigzagged down to earth, creating a loud bang and pop.

"Did ya see that?" Rachel asked, her eyes widening.

"I did," Charlotte said. She had returned earlier with Grandma Emma and Grandpa Harley. With the imminent arrival of the storm, she said she didn't want them to be alone in their house, even though their residence was less than an acre away on the same property. "Will it ever rain?"

There'd been a lot of bright flashes and loud booms, but so far there had been no rain, although the sky remained dark and ominous.

"I hope it does." Rachel flinched as another bright

bolt fell to earth, creating a loud boom. "We need it. I'm afraid of what the storm will bring if it doesn't rain soon."

"It's an unusual summer storm." Charlotte left the window to sit at the kitchen table. "I've never seen anything like this."

"Me neither." Rachel flinched at a clap of thunder. "I was hoping that this wasn't your average thunderstorm."

"We do get bad storms, but it's the flooding that sometimes concerns us. Not so much here on the farm, but hours of heavy rain can wreak havoc in the stores and shops in Lancaster and nearby villages."

"You all right in here?" Aunt Mae entered the kitchen to see the supper dishes had been washed and put away. "I'm glad you brought your *grosselders* here, Charlotte. Grandma Emma is terribly bothered by the storm. She has been praying nonstop since the wind kicked up and the thunder grew louder."

"Where are John and Joshua?" Rachel asked. She wondered if they were frightened by the storm.

"They're upstairs in their room. They love the adventure of a thunderstorm."

"Not me," Rachel said.

"Nor me," Aunt Mae replied, surprising her. She took a plate of cookies from the kitchen worktable. "I'll see if these will cheer Grandma Emma. She does love her sweets."

"Like you enjoyed your licorice?" Charlotte teased.

Aunt Mae had gotten into the licorice as soon as Noah had given it to her. In fact, she and Uncle Amos had eaten all of it in one sitting. Was it any wonder that neither one of them had wanted much to eat for supper? They had been content with breakfast food for the late meal. It had worked well for everyone. Rachel had been full from dinner out and their ice cream treat, as had her two young cousins who'd shared the day with her and Noah. Charlotte had made her grandparents a late dinner so none of them wanted to eat, either. Only Nancy had been hungry enough to eat two biscuits with her eggs and ham. It had been a quick meal to fix and easy to clean up afterward, which suited everyone just fine.

A flash through the white window curtains. A startling crack. Rachel and Charlotte rushed to the window to see if anything in the yard had been hit.

Whatever was struck, it wasn't as close as it sounded. When the downpour of rain began minutes later, Rachel was relieved. If something had been hit, the rain would help put out any possible fire.

The rain didn't last long, although the sky remained dark. Rachel heard a bang and a rumble.

"John! Joshua!" Aunt Mae scolded up the stairs. "Stop jumping on the bed!"

"Ja, Mam," John called back.

Aunt Mae returned to the kitchen. "Those boys," she said, but the softness in her expression told how much she loved her sons. Rachel had seen the same love in Mae's eyes for her daughters…and for her—her niece.

The rain began again, a steady downpour that soaked the earth. The lightning and thunder continued, and Rachel went to the window to watch for a while before she joined her cousins at the table. "Shall we play cards?" Charlotte suggested.

Grandma Emma entered the kitchen. "I'll play," she said.

They played Dutch Blitz to while away the time until bed.

They heard pounding on the stairs. "John, stop running—" Aunt Mae began, but then she saw the boy's face. "What's wrong?"

"Come upstairs. Come see the fire!"

"Fire?" Aunt Mae hurried up the stairs behind her eldest son, followed by her daughters, niece and mother-in-law. There was a good view of the smoke from the windows in the boys' room.

The dark smoke lifted despite the rain, and the wind threatened to spread the fire, wherever that might be.

"I think that's Abram's farm," Charlotte said with concern.

The storm had started to move away. Thunder continued to rumble in the distance and they could see occasional flashes across the sky. The rain had stopped, and steam rose from the main road's warm macadam as the water evaporated.

"We'd better see if Amos wants to head over to the Peachy farm," Aunt Mae said. Turning from the window, she crossed the room and headed toward the stairs.

"Amos!" she called as she descended the stairs. "There's a fire. We think it may be at Abram's house."

Amos came out of the parlor, followed closely by his father. He turned to Harley. "*Dat,* do you want to come?"

"*Ja,* of course. Abram is a *gut* man, and if it's not Abram's farm, then it must be another brother's."

"*Dat,* I want to go," Charlotte said.

"Perhaps we should all go, in case we're needed."

No one could argue with that logic. They crowded into the family buggy and went on their way. The lane was wet, but the puddles were no obstacles.

"We should alert the Lapps," Mae suggested as the buggy bumped its way toward the paved road. "We may need the boys' help."

"Ja," Amos said. "And Samuel's. I pray that no one is injured."

Mae's gaze met Rachel's. "I pray so, too."

The Lapp buggy was at the edge of the road when Amos drove near. Samuel stuck his head out the side window. "You saw the fire?"

"Ja," Amos called back. "It looks like Abram's."

Samuel locked gazes with his friend. "Hope it's not the house."

Amos's eyes widened. "Let's go." He worked the gelding into a fast trot as he drove the buggy toward the Peachy farm. Samuel and his sons followed behind them.

Rachel knew that Noah was in the vehicle with his father, but she didn't turn around. As the buggy neared the farm, the rising tide of smoke brought fear to Rachel's heart. *Dear Lord, please help them,* she prayed silently.

"It's the barn!" Charlotte exclaimed as her father parked the buggy a safe distance away.

"The animals!" John shouted.

The scent of smoke was thick in the air as they climbed from the buggy and dispersed. Amos immediately ran toward the barn, as did the Lapp men. Abram was leading one of his horses as he came out of the burning structure. The horse was blindfolded, her face covered by one of Abram's shirts. Still, the animal was skittish, perhaps sensing danger in the scent of smoke from the fire. Abram spoke softly to her as he led the horse away from the barn and fire toward the back of the house.

Charlotte, Mae, Rachel and Nancy headed toward the house, where the children stood eyeing the fire with frightened eyes. Charlotte immediately hugged the two younger girls.

"Ruthie. Mary Elizabeth," she crooned. "It will be all right."

Ruthie raised tear-filled eyes to Charlotte. "We saw a flash and heard a terrible bang, and then the barn was on fire."

"*Dat* ran outside to get to the animals," Mary Elizabeth explained. "He got our cows out, and we didn't want him to go back inside, but he went in and brought out Mattie and Blackie, our horses. Nate and Jonas ran to help him. Jonas led the cows to pasture. Nate shooed the chickens away from the barn and across the yard."

Rachel knew that Jonas was Abram's oldest son, and she remembered Nate from his teasing escapade with his sister's bonnet. Her gaze met her cousin's over the children's heads.

"Where's Jacob?" Charlotte asked, glancing around with concern.

"He's upstairs," Mary Elizabeth said. "He wanted to go with *Dat,* but *Dat* wouldn't let him. He ran up to his room. He was upset that *Dat* didn't think him man enough to help."

Rachel saw her cousin's frown. "I'll check on him." She knew where the boys' room was located from having cleaned the house before the Sunday church service that been held at Abram's.

Jacob stood at the window, blinking back tears as he watched the scene unfolding outside.

"Jacob." Rachel approached to stand at the window beside him. "Your *dat* is fine. The animals are safe, and while the barn is lost, your house hasn't been touched. It's something to be thankful for."

"But the barn…"

"They will put out the fire," she murmured, watching the commotion outside. She caught a glimpse of Noah along with Uncle Amos and the other men carrying buckets of water, swatting at the fire with shovels, as they worked to quell the blaze. She said a silent prayer for a heavy downpour of rain.

Relief came in the form of the fire department from the nearest town. An English neighbor had seen the smoke and come over to help. He had placed a call to the fire department on his cell phone. Within minutes a fire truck entered the yard and the firefighters had their thick hoses trained on the burning structure with the water supply from a tanker truck.

"Let's go downstairs and see your *vadder*," Rachel suggested.

Jacob nodded and Rachel held out her hand. He accepted and they walked together down the steps to the main floor.

Charlotte was in the kitchen, fixing food and drink for those who had worked to put out the fire. She poured iced tea and set up a plate of muffins and biscuits with butter and jam.

"They'll be hungry and thirsty," she said softly, but Rachel could hear the tremor in her voice.

She saw that Charlotte had the help of her sister, who came out of a back room. "We should make more iced tea and perhaps lemonade," Nancy suggested as she joined them.

Rachel addressed both sisters. "Jacob and I will be outside."

Charlotte nodded. "Where's *Mam?*"

"I'll find out. She's probably on the front porch."

In the yard, Aunt Mae offered the men a basin of water and soap to clean the soot off their faces and hands.

Rachel called back to let her cousins know. She stood behind Jacob with her hands on his shoulders as he stared at the barn. She followed the direction of his gaze and noted the devastation.

"It's all gone," the young boy said brokenheartedly.

"Ja." Rachel gave his shoulders a little squeeze. "But no one was hurt, nor were the animals. We have much to thank the good Lord for. Barns can be rebuilt, but family or horses cannot."

Jacob caught sight of Noah, who approached. "Have you seen my *dat?*" the little boy asked.

Noah hunkered down before the distraught boy. "Earlier. He's fine, Jacob. The last I saw him he was talking with the man from the fire department—*after* the fire was put out."

The headlights from the fire engines and the lanterns and lights that belonged to Amish church members lit up the yard in the front of the house.

Rachel's gaze locked with Noah's brown eyes briefly over Jacob's head. Feeling a sudden jolt to her midsection, she broke eye contact to search the yard and the newly soaked, smoldering barn. Her heart raced wildly as she looked for signs of Abram. "Jacob, I see him!" She pointed in Abram's direction.

Jacob caught sight of his *dat* and ran toward him. Rachel watched Jacob hug his father about the waist.

"Are you all right?" Noah asked her softly as he rose to his feet, drawing her attention.

She frowned as her eyes met his. "I should be asking you. You were the one near the fire."

The corners of his lips curved slightly. "Were you worried?"

"And if I was?"

He looked pleased. "It would be *gut* to know."

"I was worried. This is a terrible thing." Her gaze left his to settle on the men gathered near Aunt Mae. Charlotte came out onto the porch with plates of food and a pitcher of lemonade with cups. She lifted a hand to wave. Rachel waved back and turned to see Noah lowering his arm.

Noah wiped his forehead with the back of his hand, leaving a streak of dirt on his skin. Rachel raised her fingers to wipe away the dirt and dropped them before making contact. *What am I doing? This isn't appropriate behavior!*

"Rachel!" Aunt Mae called. "Will you bring clean water and fresh towels?"

"Coming, Aunt Mae!" Rachel glanced down and saw a small red mark on the back of Noah's hand. "You have a burn," she said with sympathy. "I'll get you some ointment."

Rachel left before Noah could respond, running inside to find a pot to fill with fresh water and to look for clean towels and another bar of soap. While she was inside, she searched through kitchen cabinets until she found some B&W Ointment, an Amish remedy for burns and wounds.

She handed Aunt Mae the supplies she needed and a man from the local fire department came up to the group with a first-aid kit. He offered to check anyone's injuries.

Rachel saw Noah and then hurried toward him, unscrewing the cap from the ointment as she ran. "Let me see your hand," she urged as she reached him. She held his hand within her fingers and carefully spread the burn ointment onto the tender, red skin.

She heard a sharp intake of breath and her gaze shot up to lock with his. But it wasn't pain in his eyes that she saw. It was something else…something she didn't recognize but that made her feel strange and tingly inside.

"That should help," she said as she put the cap back on the ointment.

"I appreciate it." He looked satisfied as he studied his hand.

"Keep it clean," she warned without meeting his gaze. She didn't hear his answer as she turned and hurried back toward the house. She caught a glimpse of her cousin Charlotte talking with Abram. Rachel noticed the way Charlotte leaned closer to the widower as they spoke, and she frowned.

What about Noah?

She glanced back, but Noah now stood with his father and brothers as they spoke with the English firefighters.

She had to speak with Charlotte and soon. Was Noah going to court Charlotte?

The next morning Rachel went downstairs to find Charlotte alone in the kitchen, pulling muffins out of the gas oven.

"Would you like a blueberry muffin?" she greeted Rachel with a quick smile in her direction.

"*Ja,* I would." Rachel went to a kitchen cabinet and took out plates. She reached for a glass. "Would you like something to drink?"

"Orange juice." Charlotte began to loosen the muffins from the tin and place them onto a porcelain platter.

"Where is everyone?" Rachel set plates and knives on the table.

"*Mam* and Nancy went to visit Grandma Emma. *Dat,* John and Joshua are out in the fields." She placed a muffin on each dish. "It's just you and me for breakfast. The others ate earlier."

Have I overslept? Rachel wondered.

"*Dat* asked the boys to get up earlier this morning as they had a lot to do today. *Mam* and Nancy got up to feed them."

Rachel took the pitcher of juice out of the refrigerator, returning to pour each of them a glass. "Charlotte, may I ask you something?"

Charlotte sat down, broke apart her muffin and spread fresh, homemade butter over each piece. "*Ja,* of course."

"Alta Hershberger mentioned that you and Noah would be courting soon." Rachel hesitated as she carefully, methodically buttered her muffin. "But I saw you with Abram. It looked like you are more interested in him."

Charlotte paused in the act of taking a second bite. "I am," she said softly, almost as if she was embarrassed.

Rachel took a bite and chewed it thoroughly. She blinked, startled, as her cousin's words registered. "You are?"

"I like Abram Peachy," she confessed. "I like Noah, too, but as a friend and a brother. Not as someone to court or marry."

Rachel felt her jaw drop. "But what about Noah? What if he feels differently?"

Charlotte shrugged. "Noah will be fine. You don't

need to worry about him. He is a *gut* man who will find someone to court and marry."

Rachel couldn't stop thinking about her cousin's words all that day and into the next. Was Charlotte right? Or would Noah be upset to learn that Charlotte liked Abram?

And why did *she* care? She and Noah were friends... nothing more. She liked him—it was true. She wasn't ready to have a sweetheart. Or was she?

Abraham Beiler. She fell asleep that night thinking of the man she'd thought she'd marry...recalling the accident and the pain of her recovery in the hospital...and afterward.

The next morning when she woke up, she had a headache. Thinking about the past made her sick to her stomach. Her injuries from the accident had been extensive. The doctor had told her it was possible that she might not be able to give birth.

How could she ever marry when she wasn't able to have children?

Straightening the bed linens in her cousins' room, Rachel blinked back tears.

She must be content to be a teacher, to enjoy children other than her own, to take joy in teaching them English, writing and mathematics.

She heard talking in the kitchen as she headed downstairs and entered the room.

"The barn raising will be held on Thursday. We've put an order in for the lumber, and it will be delivered Wednesday." Uncle Amos sat at the kitchen table, jotting down notes with a pencil.

"Rachel!" Aunt Mae smiled at her. "We need to prepare food for the workers who will be at the Peachy barn raising. I know you wanted to move into the cottage this weekend…"

"Abram needs a place to house his animals." Rachel smiled as she sat down across from her uncle. "The cottage can wait."

Chapter Twelve

The members of the church community in Happiness arrived at the Peachy farm early Thursday morning. The lumber had been delivered the previous day.

Rachel saw the stack of wood and pallets of roofing shingles not far from where the old barn had stood. Several friends and neighbors had worked the day after the fire to remove the charred remnants of the old barn. The land was now clean of debris and ready for new construction.

Men had already begun work on the walls when the King carriage parked in the yard. The sound of hammers and saws filled the air and mingled with the men's shouts and the cries from the youngest children at play.

Rachel carried food items into the house. Aunt Mae and Charlotte were already in the kitchen coordinating storage of refrigerated items and directing the women who came to help.

The scents of bread, fried chicken and chicken potpie filled the room as Charlotte opened the oven to check its contents. The Amish chicken potpie, different from the English version, was coming along nicely. Charlotte had put the chicken on to simmer yesterday, and then she'd added potatoes, carrots and celery, cooking them until it was time to add the homemade potpie noodles she'd made with a half cup of flour and an egg.

The kitchen smelled wonderful, and Rachel checked to see if there was anything to be done before returning outside to set the tables, some of which were under a huge shade tree. The workers had arrived at six in the morning. Food was prepared and ready for the men and boys doing the construction all day. Muffins and biscuits with butter and jelly along with eggs, ham and sausage were put out first. There were pitchers of water, iced tea and lemonade, and hot coffee inside the house for anyone who wanted it.

Rachel stood behind a table, ready to serve the men and boys who took a break to eat. Jedidiah, Samuel and Elijah Lapp came to her table for breakfast first. Jedidiah grinned as he approached.

"Eggs? Sausage?" she asked while picking up a heavy-duty paper plate and lifting the spoon in the tray of eggs.

"Biscuits with butter and jam," he said, and Rachel placed four biscuits on his plate along with pats of butter and a large spoonful of jam. She gave him the plate with a fork and knife. He thanked her and accepted the lemonade that Rachel poured for him.

She fed every one of the Lapp brothers who came to her table…except for Noah, who stayed away. There was no sign of him, and she felt disappointed.

She spied him hammering two-by-sixes together to form one of the longest wall sections of the barn. She watched in fascination as he called to the closest workers—Horseshoe Joe Zook and his two sons, Josiah and

Peter, and the four men hefted the massive wall upright and braced it into place. Another group of men had constructed a sidewall, and they hefted up the section, securing it to the length that Noah and his group had braced. They nailed the two walls together in the corner and secured the end wall in the same manner at the main front section.

Rachel watched for a time until Nathaniel Peachy appeared before her, looking for something to eat.

"Nate, helping out today?" she asked with a smile. She picked up a plate and gestured toward the food.

"Eggs and sausage, please," he said. "And may I have a muffin?"

"Ja." She set a muffin of his choosing onto his plate. "Would ya like something to drink?"

"Iced tea."

And Rachel poured him a glass and then another one as she saw her cousin John approach, looking thirsty after working in the summer morning sun.

She was kept busy serving the workers and returning inside to replenish what was eaten. The day was warm but not stifling, and the men worked up an appetite as the time passed.

She still hadn't spoken with Noah since she'd come earlier that morning. He remained busy hammering, measuring or sawing wood. Everyone seemed eager to grab a quick bite to eat, except Noah.

There were three other tables on the lawn filled with food. Five tables with benches near the house provided places for the men to sit and eat. Nancy, Anna Zook and Sally Hershberger served food from a different table. Another seven tables for sitting were on the other side of the yard.

Rachel saw Jedidiah come back for more food. This time he went to Annie Zook's table, and she saw them chatting and grinning as Annie loaded up Jedidiah's plate.

The boys old enough to help went to Rachel's table more often than not. She smiled, served them and told them that the barn was coming along nicely. But Noah still hadn't come to her table. She saw him now and again as he kept busy working on the barn. She couldn't keep her gaze off him, and once when he turned and saw her, she quickly looked away.

Charlotte gave little attention to Noah, but with Abram she was eager to help. What was she doing? Rachel knew that her cousin preferred Abram, but why didn't she think of Noah's feelings? Was that why Noah stayed away? Because he'd looked over and seen the way Charlotte was ready with drink, plate and attention for Abram whenever he stopped to eat or quench his thirst?

She frowned as she saw the way Charlotte leaned into Abram. Did others notice the interaction between the two? Or was she the only one who knew how Charlotte felt because her cousin had told her?

It was almost noon and dinnertime. Rachel went back inside to see what she could do about bringing out the meal the workers and their families would most enjoy.

Rachel had made peach cobbler from Aunt Mae's canned peaches. It had turned out well, as had the bread pudding, zucchini bars and vanilla cream she'd cooked the day before.

The kitchen was a hive of activity as the women pulled food out of the refrigerator and set some of it onto the stove to heat.

Nancy entered the house from outside. "Is there more iced tea?"

"*Ja*. It's in the refrigerator. There is also a fresh batch cooling on the table."

Rachel glanced about the crowded kitchen and asked, "Is there anything I can do to help?" It seemed as if there were too many cooks in the kitchen already.

Aunt Mae came up to her. "Would you take this outside?" This was a bowl of chicken potpie, and it smelled delicious.

"Do we have raisin bread ready?" Rachel asked as she accepted the bowl.

"*Ja*. Alta is putting on the icing now."

Rachel went out and set down the chicken potpie. She made several trips to the house to carry out more food. She had just set down a platter of buttered noodles when she felt someone's presence. Expecting to see Jacob, who had come back to her table many times, she turned with a grin.

Her grin slipped away as Rachel saw Noah waiting patiently at her table.

"You're hungry." She picked up a plate, wondering why he'd chosen that moment to come.

"*Ja*. Extremely hungry." He grinned. "There were things I wanted to finish before I stopped to eat."

Rachel nodded as she gestured toward the array of food. Other selections had joined the chicken potpie, including corn pie, both of which were kept warm with the use of Sterno. Yeast rolls, pickles, chow-chow and marinated green-bean salad were accompanying sides. There was a variety of desserts, including zucchini bars made with chocolate and butterscotch chips with walnuts and cinnamon. Rachel's peach cobbler sat on the table, smelling scrumptious. Noah eyed all the food and made his selections. He took some chicken potpie, buttered noodles and corn pie with marinated green-bean salad. When his plate was full, he took a seat at a table nearest to Rachel's serving station.

Rachel turned and saw that he was studying her with glistening, unreadable eyes. He took his time, which was his right, since this was the first break he'd taken since six o'clock this morning and it was now almost one. When he was done, he returned to Rachel's table.

"Which dessert did you make?" he asked, rubbing his clean-shaven chin.

"Peach cobbler," she answered, expecting him to look disappointed.

"I'll have some of that, then." He looked around the table. "And that." He pointed toward the zucchini bars she'd made.

Startled, she stared at him. "How did you know I made them?"

He shrugged as he ran his hands down the length of his suspenders. "They look good." He bent close to the plate she handed him, inspecting the zucchini bar carefully. "Chocolate chips?"

"Ja," she murmured as she rearranged some of the desserts. When she looked at him again, she saw his grin. His happiness made her lips curve upward.

"Anything else?"

"Ja," he said seriously. "What else did you make?"

She laughed, believing him to be teasing, but he didn't join in. "What does it matter?" she asked.

"I've been waiting all morning to eat with you. You have your dinner yet?"

She shook her head. "I've been busy serving and bringing out more food."

"Sit down and have dessert with me?"

"What about Charlotte?" She waited with bated breath to hear his answer.

"Charlotte would rather spend the time with Abram."

"And that doesn't bother you?" Rachel felt her heart start to pump harder.

"*Nay.* I'd rather spend time with you, not Charlotte." He gestured toward the table where he'd eaten his meal. "Come. Fix a plate and join me."

"I don't know…"

"Please?" He looked boyishly appealing, but she saw him not as a boy but as a man about whom she couldn't stop thinking.

Rachel glanced around to see if anyone was watching. She grabbed a plate, took a piece of peach cobbler and sat down at the table across from him at one end. Men and women didn't usually eat together…not in gatherings for church Sunday meals or on visiting Sundays. But this was a barn raising and the atmosphere was somewhat festive, despite the hard work of hundreds of those within the Happiness and nearby Amish communities who had come to help. She wouldn't be sitting with him alone. Other folks soon joined their table, filling the length of their benches. No one noticed anything amiss with her sitting at Noah's table. Everyone chatted about the food, the work and the good Lord's will.

Soon, Rachel had finished her cobbler and stood. Noah rose silently, and after one last look in her direction, he went back to work on the barn.

By the end of the day, Abram had a well-constructed

new barn built by family, friends and neighbors. It had
been a good day, blessed by God and appreciated by all.

That night Rachel lay in bed, staring at the ceiling.
Her cousins were asleep. She could hear the sound of
their soft breathing as she recalled the day's events and
the strange revelations.

Noah had no plans to court Charlotte. Rachel felt a
burning in her stomach.

He likes me. She wasn't sure how she felt about it.

When she'd arrived back at the house, she'd found a
letter in the post from her mother. Rachel had written
to her only last week, telling her about the school, the
cottage and her aunt, uncle and cousins.

In her reply, Henrietta Hostetler wrote that all was
well in Millersburg. Her mother wrote that she was glad
Rachel liked her new home in Happiness. She had news
she didn't know if she should tell, but she felt Rachel
should hear it first from her.

Abraham and Emma Beiler were expecting their first
child.

Rachel had suffered mixed feelings when she'd read
about the news. She'd reacted differently than she'd expected. She was no longer upset that Abraham had left
her for Emma. When she thought about why, only one
reason came to mind. *Noah.*

Rachel rose from bed and went to the window. It was
a warm summer night, and with the windows open, she
could hear the crickets...and the light stirring of a breeze
in the trees and bushes.

Noah Lapp. She shouldn't like him, but she couldn't
help herself. She must keep her distance, for his sake as

well as hers. But whenever she thought of his smiling face, she could feel her resolve dwindling. Noah Lapp.

School would be starting soon, and she'd be moving into the cottage and getting ready for her students.

Noah Lapp. Her head said one thing, but her heart was telling her something else. *Stay away. Enjoy his company.* Head and heart were dueling, adding to her confusion.

She closed her eyes, blocking out the night for a moment, but Noah's face filled her mind, and she knew it was hopeless. She went back to bed, tried to relax, forget about the day, thought only of the times she'd spent in Noah's presence…the laughter they'd shared…the smiles…the looks.

Dear Lord, help me to do Your will. Give me the strength to accept what may happen.

During the week that followed, the temperature rose several notches. It was too hot to do much work, so the family sat on the front porch, trying to beat the heat with inactivity, lemonade and iced tea.

To Rachel's surprise, Noah came over to sit with them daily. He arrived in the morning and stayed until just before dinnertime, when he returned home to eat the meal with his family.

Rachel enjoyed those moments he was there. Sitting in the midst of her relatives, she could watch and listen to the conversations between family members and between Noah and Uncle Amos.

Noah sometimes returned in the afternoon with one of his brothers—occasionally Jedidiah, but more often than not his younger brother Jacob, which seemed to please Nancy.

The heat wave lasted a week and a half before breaking. Once the temperature dropped, everyone worked to get caught up on chores left undone, including Rachel, who went to the teacher's cottage to set things up the way she wanted.

The house was ready for her to move in. Her bed was in place and she had all the linens she needed to be comfortable.

She planned to move in the next day. Upon hearing Rachel's intent, Aunt Mae had urged her to accept Charlotte and Nancy's company for the first night or two after she'd taken residence.

Rachel didn't mind. Truth was, she wasn't sure how she felt about living alone, but she had been in her uncle's household long enough. She had things to do in the schoolhouse. It made good sense for her to be close enough that she didn't have to worry about rushing to get to school. She could rise, eat breakfast and walk down a short gravel driveway to open and ready the classroom.

She enjoyed her first night in the cottage with her cousins. Charlotte, Nancy and she giggled long into the night before finally falling asleep in the same room. Rachel and Charlotte slept in Rachel's double bed, while Nancy slept on a comfortable pallet made with a thick layer of quilts on the wooden floor right next to the bed.

They stayed for the first three nights after Rachel's move. During the second day, Noah and his brother Jacob appeared on Rachel's doorstep. Charlotte let them inside.

"Is everything working all right?" Noah asked, glancing about as if to see that all was in order.

"Fine. Everyone is *gut*," Charlotte said.

"Rachel," Noah greeted. "You like the bed? Is it comfortable?"

Rachel flushed. "*Ja.* Charlotte and I slept well last night."

"We just stopped by to see that all was in order. If you need anything, you know our house is not far."

Rachel nodded. She saw that Jacob and Nancy were grinning at each other. She controlled a little smile.

"Would you like breakfast?" Nancy asked.

"*Ja—*" Jacob began.

"*Nay,*" Noah said simultaneously.

"We've got fresh cinnamon rolls." Charlotte held up a plate of the fresh-baked, newly iced cinnamon rolls. The aroma wafting from the treat smelled delicious.

Jacob and Noah exchanged looks. "Noah?"

Noah sighed and then smiled. "They look and smell wonderful. Do ya have enough?"

"We have another half dozen in the oven," Charlotte said, gesturing toward the kitchen table.

Rachel watched helplessly and with a secret thrill as Noah made himself comfortable in a chair next to Jacob's. Recalling her manners, she went to the stove and held up a metal coffeepot. "Would you like a cup?"

Noah held her glance as he nodded, and Rachel quickly turned to take cups out of the cabinet. Her face felt warm and her heart beat rapidly.

"I'll have a cup," Jacob said and Rachel nodded. As she carefully poured each brother a cup of coffee, Rachel found the moment she needed to gather her composure.

Her heart beat a rapid pace, but she believed she hid her reaction to Noah's presence.

Chapter Thirteen

What is the matter with me? Rachel wondered.

She set down the coffee cups and went to get the pitcher of cream out of the refrigerator and butter for anyone who wanted to spread some on a cinnamon bun.

It had been some time since Rachel had spoken with Noah, other than in the company of her relatives on the King family front porch.

"We're here to finish putting up Rachel's clothesline," Jacob said. He held up a roll of rope. The Lapp boys had put up the T-bars a day earlier.

Rachel nodded.

"I'll get started," Jacob said.

"I'll help," Nancy chimed in, and she hurried to follow Jacob out the rear door.

Charlotte, Noah and Rachel remained in the kitchen.

"Another cinnamon roll, Noah?" Charlotte asked cheerfully.

"*Nay.* But I wouldn't mind another cup of coffee."

"Rachel, I have to get over to Abram's to watch the children." Charlotte untied her patchwork apron. "Would you mind getting Noah's coffee?"

"Not at all," Rachel said, experiencing a sudden fluttering beneath her breast. She went to the stove for the coffeepot and brought it over to the table to pour Noah a second cup. While there, she poured some for herself.

The sugar was on the table. "More cream?" she asked as she returned to check the pitcher. She was conscious of the fact that she and Noah were suddenly alone. The flutter within her chest quickened.

Noah handed her the pitcher of cream. "There is enough."

Rachel poured in a small amount after she added a spoonful of sugar. She handed the pitcher back to him, for she'd noticed that he'd given her the cream first. She stirred her coffee and then glanced over at him. He was watching her, a slight smile playing about his lips.

"I appreciate the breakfast," he said, his warm brown eyes twinkling.

"Charlotte made the cinnamon rolls."

"But you made the icing," he said.

She frowned. "How did you know that?"

"You've got a bit of icing on your apron." He leaned toward her and lowered his voice. "The icing is the best part."

She felt an infusion of warmth. It wasn't appropriate for her to be alone with him, not when she was feeling this way. She stood and went to the sink to pour out the last of her coffee, which had tasted bitter to her. "Noah—"

"Ja?" Noah rose from his seat and approached. Rachel seemed skittish. Was she nervous around him? After the outing they'd shared and the search for little Jacob Peachy?

It was wonderful to see her. He wanted to spend

more time with her, but he could tell that something was bothering her. Had she been hurt in the past? He liked her, and he'd thought that she liked him, but lately she seemed distant.

He wanted to court her. Should he tell her? Or would it only frighten her more? He could make himself helpful to her, ready to fix anything in the school or cottage. He could fetch her supplies or offer to take her into town again.

Rachel was startled to turn from the sink and find Noah right behind her. She glanced up at him, wondering why exactly he had come. He didn't need to enter the cottage to put up the clothesline. Unless he had wanted to see her....

Now that she knew he and Charlotte weren't interested in each other, she should feel relieved, even happy...but how could she when she was afraid to become involved? There was much he didn't know. She couldn't risk it...yet.

They stood in close proximity for a long moment, and the tension between them was thick and laced with a tinge of excitement...at least for Rachel.

She thought Noah was about to say something, but he must have thought better of it, for he withdrew a few steps.

"I'd better get outside to help Jacob with the line."

Without saying a word, Rachel nodded.

"You will tell me if there is anything that needs fixing?" Noah stood at the door with his hand on the knob.

"I will," she assured him, not able to meet his gaze.

"Sink is all right? Any doors squeaking or sticking? Shower work well?" He listed several things that must have concerned him.

"Everything is fine," she said quietly.

Noah smiled, and his genuine warmth radiated across his features. "I hope you will be happy in your new home."

"It is wonderful. I will enjoy living here."

Then after a quick nod, Noah exited through the back door, and as he disappeared from view, Rachel went to stand in the doorway to catch another glimpse of him. She saw him approach his brother and Nancy, who were teasing each other, if their laughter was any indication. She watched Noah and Jacob exchange words, and then she continued to study Noah as he and his younger brother secured each length of line on the wooden T-bars, allowing plenty of room for her to hang her laundry.

A new washing machine would be delivered later this week. Until it came, she would rinse her clothes out in the sink or go to her aunt's to do laundry but return to hang her garments on her newly constructed clothesline.

As if he sensed that she was watching, Noah turned toward the house and waved.

She stepped outside and waved back. "It is a *gut* clothesline," she called across the yard.

He nodded and grinned, and then he left with his brother a few minutes later.

Noah was everywhere. She couldn't have ignored him if she'd wanted to, which she realized she honestly didn't. Still, Rachel did her best to discourage Noah Lapp's attention whenever he came to the schoolhouse—which was often—and whenever he visited the cottage, which was at least once every other day. And during church service and the meal afterward, Noah was always near... watching her...making her aware of his presence.

If something needed fixing at the school, he appeared as if summoned. When the lock on the cottage's back door got stuck, he was there to reposition the lockset with hammer, chisel and screwdriver.

One morning after her cousins returned home, Rachel had awakened to find flowers on her front doorstep. Only one person came to mind when she saw the flowers...the same man who had picked wildflowers for her and Charlotte the first time she'd visited the schoolyard.

Sunday arrived and church service was held at Joseph and Miriam Zook's farm. Everyone came in their Sunday-best black, including the children, who behaved well during the service.

Rachel again noticed Noah's presence during the service and afterward during the meal, but he didn't approach to speak with her. She didn't know how she felt about that. She kept her distance, glanced over at him from time to time to see if he was watching, noticing her, but his attention had turned elsewhere. To her disappointment, he talked with everyone, it seemed, but her.

She ate, enjoyed the company of the community women. As usual, Alta Hershberger had a lot to say about many people, and while she listened politely, Miriam Zook didn't join in the discussion as she usually did. Rachel narrowed her gaze as she studied her. Was Miriam all right? She approached the woman when she had the opportunity to talk with her alone.

"Miriam?" she said softly. "Aren't you feeling well?"

Miriam smiled and regarded her with kindness in her gaze. "I am well, Rachel." She paused to instruct her daughters to put out the desserts. "Are you settling in at the cottage?"

"Ja," Rachel said, taking the hint that if something was bothering the woman, Miriam preferred to keep it to herself. "It's a comfortable house. Have you been by to see it lately?"

"Nay. I meant to, but there was so much to do with my parents. *Mam* is not well. She just came home from the hospital. *Dat* had a hard time while she was gone. It is good that both are back home in the *grosselders'* house. It's been a worry."

Rachel felt instant compassion. "Is there anything I can do to help?"

Miriam smiled as she brushed crumbs off her apron. "You are a dear. We are doing better now. I appreciate your offer. If I need you, I'll let you know." She gestured to her daughter Annie to take the chocolate cake and shoofly pie. "Alta means well," Miriam said. "She is a *gut* God-loving woman. We all are curious about our friends and neighbors."

Rachel nodded. It was true. Wasn't that why *The Budget,* the Amish newspaper, was a popular read?

As Miriam continued to oversee the kitchen, Rachel grabbed a pan of blond brownies and rejoined the other women who were moving food on the tables outside.

She was thoughtful as she shifted plates and made room for the pan as well as the other desserts that Annie and her sister Barbara brought out for all to enjoy. *The Budget* had news from Amish communities all over the country. Neighbors reported everything from who was ailing from what to the weather, as well as deaths, births and any other news deemed reportable by someone in the community.

Rachel felt her stomach tighten as she recalled her accident. She knew it had been reported in the Amish newspaper. Not by her family, she knew, but by a neighbor. She hadn't realized at first. When Rachel was in the hospital, the outpouring of love and caring toward her had been tremendous. She'd received cards and letters from family and friends. It was when she began to receive mail from folks outside Millersburg that she had guessed. The fact disturbed her, at first, until she realized that no one knew the true extent of her injuries. They'd just learned that she'd been hurt seriously enough for family and friends to ask everyone to pray for her.

Katie Lapp and Noah came up to the table and Rachel shook off her mood. It was the first time Noah had approached her all day.

"The desserts look delicious," Katie said with a smile. "I believe my son would like a piece of the chocolate-chip chocolate loaf."

Rachel couldn't keep from grinning. "No surprise there." She cut him a slice, and as she handed him a plate, she locked gazes with him.

"Rachel," he said with a small smile.

Heart thumping hard, Rachel tore her gaze away to smile at his mother. "Would you like a piece?"

"A tiny slice for Hannah." Katie turned as one of her younger sons, Daniel, approached with Hannah on his hip. "Daniel, would you like dessert?"

Young Daniel's eyes lit up. "*Ja!* Got any peach pie?"

Rachel nodded and cut Hannah's piece of the loaf before she reached for the pie to cut Daniel a generous helping.

The young boy grinned his thanks and handed his

sister over to his mother before taking his pie and fleeing to enjoy it at the men's table.

"You need your diaper changed, little one," Katie crooned to her daughter. "I'll be back for Hannah's dessert," she said to Rachel.

"I'll bring it to you in a few minutes, *Mam,*" Noah said.

Katie left and Noah and Rachel faced each other alone. There were people milling about the yard but it seemed to Rachel as if they were the only two people on the earth.

"I haven't spoken to you all day," Rachel said after a few seconds of silence.

Something flashed in Noah's expression. "Did ya miss me?"

Rachel eyed him carefully. *"Ja."* Her stomach tightened.

Noah's grin held pleased satisfaction. "You don't find my company annoying?"

"Nay!" She frowned. "Why would you think that?"

He shrugged. He looked wonderful in his Sunday best. His sandy-brown hair was neatly trimmed, his face clean-shaven. His white shirt, black vest and pants fit him well, she noticed. His eyes gleamed beneath his felt wide-brimmed hat.

"I was afraid you might have thought me too helpful." Noah broke off a small piece of chocolate loaf and ate it. Rachel watched fascinated as he chewed and swallowed.

When she realized that she was staring, Rachel quickly looked away.

"There is a singing tonight," Noah said.

Rachel nodded. It was church-service Sunday.

"Will you let me drive you home afterward?" He held his fork in midair, and several heartbeats passed as Rachel digested what Noah was asking. It was one thing to have him walk her across the yard at her aunt and uncle's farm. But the journey from the Zook house to the teacher's cottage was longer and would require more time alone with him…unless his brothers would be accompanying them.

"Jacob will be taking Nancy," he quickly added, as if he had read her mind.

Did she like Noah Lapp enough for him to consider her his sweetheart?

Ja, she thought. Hadn't she gone over this in her mind again and again?

"I will be happy to ride home with you this evening, Noah Lapp," she said quietly, for she wanted no one else to hear.

His features lit up and his grin widened. "I missed talking with you today, Rachel Hostetler."

"Me, too." She felt suddenly nervous, as if meeting him for the first time.

"I'd better take Hannah her dessert." Noah held out his plate for another helping, and Rachel laughed and sliced more chocolate loaf. "I will talk with you later," he said softly.

"I will see you later, Noah." Rachel watched him walk away with two plates of dessert, and the day suddenly seemed brighter…while the night loomed excitingly ahead.

Chapter Fourteen

The gathering at the Zooks' ended at eleven-thirty that night. Everyone had a wonderful time. This night the singing was held in the Zook home rather than outside or in the barn. Miriam and her younger children stayed in the kitchen to help with the food before the children retired upstairs. Joseph Zook, the head of the household, had gone to William Mast's house for a time before arriving home and joining his wife in the kitchen for a bite to eat before heading upstairs with her. Their daughters Annie and Barbara were at the singing along with their eldest son, Josiah.

Annie had confided to Rachel that her parents enjoyed hosting the singing for the young people. It reminded them of their days of courting when Annie's *vadder* had driven her *mudder* home.

Rachel liked hearing the story of the Zooks. Horse-shoe Joe and Miriam obviously cared for each other still, and it was nice to see another example of a successful marriage.

Neither Noah nor she had joined the church yet. Most of the young people at the singing had not. Joining the church was the decision of the individual. The older young people could enjoy a time of *rumspringa* to help them decide. During *rumspringa,* young people could discover a taste of the English way of life. Amish elders were lenient about the actions of young people during *rumspringa,* sometimes ignoring when they heard a radio playing out in the yard or when one of their sons temporarily exchanged his Amish garments for English clothes for trips into town.

Their being lenient didn't mean they liked *rumspringa.* They tolerated it as long as their children's actions weren't destructive or didn't end in arrest. The Amish community felt it necessary for young people to test the waters of outside life to help them make the decision of whether or not to join the church. Once they joined the church, then they had to abide by the *Ordnung,* the rules set by the community. If they did not, they could be shunned or banned, a terrible fate for a member of the community. But if a teen decided not to join the church, he could leave and not be shunned, for it was only after one made the commitment to join the church and to God that the *Ordnung* took priority.

Noah stood outside by the wagon when Rachel exited the Zook farmhouse. He approached when he saw her.

"It is a nice night," he said. "It should be an easy ride home. I have the lantern for the trip." He held up the light. There were also lights on the back of the wagon to alert any automobiles of their presence on the roadway.

"Have you seen Jacob?" he asked.

"Still inside." Rachel looked over at the house. "Here they come now."

Jacob and Nancy walked outside together, chatting and smiling into each other's eyes. Elijah, Noah's other brother, followed behind them. Charlotte was accompanying him, but as friends, not as sweethearts, for Charlotte liked Abram Peachy and Elijah liked Rebekka Miller, who had been unable to come to this evening's singing. Jedidiah stayed behind at the Zooks'; he would ride home with Benjamin Mast. He wanted to spend a few more minutes with Annie.

Noah helped Rachel onto the front seat and then climbed up next to her while everyone else piled into the back.

Laughter and socializing went on in the back of the wagon. Noah and Rachel were quiet as Noah guided old Bess onto the road toward home. But it wasn't a tense quiet, more like a pleasurable silence during which she and Noah exchanged warm glances and smiles.

As they traveled away from the Zook farm, Rachel felt a light brush on her left hand and looked down as Noah clasped her fingers.

No one in the back had noticed. Once or twice, Charlotte had to remind the merrymakers to lower their voices, as it was late and people in the neighboring homes they passed wouldn't appreciate having their sleep disturbed. After each scolding, the voices would lower and the giggles would soften until someone said something to make them all forget and their laughter would ring out loudly and Charlotte would hush and scold them once again.

"Noah." Jacob leaned over the back of the front seat, and Rachel quickly removed her hand from Noah's. "How about we take a side trip?"

"A side trip?" Rachel asked. She met Noah's glance, which looked soft beneath his hat brim in the lantern light. His brother's words made him frown. He obviously didn't care for Jacob's idea.

"*Nay,* brother," he replied. "*Mam* will be wondering where we are."

Jacob made a face. "*Ja,* I suppose she will be." He seemed to think for a moment before he said, "We can go another night!"

Noah shrugged. "It's possible," he said and then didn't say anything more.

Jacob turned back to the others, and the group continued to enjoy the ride, although they were disappointed that the night would soon end.

They arrived at the King farm, and Jacob climbed out of the wagon and helped Nancy to alight. Elijah in turn helped Charlotte. Noah and Rachel sat in the front seat for a while longer.

The silence was peaceful, but it seemed as if there were things to be said, only neither was speaking.

"It's late," Rachel finally said.

Noah nodded and turned to face her. "Rachel…"

"*Ja?*" She looked uneasy.

He studied her face, her brown eyes, her pink lips. "I'd like to court you." He saw her eyes widen.

"Noah…"

"I like you. You like me." He watched her and saw the truth in her expression. "We can enjoy each other's company."

"I don't know if I'm ready," Rachel whispered, although her heart was saying *ja, ja!*

"Ready," he murmured. "Rachel, did someone hurt you?"

She drew a long breath and inclined her head.

"You want to tell me about it?"

She shook her head vigorously. She wasn't yet able to discuss her former betrothed, the accident and Abraham's decision to marry her best friend.

Noah was studying her. Rachel tried to smile but failed miserably.

"I don't want to push you," he said, "but will you think about it?"

"*Ja,* I will think about it," she said softly.

"You aren't against the idea?" His expression was solemn.

She smiled, a genuine smile. "*Nay,* Noah, I'm not. I do like you, only…"

"You're not sure you're ready to court anyone?"

Her look was his answer. He grinned. It wasn't that she had a problem with him; the problem lay in her past, whatever that was.

"Will you meet me in the schoolyard tomorrow night?"

Close to the cottage, but out in the open, she thought. "What time?"

"After supper…about eight o'clock?"

She inhaled sharply. "I'll be there."

"I had a nice time tonight," he said.

She regarded him with warmth. "Me, too."

Jacob and Elijah were nearing the wagon. "Time to take you home."

Noah's brothers climbed into the back, and Noah guided old Bess back down the lane and onto the road toward the cottage where Rachel now lived.

Noah climbed down and assisted Rachel from the wagon seat. He walked her to her door, and she was conscious of the fact that his brothers were near, watching. He must have been aware of them also, for he spoke softly after he'd opened the door for her.

"I'll see you soon, Rachel Hostetler."

"See you soon," she echoed.

He entered before her, checking the house to make sure all was well. He allowed her to go inside once he knew that she'd be safe.

"*Gut* night." He touched her hand.

She laced her fingers through his briefly before pulling her hand away. "Until tomorrow," she said and then went inside the house and watched from the doorway as he rejoined his brothers. After one last look, he drove the wagon away, and Rachel shut the door and locked it behind her before heading to her bedroom, where she thought of the day, the night and her next meeting with Noah.

He wants to court me.

She was thrilled; she was excited. But she couldn't be his sweetheart. The accident…

Or could she? The doctors hadn't been sure. What if they were wrong and she *was* able to have children?

Tomorrow night she would meet him. She felt a wild little thrill.

She made sure both doors and all the windows were locked except for the one room where she needed fresh air—her bedroom. Still, she opened that sash from the top and not the bottom, and put a chair piled with books beneath the window. If someone tried to enter through the open window, she would know about it.

She smiled as she put on her night garment. After brushing her hair, she climbed into bed. *Tomorrow will come soon enough. It is time for sleep.* Morning would come quickly, and there were things to be done in the schoolhouse...and she'd offered to help Aunt Mae with the baking.

Her last happy thought before she fell asleep was of Noah's excited expression when she'd agreed to meet him in the schoolyard.

Noah was standing by the swing set when Rachel entered the schoolyard. Her heart leaped at the sight of him. He looked wonderful in a green shirt with his triblend pants held up by suspenders. His wide-brimmed banded straw hat was pushed back to reveal the look in his eyes as she approached. Her heart started to pound hard.

"Rachel," he said with a formal nod, but his gaze was anything but formal.

"Noah." She glanced about the schoolyard and lane. "Did you walk?"

"*Nay.* I took the only buggy that was available." He gestured beyond the yard to where he'd tied up the horse. He had brought the single-bench courting buggy. "I don't suppose you'd like to go for a ride?"

Rachel eyed the buggy and then turned her gaze onto Noah. She trusted him. Hadn't he saved her when she was clinging for dear life on the runaway buggy?

The mare was Janey, a gentle soul who heeded Noah's commands.

"I'll go for a ride."

Noah felt a sudden lightening within. Rachel must trust him to agree to take a ride in the courting buggy. Not that they were officially courting yet. If he had his way, he'd be courting her soon, but he would go slowly. He didn't want to frighten her. He'd go slowly as long as he could.

He held out a hand and she accepted his help as she

climbed into the buggy. The buggy moved under her weight, but Rachel smiled as she settled down onto the seat.

Noah climbed up to sit beside her. "You ready?" he asked softly.

She nodded as she straightened her skirt over her legs. "Where are we going?"

"We can travel down the paved main road a little or we can continue down this dirt lane, past the cottage and onto Lapp land."

It was light, but darkness would be descending soon. She preferred the farm lane rather than the road. She didn't trust the cars that might speed past—or the drivers who might not see them. "Your land," she said.

"Onto our farm we'll go then," he said, pleased at her response.

A light rain had dampened the lane earlier, tamping down the dust. As Noah guided Janey past the cottage and onto the part of the lane used mostly by his family, Rachel enjoyed the cooler evening temperature and most especially Noah's company.

They said little at first. Rachel thought that it might be because they felt comfortable and content in each other's company.

Noah pulled up on the leathers to stop the buggy. "Look!" He gestured toward animals in the field on the left.

Rachel beamed. "Deer! And so many."

There must have been five or six deer standing in the field. They ran and jumped across the lane far head of them and then disappeared through a windbreak of trees and out of sight.

Noah grinned at her as, under his guidance, Janey

continued down the lane. "We may see raccoon or fox," he said.

Rachel narrowed her gaze as she searched the surrounding scenery for signs of animal life. Noah continued to drive for a time until they reached a stream where he parked the buggy and helped her to alight.

"I used to play here a lot as a child. I usually got in trouble for slipping and falling into the stream. *Mam* was never happy to see me arrive home drenched in water and mud." He smiled at the memory. "She wasn't angry—not really. She gave me a scolding, but I got the sense that she didn't really mind…as long as I wasn't hurt and got home safe."

"Your *mudder* is an amazing woman," Rachel said sincerely. She liked Katie Lapp. Katie had been kind to her from the first, understanding what had happened to her during and after her accident, mentioning it once to let her know she understood and then never mentioning it again. She had seemed to sense Rachel's need for privacy and the secret that Rachel kept from all but her family.

There was a large boulder half-submerged in the dirt; it made a good perch on which to sit and reflect as one listened to the gurgling stream.

Noah smiled as he gestured for her to sit. Rachel sat and he settled on the rock beside her.

She could smell his clean scent, hear the subtle inhale and exhale of his breath. His nearness made her heart sing.

They sat for a time in silence, disturbed only occasionally as a thought came to one or the other.

"Where does the stream go?" she asked.

Rachel had the strongest urge to take off her shoes and wade into the cool depths of the stream.

Noah bent and removed his shoes. Rachel didn't wait but a heartbeat before she untied her own shoelaces and rolled down her black stockings. In unison and without words, they reached out to clasp hands as they stepped into the stream and felt the cool water swirl about their bare ankles and the mud beneath their toes and the soles of their feet.

"Be careful of the rocks," Noah warned just as Rachel moved a step and felt a hard edge beneath the water. She gasped and started to tumble, but Noah grabbed her closer, steadying her. The feel of Noah's chest pressed close stole Rachel's breath and made her face heat.

He released her quickly but that one quick moment stayed in her memory, leaving an imprint.

"Are ya hurt?" he asked as he helped her out of the water.

"Nay," she said breathlessly. "I was startled, that's all." She managed a smile of thanks. "It would have been a long ride home if I'd gotten soaked to the skin."

Darkness had descended quickly. Rachel could barely see enough to put on her stockings. After he put on his shoes, Noah went to the buggy and pulled a flashlight out from under the seat, and switched it on so that Rachel could see. She put on her shoes, and with Noah's help, she scrambled to her feet.

"I'll take ya home," he said.

She nodded. "I enjoyed the outing."

"Ya did?" He walked to her side of the buggy and held out his hand.

She placed her hand in his. *"Ja."*

"Gut." Clasping her fingers, he helped her step up into the buggy. "You'll meet with me again?"

Rachel made herself comfortable as she took her seat. "I'll come again."

Noah was pleased as he circled the buggy to grab hold of Janey's lead, turning her back in the right direction, before he stopped to hop up onto the driver's side. It had been a wonderful night with the girl he was sure was God's choice for him. He just had to be patient and convince her that he would be the best husband for her.

A light breeze stirred the air, making the ride back pleasant. They were silent for a time until Rachel exclaimed with wonder, "Look, lightning bugs!"

She'd always loved them as a child and the sight of them still gave her enjoyment. There were tiny flashes of light in the wooded area not far from the lane. They looked a lot like the Christmas lights that the English had in their homes and businesses.

"They are nice to see," Noah agreed, and then the *hoo hoo ho-oot* of an owl once, and then again, drew his attention toward a treetop. He searched for the bird but couldn't see it. Still, he knew the call. "Great horned owl."

Rachel cocked her head to listen. The sound came again and she smiled. "Do you have any barn owls? We have them on the farm in Millersburg."

"We did. Haven't seen or heard from any in a long time."

The mare's hooves made a muffled clip-clop in the dirt. Rachel enjoyed the sound and Noah's company. Tomorrow school would start, and she would be busy with her students.

.The wagon jerked. Old Janey whinnied and snorted as she balked at continuing.

"Walk on! Walk on!" Noah commanded, but he could sense that something was wrong. He aimed the flashlight along the woods line and caught the glint of two eyes and the outline of an animal.

Rachel froze with fear. *"Noah!"* she screamed.

Chapter Fifteen

"Coyote! Hold on, Rachel!" he said just as the coyote broke from the trees to run toward the buggy.

Rachel stifled a gasp of fright as old Janey went wild and half reared in the traces. Rachel held on tightly as Noah fought to control the plunging mare. The coyote stopped in the middle of the lane in front of them, stared at them a moment, then dashed away into the fields.

"Gently! Gently! Easy now, Janey," Noah crooned. "You all right, Rachel?"

"Holding on!" She was familiar with coyotes; they'd been a problem in Ohio, especially on a neighbor's farm. The sight of one filled her with terror, but that fear was nothing compared to the deep-seated panic that the buggy would overturn and she would be trapped in the tangle of wood and spinning wheels.

"*Gut!* Easy, girl. Easy." Noah held on to the leathers, soothing the horse with his voice. When Janey settled a bit, he jumped down from the wagon and moved carefully toward the animal's head, where he continued to speak softly to ease her fear.

Janey trembled and danced nervously, ears twitching and eyes rolling back to show the whites. Rachel clutched the edge of the wagon seat.

"*Gut* girl," Noah was telling the horse.

Slowly, Rachel's tension eased. "Is she all right?" Rachel asked. "And what about the coyote?"

"*Ja,* Janey is fine. She could sense the coyote before we saw it. Don't worry. The animal is long gone. I'll tell my *vadder* and brothers to keep an eye out for it, but I doubt we'll see it again. I think we frightened it as much as it scared Janey."

"May I have the flashlight?" Rachel asked as she climbed down from the wagon.

Noah handed it to her. She shined the light on the woods and across the field. There was no sign of an animal…neither a movement in the brush nor a glint of two strange eyes.

"We have coyotes in Ohio," she told him. "They ate a neighbor's chickens and then they went after his black Lab. The dog was killed."

Noah studied her face in the lamplight and saw how upset she was. It hadn't helped that the buggy had almost overturned. It must have reminded her of her first day in Lancaster County.

"I think he is long gone, Rachel," he said softly.

She shuddered. "I hope you're right."

Janey trembled and balked, still shaken by the coyote encounter. "We'd best walk her back," Noah said. "Can you make it?"

"It's not far. I'll be fine," Rachel said. She wasn't in a hurry to get back into a buggy being pulled by a spooked horse.

Noah held on to the bridle and with Rachel beside

him started to walk back toward the schoolyard. "Rachel…you all right?"

"*Ja.* I am fine."

Noah paused to examine her features. What he saw reassured him. "Let's get you home, then." He rubbed the horse's neck. "You too, Janey."

The air was still; the song of insects filled the night. The darkness around them lit up here and there with the flash of fireflies. Rachel heard Noah's muffled footsteps mingled with the sound of hers and the dull rhythmic thuds of the mare's hooves on the dirt road. She chanced a look at Noah and saw the outline of his features in the outer glow of the flashlight he held. His brown eyes glistened in the light, his expression looked serious. Rachel had the strongest urge to grab his hand and hold on tightly, but she kept her head and continued to walk silently beside him.

After a fifteen-minute walk down the dirt road, Noah caught a glimpse of the teacher's cottage ahead. As they approached, he noted with a soft inner smile the flowers planted on each side of the front door. He had seen Rachel and her cousins digging in the dirt not long ago. They had done a nice job of arranging the petunias, marigolds and vinca plants.

"Home," Noah announced as they reached the cottage. "I'm sorry you had to walk back."

Rachel met his gaze. "I'm not." She appeared to hesitate, as if wanting to say something more, but was unable to find the right words. "I enjoyed the buggy ride."

"And the walk?"

She beamed at him. "*Ja.* The walk was the best part."

"I'll see you tomorrow?"

"*Schuul* starts tomorrow," Rachel told him.

He'd known about school, but he'd hoped she wouldn't use it as an excuse not to meet with him. "*Ja,* but it will end by three o'clock or so." Noah reached out, captured her hand. "You will think about what I said?"

"Noah…"

"It's all right, Rachel." He reached over to open the door. He peeked inside to make sure all was well. "*Gut* night," he said softly. He wouldn't push her, but he wondered if he'd kept his heart from showing in his eyes. "I will see you soon."

He saw her swallow.

"*Ja.*"

His smile was crooked. "Have a good first day of *schuul.*"

Rachel watched as Noah walked Janey and the buggy onto the road and continued to stand at the door until Noah disappeared from sight.

Early the next morning, Rachel stood at the door to the one-room Amish schoolhouse and smiled at her new students as they filtered inside. She nodded at each child who passed her, mentioning those she knew by name.

"John. Jacob. Mary Elizabeth." She smiled at several other children whose names she had yet to learn.

Within minutes, every child had taken a seat, and Rachel stood in the front of the classroom and introduced herself, speaking in the Amish German dialect.

The older children already received most of their education in English. This school year would be the first time for the youngest children to begin their English lessons, but time and their quick minds would soon have them chattering away like the others.

The day went well. The children seemed eager to be

back in the classroom, except for one or two boys whose attention drifted until Rachel called it back.

At lunch break, the children opened their packed lunches and ate at their desks before going outside to play. As they did during class, the older students helped the younger new students get adjusted. They showed them the swings in the schoolyard. While the younger children played on the swings, the older boys played catch with a baseball. Soon it was time for the afternoon lesson to commence. The littlest of her students practiced writing As and Bs while the older ones read from a reader designed to teach them about community life.

Rachel dismissed the class just after two-thirty in the afternoon. "I will see you tomorrow morning," she said with a smile. She had given them little homework on their first day of class. The children had enough to do to help out at home; they didn't need to be overworked by school.

After her students left, Rachel straightened the classroom before she exited the school and locked the door. She turned to head home and then gasped. Noah Lapp stood about three yards away, as if waiting for her.

"How was your first day as our Happiness teacher?" he asked conversationally, but she thought she detected a hint of anxiety beneath his pleasant demeanor.

"We had a *gut* day. The children were happy to be back in class." She paused. "Most of them were. My cousin John is still unconvinced he needs to come to school." Rachel studied him a moment as he accompanied her toward the cottage, sensing something odd in his mood. "Is something wrong?"

Noah attempted to smile. *"Nay."* He halted near

her front steps and waited for her to unlock the door. "Rachel—"

She faced him. *"Ja?"* Today, he wore a short-sleeved maroon shirt with his triblend denim pants. It looked as if he had combed his hair recently before putting on his wide-brimmed straw hat.

He held her glance and then looked away toward the road, almost as if in a daze. After several seconds of silence, he finally said, "You had a nice time last night, *ja?"*

She nodded. "I did."

"I'm sorry if you were frightened." He seemed distressed about the coyote sighting and the unplanned walk back.

Rachel caught and held his gaze, her smile soft. "Noah, I would have been more frightened if you hadn't been there taking control."

He seemed pleased by her response. "The coyote—"

Rachel felt herself tense up. *"Ja,* I didn't like that part, but we had a nice time at the stream and before…and I didn't mind the walk. Really." She waited a heartbeat and then asked, "Did you find him?" She straightened her white *kapp,* pretending to be indifferent, that the idea of the coyote in the area didn't bother her.

"Ya don't need to worry about him any longer. He made the mistake of venturing onto an Englisher's farm and raiding his henhouse. The man took prompt care of him."

Rachel flinched. She didn't want the animal to hurt or bother anyone, but neither did she want to see it harmed. Noah was quiet for a time. She stood studying him, wondering what was on his mind.

He seemed reluctant to speak and what he said startled her. "Rachel, I know someone hurt you in the past, but I won't hurt you. You believe me?"

She felt her heart thumping. This wasn't a subject she was ready to discuss with him. Seeing how genuinely upset he seemed, she said softly, "I believe you won't hurt me." She touched his shoulder and then pulled back as if burned. "Sometimes things happen that cause someone to be hurt."

"I will wait for you, Rachel Hostetler," he said, his expression earnest. "I will wait until you trust me enough to believe in me…until you'll say yes to our courting." He left, heading toward the main road.

"Noah—" she called out, unable to help herself.

He stopped and faced her.

"I will see you tonight?" she asked. She no longer cared if he knew that she wanted to spend time with him.

"It is my brother's birthday," Noah said quietly. "Will you come to the house?"

"I don't know—"

"Come," he urged. "My mother will be glad to see you. The Kings are coming, too."

Her aunt and uncle would be there? That fact gave Rachel comfort. No one would think anything of her presence if her relatives were there.

"I'll come," she said.

"I'll stay and wait for you then. *Mam* is making Joseph's favorite."

Rachel entered the house. "Come in, then, while I put away a few things. So it's young Joseph's birthday."

Noah seemed larger than life as he followed her into her kitchen. "*Ja*, the youngest Lapp child before Hannah."

Rachel set her lunch bag on the counter, and then she opened a cabinet and took down two glasses. "Iced tea?"

"That would be nice." He sat at her kitchen table and Rachel poured him a glass and set it before him. She put out a plate of cookies and he grinned as he grabbed one and took a bite.

"I will be back in a few minutes," Rachel said as Noah enjoyed a chocolate-chip cookie and drank his tea. He waved at her as he helped himself to a chocolate cookie iced with chocolate frosting.

Rachel headed to her room and took off her school apron, replacing it with a clean one. She'd worn her spring-green dress for the first day of school. She splashed water on her face before she returned to the kitchen to find Noah staring out the window, apparently deep in thought.

"Noah."

He jumped as if startled and rose to his feet. "Ready?"

"Do you think Joseph will like some of these cookies?" she asked.

Noah smiled. "*Ja,* he will, and if not, his big brother does."

Rachel laughed. She checked to see that the back kitchen door was locked before she and Noah left the house by the front door.

"I thought we could walk," Noah said when he saw her look for his buggy.

"It is a nice day for a walk," Rachel agreed as she fell into step beside him. They went through the schoolyard and then cut across the field until they reached the dirt driveway that led to the Lapp home.

As they followed the lane toward the house, they heard the wheels of a buggy and the clip-clop of the horse that pulled it.

"Noah! Rachel!" It was the King carriage. "Want a ride?"

Noah shook his head. "We're almost there. Mae, Amos. Glad you could come by this evening. Charlotte, Nancy." He nodded at each one in turn. "Is that John and Joshua I see hiding in the back of the buggy?"

Rachel could hear Joshua's giggle before she saw him peek up alongside his older brother. "John," she said. "Any trouble with homework?"

"*Nay*. Not much to do. It didn't take me long."

"I thought I'd go easy on the first day. Be prepared!" She saw John's eyes widen, and she laughed to let him know she was teasing him.

She spent a pleasant evening at the Lapp residence. It was wonderful to see Katie again. Rachel genuinely cared for the woman, and Katie seemed to know how much she enjoyed holding Hannah, for it wasn't long before the baby was asleep in the young woman's arms.

The evening was pleasant, not cool but not too warm. After supper, they sat on the front porch, and even the men joined them. Soon, the time came for her to go home. She had another day of class the next morning, and she needed a good night's sleep.

Noah volunteered to escort her home. He matched her steps as they strolled down the lane and then entered the field. Rachel appreciated that she felt easy and lighthearted whenever she was in Noah's presence.

Noah noticed that Rachel seemed to enjoy the evening and that she wasn't in the least afraid as he walked her home. If she thought of the coyote, she didn't mention it.

"Everything all right at *schuul?*" he asked. "Any problems with the construction?"

"*Nay*, the construction is fine and all went well." Rachel felt his presence like a warm blanket of protection. She'd never felt this way about anyone. He made her feel safe, cared for…special.

She stepped inside, and he hesitated in the door opening. "Rachel…"

She turned to him and said, "*Ja.* Noah—"

Noah looked confused…and then as he studied her face, he felt warmth radiating inside his chest. *"Ja?"* He waited hopefully.

"You may court me." She stared at him. "If you want to—"

"If I want—" Noah whooped for joy as he lifted her within his strong arms and spun her around before setting her down again. "Rachel, I—"

Rachel had laughed as he'd spun her. "I know," she said. "Me, too."

He grinned as he caught and held her hand. "We can go for a ride tomorrow. John can chaperone us. We can—" He suddenly frowned. "I'll need to talk with someone about us, but who?"

Rachel shrugged. "My parents are in Ohio. My only relatives here are Aunt Mae and Uncle Amos, and they love you. Talk with Uncle Amos. I don't think there will be a problem." Eyes softening, Noah continued to study her. Rachel loved the giddy way he made her feel. "I hate to say this, but it's late, and I have a class to teach tomorrow morning."

"*Ja.* I will go," Noah said, "but Rachel?"

She tilted her head as she gazed up at him. "Is something wrong?"

"*Nay.* I only wanted to tell ya that you've made me a happy man tonight."

The look in his eyes made her feel dizzy with joy.

Rachel gazed at him with tenderness. She dared to lift a hand and caress his cheek. "And you've made me a happy woman, Noah Lapp. Now, you'd best get home before your *mam* and *dat* wonder what happened to you."

He spun to leave and turned back to flash her a warm smile. "*Gut* night, Rachel. Pleasant dreams."

"*Gut* night, Noah. I had a nice time tonight."

"Me, too," he said, and then he left, but not before glancing back several times to see if she was still at the door watching him, and she was.

The weeks that followed were filled with wonder and happiness for Rachel. She taught school with the enjoyment of one who loves to teach. Noah came by the school often for one reason or another. It was the Friday after her dinner with the Lapps that she and Noah were seen out and about in the wagon together with only Rachel's cousin John King as chaperone. Rachel was surprised when Noah first came with the large wagon instead of the courting buggy, but considering what had happened the last three times she'd ridden in one, she was secretly glad. Still, did folks realize that she and Noah were courting? If they didn't at first, they would soon. Noah and she were seen often in each other's company, always accompanied by one cousin or another—mostly John and occasionally little Joshua.

Aunt Mae and Uncle Amos couldn't be happier. If they were surprised by Noah's interest in Rachel, they didn't show it.

"You're a *gut* girl, Rachel. We are happy you have taken a liking to Noah," Aunt Mae said. "Noah is a *gut* boy."

"He is a *gut man,* Mae," her husband corrected softly.

"*Ja,* this is so," Aunt Mae said, "but it seems only yesterday when he and our girls were small children."

Rachel wondered how her aunt and uncle felt about her relationship with Noah after it became obvious to the community that Noah had chosen Rachel over Charlotte. It was during the second week of her and Noah walking out together that Rachel learned that several women had approached Charlotte to commiserate with her the loss of Noah's affections. Charlotte had reacted with laughter at the notion and expressed to all her genuine happiness at her cousin's good fortune to have Noah court her.

"Abram and I have been seeing each other secretly," Charlotte had confided to Rachel. "Abram is shy, but he seems to enjoy spending time with me." Charlotte told Rachel that she had high hopes that their budding friendship would lead into something special and long lasting.

It was an early Saturday morning when Charlotte came to visit Rachel at the cottage. She knocked and Rachel was pleasantly surprised to see her and invited her in for breakfast.

"You haven't eaten?" Rachel said.

"*Nay,* I wouldn't mind a bite."

"I can make you eggs and I have coffee cake."

"Coffee cake will be fine," Charlotte said, taking a seat at Rachel's kitchen table. "And tea, please."

Rachel felt her cousin studying her as she poured a cup of tea and cut Charlotte a piece of cake. She looked up and met her gaze. "What?"

"It becomes you," Charlotte said with a little half

smile. When Rachel looked confused, Charlotte continued, "Courting. Or should I say, Noah becomes you."

Rachel blushed as she sat down. "He is wonderful."

"I told you so," Charlotte said, sounding satisfied.

"And I thought you were saying so because you were in love with him yourself."

"What?" Charlotte looked stunned. She thought a moment and then began to chuckle. "I never thought… I guess you might have seen it that way. I wanted you to know how amazing he is so that you'd see him for what he is—the man for you."

"I can see that now…" Rachel sipped and swallowed some tea. "Sometimes I feel so happy that it scares me." She hesitated and then admitted, "You know what happened with Abraham Beiler."

Charlotte shook her head. *"Nay,* not really. I know you and he were in a buggy accident…"

"We were courting, Charlotte. I got hurt and spent some time in the hospital," Rachel said lightly, unwilling to go into detail about the horror of that time. "That was the last day of our courtship."

"Oh, Rachel…"

"Noah is different," Rachel said. "He makes me feel special…and loved."

Charlotte smiled. *"Gut,* because he loves you."

Rachel felt a jolt to hear her cousin say it. Noah and she hadn't reached the point of such discussion. They were enjoying their courtship, but the depth of their feelings had yet to be stated.

"You couldn't do better than Noah, Rachel." Charlotte sipped her tea.

"And I hope all works out well with Abram."

"I think it will," Charlotte said as she put down her cup. "Abram is coming to the house this afternoon. He says he wants a word with *Dat*." She lowered her voice. "I hope it's for the reason I want it to be."

Rachel got up and went over to hug Charlotte. "It will be. I can feel it in my heart that today will be special for you."

They ate their coffee cake and drank their tea. Soon, Charlotte got up to leave. "Tell me all about it tomorrow," Rachel said.

"You won't come to dinner?"

"*Nay.* Noah is coming to take me to his house. Katie is making something special, he says."

The cousins hugged and wished each other a fine day, and then Rachel set to work cleaning the cottage and baking something delicious to take to the Lapp table this evening.

Katie Lapp was glad to see her. Rachel beamed at the woman as Katie accepted her cherry-chocolate pie and then led her into the kitchen, where she invited Rachel to sit down.

"I'd like to help," Rachel said.

"No, please. You sit and relax. You work hard enough as it is. If you like, you can hold Hannah." Katie left a moment and came back with her daughter in her arms.

Rachel gladly accepted the little girl and set her on her lap. She played with the child's fingers to entertain her.

"You've made my son happy," Katie said as she set down a cup of tea before Rachel, who nodded her thanks.

"I've never met anyone like Noah," Rachel said. "He is kind and generous." She paused a moment. "You raised a *gut* son." She was having fun with Noah. She didn't want to think about it ending. She didn't want to believe that there was a chance that she couldn't have children. The possibility that a child wasn't in her future could ruin her relationship with Noah. Maybe she could make an appointment with a doctor to see if it was true....

It wasn't long before dinner was ready and Rachel helped Katie put out the meal. Katie, Hannah and Rachel were the only females at the table filled with eight men, including little Joseph. It was clear to Rachel that the Lapp males liked to eat and enjoyed Katie's cooking. Tomorrow was Sunday. There were other food items already prepared for the next day when there would be no work, including cooking, except for the simplest chores that couldn't be avoided, like caring for the animals.

"We'll be visiting the Kings tomorrow," Katie said. "Rachel, you'll be there as well?"

"*Ja.* I miss my aunt and uncle. It will be *gut* to spend the day with them."

Not long after the meal, Noah took Rachel home. He halted at the door, reluctant to leave her. "My family loves you."

"I love them, too."

He flashed her a grin. "And me?"

Rachel's heart skipped a beat. "We wouldn't be courting if I didn't like you."

"Only like?"

She sighed. "Noah..."

He held up his hand and stepped back a few paces. He gazed at her with affection. "I will see you tomorrow."

"See you tomorrow," she echoed.

Noah stepped up to her quickly, took hold of her hands. "Think of me tonight," he said as he gave her fingers a gentle squeeze. Then he released her and was gone.

Chapter Sixteen

The following Wednesday, Rachel dismissed her students and then straightened the classroom as usual. She didn't expect Noah to stop by, for he had errands to run for his father, so she lingered, planning her lesson for the next day and erasing the chalkboard in the front of the room.

The pain, when it hit her, was sharp and made her cry out and clutch her abdomen. She gasped and moved to her desk chair, taking a moment to sit down. She took several calming breaths and the pain subsided for a few seconds before coming back full force.

Dear Lord, she prayed, *don't let this be my injury from the accident!*

When she'd gotten hurt in the buggy accident with Abraham, she had been told that her injuries were serious…that they might come back to trouble her in the future.

Tears filled her eyes as she hugged her abdomen. *What if this pain is the result of the old injury?*

She stood and felt nauseous, the pain was so great.

How was she to get help? She couldn't walk anywhere. She pressed lightly on her abdomen and inhaled sharply.

"What am I going to do? Please, Lord, help me." Then she heard a voice and thought she'd imagined it.

"Rachel!" Charlotte called excitedly. "Rachel, I've got something to tell you!" Her cousin entered the schoolhouse and froze as she saw Rachel. "Rachel!" She hurried to her side. "What's wrong?"

"Terrible pain in my belly. Hurts bad." Rachel tried to rise and then gasped and clutched her midsection. "Can you take me to the doctor?"

"Noah," Charlotte said, "I should get Noah."

"Nay! Please don't worry him. You can tell him after I find out what's wrong."

"I don't know," Charlotte hedged. "He'll want to help."

"Nay! Please, Charlotte, promise me. I don't want to upset him." She didn't want him to learn about her injuries in this way. She had tried to put what the doctors had said out of her mind, but now she was getting a painful reminder.

"I promise." Charlotte helped Rachel to her feet. "Good thing I brought the buggy. But I'm not taking you to the doctor. You need a hospital."

Hospital. Rachel closed her eyes tightly. She had spent more time than she'd ever wanted in a hospital, but she knew her cousin was right. "How far is it?"

"I'm not sure. It must be four miles or more." Charlotte studied her with concern. "How about *Dat?* Can I get him?"

"Nay." Rachel opened her eyes and swayed. "Just take me, please." Tears slipped from beneath her lowered lids.

Charlotte helped Rachel into the buggy and then ran

around the back of the vehicle to hop into the other side. "How is the pain?"

"It's eased for a minute, but—" Rachel grimaced as the pain returned.

Charlotte clicked her tongue and guided the buggy onto the road in the direction of the local hospital near Lancaster. "We should stop and tell *Mam*."

"*Please,* Charlotte." She didn't want everyone to know. She'd had to suffer the physical pain and the emotional hurt of knowing that the past buggy accident might have caused enough injury to cause her current pain and possible barrenness.

She loved Noah. She didn't want to lose him. She shouldn't have agreed to their courtship, but she wanted to be with him, and she had begun to believe the doctors had been wrong. Besides, they hadn't actually said that she couldn't have children. Only that it might be difficult for her to conceive and give birth.

The ride toward the hospital seemed to take forever. Rachel sat with her eyes closed, hunched over and praying through the pain. Soon, she felt the buggy shift and turn right. Rachel opened her eyes and saw the Peachy farm.

Her cousin faced her. "I'm getting Abram to help us."

"Charlotte—"

"You're feeling worse, Rachel. I'd feel better if Abram drove you to the hospital."

A sharp pain made Rachel gasp and cry out. She wasn't in any condition to object.

Charlotte pulled the buggy into Abram's yard and then ran toward the house. "Abram! Abram!"

Within seconds, Rachel heard quick footsteps as someone approached. The buggy dipped as he climbed in. But it wasn't Abram Peachy, as expected; it was Noah. Rachel looked at him and tried to smile but tears filled her eyes as the pain ripped through her abdomen. Despite her words to Charlotte earlier, she was glad to see him.

"I'm taking you to the hospital," he said, and she jerked her head in a nod.

Abram and Charlotte came out of the house, hurrying toward the vehicle.

"I'm going to take her!" Noah called out. "No time to waste!"

"Go, Noah! Abram will take me home. *Mam* will want to know." Charlotte shot Abram a glance.

"*Ja.* I will take her home. Go!" Abram put a comforting arm around Charlotte's shoulders.

Noah guided the buggy around, and then with a loud *yah,* he flicked the leathers to spur the horse-drawn vehicle down the lane and onto the main road.

Flashing her a quick glance, Noah felt an awful burning in the pit of his stomach at the sight of Rachel's tears. She was in terrible pain, and he felt helpless. *Dear Lord, please help me get her to the hospital safely.*

Rachel sobbed quietly. She held her belly, her gaze focused on the road ahead. She looked pale and very ill.

"Noah," she finally said, "I'm going to be sick."

He pulled back on the leathers, and after the horse slowed, he guided the buggy to the side of the road, where he jumped down and raced around the vehicle to help Rachel. She made it only two steps before she vomited. Concerned, Noah eyed the buggy, thought about their distance to the hospital, and the realization terrified him.

Rachel was too sick to feel more than only slightly

embarrassed. The cramping had made her nauseous and the ride in the racing buggy hadn't helped.

When she was done, she turned to find Noah flagging down a car.

"Please," he told the driver who finally stopped to help. It was the Englisher who had helped to put out Abram's barn fire. "Rachel is ill. We need to get to the hospital. Can you take us?"

"Of course," Tom Drulis said. "Get in." The gray-haired man had a kind face. He gestured toward a nearby house. "Can you move the buggy over there? I know the Beckers. I'll tell them someone will come back for it later."

Noah was grateful, and after seeing Rachel safely into the backseat of the car, he quickly moved the buggy to a hitching post in the Beckers' barnyard. Kyle Becker came out of the house, and Tom spoke with him. The farmer assured Noah that he would water and take good care of the horse.

Soon, Noah joined Rachel in the backseat of Tom Drulis's car, speeding toward the hospital. Noah put his arm around Rachel and held her as she cried through her pain. They arrived in less than ten minutes. It would have taken Noah a good half hour or more to reach the hospital in the buggy, and the Kings' horse would have suffered.

Noah thanked Tom Drulis profusely as he helped Rachel out of the man's car. Tom promised to return later to see if he could help.

As they entered the building, Noah noted the hospital's strange medicinal smell. He eased Rachel carefully into a chair and then hurried to speak with the triage nurse.

"See the girl there?" Noah said anxiously. "Her name is Rachel Hostetler. She has had sharp pains in her lower belly for some time. She got sick on the way over. I think there is something terribly wrong!"

The nurse looked up with a bored expression until she met Noah's gaze. She frowned and then glanced toward Rachel. Rachel sat in the chair, hunched over, sobbing. Noah saw the quick change on the woman's face as she came out from behind her desk and approached. She gently asked Rachel about the pain. She helped Rachel over to the triage area and took her vitals. Noah followed closely. "She has a fever," the woman said with a frown. "Someone is coming to take her back now."

Rachel barely heard what was being said, she hurt so much. She thought someone said something about being taken back, and then she thought that the woman asked Noah to wait outside in the waiting room.

"Nay!" Rachel said. "Can't he come with me? Just for a little while?"

"Until the doctor comes in to examine you," the nurse said.

They moved Rachel into a curtained area in the emergency room. Noah was barely there two minutes when he was asked to leave.

Holding her gaze, Noah clasped her hand and gave her a reassuring squeeze. "I'll be here when you need me," he said before he left as ordered.

The doctor who came in to see Rachel was a woman. Dr. Moss introduced herself and asked if she could examine Rachel. Rachel lay back on the examining table, and when Dr. Moss pressed on her abdomen, she flinched and then cried out as the woman probed a specific area.

"Any nausea or vomiting?" she asked Rachel.

"Ja," Rachel whispered miserably. She told Dr. Moss about getting sick and then about the buggy accident and severe abdominal injury she'd suffered. "They said I might have trouble with it again."

Dr. Moss frowned. "I'd like to run some tests, including a blood draw. You're running a fever. I think I know what's wrong, but I want to make sure before we proceed."

Rachel felt her throat tighten as her tears overflowed. She knew what the doctor was going to tell her—that the internal injury she'd suffered had become infected. *Please, Lord, help me to be strong.*

Noah was pacing the waiting area when Abram, Charlotte, Mae and Amos arrived. Tom Drulis had stopped by the Kings' to inform the family and had offered to drive them into town. Upon seeing Noah, Mae rushed over.

"How is she?" she asked. Noah saw Mae's concern.

"She's still inside. The doctor hasn't come out yet." He felt sick with worry. Rachel meant so much to him; he didn't want anything to happen to her. He hated seeing her in pain.

It seemed like a long wait before the doctor came out with news.

"How is Rachel?" Noah asked anxiously.

"Rachel is going to need emergency surgery," Dr. Moss said. "She has acute appendicitis and they are prepping her for the O.R. now."

"Will she be all right?" Mae asked.

"As long as we get to the appendix before it ruptures. She's in a lot of pain, so we need to get her to the OR now."

Noah rubbed his forehead beneath the brim of his hat. "May I see her?"

Dr. Moss looked to Mae. "You are her relative, and there is only time for one quick visit."

"It's fine. Let Noah see her. She'll want to see him." Mae turned toward Noah. "Tell her that we'll be here for whatever she needs."

"I will." Noah met Mae's gaze. "I appreciate this. I know how worried you are about her."

"Go, Noah. Cheer her up."

"If you want to see her, you must go quickly," Dr. Moss said.

Noah was taken into the emergency room, to the curtained area where Rachel lay. She wore a hospital gown and was covered modestly with a blanket. She still wore her *kapp;* the rest of her clothing had been put elsewhere for safekeeping.

"Rachel," he whispered as he hurried to her side. "I'm sorry." She looked pale and vulnerable. She was hooked up to an IV and a machine monitored her heartbeat. He felt helpless that he couldn't do more for her.

Rachel managed a small smile. "Why are ya sorry, Noah? It's not your fault that I have appendicitis. You got me here quickly."

As she spoke, medical workers came to take her to the operating room.

"Your aunt Mae and Charlotte are outside. Aunt Mae wanted me to tell you that they will be here for whatever you need." He gently took hold of her hand. "I'll be here for you, Rachel. Always."

"You're a *gut* man, Noah Lapp," Rachel said and then she grimaced and closed her eyes, clearly in pain.

"Time to go," the nurse said.

She opened her eyes and met Noah's gaze. "I'll be all right," she said, and then she was taken from the area and Noah was led outside, back into the waiting room.

The Lapps arrived, all seven of Noah's siblings along with his *mam* and *dat*. Carrying her daughter, Hannah, Katie rushed up to her son. "How is Rachel?"

"She has appendicitis," Noah said.

"Mae told me, but *how is she?*"

Noah's mouth curved slightly upward. "She says she will be fine. She is in a lot of pain. I wish I could do something to help her."

"You already did," Mae said, joining the two of them. "You had the good sense to have someone drive her in a car and God blessed us in that it belonged to Tom Drulis." Mae touched his cheek. "Take heart, Noah. I have faith that Rachel will be well soon."

Noah nodded, but then bowed his head and said a silent prayer. After a time, other members of their church community filled the waiting room, coming in support of Rachel, Noah and the Kings. A hospital worker entered the room and told them they couldn't stay. "There isn't enough room for all of you," the woman said.

The Zooks, the Masts and the Hershbergers took their leave, asking Mae to keep them informed about Rachel's recovery.

"See that she rests," Alta Hershberger instructed Mae.

Noah saw Mae control a small smile. "I will," Mae assured her.

After a few moments of silent prayer, most of the church community members left. Only Mae, Charlotte, Noah, Katie and baby Hannah remained.

Two hours later, the emergency-clinic door opened and Dr. Moss came out, still in surgical scrubs. "Rachel did well," she told them. "If we'd been much longer, the appendix would have ruptured. She will be sore when she wakes up, but fine."

"May we see her?" Noah asked, anxious to be with her again. He needed to see for himself that she was better.

"I'm afraid not," the doctor said. "She's in the recovery room. We don't expect her to be ready for visitors until tomorrow morning. She's likely to sleep the rest of the afternoon and night." She glanced about the waiting room, and seemed to take note of those who had stayed for news of Rachel. "You should go home and get some rest. Rachel won't even know you have gone. You'll be able to see her first thing tomorrow. Is there some way I can reach you if needed?"

"Whittier's Store near us has a telephone," Noah said. "They often take messages for us." He waited while the doctor retrieved pen and paper from a worker's desk before he gave her the number. "Mention my name, and Mr. Whittier will make sure I get the message."

Dr. Moss jotted down the information. "Go home," she urged again. "You can see Rachel in the morning."

After the doctor left, Noah sat down. "I don't think I should leave her."

"Noah," Katie said softly. She gently touched her son's cheek. "You've been through a lot. Rachel will want to see you tomorrow. You should rest today so that you are at your best for her in the morning."

Noah met his mother's loving gaze and felt overwhelmed by the events of the day. He *was* exhausted... tired, worried and frightened for the woman he loved. What *Mam* said made sense. He needed a good night's sleep.

He stood. "I'll go home…for Rachel. I need to fetch Amos's buggy. I left it at a neighbor of Tom Drulis's when Tom drove us here."

"Amos has our buggy. Yours is outside," Mae said. "Tom picked up Jedidiah, who drove ours the rest of the way to the hospital. Your brother rode home with the Zooks, leaving us the buggy. Samuel brought your family buggy and then he and your other brothers got a ride home with the Hershbergers and Masts."

Noah approached Mae. "You will come with us?"

The woman smiled. "*Nay.* Amos is not far; Tom went back for him and our youngest. Amos took Joshua for an ice cream. He'll be back to take us home."

Shortly afterward, Noah, his mother and his sister climbed into the family buggy and headed home. Noah was quiet during the journey. Suddenly, he needed his mother to know how he felt. "*Mam,* I love her."

"I know you do." Katie shifted her daughter more comfortably in her arms.

"Someone hurt her in the past. I don't know who."

"Ja." Mam looked as if she would say something more, but kept silent.

"I want to marry her. I'll wait until she agrees. I will be patient." He exhaled sharply. "She is worth the wait."

His mother's answer was to place a hand on his arm and give it a quick, light squeeze.

They were silent for a time. Hannah had fallen asleep on Katie's lap. The only sounds were the horse's hooves on macadam and the squeak of the buggy wheels as they turned over pavement.

"Noah, I have something I need you to do," Katie said after a time. "There is a pile of *The Budget* in the barn.

I'd like you to gather the newspapers and bring them into the house. I would like your help sorting through them."

Rachel was in the hospital, and *Mam* was thinking about cleaning out the barn? He shrugged. "All right."

"Noah."

"Ja, Mam?" He turned toward her.

"Rachel will be fine."

He managed a smile. "I pray to the *gut* Lord that it is so."

Katie nodded. "It is always the best thing to do."

Chapter Seventeen

Early the next morning, Noah helped his mother into the buggy and then ran around to hop into the seat beside her. "Do ya think she'll be awake when we get there?" he asked.

Katie shifted to make herself comfortable and waved through the window to her eldest son, who would be in charge of the children until their return. "She may...especially if she slept all of yesterday afternoon and last night."

Noah flicked the leathers to spur the horse on. Today they were taking their horse Jerry John; he was eager to make better time with the young gelding.

"You never told me about Rachel's accident," he said.

"It wasn't my secret to tell." Katie straightened her *kapp* as she glanced at her son. "With all that's happened, I thought a little information might be helpful to you."

Noah couldn't control a grin. "And by having me 'help' sort through the newspapers..."

Katie nodded. "You just might stumble onto the issue with news from Millersburg...about a young woman involved in a courting-buggy accident." Her small smile faded as Rachel's misfortune that day seemed to have taken hold of her thoughts. "You went to see Mae?"

"*Ja.* She told me what happened. How Abraham Beiler left her while she was still recovering in the hospital." Noah scowled. "What type of man does that to a woman?"

"A guilt-ridden one, I'd say." Katie waved to a neighbor along the road. "Don't judge him too harshly, Noah. It wouldn't surprise me if he left because he couldn't face her."

"But to marry her best friend within months?" Noah shook his head. "I will try hard to think kindly of him." He brightened. "If not for his actions, then Rachel wouldn't have come to us, and I would not have met the woman I love."

His mother smiled at him and then turned to look out the side buggy window. She was silent for a time. Suddenly, she turned to him, placed a hand on his arm. "You know she suffered injuries in the accident," she said softly.

He patted her hand. "I know. Mae explained, but it makes not a bit of difference about how I feel about her. Knowing the truth, I love her even more."

Katie looked satisfied. "She loves you, but she is afraid of getting hurt again."

Noah knew how vulnerable Rachel was and there was no way he would ever hurt her. "I know. I will wait until she is ready...until I can prove to her that she has nothing to fear in our future together."

He could sense his mother's surprise. "You asked the Kings' permission."

"*Ja.* I wanted to do this right. They know that I will

not rush her. They are happy that we have found each other."

"As your *dat* and I are," Katie commented with a grin.

The ride, which Noah expected to last forever considering how eager he was to see Rachel, was over much more quickly than he thought it would be. He pulled into the hospital parking lot and around to the hitching post in the back of the building. He secured Jerry John and then helped his mother alight.

Katie smiled at him as he helped her step down. "You will make a fine husband."

Noah blinked. "Are you looking to have grandchildren?"

"I have a babe of my own still. Grandchildren, if and when they come, are blessings from God. I was not referring to that part of marriage."

Noah felt his stomach tighten as the truth of Rachel's pain hit him. "I know."

He reached into the buggy and withdrew a bouquet of wildflowers. He remembered how pleased she'd looked the first time he'd given her flowers. He hoped the posies would cheer her.

Katie looked at her son's face and the flowers he held carefully in his hands. "We should check on Rachel. I think she will be looking to have visitors now."

The pain in Rachel's abdomen wasn't as bad as it had been last night. She had awakened in the middle of the night, crying out, disturbed by the hospital surroundings. She had thought it was a year ago again, and the pain was from the buggy accident. She had sobbed as all the terror and heartache had come rushing in.

Upon hearing Rachel's cry, the night nurse had come

into the room and calmed her, explaining that she'd had an appendectomy. The woman had given Rachel something for the pain, and finally Rachel had been able to go back to sleep, sore but with the pain manageable and the terror of the past eased.

This morning another nurse had come and adjusted Rachel's bed so that she was more comfortable. Rachel had dozed on and off for a time until just a short while ago, when the pain had disturbed her sleep. She wondered where everyone had gone—Noah, Charlotte, Aunt Mae and Uncle Amos.

A hospital worker came into her room. The bed beside hers was empty; the woman who'd had gall-bladder surgery had been discharged the previous afternoon, the nurse had told her. Someone else would no doubt be moved into the room today.

"Would you like some Jell-O?" the girl asked. She had blond hair, not unlike Charlotte's, and she looked about sixteen in her pink uniform. Her name badge read "Jessie."

Rachel shook her head.

"I'm sorry," Jessie said, "but it's all you can have. You can have that or a cup of tea. You're on a liquid diet today."

Rachel managed a smile. "Thank you," she said easily in English, "but I don't need anything right now."

Jessie nodded as if she understood. "I'll come back later. Perhaps you'll want a cup of tea then."

"Thank you," Rachel said. She closed her eyes briefly and brought up the image of Noah's face. He had been so comforting and caring during the ride to, and at, the hospital. Where was he?

She felt a burning in her stomach. Abraham Beiler

had never come to see her. *But Noah is different, and he will come.*

She heard a familiar voice outside her room and thought, *Noah!* She opened her eyes as Noah and Katie Lapp stepped through the doorway.

"Rachel!" Noah hurried to her side.

"Noah!" she breathed. He was here, and she had never been so happy to see anyone.

"How are you feeling?"

She gave a crooked smile. "Sore, but much better... because of you."

"Rachel." Katie Lapp stepped forward. Rachel regarded the woman with warmth. "Katie. I'm so glad you came to see me." She gestured toward the chairs by the bed. Noah took the one closest to her head. Katie sat in the chair beside him.

"We were all worried about you," Katie said. "The waiting room was full—we were told that we couldn't all stay."

Tears glistened in Rachel's eyes. "Everyone came. That is wonderful to hear." She was moved by the concern of her new church community. "Please tell everyone how much I appreciate their concern." Noah handed her a bouquet of wildflowers. "These are beautiful, Noah." Smiling, she set them in her plastic water cup. Noah helped to hold the cup still for her.

"The Kings will be here later," Noah said. He reached out to grab hold of her hand. "*Mam* and I wanted to come first thing. Jedidiah is in charge of the children today."

Amused at the thought, Rachel raised her eyebrows. "I bet he isn't happy about that."

Katie smiled and regarded her with twinkling eyes. "It isn't the first time one of my sons has helped out.

With seven sons and a baby daughter, it is often necessary for one of them to lend a hand in the kitchen or garden."

"Did you see the doctor this morning?" Noah asked. He still held her hand, and Rachel enjoyed the contact.

Rachel flashed Katie a quick glance before returning her attention to Noah. "She was in earlier. I am doing as well as expected."

If it bothered Katie to see her son's open display of affection, Katie didn't show it. "You will stay at the Kings' during your recovery?"

Rachel frowned. "I had hoped to stay in the cottage."

Katie gave a nod. "We thought as much. We will take turns staying with you until you are well enough to be on your own."

"I didn't expect that—"

"Rachel," Noah interrupted softly, "it will be for your own good, and you know the women will enjoy it."

Rachel recalled the fun she'd had when her cousins had stayed with her the first few nights after she'd moved in. *"Ja,"* she said. "I know my cousins will."

The three of them talked for a time until an hour flew by. Katie rose. "I think I will go downstairs for some tea. Would you like some?"

Rachel shook her head. She thought she saw Katie and Noah exchange quick glances, but she might have been mistaken. "I'll have a chocolate milk shake," Noah said, and Rachel laughed.

"Of course it would be chocolate," she said.

Katie left and Rachel was alone with Noah. Noah stroked her hand and regarded her with a solemn expression. He seemed anxious, and Rachel frowned. "Noah, are ya all right?"

He seemed to pull himself up, and then his smile for her held genuine warmth. "I am well, Rachel, but I was so afraid for you. Terrified that I would lose you."

"And as you can see I am fine. The doctor said the surgery went well."

"The Lord was watching over you. I'm relieved the doctor could operate before your appendix ruptured." He released her hand and stood for a moment. He gazed down at her. "Rachel, it is you that worries me. Charlotte said that you didn't want me to know…about how sick you were."

Rachel looked away briefly. "That was true—at first. But when you came, I felt glad. I knew you would take *gut* care of me…get me to the hospital quickly." She grabbed hold of his hand so that her fingers surrounded and squeezed his gently. "I didn't want you to worry." And she'd wanted to know for certain exactly what was wrong before letting him know. A crazy notion, she realized.

His expression softened as Noah sat and regarded her with warmth. "I'm glad to hear you say that." He moved to the edge of the chair, took hold of both her hands. "Rachel Hostetler, I want to marry you. Please marry me so that we can be together forever."

Stunned, heart beating wildly, Rachel could only stare at him. She loved Noah with all of her heart, but how could she say yes? How could she marry him if she couldn't give him a family?

"Noah, I love you, but I don't think I should marry you." She didn't see the hurt she'd expected; the only thing she saw was his fierce determination.

"Why not? You say you love me."

"There are things about me you don't know."

"You are already married?" he said jokingly, but the words fell flat.

Rachel shook her head. This was no joking matter, and she realized then that despite his expression, Noah was hurting. She knew she had to tell him everything. She knew it would cause him pain once he realized the reason they couldn't marry…but still, she had to tell him.

She blinked against tears. "A year ago this past winter, I was in a buggy accident, and I got seriously hurt. I spent weeks in the hospital."

She studied his face but couldn't read his expression. She hesitated until he nodded for her to go on. "It was a courting buggy…"

As if sensing her pain, Noah stroked her hands reassuringly. Her skin tingled under his touch.

"Noah, I was seriously injured…*here*." She pulled a hand away to place it on the covers over her abdomen. She bit her lower lip and tears spilled from her eyes.

Noah hated seeing her tears. He could feel her pain as if it were his.

"You recovered," Noah said, "and you will do so again."

"Noah, I may not be able to have children," she said quickly. "You are so good with them; it wouldn't be fair to you…"

He smiled. "That's it? You can't marry me because it's possible you can't have a child?"

Rachel was stunned by his reaction. Noah looked almost relieved. But relieved by what?

"Rachel," he said. "I love you with all of my heart. I truly believe that the Lord wants us to be together. It doesn't matter if you can't have a child. I love *you*."

"But children—you will make a good father."

"Then we will adopt. There are children who need homes. Together, with our love, we can provide a *gut* home."

"Noah…"

Noah could tell that Rachel was afraid to believe that the solution was this simple. He knew that with Rachel by his side, he could live life as God intended…he could happily meet life's challenges head-on.

"I know all about the accident, Rachel," he admitted, "and Abraham Beiler. I am sorry you had to suffer through that. I am not sorry that Abraham Beiler was a fool, for if he hadn't been, then you and I wouldn't have met." He leaned forward, even closer to the bed. He recognized when she felt a tiny seedling of hope.

"Marry me, Rachel. Make me the happiest man alive and be my wife."

She started to cry. "Oh, Noah! I do love you."

"And?"

"I will marry you, if you are certain."

He realized hers were happy tears. "I have never been more certain in my life."

"Then, *ja,* I will marry you, Noah Lapp." It was as if the sun shone forth from her glistening brown eyes.

Noah laughed. "We can be married in November, the time for weddings. By then you will be well enough to stand by my side." He stood and came around to the other side of the bed. He leaned down and kissed her.

As their mouths touched, Rachel felt an overwhelming happiness. "I love you," she said when his head lifted. In answer, he kissed her again.

"And I love you," he said as he slowly straightened.

It was then that Rachel saw Katie Lapp in the doorway with Noah's milk shake in her hand. She blushed.

Noah noted Rachel's embarrassment and realized that someone had entered the room. *"Mam?"*

"Ja, Noah," Katie said, sweeping into the room to set Noah's milk shake on Rachel's bedside table. "I see you asked and got your answer."

Noah grinned at his mother. *"Ja.* She gave me the answer I'd hoped for."

Katie looked pleased. "It will be *gut* to have another daughter," she told Rachel.

Rachel beamed at her as she silently thanked the Lord for answering her prayers. "And it will be wonderful to belong to the Lapp family."

Epilogue

In early November, long after the fall harvest, the church community gathered together on a Tuesday in the home of the King family to celebrate the marriage of Noah Lapp and Rachel Hostetler. The occasion was a joyful affair, which promised to last from early morning until early evening for the elders; the young people would later head into the barn to continue the party well into the night. Rachel's family had come to Happiness from Millersburg, Ohio; Ezekiel and Henrietta Hostetler had been pleased to meet Rachel's intended and to witness firsthand their daughter's joy.

Noah and Rachel's intent to marry had been "published," or announced before the community, five weeks previously. Only a few close friends and neighbors had truly known about or suspected the couple's courtship. The seriousness of their relationship wasn't officially recognized until it was published.

The day he had taken Rachel to the hospital, Noah had been at Abram Peachy's house presenting to the deacon his desire to marry. Under normal circumstances, Abram would have gone to Rachel's family, usually her parents, to inquire of the wishes of the prospective bride-to-be. Rachel's illness and hospital stay had changed things. Under the circumstances, Noah had been unable to hold back from asking Rachel to be his wife, and everyone had understood.

In October, after Fast Day and on the day the Amish take fall communion, Noah and Rachel requested proper certifications of church membership. On the second church Sunday after their request, Noah and Rachel happily became members of the church, as was desired and necessary in preparation for their union. The Sunday the banns were published, Rachel and Noah didn't attend church service, but ate dinner together quietly in Rachel's kitchen.

Usually a newly married couple would live with the bride's parents, but not in this instance. After their marriage Noah and Rachel would live in the teacher's cottage until another house could be built for them on Lapp land. Rachel would remain a teacher until then or a time when a new teacher could be found to take her place.

After the couple vowed before all that their union was ordained by God, there was singing and preaching and finally all enjoyed food, seated in various places in the house. Partition walls had been removed to unite rooms and the guests. The bride and groom sat at the *Eck* table in the most viewed corner of the Kings' extended living room. The bridal party sat with them, each man or boy in the wedding party—in this case five of Noah's brothers—was situated across the table from a woman of his choosing. These men had escorted the women to the table while holding their hands. Jedidiah sat across from Annie Zook while Jacob chose Rachel's cousin Nancy. Noah's brother Elijah finally enjoyed his chance to spend time with Rebekka Miller. Daniel and Isaac weren't inclined to choose partners, but as was custom at an Amish wedding, partners were chosen for them— Mary Hershberger for Daniel and Martha Mast for Isaac, and the two brothers did not object as they escorted the women to their chairs. Both girls were older than these Lapp brothers, but it didn't matter. The partnering was for celebration purposes only.

Seated with his new bride in the *Eck* corner, Noah turned to Rachel and drank his fill of her. There was a radiant smile on her face as she eyed the wedding guests. He saw she was particularly interested in watching her cousin Charlotte with her betrothed, Abram Peachy. The couple's intent to marry had been published only recently, and a December wedding was planned. Noah agreed that Charlotte had never looked happier. Abram's children loved her, as did their father, who couldn't keep his eyes off her.

As if sensing Noah's attention, Rachel slowly faced him.

"Rachel Lapp," he said with a smile.

She grinned, looking more relaxed and happy than he'd ever seen her. He knew he had helped to put that twinkle in her brown eyes and that upward curve to her pink lips. She wore her new navy-blue linen Sunday-best dress, sewn by her aunt for the occasion. Her white prayer *kapp* was also new, fashioned of white organdy in the Happiness community style, her apron and cape in matching white. She would wear the dress and *kapp* again come next church Sunday. The apron she would put away for her funeral someday.

"Noah, my husband," she murmured softly. Rachel studied him with love. He wore a suit sewn for him by his mother. Hooks and eyes secured his black coat and vest over his white shirt. Black pants were held up by suspenders under his vest. He had donned a black bow tie, which, she knew, felt unfamiliar to him, for this was the one occasion he would be allowed to wear one. Earlier, he had taken off his black wide-brimmed hat and hung it on a wall hook. Rachel could easily see his face, and she loved what she read in his expression.

She leaned close to whisper, "I love you."

He grinned. "As well you should, since you just declared so before the eyes of the Lord God and the members of our church."

She made a face and he easily slipped his hand around her back. He dipped his head to whisper in her ear. "I will love you forever, Rachel Lapp."

She shivered with pleasure at his breath in her ear, against her neck. "And I will love you forever, Noah." Then she took a quick glance to see that no one was watching at that very second, and she turned her head to plant a kiss on his cheek.

She leaned back in her chair. "I have truly found happiness in Lancaster County," she breathed softly.

"*We* have found true happiness together," Noah murmured, holding her close.

* * * * *

PLAIN PERIL

Alison Stone

To my big sister, Lisa, whose gift was reminding all of us to Live, Love, Laugh. To Scott, Scotty, Alex, Kelsey and Leah. Love you guys, always and forever.

And we know that God causes everything to work together for the good of those who love God and are called according to his purpose for them.
—*Romans* 8:28

Chapter One

The long shadows from the branches clacking against the bedroom window stretched across the two small lumps in the queen-size bed. Hannah tucked the hand-stitched quilt—the one her grandmother had made—under her six-year-old niece Emma's chin and smiled. A pathetic smile. The poor child stared back, a cross between grief and contempt on her precious little face. On the other half of the bed, Sarah, Emma's nine-year-old sister, had already lost the battle against the flood of tears, and sleep had taken her. Merciful sleep.

Hannah blinked her gritty eyes a few times and drew in a deep breath, praying for wisdom.

"I want *Mem*." The plea in Emma's tiny voice tore at Hannah's heart.

I want your mem, too. But Hannah kept those words locked in her heart along with her conflicting emotions. She kissed her niece's cool forehead. "Sleep, little one. I'll be here in the morning."

Emma pursed her lips, unimpressed with the promise of another day with Aunt Hannah.

How many more mornings could Hannah maintain

this routine? She had already been here for three days, and she only had two weeks before she had to return to her job as a bank teller in Buffalo. She tried to quiet her mind and prayed the young girls' father would return home soon. Everyone had anticipated that her sister's husband, John, would returned for his wife's funeral.

Everyone was wrong.

Hannah's chest tightened. The circumstances surrounding John Lapp's disappearance were sketchy at best. Would leaving these two sweet girls with the father who had abandoned them at the most critical time in their lives be the best option—even if he did return?

A little voice told Hannah John was not going to return.

Emma crinkled her nose at Hannah. The familiarity of the gesture took Hannah's breath away. How many times had she seen Ruth make that same face when she was a little girl? *Poor Ruthie.* Hannah smoothed her niece's hair, and the child jerked away.

Hannah's heart broke a little bit more.

"*Guten nacht*, Emma. I love you." Hannah took a step toward the door. Every inch of her ached for her precious nieces who had lost their mother in a horrible farming accident, after which their father had apparently run off in grief upon finding her body partially buried in the grain silo.

She shook her head, trying to dismiss the horrific image. She ran her hand along the smooth railing on the stairs. The swooshing of her long dress brushing against her legs felt strange yet familiar. She slowed at the bottom of the stairs, allowing her eyes to adjust to the gathering darkness. She hadn't bothered to turn on the gas-powered lights before she had headed upstairs to tuck the children into bed.

Now she didn't mind lingering with the long shadows. It suited her mood. She wondered fleetingly what time it was, then realized it didn't matter. The children and the chores on the farm dictated her day. Not a clock.

Through the front window, she noticed the sun low on the horizon. Soon the entire house would be cast in darkness. Then she'd be left with nothing but her thoughts because sleep didn't come for the guilt ridden. A chill skittered up her spine, and her neck and shoulders ached from exhaustion. She dreaded the long night in her childhood home in the middle of nowhere.

She wished she had something mindless to occupy her time, like TV or her iPad, two things she had reluctantly given up when she stepped foot into her sister's Amish home.

Her dead sister's home.

Her eyes drifted to the far wall in the room, an empty spot where her sister's simple pine casket had held her body as friends and neighbors came to give their final respects. She closed her eyes and felt the familiar tingling, the promise of more tears. How could it be that her younger sister was dead? She sighed heavily. Hannah had abandoned her Amish ways, but she hadn't abandoned her faith. She'd get through this. For the sake of her nieces, she had to.

Hannah found herself in the kitchen putting on the teakettle. She stared over the yard and daydreamed about the days she and her sister—two years younger—had run in and out of their mother's fresh sheets hanging on the line. The scent of clean laundry and newly cut hay. Not a care in the world.

A nostalgic unease wormed its way into her memory. No cares as long as *Dat* was busy working on the farm because as soon as his chores were done, he'd find a reason to scold Hannah while allowing Ruthie to play undisturbed with her dolls.

Hannah never understood the favoritism. Now, more than a decade after she had slipped away from Apple Creek in the middle of the night, she felt the emptiness. An emptiness that had kept her away.

Until now.

A knocking at the door startled Hannah. She turned off the gas stove. Her pulse whooshed in her ears as her long gown whooshed around her calves. Had her sister's husband, John, finally returned? Doubt whispered across her brain. Why would he knock on the door of his own home?

Why would he abandon his daughters after their mother's tragic death? John was obviously not well.

She drew in a deep breath and reached for the door handle. What could she possibly say to him? Could she muster the compassion her brother-in-law needed? She feared she'd be unable to hold back the torrent of angry words criticizing him for not manning up when it came to his bereaved children. She yanked open the door, praying for the former. The greeting froze on her lips.

"Miss Wittmer, I'm sorry to bother you so late. I'm Sheriff Spencer Maxwell. We met earlier today."

Alarm sent goose bumps racing across her skin.

"Yes, Officer?" Self-consciously, Hannah smoothed her apron and skirt, an outfit she wore out of deference to her grieving mother. Hannah's English wardrobe would have been an in-your-face reminder that her mother had lost not one, but two daughters. The handsome sheriff had paid his respects at the funeral earlier today in the barn. He was one of only a few outsiders to mingle among the hundreds of Amish. That's the reason she noticed him, or so she told herself.

The sheriff removed his hat and pressed it to his chest revealing short-cropped hair and kind eyes. "I almost didn't stop when I noticed the lights weren't on, but I took a chance."

Something in his tone made the fine hairs on the back of her neck stand on edge. "It sounds important." She didn't invite him in, fearing the neighbors would question why a single Amish woman—she referred to herself as Amish in the loosest of terms—had invited a man into her home. Part of her wondered why she cared. "Do you have news regarding my brother-in-law?"

"No, I'm sorry. I don't." His even tone gave nothing away. "But I do have something important to discuss."

Hannah listened for any sounds from the bedrooms. It was quiet save for the chirping of the crickets floating in through the open windows on the warm summer evening. Hannah hoped Emma had finally drifted to sleep. Hannah stepped onto the porch, pulling the door closed behind her. "Let's talk out here."

Hannah sat on one of the rockers, fearing her legs wouldn't hold her upright. She was still struggling to get over the news that her sister had died. Her twenty-seven-year-old sister.

Sheriff Maxwell walked the length of the porch slowly then turned around and stopped in front of her. He leaned back on the porch railing. He seemed to be collecting his thoughts, but his hesitation made her feel suspicious, like when a man wandered into her bank with sunglasses and a baseball cap tugged low over his eyes.

"Please sit, Officer Maxwell. You're driving me crazy and if you don't sit, I'm going to lose it."

The sheriff angled his head and studied her for a minute. She knew the look. Something wasn't adding up in his head. She had seen it many times, mainly in Buffalo. It was the double take of a bank patron when the word *yah* slipped from her lips. Or the pestering of her coworkers who couldn't understand why she didn't join them for happy hour. Or her roommates, who playfully mocked her unassuming wardrobe.

Now her English vocabulary was invading her Amish ruse.

The sheriff lowered himself into the chair next to hers and ran his hand along the smooth wood of the arm. "You seem different than the other Amish women I've met."

And there it was.

Hannah flattened her hand against her prayer covering and forced a smile. "Is my bonnet on crooked?" After burying her sister and suffering withering looks from her former Amish neighbors and so-called friends, she was in no mood to be scrutinized by the sheriff, too.

The setting sun reflected in his brown eyes, and his brows shifted, as if he were adjusting his line of thinking. Regret at her snippy comment teased her insides, but not enough to apologize.

"I didn't mean to pry." He tapped his fingers on the arm of the chair. "I have some difficult news."

Hannah hiked her chin and tried to ignore her racing heart. "At this point, I'm numb to bad news."

"You've had a rough time of it." Sheriff Maxwell's Adam's apple moved in his throat, and his hesitation made her panic swell, forcing all the air from her lungs.

She wasn't as numb as she claimed to be. He shifted toward the edge of the rocker and looked like he wanted to reach out and take her hand, but thought better of it.

Hannah sent up a silent prayer.

Dear Lord, please be merciful and let me handle whatever it is this man has come here to say.

"Yesterday, I drove out to Bishop Lapp's farm."

"John's father." The elder Lapp had to be escorted by the arm into the barn for his daughter-in-law's funeral. His stooped posture radiated his grief. The bishop had only a few terse words for Hannah. It didn't come as a surprise, considering the bishop's loss and Hannah's non-grata status in the community.

"The bishop's other son, Lester, dismissed me without hearing what I had to say." The sheriff stared toward his vehicle parked on the side of the road; its presence no doubt had the neighbors' tongues wagging. Wireless technology had nothing on the old-fashioned rumor mill in Apple Creek.

"Bishop Lapp must be having a difficult time." Hannah said the first polite thing that popped into her head. She had no firsthand knowledge on how he was doing. Since Hannah had never been baptized, she wasn't officially shunned, but the bishop was determined to freeze her out all the same.

"I understand, but I need to talk to him about his son, John."

"I'll be of no help there."

"It's important you know where the investigation is headed, especially since you're staying in John Lapp's house."

A hot flush swept over her body. "This was my family's home before John moved in with my sister."

"I understand." Spencer sounded contrite, but determined.

She tugged on the folds of her skirt to allow the fresh evening air to cool her shins and bare feet. "You're investigating my sister's accident?"

"Yes. It's customary for the medical examiner to be called out after a death like this. Law enforcement needs to make sure there was no foul play involved."

Apprehension prickled Hannah's scalp. She winced and scratched her hair through the fabric of the cap. Her tight bun was giving her a headache. "My sister's death was an accident. A tragic farming accident." That's what everyone had repeated over and over as they paid their final respects and then again when they delivered casserole dishes with wordy instructions on how to warm them up.

Such a shame. A tragic farming accident. And those poor girls, to lose their mother...

They'd shake their covered heads then bustle into the kitchen and make tsking sounds at her nieces, who sat cross-legged on the floor, stacking blocks.

What was left unsaid, but blatantly obvious in their Amish faces, was that if John had been a better husband, Ruthie wouldn't have been left with the brunt of the chores while her husband fraternized and schemed. What exactly he had been scheming, Hannah's mother wouldn't tell her.

Apparently, John Lapp hadn't entirely shed his youthful, rebellious ways.

This wasn't news to Hannah.

Sheriff Maxwell stood and faced her. The setting sun behind him cast his face in shadows. Tension hung heavy in the air. "There's no easy way to say this." The shaky quality of his voice made icy dread pool in her stomach.

"Tell me." She wrapped her fingers around the arms of the chair and squeezed.

"Before your sister ended up in the silo, she was already dead."

Miss Wittmer slumped in the wood rocker. Spencer's first instinct was to reach out, grab her, but she clutched the arms of the chair and stiffened her back, as if determined to be strong, regardless of the devastating news. The color draining from her face told a different story.

She drew in a deep breath. "I… I don't understand." The Amish woman rose and stood next to him. A thin strand of brown hair poked out from underneath her bonnet. She turned to face him, her eyes shiny with unshed tears. "Are you telling me my sister was murdered?" Her tone was shaky, brittle.

"I'm afraid so." Spencer let his hand hover near her elbow, ready to grab her if she should faint. She stood absolutely still, and he thought he heard Miss Wittmer's gasp above the incessant chirping of the crickets. As a cop originally from the inner city, he still hadn't gotten used to the racket nature created.

She shook her head briskly, as if trying to shake away the image, or perhaps his words. "My sister was murdered." It was no longer a question.

This time there was no mistaking her gasp. Spencer clutched her elbow. She crumbled to her knees, her thin frame swallowed in a pool of black material. She bowed her head. Spencer had seen loud grief—the wail of a mother who had lost her child in a drive-by shooting. He had never seen such a quiet, heartbreaking display. He didn't know how to react, and he didn't know which was worse.

Spencer crouched next to the woman and held her arm. "Let me help you up. I can get you some water. A cold washcloth. Something."

"Who did this?" Her words came out, barely a whisper.

"We're investigating."

The woman brushed his hand away and grabbed the railing and pulled herself to her feet, a mix of embarrassment and anger lacing her tone. "Ruthie told me she was afraid."

Spencer's pulse ratcheted up a notch.

Miss Wittmer yanked off her bonnet. The moon rising above the trees lit on the golden strands of her dark hair. If she weren't an Amish woman, he would have thought she had highlighted her hair. She smoothed a hand over the few loose strands that had sprung free from the bun at the nape of her neck.

She sat, resigned. "She told me she feared too many things were changing." She leaned back and wrapped her fingers around the arms of the chair. "My sister and I hadn't seen each other for over a decade, then about five months ago, she called me. She wanted to see me."

Spencer rubbed his jaw. "I guess it's my turn to be confused. She called you?"

Miss Wittmer looked up at him, a battle waging behind her watchful eyes. "John had a phone installed in the barn." She shrugged. "Claimed he needed it for work."

"And you have a phone, too?"

"I'm not Amish."

Spencer bit back a comment.

"I left Apple Creek and the Amish community eleven years ago." Miss Wittmer dragged her lower lip through her teeth. "It—" she lifted her palms "—this life wasn't for me. Once I left, my father refused to allow me to visit."

"You were shunned." Spencer had been sheriff of Apple Creek for only a year, but he was slowly learning the ways of the Amish.

She shook her head. "I was never baptized, so technically, there was no reason to shun me. But my father was a controlling man. He was part of the reason I left. I felt suffocated. And I suppose there was always the fear that if I came back home for a visit and talked about my wonderful, worldly life, who's to say my sister wouldn't want to leave with me." Heavy shadows masked her expression, but Spencer thought he detected an eye roll when she referred to herself as *worldly*.

"The clothes." He gestured to her long gown, her apron, the bonnet in her hand.

"It's easier this way. I wanted to make sure I respected both my sister and my mother." She grabbed a fistful of material by her thigh and fluttered her skirt. "This is my sister's." Her words came out droll, sad, lifeless as if to say, "She won't be needing it anymore."

A thought nagged at Spencer, and he didn't know how to broach it. He decided to be direct. "If you were estranged from your family, why did they contact you when your sister died?"

A mirthless laugh escaped her lips. "My mother, who wouldn't dare use the phone herself, sent word through a neighbor. I'm her only surviving child. My father's gone. Now my sister's gone." She sighed heavily. "And someone needs to take care of the children...until John returns." The tone of the last three words convinced him she understood John was unlikely to care for his children when and if he did return.

"No other family can care for the children?"

"John's family is busy searching for their son and brother. They believe he ran off in grief after finding Ruthie in the silo. Perhaps blaming himself. His new job has taken him away from the farm." She rocked slowly in the chair. "My mother is not as strong as she used to be. She'd never be able to manage two young girls." She stopped rocking. "I'm worried about my *mem*. The news Ruthie was murdered will devastate her all over again."

"I'll do my best to find whoever did this." He studied Miss Wittmer's face to see if she had the same suspicions he had. "Why was Ruthie worried things were changing?"

"Ruth embraced the Amish way. When we were kids, she spoke of raising her family here. She was doing that. She had two beautiful daughters. By all outward appearances, she had what any humble Amish girl could want."

"What about her husband? Was her husband a good guy?" John Lapp had come under his radar once or twice, which definitely wasn't a good thing.

"I didn't know John. He returned to Apple Creek shortly before I left. He was one of a group of young men who had left the area to work on a ranch out West. A handful of them returned and embraced the Amish way and were baptized and married." She drew in a deep breath and let it out slowly. "It was the talk of the community. The families considered themselves blessed because their wayward sons had returned."

"The prodigal sons." Spencer referred to the parable he remembered from his childhood days in Sunday school. Before he realized God didn't bless all His children, especially poor ones born into bad neighborhoods where guns and hanging out on street corners crowded out God and Sunday church services.

"Something like that." Miss Wittmer seemed unimpressed. "But no one killed a calf in celebration of their return. Everyone went about their business. If you haven't noticed, *we* are a humble people." She wiggled her bare toes.

"Do you know if your sister and John had a good marriage?"

"When we got together for the first time five months ago—my sister drove the wagon to the McDonald's in the next town—she said she was worried that John didn't seem content. She feared he might leave her and the girls. John had given up farming for the most part and had taken a job making fancy swing sets."

Spencer pointed toward the road with his thumb and squinted. "The place down the road? A lot of Amish men are employed there." The Amish were notorious for being hardworking, skilled laborers. No shame in that.

"That was the first change. John also spent more time with the men whom he had left with years earlier."

"Do you know these men?" Rumors reached the station that there had been some discord within the Amish community. When he tried to investigate, the alleged victims, men who had their beards cut in the middle of the night, refused to talk to him. Even Ruth Lapp had sent him away when he had come to this very farm to question her about her husband's possible involvement. But there was no mistaking the fear in her eyes. Ruth Lapp was afraid of something.

Miss Wittmer got a distant look in her eyes, as if

she were replaying a memory. "Ruth never gave me the names of the men John was hanging out with. I've been gone a long time. The names may not have meant much to me." She ran her pinched fingers down the long tie on the bonnet in her hand. "There was something I found strange. My sister made what I thought was a passing comment about taking care of her girls. I laughed at her." Regret and grief flashed in her eyes. She sniffed. "When I realized she wasn't joking, I assured her she was doing a great job as a mom but if the time ever came, I'd make sure Emma and Sarah were well taken care of."

Her gaze drifted up to meet his. "Do you think she knew something was going to happen to her?"

The memory of Ruth Lapp shooing him off the farm so that her husband wouldn't find him here had haunted him from the moment he heard of her untimely death.

"Your sister seemed afraid, but she wouldn't open up to me."

Miss Wittmer's head shot up. "Why didn't you do something. Protect her?"

Spencer shoved his shoulders back despite the punch to his gut. "She assured me everything was fine. She told me to go, reminding me that the Amish and law enforcement have a tenuous relationship at best. There wasn't much more I could do if Ruth didn't talk to me."

Miss Wittmer bowed her head, and her shoulders sagged. "I was helpless when it came to my sister, too. I had no right to snap at you." Clasping her hands in her lap, as if she were bracing for something, she asked, "How do you know my sister's death wasn't an accident?"

"The county medical examiner didn't find any corn

in her mouth or nose. If your sister had suffocated in the silo, she would have inhaled the corn."

Miss Wittmer closed her eyes. "He killed her, didn't he? John Lapp killed my sister."

Spencer cleared his throat. "We're still investigating. The Lapp family has been unwilling to talk to me. I'll give them a day or two to reconsider."

Miss Wittmer rubbed her arms, despite the mild evening. Her bonnet had been abandoned on her lap. "How cooperative do you think they're going to be when you accuse their son of killing my sister?"

"It's part of my job."

"I don't envy you." She planted her elbow on the arm of her chair and rested her chin in her palm. "I don't envy either of us."

Chapter Two

Hannah tossed and turned on a small cot in the first-floor bedroom of her childhood home, now her sister's home. Even the white noise of the crickets couldn't lull her to sleep, not after the news she had received from Sheriff Maxwell. He had left her with a warning to be careful, his cell phone number and a promise to have his officers patrol her property.

Small consolation in the dead of night in the middle of nowhere.

Not even knowing that her mother slept nearby in the adjacent *dawdy haus* could calm her nerves.

The small bedroom grew stifling, yet she still couldn't bring herself to move to her sister's more spacious bedroom upstairs. Hannah slipped out of bed and slid the window open. She dismissed her silly fears that someone would climb through her window because if someone really wanted to get in, all they had to do was stroll through the front door. It didn't have a lock.

Hannah flopped down on the cot and sighed. She pulled the sheet up to her chin and stared toward the open bedroom door, imagining the shapes morphing into an intruder, namely John. She was driving herself crazy. Her nerves felt like they were jacked on too much caffeine.

Had John really killed her sister? The sheriff had warned her they didn't have enough evidence to prove John had been involved. But still…

Hannah struggled to quiet her mind with prayer and the hope of sleep. The chirping crickets filled her ears, and she realized the noise could also mask footsteps on creaking floorboards.

Tingles of dread crept up her spine.

"You're being silly. You lived in the city and never were this afraid," she whispered into the night.

You never tried to fall asleep with the knowledge your sister had been murdered.

Sitting up, she leaned against the wall and tipped her head back. The piece of snitz pie she had eaten before bed didn't seem like such a good idea. She was making herself sick with anxiety.

Just when her rational side had talked her irrational side out of a full-blown panic attack, the blaring of a car alarm sliced through the cacophony of chirping. Hannah bolted upright and snapped her attention toward the window. Her car was parked behind the barn and covered with a tarp.

She pressed a hand to her thumping chest and drew in deep breaths.

The alarm will turn off by itself. It will turn off by itself.

How many times had a car alarm gone off in the city? Especially on her street filled with college students and their varying schedules. Car alarms were sensitive. An animal probably scampered across the tarp. Or a tree branch dropped on it. Or…or…

No, it did not mean someone was out there waiting for her. Her apprehension grew with the strident pulsing of the alarm. She drew in another deep breath through her nose and released it.

Hannah threw back the sheet and climbed out of bed. She pushed back her shoulders. *I'm being ridiculous.*

She grabbed her cell phone from the end table and dialed six digits of Sheriff Maxwell's phone number, ready to press the seventh digit if needed. She grabbed a flashlight and her car keys from the kitchen on her way out the door. She stopped long enough to stuff her feet into boots.

Her focus tunneled. She made a direct path to her car, tucked neatly between the barn and a dense crop of trees. Striding across the yard, she rolled her ankle in a rut. "Whose great idea was it to park my car way out here? Oh yeah, mine," she muttered. Hannah was doing everything possible to comfort her mother, even if it meant hiding everything that made her an outsider.

The alarm came at Hannah in varying waves of ear-piercing obnoxiousness. Wincing, she lifted her key fob and aimed it in the general direction of the car and hit the alarm button. The sudden silence deafened her. Even the crickets were mute. She glanced back toward her mother's dark residence. Apparently, the noise hadn't disturbed her.

Hannah debated about returning to the house, but decided to quickly check on her car. She rounded the corner of the barn, and the beam of a flashlight blinded her. Her heart leaped in her chest, and she turned to run.

"Wait." A deep, commanding voice vibrated through her.

Hannah didn't wait. She had to put distance between

herself and the man trespassing on the farm. She was out here alone. She had to protect the girls. She bolted toward the house, calculating how she'd reach the girls' room and wedge something against the door.

She stumbled in a wagon wheel rut and pitched forward. Crying out in panic, she braced herself. Pain shot up the heels of her hands as they met the earth. Her knees slammed down hard on the packed dirt.

"Miss Wittmer, it's Sheriff Maxwell."

On all fours, Hannah dropped her head in relief. She pushed to her feet and brushed the dirt from her palms and her pj's. She spun around. "What are you doing? You scared me to death."

"What are *you* doing out here? You shouldn't be wandering alone outside." The sheriff arched the beam of the flashlight across her dirty pj bottoms and her University at Buffalo T-shirt, complete with boots she obviously should have laced up.

"Don't answer my question with a question." Hannah crossed her arms and huffed. She had a tad more confidence in her English pj's than she had wearing her sister's Amish dress. No one expected her to fake Amish while she slept, did they?

"I was patrolling the area and heard the alarm." Sheriff Maxwell flicked his flashlight toward her vehicle. "Yours?"

She didn't bother to answer the obvious. He tossed back the tarp, revealing her three-year-old Chevy Malibu. "Someone slashed your tires."

Hannah plowed a hand through her hair, and a mix of annoyance, resignation and fear wound their way up her spine. "Did you see anyone?"

The sheriff shook his head. "I'm afraid not."

She glared at him skeptically. "Why are you lurking around here?"

"I'm not lurking. I'm doing my job." An annoyingly coy smile played on his lips.

"If you were doing your job—" she held out her hand toward her car, the one with twenty-seven remaining car payments "—then this would have never happened."

"Fair enough." His smooth voice rolled over her. "But doesn't it make you feel better to know I'm not far away if you need me?"

Hannah smoothed the tarp back over her car. "Let's be clear about something. I don't need anyone."

He seemed to give her a once-over. "That's debatable."

Hannah swept her hair into a ponytail and fastened it with a rubber band from her wrist. "Fair enough." She repeated his words. "I am glad you're here. Find out who did this. But make sure you're not lurking around too much. I don't want the neighbors talking. They already give me enough grief."

Hannah spun around—her snippiness fueled more from her adrenaline-soaked nerves than from anger— and marched up to the house, keenly aware that Sheriff Maxwell was watching her.

The next morning, Hannah slipped into her sister's black Amish dress, an outward sign she was grieving. She peeked in on her sleeping nieces and decided to check on *Mem*. Through the screen door of the adjacent *dawdy haus*, Hannah saw her mother sitting at the kitchen table with a cup of coffee. When Hannah knocked, her mother pushed back from the worn pine table slowly. Hannah couldn't be sure, but she thought she saw her mother wince.

"Are you okay?" The screen door squeaked, and Hannah stepped into the small space. Memories crowded in on her. Hannah had spent long hours here visiting her own grandmother. Her mammy was the one person who loved her unconditionally. When Mammy died shortly before Hannah turned sixteen, Hannah had found herself rudderless between an overdemanding father and a too-passive mother.

"Tired is all." Her mother waved away her daughter's concerns. "Would you like coffee?" She took a step toward the stove.

"No, I can't stay long. I want to make sure I'm in the house when Emma and Sarah wake up."

Her mother shook her head in disbelief. She did that a lot since Ruthie died.

"Did you hear the commotion outside last night?"

Her mother paused. "Commotion?"

"My car alarm went off." She omitted the part about the slashed tires. She hated to add to her mother's grief.

"Neh." Her mouth pursed her lips. "My hearing is *neh gut.*"

Hannah leaned against the counter and watched her mother slowly sit back down. Her mother took a sip of coffee then touched her head. "Your *kapp.*"

Hannah tugged on her apron with both hands. "But I'm wearing a dress."

Her mother looked down without saying anything, renewed disappointment etched in her pale features. An expression Hannah had seen many times. An expression that had both frustrated and confused Hannah as a teenager. Why didn't her mother say what she meant?

"*Mem*, I came back for Sarah and Emma…and you." Hannah pulled out the chair across from her mother and sat. She angled her head to see into her mother's eyes. "I don't know what my future holds."

Her mother lifted her brows. "Your sister said you were coming home." Her hopeful tone broke Hannah's heart.

Hannah dipped her chin, surprise making her momentarily speechless. "Ruthie told you about our visits?" Ruthie had sworn her to secrecy.

Her mother nodded. *"Yah."* She fingered the handle of the coffee mug. "Are you ready to be baptized Amish? Find a nice Amish boy and marry? Maybe next year you can prepare—"

"No." The single word came out sharp, angry. Hannah flattened her palms on the table and drew in a calming breath and said more softly, "Not yet, *Mem*. Not yet." Hannah scratched her forehead. "I'll admit, I wasn't happy in Buffalo." She was lonely and didn't enjoy her job, but she hadn't decided to return to the Amish way of life. Not permanently anyway. She was toying with the idea. Searching for happiness. Wondering out loud to her sister if she had been naive in her decision to leave the Amish community in the first place.

Perhaps saying as much to please her sister.

Or perhaps, in a way, dissuading her sister from making any big decisions that would alter her life irrevocably. As Hannah's decision had forever changed her life.

Hannah covered her mother's hand. "I'm here for the short-term until I know the girls are okay. Please, don't get your hopes up about me returning for good."

Disappointment creased the corners of the older woman's sad eyes. "I thought with *Dat* gone…"

Although the rift between Hannah and her father was apparent to anyone with eyes, it pained her to hear her mother talk about it.

"*Mem*, please, let's talk about this another time. We're all trying to come to terms with Ruthie."

"*Gott* has a plan."

Hannah's body tensed. "I wish God's plan was to leave Ruthie here on earth with us. With her daughters."

Her mother's lips quivered. "Life is hard. You have to make decisions that are *gut* for the family. You can't be selfish."

The sting of her mother's comments wounded her. Had Hannah been selfish?

"One day at a time, okay?" Hannah hated throwing out a silly platitude, but she wasn't ready to make life-altering decisions right now.

Will I ever be ready?

Hannah didn't want to discuss Ruthie's husband, but it couldn't be avoided. Not with John running around out there, somewhere. "Did Ruth ever say anything negative to you about John?"

Her mother's eyes flashed momentarily dark. *"Neh."* She shook her head vehemently. "I don't know how things work in the English world, but a woman does not speak ill of her husband. And if she does, she's just being gossipy."

"I'm not gossiping." She placed her elbow on the table and rested her chin on the heel of her hand. "Was John ever mean to Ruth?"

"John Lapp is the bishop's son." Agitation shook her mother's hands, and she refused to meet Hannah's gaze.

"John left Apple Creek when he was a teenager. He

was gone for a long time. Maybe he wasn't the son the bishop had raised."

Her mother lifted her chin. "John came back. Was baptized. Married. It was *gut*." Which was more than Hannah had done. The accusation in her mother's eyes made Hannah's cheeks fiery. Couldn't her mother see she was doing everything she could? Everything short of promising to be baptized Amish.

"You like John Lapp?"

"Your sister and her husband took care of me. I am grateful to them."

Unease settled in Hannah's belly. Learning Ruthie was murdered would kill her mother. Hannah pushed away from the table. The whole truth would wait for another day.

Hannah brushed a kiss across her mother's soft cheek. Her mother pulled back and widened her eyes, startled by the display of affection. Hannah started to leave but turned back one last time. Her mother was holding her fingertips to her cheek, where Hannah had kissed her.

"Burning the midnight oil, huh?" Mrs. Greene, Spencer's elderly landlady, sat in her wicker rocker on the front porch, nursing her tea.

The screen door slipped out of his hand and thwacked against the door frame. "Sorry about that. Didn't see you sitting there."

"Got no air-conditioning in there. Cooler out here. Can't imagine how hot it's gonna be later if it's already this hot at—" She squinted up at him "—what time is it?"

"Early." Too early, considering he hadn't gotten much sleep last night. The red numbers on the digital clock by his bed read a blurry four-something by the time he left Miss Wittmer's and climbed into bed. Despite assigning another officer to check in on the Lapp farm, he felt unsettled.

What was it about the brown-eyed beauty that had gotten under his skin? And what kind of danger was she in with John Lapp still out there?

Spencer eased down, balancing his coffee and sat on the top step. Mrs. Greene spoiled him. She brewed the best coffee and left a to-go mug on the hall table inside the front door every morning. She claimed she missed having her boys around. All of them had grown and moved on with their lives, leaving her to dote over the tenants of her two upstairs apartments, only one of which was occupied.

"You finally meeting some people in this town? Doing things besides work?" Mrs. Greene had a say-whatever's-on-her-mind way of talking that didn't always allow room for him to get a word in edgewise.

Smiling, Spencer lifted his coffee and inhaled its rich scent. "Last night was work."

Mrs. Greene made a tsking noise. "How are you ever going to have a life if all you do is work?"

Spencer leaned back on the railing and shifted to look at Mrs. Greene. "I need to find you a hobby so you don't pay so much attention to me."

"Someone's got to pay attention to a handsome man like you. You can't tell me you haven't found one pretty woman in Apple Creek who you'd like to take for a nice Friday fish fry."

Spencer laughed, nearly choking on his coffee. "Is that what women like to do around here? Go to a fish fry?"

"That's what they did in my day." Mrs. Greene seemed to go somewhere for a minute before snapping out of it. "Nice crispy haddock and tartar sauce. Yum."

Spencer watched the content expression on Mrs. Greene's face. The look of a woman who had lived a good life and was now satisfied to sit back and watch the world go by—and to micromanage his.

"That girl you left behind in Buffalo hasn't come to her senses yet?"

Why had he told Mrs. Greene about Vicki? Because she had a way of prying things out of people, that's why. Spencer shook his head and rolled his eyes, feeling very much like a schoolboy under the inquisitive gaze of his grandmother, who always had an interest in everything he did. Unlike his parents, whose only interests involved all the things they required him to do.

"I've been here a year. I don't think she's suddenly going to show up at my door."

Mrs. Greene thrummed the pads of her fingers on the arm of her wicker chair. "Country's not her thing, you say?"

"Vicki was definitely a city girl." And last he heard, she was engaged to a surgeon. So very Vicki. Looked like she was going to get everything she wanted out of life.

He and Victoria had both been in law school when they started dating. She told him she had signed up for one kind of life, and Spencer had turned the tables on her by signing up for the Buffalo police exam.

"Heard she's engaged," Spencer found himself saying.

"I'm sorry."

He narrowed his gaze and stared at the long strands of grass growing up around the railing posts where the lawn service had forgotten to trim. "I'm not. Now I don't have to feel guilty for stringing her along for so many years."

Mrs. Greene made a disagreeable sound. "That's not like you to string someone along. Don't be so hard on yourself."

It was tough not to be hard on himself when even his own father claimed disappointment. His father had been a police officer, but he had wished something more for his son. Spencer was the first college graduate in the family. A lawyer—a nice, stable, *safe* profession.

Spencer grabbed the railing and pulled himself to his feet. "Maybe it's time I got back into the game." Miss Wittmer's pretty face came to mind. He smiled wickedly at Mrs. Greene. "Maybe I should find me a nice Amish woman."

Mrs. Greene's eyes flared wide. She waved her hand in dismissal. "Don't be getting any crazy thoughts. The Amish don't take to the English. Not for datin'."

Spencer felt a smile pulling on his lips. He walked over and tapped Mrs. Greene's knee. "No, no crazy thoughts. I'll just stick to my job."

And his job was to make sure nothing happened to Miss Wittmer and her two nieces out there on the Lapp farm. Until he had John Lapp in custody, he feared he wouldn't be getting much sleep.

He couldn't screw this up. Not like he had let down Daniel, the teenage boy in Buffalo who had ended up another grim statistic. He wouldn't let that happen again. Not on his watch.

Chapter Three

Hannah slipped back into the house after visiting her mother in time to find Emma coming down the stairs in her sleeping gown, one hand on her doll, the other fisted and rubbing her eyes. Sarah came down only when it seemed hunger had gotten the best of her.

After feeding her nieces breakfast of, in their opinion, too-lumpy oatmeal and runny *dippy ecks*, Hannah had the girls get dressed then ushered them outside. She needed to check on the farm animals and thought perhaps the outdoors would brighten the young girls' dispositions.

Hannah reached the door of the barn as the sun was haloing the roofline of the gray, weatherworn barn. Sarah and Emma seemed content to plop down on the slight incline leading toward the barn and drag long strands of grass through their fingers. As long as the young girls stayed close to the barn, there was nothing they could get into. The freedom the Amish children had to explore was far different than the constantly monitored existence of English children.

A little voice in her head warned her that her non-motherly way of thinking was likely to get her—or her new charges—into trouble. She considered taking each by the hand and advising them to stay close, then decided it was best not to draw attention to her slipping into the barn to check on the animals.

With two hands, she peeled back the door and stepped inside. The familiar smell of manure assaulted her nose even though the barn had been swept clean yesterday for her sister's funeral. She lifted her apron to her nose, wondering how she had ever gotten used to such a foul smell. Glancing over her shoulder, she saw Emma and Sarah kicking a volleyball back and forth. Their long blond hair dangled down their backs.

The morning light filtered through the slats of the barn. The cow mooed as if happy to see her. A neighborhood boy, Samuel, had come over both in the mornings and afternoons to milk the cow and feed the horse the past few days. Samuel had told her he couldn't come this morning, but he'd be available this afternoon.

Planting her hands on her hips, she let out a heavy sigh. Even though John's move away from farming for a living had been a point of contention for her sister, Hannah was grateful. Now she only had to worry about a few animals and no crops. Seemed a shame, though, considering all this land her family's property sat on.

Hannah grabbed a milking stool and sat. She glanced at her soft hands, now foreign to the rigors of physical labor. A shadow crossed the open door, and Hannah's hand immediately went to her head. She had taken the time to twist her hair into a messy bun, but she wasn't wearing her cap.

"*Gut* morning." The words flowed naturally from her

mouth. She held up her hand to block the sun as a man strolled into the barn.

"Morning, Miss Wittmer." The casual, warm greeting brought her up short.

"Sheriff Maxwell." Hannah drew in a deep breath and found herself wishing she had on her English wardrobe complete with a little eyeliner and smoothing hair gel. She lowered her hand and forced a smile. "We have to stop meeting like this."

"Call me Spencer."

"Then you'll have to call me Hannah." She scrambled to her feet then looked past him to see her nieces hanging on to the door frame, studying the visitor.

"Go back to playing, girls. The sheriff won't be here long."

"No, I won't." Spencer shifted his stance. "Is there anyone who can take care of the animals for a while?"

"Why?"

"I think it would be safer if you and the girls left the farm for a while. Until we get this all sorted out."

"I can't pick up and leave." She lowered her voice and leaned closer to him. "This is the only home my nieces have known. They lost their mother. And my mom lives next door…and I don't know offhand who could care for the animals full-time." Her brain swirled with all the responsibilities.

"Sounds like you have a lot of reasons to stay."

"I have a lot to figure out." Outside the barn, her nieces returned to their seats on the grassy incline and plucked long blades of grass and twisted them around their fingers.

"Maybe you can find other family to stay with the

girls until we locate John and figure out what's going on here."

"My sister was all I had. As far as reaching out to other Amish families, I won't be welcomed."

"I'm sure a family would welcome your nieces."

His words felt like a knife stabbing her heart. "I'm not going to leave my nieces." She had promised her sister she'd make sure the girls were cared for. Hannah couldn't run away.

Spencer studied her with unnerving intensity. Then he snapped out of it and jerked his thumb toward the cow. "Didn't mean to interrupt your morning chores. You can milk a cow?"

She laughed, genuinely laughed, for the first time since she had received word of her sister's death. "I'm certainly capable of milking a cow or two." She tucked a wayward strand of hair behind her ear. "This is the first morning I've had to deal with farm life since I arrived. I'm facing one thing at a time. First my nieces, then the farm animals."

"All God's creatures."

Hannah stared at him for a minute. The smile lines at the corners of his eyes softened all his features. Yet his broad chest and solid arms would intimidate any criminal. She scooped up a metal bucket, fully aware that he was watching her. "An Amish boy has been helping me. That's one thing you can say about the Amish. They always look after their own."

"They do." The two simple words held more weight than she dare explore.

She shifted the solid milking bucket from one hand to the other. She patted the backside of the cow, running her hand over its coarse fur. "How do you feel about a city slicker milking you?" The cow shuffled its back feet and let out a deep moo that vibrated through her chest. Hannah patted the animal again. "I'll take that as a yes."

Hannah pulled up a stool and straddled it. Out of the corner of her eye, she noticed Spencer standing close. Did he doubt her abilities? Inwardly she laughed. What did *he* know about farm life?

Hannah glanced at the empty bucket to make sure it was clean enough for fresh cow's milk. Three tiny holes marred the bottom of the metal bucket. The milk would leak out.

She put the bucket down and stood. She brushed past Spencer, his clean scent mixing in with fresh hay and too-fresh manure. She picked up a second pail from a nearby table. It also had several neat holes in the bottom, as if someone had taken a nail and driven it through the metal with a hammer.

"Something wrong?" Spencer's voice sounded from behind her.

Biting her lip, she turned the pail over. Bold red letters spelled out the word *English*. A red slash cut across the entire bottom of the pail, as if to say, *No English Allowed*.

Her knees grew weak. Suddenly, the heavy cotton of her Amish dress clung to her neck, strangling her. She pushed past Spencer and returned to the first pail and found the same thing. She shoved the pail into Spencer's chest.

"Look. The person who slashed my tires was busy last night."

Spencer's brow furrowed as he glanced down at the bucket in his hands.

"You have to find John. If it's John who's doing this,"

she quickly added. "He mustn't be in his right mind."
Hannah tugged on her bun to loosen it. "To kill my sister and now try to chase me away. What does he hope
to accomplish?"

"I can't speculate on his motive." Spencer inspected
the pail. "We're doing everything we can to find him.
To get answers."

"Maybe it's just kids. A prank…" Even as she said it,
she doubted it. But John…that didn't seem right, either.
The thought of spending another long, restless night in
this house made her wish she had the ability to speed
up time. There were no locks on the doors, but maybe
she could move furniture in front of the doors at night.
She said a silent prayer in hopes of calming her fraz-
zled nerves.

She bowed her head then lifted it and met his gaze
directly. "I refuse to abandon my nieces. Because—"
she swiped the bucket out of his hand "—that's exactly
what he wants me to do."

When Spencer emerged from the barn a half step
behind Hannah, the little girls were each holding an
Amish woman's hand. The girls tugged and pulled on
the woman's arm as she marched directly toward them,
an expression, a combination of disgust and scolding on
her plain features.

"There you are," she said, narrowing her gaze at Hannah. "These girls have been wandering around half-
dressed."

"They are perfectly dressed." Hannah fingered the
older girl's blond curls. "If it's their hair you're concerned with, I didn't have a chance to do their braids

yet. I wasn't expecting visitors." Hannah touched her own messy bun.

The woman's gaze shot to Spencer, and her nose twitched.

"Morning. I'm Sheriff Maxwell." He held out his hand then let it drop when it was obvious the woman wasn't going to accept it.

The woman sniffed the air. "I'm Fannie Mae Lapp." She lifted the girls' hands. The pout on the older girl's face was unmistakable. The younger of the two was on the verge of tears. "I'm the girls' *aenti*." She glared at him as if he were going to challenge her claim.

"Is there a problem, Sheriff?" He recognized Lester Lapp, John's brother, strolling across the grass. Lester had been his father's, the bishop's, guard dog, not allowing law enforcement to speak to anyone in the Lapp family since Ruth's death and John's disappearance. Lester strode down the slight incline from the house to the barn, his arms swinging confidently by his sides. "I came out as soon as we heard you were here. The bishop is also here." His tone held a warning. "If you have news regarding my brother, you can share it with me. My father is still weak from grief."

"I have no news about John." Spencer wasn't about to share news of Ruthie's murder in front of her daughters. "But I'm afraid we've had some—" he glanced down at the girls "—*events* on the property that need to be addressed." Spencer crossed his arms. "It's best if we don't talk in front of the children."

"Girls, run up to the house for me." Hannah tossed the metal bucket on the hard-packed mud. It tumbled and landed with the graffiti facing away from the guests.

Lester gave Fannie Mae a subtle nod, giving her permission to take the children up to the house. The older niece yanked her hand from her aunt's grip and ran ahead. The little one seemed tired of being led around, reminding Spencer of a rag doll dangling by a boneless arm.

"What's going on?" Lester fingered his unkempt beard and kept his eyes trained on Hannah. "Sheriff Maxwell seems to be spending a lot of time on my brother's farm. I'd hate for the neighbors to start talking. There is much work to be done if you expect to be accepted in Apple Creek." He was speaking directly to Hannah.

Was Hannah planning on joining the Amish community permanently? Something in Spencer's heart shifted, and he wasn't proud of himself. Regardless of his initial attraction to this spunky woman, she had to make a decision that was best for her even if it meant there would be zero chance of a *them*. His disappointment seemed silly considering they had only just met. However, there was something about her simple, straightforward manner that was the complete opposite of high-maintenance Vicki.

"Lester, I'm going to forgive your bad manners on account of your tremendous loss," Hannah said, not mincing words.

"I don't need your forgiveness." A vein bulged in Lester's forehead.

"What's going on here?" Bishop Lapp navigated his way down the slope with his cane. He looked warm in his black overcoat as the sun climbed higher in the sky.

Lester's expression immediately softened. He met his father and guided him to the dirt-packed entrance of the barn.

"I have difficult news," Spencer said. The bishop had

aged dramatically these past few days. Spencer cleared his throat and then told Lester and Bishop Lapp of the suspicious circumstances surrounding Ruth's death.

"Are you saying John hurt Ruth?" Lester crossed his arms over his chest, one of his fingers snagging on his suspenders. "*Neh*, impossible." He shook his head adamantly for emphasis. "It was an accident. A tragic accident."

"I'm afraid the medical examiner's findings contradict that."

"And you? How do you feel?" Lester asked.

"I have more questions than answers right now. I need to talk to John. Have you heard from him?" Spencer watched their expressions carefully, trying to detect deceit.

Lester tipped his head, hiding his eyes behind the brim of his straw hat. "*Neh*. We're worried."

"My son had nothing to do with his wife's death." The bishop narrowed his gaze. He reached out and clutched a post to steady himself. "You haven't been in town long, Sheriff. But one thing you must already know. The Amish are a peaceful people. This medical examiner…he is wrong."

"Someone slashed my tires last night." Hannah stepped forward. "Any idea who would do that?"

"It wasn't John. He hasn't been around. Don't you think if my brother was around, he'd be consoling his children? He must not be in his right mind due to grief. There's no other reason he'd stay away so long." Lester took off his straw hat and rubbed his head. "None of this makes sense. What reason would John have to hurt Ruth and then come back and destroy property?"

Spencer watched Lester. The man appeared genuinely distraught. "You're all under tremendous stress right now. I'm not accusing anyone of anything. It's my job to uncover the truth."

"We want the truth, too." The bishop's voice sounded shaky as he mopped his brow with a handkerchief.

"Do you have any idea where John might have gone? Someplace he feels comfortable. Safe."

"He felt safest here at home." A tall Amish man with broad shoulders ambled toward them. Spencer recognized him from around town. "Can't imagine what would keep my good friend away when his daughters need him." A look of disgust swept across the man's face as he took in Hannah before his features smoothed into an appropriate look of solemnity. Or had Spencer imagined it?

Spencer held out his hand. "I'm Sheriff Maxwell."

The man nodded but didn't take his hand. "I know who you are." He looped his thumbs through his suspenders. "I'm Willard Fisher. I live down the road where it meets Plum Crossing. John and I help each other out when we can. My boy Samuel has been caring for the animals while he's gone." He shook his head in disbelief. "I was away visiting family in Ohio. I wish I had been here to console him after his wife's accident."

Lester puffed out his chest, as if in competition with the new arrival. "My brother was overcome with grief. He found his wife's body. I can't imagine what I'd do under the circumstances."

"Have faith." Willard's mouth flattened into a grim line. "Have faith in *Gott* and continue on."

"Do you know if John or Ruth had issue with anyone? Someone who might have wanted to hurt her?" Spencer shifted his stance, feeling as if he had to brace himself against the men's displeasure.

The bishop shook his head. "We lead simple lives."

"Are you saying Ruth's death wasn't an accident?" Willard frowned.

"That's exactly what I'm saying."

Willard and Lester glanced at one another while Hannah looked like she was tired of holding her tongue.

Spencer's cell phone rang. He glanced at its display. "I have to get this. Excuse me." As he stepped away, the back of his head prickled with the men's laser-like gazes.

Hannah picked up the metal bucket and hung it upside down on the post near the barn. She watched the men to see if anyone had a reaction to the graffiti written on the bottom of the bucket.

"Don't let your English ways interfere with our peaceful life here." Lester's fiery gaze slid from the sheriff to her.

Willard crossed his arms over his broad chest, but didn't say anything. He obviously agreed. No one wanted an outsider living in their midst. She could dress up in her dead sister's clothes, but no one would truly accept her until she embraced the Amish way and was baptized and found a suitable Amish husband.

Hannah's pulse whooshed in her ears. "My sister was murdered. You can't ignore that. The sheriff has to do a thorough investigation. If John was involved, you can't protect him."

Lester shook his head. "My brother had nothing to do with Ruth's tragic death. It was an accident."

Hannah lifted her trembling hands to dismiss him. "I can't listen to this."

She strode past Lester. He hollered after her, "Will you be joining us for church service tomorrow? We are having service in our home."

Hannah turned and tugged on the collar of her dress. The thought of sitting in a sweaty barn for three hours listening to Bishop Lapp talk did not appeal to her, but she knew she had to make an effort on account of the girls. Her air-conditioned church back in Buffalo had spoiled her. It wasn't God she was opposed to, it was falling back into her old Amish lifestyle before she made a true decision. Things were happening so fast.

"I have a lot of work to do around here," she muttered, her brain racing for an excuse.

"It's Sunday," the bishop said. "A day of rest."

"John and Ruth would want the children to go to church service," Lester piled on.

Low blow.

"I'm not sure how I would get there." Her car wasn't an option even if her tires weren't slashed.

"My family can take the girls," Willard offered.

Hannah's gaze shifted to the stern man and wondered where his son Samuel had gotten his soft-spoken demeanor. "I can take the girls to the service. *Denki.*" The Pennsylvania Dutch word for *thank you* slipped out of her mouth so naturally it caught her off guard. She'd take the horse and buggy, something she hadn't done for years.

Hannah thought she detected a low chuckle from Willard, and her cheeks immediately fired hot.

"We look forward to seeing you there." The bishop tapped the earth with his cane to emphasize his point. "You cannot live in two worlds."

"I'm doing my best," Hannah said. "My priority is caring for my nieces."

Willard picked up the bucket and turned it over, studying the graffiti. "You found this in the barn?"

Hannah swallowed around a knot in her throat. "Yes, seems someone wants me to leave."

Willard hung the bucket back on the post. "Shame to ruin a perfectly good bucket." He turned and looked at Hannah. "Is my son doing the chores to your satisfaction?"

"Samuel's been a big help, thank you." Hannah felt the need to defend Samuel, and she wasn't sure why. "I hope his helping me here hasn't caused you more work on your own farm."

"You need the help. John will be home soon, then Samuel will be back on my farm." Willard said it so matter-of-factly, she wondered if he knew something she didn't.

Unexpected emotion rolled over Hannah. She lowered her voice. "I do hope John comes home soon and this—whatever this is—is all cleared up."

"He will," the bishop said. "It's best if you follow the *Ordnung* while you are here. I do not want my granddaughters to be influenced by worldly things. I will pray that once you are settled, you will decide to bend a knee." The bishop made a few shuffle steps to turn around. He picked each step deliberately as he walked toward the house. A knot twisted her stomach. Would she ever be ready to be baptized in the Amish church?

Lester stepped forward. His features softened, yet the angle of his mouth seemed strained. "Fannie Mae and I will raise Emma and Sarah. *Gott* has not yet blessed us with children."

A mix of relief, apprehension and dread washed over Hannah. Lester had offered her a way out.

"This life isn't for you. You can return to Buffalo. We'll take care of the girls." Lester hesitated a fraction. "Until John is back and fit to care for them."

Uncomfortable, Hannah glanced behind Lester and noticed Spencer sitting on the porch steps talking animatedly to the girls. They had bright smiles on their faces, the first she had seen since returning to Apple Creek.

Hannah refocused on Lester. "If I left the girls in your care, could I visit them?"

A muscle pulsed in his jaw. "*Neh*. Your life in the outside world would only confuse them. Raising her children here was important to Ruth. Ruth is gone, but don't take her children away from everything that is important to them."

Hannah hated Lester's message, but she knew he was right. She backed away from him and made a show of swiping imaginary hay from her skirt. "I'll have to think about it."

"Fannie Mae will be a good *mem* to them."

Hannah's gaze drifted to Lester's wife, standing apart as Spencer played with the two girls. Perhaps the woman didn't know how to interact with children because she didn't have any of her own. Indecision weighed heavily on Hannah, sucking the air out of her lungs.

"You should give this serious consideration." Lester adjusted his straw hat by its brim. "I believe *Gott* has bigger plans for me in this community. I don't want my family distracted by the outside world."

"*Gott* decides such things. Not man. Be humble," Willard scolded Lester.

Lester bristled. Perhaps Lester, like Hannah, had forgotten Willard was standing within earshot.

Hannah ran a hand across the back of her neck. "You want me to leave and to leave quietly?"

Lester's dark eyes bored into her. "I want what's best for my brother's children."

"My sister would want me to be their guardian."

"The children still have a guardian. *Their father.*" Lester's eyebrows disappeared under his hat.

"I will be their guardian until that matter is settled." Hannah bustled past Lester and strode up the hill. The ache in her brain pounded in time with her racing heart.

"Everything okay?" Spencer stood when Hannah reached the porch. The compassion in his eyes diffused a fraction of her anger. Six-year-old Emma jumped to her feet to stand next to Spencer, looking up at him with big blue eyes as trusting as her *mem*'s.

Hannah glanced at Fannie Mae quickly, then back at Spencer. "Everything is great. Girls, would you like some fresh-baked muffins?" Hannah wanted to make up for the lumpy oatmeal from earlier, but feared her baking skills were also rusty.

Emma and Sarah raced Hannah inside. The screen door slammed in its frame, shutting out the outside world, even if only temporarily.

Chapter Four

Hannah adjusted the buckle on the horse's harness and tugged on the end of the leather strap. Quietly, she muttered to Buttercup, reassuring her sister's beautiful horse as she hitched the animal to the buggy. This was the second time she'd done this in the past twenty-four hours, and it was beginning to feel like old hat.

Hannah had done a lot of reflecting since yesterday's church service. It had been more than a decade since she'd sat on the backless benches at an Amish service, praying and singing the hymns from the *Ausbund*. The language she had tried to put behind her when she moved to Buffalo came back with ease. She felt a certain peace she hadn't felt in a while. A peace she struggled to find as an outsider in the English word. Yet she didn't know if she'd be able to commit to the Amish way.

Would she ever be ready?

Hannah had no idea. But for now, she had to get answers. No one other than the sheriff wanted to entertain the idea that John might have played a role in her sister's death. She had decided if anyone truly knew John, it was his friend Willard. Willard was one of the men who had left Apple Creek with John and later returned. She had learned this much from her mother last night.

And something about Willard set Hannah's nerves on edge.

Hannah adjusted the final strap on the horse's harness and stepped back to admire her work. Hitching a horse to a buggy took a lot more time and effort than hopping into her car and jamming the key into the ignition. But there was something very satisfying about it.

Hannah had left Emma and Sarah and some building blocks with her mother, promising she wouldn't be long. She patted Buttercup's mane when she was done hitching her to the buggy, satisfied that some tasks, however complicated, came naturally. She wondered if her ex-boyfriend back in Buffalo would call her inept now? No, more than likely he'd be too busy mocking her choice of clothing.

Wow. She hadn't thought about him since she got the phone call about her sister. Maybe she had moved on. Too bad it took her sister's death for her to do so.

A cool breath prickled the hair at the back of her neck despite the warm summer sun beating down on her. She glanced around the deserted farm.

Hannah hustled into the buggy. "Trot," she commanded the horse. The buggy bobbled and dipped over the ruts. She smiled to herself with satisfaction. Willard lived in walking distance—Samuel walked back and forth most days to do his chores—but Hannah hoped she'd have time after talking to Willard to run into town to pick up a few necessities.

Once on the country road, Hannah flicked the reins, and the horse picked up his gait. The country air caressed her face. The fresh smell of cut grass at a nearby home tickled her nose, and the warm sun kissed her face. She had forgotten how peaceful it was to be out on a country road all alone.

Except for the occasional car or truck whizzing by.

Beyond the curve, she saw Willard's place. She tugged on Buttercup's reins and pulled off the main road. She hopped out of the buggy and looped the reins around a post on the split rail fence lining the front of their property. As she walked toward the front door, her heart raced wildly. She didn't know what she was going to say to this man. She couldn't very well come out and ask him if he thought his friend was a murderer. Willard didn't exactly exude what she'd call the warm fuzzies.

Apprehension made her footsteps deliberate. Maybe she should let Spencer handle the investigation. But Willard was unlikely to talk to someone in law enforcement. She straightened her back and climbed the last step. Perhaps he would be more open with an Amish woman, a hesitant one at that.

Hannah lifted her hand to knock and stopped when she saw her old friend Rebecca walking toward the door. The shocked expression on her friend's face surely matched the one on her own. "I heard you were back, Hannah." Rebecca made no effort to open the screen door.

"Rebecca, what are you doing here?" Hannah took a step back, wondering if she had gotten the wrong house. "I'm looking for Willard Fisher."

"My husband is doing chores in the barn." Rebecca glanced behind her, fidgeting with the fabric of her skirt.

"You're married to Willard? But his son…" Her words drifted off. Samuel was too old to be her dear friend's child.

"I am the boy's stepmother. His mother died when he was very young. Samuel is like my own."

The word o*h* formed and died on Hannah's lips. "But you weren't with him at the church service yesterday."

"My youngest was ill. I kept both little ones home." As if on cue, two small children ran up and clung to their mother's skirt. Rebecca gently touched one head, then the other. "This is Katie and Grace."

Hannah smiled. Nostalgia edged her grief. *This* was the life she had walked away from. "Hi, girls." She lifted her gaze to their mother. "May I speak with Willard? Perhaps I can go to the barn."

"No, he doesn't like to be disturbed." Rebecca pushed open the front door with her bare foot. Behind her, the girls peered around their mother. "I suppose he won't mind if you come in and wait a minute. He should be in for lunch soon." Rebecca spun on her heel. Hannah followed her to the kitchen where Rebecca continued to make lunch, but didn't offer Hannah a seat or anything to drink.

Hannah decided this must be what it felt like to be shunned.

"Go wash your hands," Rebecca said to the little ones.

The two children, Hannah guessed, were around five or six. Close to Emma's age. She wondered if they were friendly with her nieces. She was about to ask them when they spun around and ran away, presumably to wash their hands.

"I'm sorry about Ruthie."

"Thank you." Hannah cleared her throat, eager to change subjects. "Samuel has been a big help to me on the farm."

Rebecca nodded. "I suppose there's not much to do on

the farm nowadays with John working down the way."
Her friend was too polite to make mention of the fact
that currently John wasn't working anywhere.

Hannah touched her cap, suddenly self-conscious. "I
suppose it's true. There are no crops to worry about, but
the animals still need care. I appreciate Samuel's help."

Rebecca nodded again. She put aside the knife she
had been using to spread the apple butter on bread and
said, "Ruthie was like a sister to me."

"Ruthie felt the same way about you." Guilt snuck up
and twisted Hannah's insides. "I'm sorry I left Apple
Creek without saying goodbye to you. You had always
been a dear friend."

Her friend shrugged and turned back around and continued to prepare her family's lunch.

Hannah leaned her shoulder on the door frame. "I
couldn't tell you I was leaving. I couldn't tell anyone."

Rebecca turned around with a spoon in her hand.
Something red from the spoon plopped onto the floor.
The hurt expression on her friend's face wounded her.
"I thought we were *gut* friends. It wonders me why you
snuck away from Apple Creek in the middle of the night.
I never imagined you a fence jumper. The bishop, your
parents, everyone came to me with questions." Rebecca
drew in a shuddering breath on the verge of tears. "I
didn't have any answers."

"That's why I couldn't tell you. I didn't want to put
you in that position." Hannah tugged on the collar of her
Amish dress. Right now she longed for cooler English
clothes and air-conditioning.

Rebecca turned around and resumed preparing the
lunches. "*Yah* well, I thought you were happy here."

"I wasn't." Hannah didn't tell her friend about her

father's verbal abuse. And how could she explain her discontent with a life her friend embraced?

"I wish you had told me." Rebecca's words were so soft Hannah had to strain to hear them.

The back door slammed, and Willard stomped into the kitchen. He came up short when he saw Hannah. He spun around and told Samuel to grab his sisters and go back outside. Something flickered across his face and then disappeared. A bead of sweat rolled down Hannah's back.

Willard glared accusingly at his wife. "You have a visitor?"

"I'm here to see you." Hannah quickly spoke up, not wanting her friend to get into trouble.

"Do you have news regarding John?" Willard asked, his voice gruff.

"No, I was hoping to ask you about John. I know you were good friends. How was he? I mean, before Ruthie died?"

Willard washed his hands in the sink, dried them on a towel and then hung the towel on a wood peg. *"Gut."*

Hannah smoothed a hand across her bib. "My sister was worried about him."

"You spoke with Ruth?" Willard's tone was strangely flat.

Hannah nodded, feeling like a fifteen-year-old who had been caught kissing a boy behind the barn, not a grown woman who had every right to spend time with her sister. "We met a few times and chatted. We're family. We missed each other."

Willard pulled out a chair and slammed the legs down on the floor. Rebecca flinched. "You made your choice when you left Apple Creek."

"Hannah just lost her sister. Don't be…" Rebecca deflated under her husband's withering stare. Rebecca had swiftly come to her defense often when they were kids. It had been Rebecca, Ruthie and Hannah. The three musketeers. The only consolation Hannah had when she left was that Ruthie still had Rebecca. But it seemed now Willard had Rebecca and kept a tight rein on her.

"Don't be…what?" Willard repeated.

Rebecca seemed to swallow hard to gather her nerve. "Hannah made a bad decision when she left Apple Creek, but we can have compassion now as she deals with her sister's death. Perhaps this is *Gott*'s way of bringing her back home."

Hannah stifled a grimace at the notion God had used her sister's murder to bring her back into the fold.

"We need to find forgiveness," Rebecca added.

"Are you looking for forgiveness?" Willard picked up his spoon and scooped up a mouthful of soup, never taking his eyes off Hannah.

"I am here to find out about John." She struggled to keep her jaw from trembling.

Willard dabbed his mouth with a napkin. "John seemed fine. He was a hardworking Amish man dedicated to his family. We both had lost our way, much like you—" she knew he had to get a dig in there "—but we had both come to realize living apart from the temptations of the outside world was the way our parents and their parents before them wanted things."

"I can't believe Ruthie's gone." Rebecca turned and filled four more bowls and set them on the table across from her husband.

Willard flattened his palms on the table on either side of his soup bowl. "Rebecca can mind Emma and Sarah

Lapp until their father returns. I understand you have a job in Buffalo you have to get back to."

Hannah did a double take. The Amish grapevine was amazing.

"I am capable of caring for my nieces." Hannah hiked her chin.

Rebecca watched her husband carefully. She stood behind her chair, waiting for something, and then Hannah realized she was preventing her friend from eating.

"I better go."

Rebecca led her to the door and whispered, "I'm sorry I couldn't invite you to stay for lunch. Willard is quite strict and believes we should stay separate from the English. No exceptions." Her voice wavered. "I'm sorry."

Hannah brushed the back of her friend's hand. "But it's me, Rebecca." Her friend seemed unmoved, so Hannah nodded. "It's okay."

Rebecca retreated into the house, and Hannah could hear her calling the children in to eat. Loneliness weighed heavily on her, and she swallowed down a lump of grief in her throat.

Forever the outsider.

Each day was running into the next, and Hannah struggled to remember what day it was. She rolled out of bed and pulled on jeans and a sweatshirt, figuring no one would see her at this hour. 5:00 a.m. was horribly early to have responsibilities like farm animals. Samuel had told her yesterday he had to help his father on the farm this morning, but he'd do his best to stop by and help in the afternoon. Part of her wondered if Willard just wanted to make it more difficult for her so she'd be forced to concede.

However, to be fair, the Fishers had a farm of their own to run.

Hannah gave herself a pep talk and splashed cold water on her face. She better get used to getting up this early if she planned on staying. *If.* She slipped her cell phone into her back pocket. It gave her a sense of security. She was grateful she had thought to bring the car charger for her phone. She still hadn't gotten used to being out in the country in the middle of nowhere, and she hadn't installed the locks on the house, a small part of her fearing she'd be breaking the rules and giving the elders another reason to ask her to leave. In the darkness of early morning, her reasoning sounded silly. She had to keep her nieces safe.

She stalked quietly through the darkened house. She grabbed the flashlight from the kitchen counter and stepped outside, pulling the door closed behind her. A warm summer breeze carried the farm scents of her childhood and with it not nostalgia but a longing for something more. A longing that had grown from her preteen years into her teen years, into something she couldn't dismiss. Something bigger that could only be found beyond the fences of the Amish community.

But *had* she found more in her boring job in Buffalo? A feeling of acceptance, of belonging, eluded her. Her condescending former boyfriend and her roommates didn't understand or want to understand her conservative ways. Hannah had found cheap rent near the university, but not like minds.

Hannah glanced toward her mother's residence. Dark, just as she expected it to be. She wondered, not for the first time, if the Lapp family would care for her mother if Hannah returned to Buffalo. The Amish rallied around one another, right?

Her mind drifted a lot in the early-morning quiet hours. She remembered Ruthie—during their secretive meetings over French fries and shakes—telling her how wonderful it would be for the girls to know their aunt. For Hannah to one day get married and raise her family nearby. If only Hannah would come back to Apple Creek and be baptized.

A wave of guilt slammed into Hannah. Why had she been so quick to brush off her sister's request? What if Hannah had returned? Would she have seen the deteriorating relationship between Ruthie and John and been able to intervene? If that had indeed been the case.

Hannah grimaced when her sneaker hit something smooshie as she entered the barn. She lifted up her foot and noticed a dark shadow of who-knows-what. She groaned. She *so* wasn't cut out for this. The bishop's words scraped across her brain. All she had to do was turn her nieces over to their aunt and uncle, and she could return to her regular life.

Her regular life.

No cow dung. No horses. No predawn chores.

Her boring, unfulfilled, regular life.

She had escaped the Amish life only to find her life still unfulfilled.

She shook her head and kept moving forward. The cow mooed halfheartedly, and she patted his backside. "That's how I feel, too, buddy."

Hannah turned on a kerosene lamp, spreading a warm, yellow glow across the barn.

She knew how to milk a cow by hand—one of the perks of growing up on a farm—but she had gotten accustomed to running to the grocery store for a gallon of milk. For the past decade, her biggest concern with milk had been making sure she consumed it before the expiration date. Which wasn't always an easy task when she was the only one drinking it.

Hannah pulled up a stool and talked to the cow reassuringly. She had found a usable pail in the far corner of the barn.

A crash—the tinkling of breaking glass—sounded behind her. The barn was immediately cast into darkness. She froze and swallowed her growing panic. Her thumping heart drowned out the silence.

"Is someone there?" she croaked out.

A crackle. Then another.

Fear swept across her arms, and sweat pooled down her back. She grabbed the flashlight next to her stool and directed it toward where she had placed the lamp. The kerosene lamp had crashed onto the barn floor. The flammable liquid spread across the loose hay scattered on the floor.

Panic edged out all rational thought.

Fire! The animals!

Hannah bolted past the flames. She had to do something. Then as if by divine intervention, she remembered the blanket in the barn near Buttercup's stall.

She grabbed the blanket, the heavy, scruffy burlap, her only hope. Buttercup neighed in protest, as if sensing Hannah's panic. She tossed the blanket onto the flames licking across the loose hay, eager to sweep across the barn floor. She stomped on the blanket a few more times to make sure the flames were extinguished.

Shaking and unsure of herself, afraid to leave the barn

in case a hot spot flared up, she reached into her back pocket and pulled out her cell phone.

If Bishop Lapp and his eldest son hadn't convinced her she had no business working this farm and caring for her nieces, this fire had.

Spencer's cell phone interrupted his dream. He couldn't recall the specifics, but he was pretty sure a real-life nightmare was haunting his dreams. He wondered if he'd ever get past that night in Buffalo.

He shook off the guilt and sleep and answered the phone with a curt, "Maxwell."

Hannah sounded equal parts frightened and embarrassed when she explained the accident that had led to a small fire. She had convinced herself, but not him, that she had extinguished it. He dressed quickly and drove out to the Lapp's farm in a record eleven minutes. After recent events, he wasn't assuming anything was an accident.

When he arrived, he found Hannah right where she said she'd be, at the door of the barn where she could keep an eye on the animals and the house where her nieces slept.

He pulled his truck onto the grass and climbed out. The sky was pink and purple with fingers of white clouds. Funny how he noticed things out here. In the city, he had forgotten to look up at the sky.

Hannah leaned against the barn door dressed in jeans and a sweatshirt, her long brown hair flowing over her shoulders. *This* was the woman he found himself drawn to, but he had to push that thought from his head. If she was going to return to her Amish roots, he didn't want to be standing there with a broken heart.

And his job was to protect her. Period.

Hannah levered off the edge of the barn door and pointed at the charred blanket on the ground. "I must have put the lamp too close to the edge. It fell over... I could have burned the entire barn down." She glanced nervously toward the house. "The wind could have carried the flames to the house. My nieces..." Anger creased her forehead. "Maybe I'm not cut out for life on a farm raising my sister's daughters. Maybe everyone is right."

Spencer inspected the charred blanket. "You were smart. You contained the fire. It's okay." He tossed the blanket outside and touched her upper arms lightly. "Look at me."

She bowed her head and sobbed quietly. Her legs seemed to go out from under her, and he wrapped his arms around her. She rested her head on his shoulder and stilled for a moment. The floral scent of her shampoo tickled his nose. He refused to let down his guard. This was strictly a professional relationship. Suddenly, as if reading his mind, she stiffened and stepped away from him, batting away at the tears that glistened on her cheeks in the morning sun.

Sirens sounded in the distance. A horrified look flashed in her eyes. "Did you alert the fire department?"

"Yes, I couldn't risk wasting precious time if the fire had gotten out of control."

"Oh, no. Now the neighbors will really be talking."

"Stop worrying about them."

"My mother!" Hannah's eyes grew wide. "I better go tell her everything's okay."

Spencer nodded then strode across the driveway to

meet the fire engine. A firefighter jumped out of the truck and followed Spencer into the barn.

A few minutes later, Hannah joined him in the yard. "My mother's had to deal with a lot lately."

"Is she okay?"

Hannah nodded. "And believe it or not, Emma and Sarah are still sleeping."

"The firemen are going to saturate the area around the charred hay to make sure there're no hot spots."

"Okay."

"You've been through a lot, too. Sit down." Spencer guided her to the grassy incline.

Hannah let out a sigh. She held a fisted hand to her mouth. "I don't belong here."

"You're fine, everything's fine." Spencer rubbed her back in small circles, trying to reassure her.

"I wanted to do right by my sister. By my sister's children. But I'm not meant to run a farm." She swept her hand in the air in front of her. "I can't even commit to the wardrobe, never mind their ways." She shook her head. "I had hoped to take it day by day, but…" She threaded her fingers through her hair. "I almost burned down the barn."

Spencer tilted his head in an attempt to get her to shift her gaze from the barn to him. He was rewarded with a sad smile.

"For a city girl, you really thought fast." He stood and picked up the discarded blanket. The fire had burned two large holes into the fabric with a smattering of tiny dots. He folded it and tossed it down again.

She shrugged and hugged her knees to her chest.

Spencer scanned the barn. Something about this

rubbed him the wrong way. "Did you see anyone out here this morning?"

Hannah's eyes flashed wide. "No. You think someone knocked over the lantern? Tried to burn down the barn?" She flattened her hand on her midsection and looked like she was going to be sick.

"Just the other night someone slashed your tires." He scrubbed a hand over his whiskered jaw. "Too many things to be considered a coincidence. Listen…" She accepted his outstretched hand, and he pulled her to her feet. She swiped at the back of her jeans.

"I fear the next time someone goes after you, they aren't going to slash your tires or knock over a lantern."

"What?" The word came out as barely a whisper.

"I've seen these things escalate." First the child gets in trouble in school, then he starts hanging out with the wrong crowd, he's arrested for shoplifting, then shot in the head during a gang initiation gone bad. But that was his dark secret. His personal failure.

Not hers.

Hannah blinked at him in shock. A knot formed between his shoulder blades. Regrets haunted him. He had tried to save a young city kid, but drugs and gangs were too prevalent to spare a boy living in poverty. "I won't let anything happen to you." He had failed to keep that promise before.

Never again.

Hannah ran a hand across the back of her neck. "I'm not in any real danger, am I? The tire slashing was a prank, right?" She looked up at him, trust in her bright brown eyes.

"I'm not a fan of coincidences, remember?"

She sighed heavily. "Why would someone do this to

me? If John wants me to leave, then he needs to come home, prove his innocence and raise his children." Her soft voice hardened with anger. "Besides John, I don't have enemies." She locked gazes with him. "The Amish don't believe in violence. No one from this community would try to hurt me regardless of how they feel about me personally." The hesitancy in her voice told him she wasn't buying it, either.

"John Lapp is our primary focus."

"Then he needs to show his face. Be a man." Her lower lip shook with rage.

"These are not the actions of a rational person." It was speculation, but the best idea he had right now.

Hannah threaded her fingers through her hair and closed her eyes briefly. "Maybe this fire was caused by my own carelessness." Her shoulders dropped. "I'm sorry I woke you up early. The fire had me freaked out. I was worried it would flare up again." Hannah brushed the palms of her hands together as if she had put this entire situation behind her. "It appears the fire department has taken care of that." The firefighters wrapped up their hose and tucked it away.

One of the men wandered their way. "You're good, ma'am. Just be careful with the kerosene lamps."

"I will. Thank you."

The firefighter waved to Spencer. "Take it easy, Sheriff." The firefighter climbed onto the truck. The fire engine eased out of the driveway and onto the main road.

When the fire engine was out of sight, Spencer turned to Hannah. "We don't know the fire was an accident." They locked gazes for a long moment. "You need to be careful."

"I'm out here alone with the girls. My mother lives

on the property, but her health keeps her inside most of the time. What am I supposed to do?"

"I'll make sure you're protected."

She dragged the heel of her hand across her forehead. "You can't guard me out here. You have a job."

"I'll have extra patrols come by. I won't let anything happen to you." But he had been having extra patrols and still this happened.

"Maybe it is time for me to leave."

Spencer brushed his knuckles down the sleeve of her sweatshirt. "You've had a stressful week, and I know you think you're in over your head. Don't make any rash decisions until you have a chance to consider all your options." He wanted her to be safe, but for selfish reasons he didn't want her to leave Apple Creek. A twinge of guilt pinged him.

"I better check on the girls." Hannah pulled the sleeves of her sweatshirt down around her hands. "Can I make you breakfast?"

He held up his hand, intending to refuse when Hannah added a little too breezily, "It's the least I can do for dragging you all the way out here before sunrise."

Spencer followed her to the house. When she opened the door, they found Emma sitting in a chair hugging her plain, faceless fabric doll.

Hannah glanced at him over her shoulder. The smile slipped from her face. "Have you been up long, sweetie?"

Emma bowed her head and buried her face into the doll and squeezed its middle tight.

"The fire truck must have been scary. I promise everything is okay now." Hannah crouched in front of the little girl and smiled. "Where's your sister?"

"In bed." Emma sniffled. "I thought you were gone.

Like *Mem*." Emma hid her feet under her nightgown and pulled her knees to her chest. "And I saw that big truck like when *Mem*…"

Pink blossomed on Hannah's face, and she looked as if she was fighting back tears. "Oh, no, sweetie. I went outside to do chores. Careless Aunt Hannah knocked over a lamp. That's why the firemen were here. I wouldn't leave you. Ever."

Emma looked up, hesitantly at first, then a shy smile crossed her face. She scooted to the edge of the chair and slipped her hand into Hannah's.

Spencer cleared his throat, feeling like a true outsider. "I should head out."

Hannah kissed Emma on the cheek and turned to Spencer. "I believe I owe you breakfast."

Chapter Five

After breakfast, Hannah and Spencer lingered over coffee while the girls returned to their dolls. Hannah wondered if her sister would have minded if she purchased the girls real dolls with blinking eyes and fancy clothes, then decided the faceless, plain ones were more suitable. For now.

Hannah set her mug down. "So, Sheriff, you know all about me, and I know nothing about you. What brings you to the sleepy town of Apple Creek?"

"The job. I got tired of being a police officer in the city. Apple Creek had an opening when the last sheriff resigned after his son was indirectly tied to the disappearance of a five-year-old Amish girl."

Hannah shuddered. "Poor sweet Mary Miller. I remember when she went missing. What a tragedy." Amish parents kept a closer eye on their children for a long time after Mary went missing while shopping at the general store with her older brother. She lowered her gaze and said a quiet prayer for the girl's soul.

"Anytime a child is hurt or..." A faraway look flitted across his eyes. "It's the hardest part of this job."

"I can't imagine."

"Anyway…" Spencer took a deep breath, snapping out of it. "I thought a job change would be good."

Hannah narrowed her gaze. "Seems like it would be a lot more exciting to work in the city rather than coming to the aid of an Amish woman in the middle of farm country."

"Can't say I've ever helped an Amish woman in Buffalo."

"Probably not." She laughed. Something about this man lightened her heart.

"Where in Buffalo did you live?" He rarely broke eye contact when he spoke, making her self-conscious.

"I have a small apartment in the university district. I'm living there month-to-month with two roommates, both college students."

Spencer seemed to consider this a moment. A smile pulled on the corners of his lips. "I can't see you hanging out at college parties."

Hannah waved her hand. "I'm a little too old to be hanging out with the college crowd. My roommates are grad students. Not the partying type. But if you listen to them, you'd think I was the most boring person in the world."

The creases around his eyes deepened when he laughed. "I'm sure you're not *that* boring."

Hannah averted her gaze, and her cheeks grew warm. "I grew up in a very conservative lifestyle. I wasn't prepared for the things that go on in the English world." She lifted her gaze and met his.

"You just haven't met the right people yet." His smooth voice rolled over her, and she couldn't help wonder what he meant.

His intense regard unnerved her, so she reached across the table and nudged his arm in hopes of lightening the mood. "Okay, funny man. I wasn't going to pry, but tell me why you'd leave Buffalo for a town whose nearest Wegman's grocery store is a forty-five-minute drive."

Spencer leaned toward her, resting his elbows on the table. "There's more to life than the Cadillac of all grocery stores."

Hannah narrowed her eyes. "Oh, I don't know." She laughed, then grew sober. "I'm really curious about you. Why did you leave Buffalo?"

Spencer's chest rose and fell on a heavy sigh. "A police officer sees a lot working in the city." The raw honesty on his face exposed a chink in his armor. Their brief connection made her feel equally exposed.

She pushed back the chair and stood, giving him her best I'll-let-you-off-the-hook-for-now expression. "I better red up the room, as my kinfolk would say, and turn back into Amish aunt." She plucked at her sweatshirt. "Sometimes I feel like spinning around like Wonder Woman to change back and forth." She giggled. "Oh man, I'm getting punchy."

Spencer lightly touched her wrist as she passed. She paused and glanced at his tan hand against her pale skin. A feeling of being protected, safe, coiled around her heart.

"Don't let anyone pressure you into doing or being something you're not."

Hannah stared at him for a long moment. "I won't." The words sounded unconvincing even in her own ears.

Hannah cleared away the dishes and moved to the sink. She enjoyed the companionable silence as she washed, and Spencer dried. Never in a million years would her father have done what he called *women's work*. Almost done, Hannah put the frying pan under the faucet and a powerful gush sent water bouncing off the pan and into their faces.

Scrunching up her nose, Hannah turned to Spencer. The front of his brown hair was soaked, and big drips ran down his face. She grabbed the dish towel from him and dabbed at his cheeks. Laughing until her vision blurred, she apologized profusely.

After a moment, he pulled her hand away from his face. Their eyes locked, and tension stretched between them.

Spencer was the first to break the silence. "I'm fine. Really. It's just a little water."

The sound of someone clearing his throat made Hannah jump. Pinpricks of unease swept across her skin. She dropped her hands to her sides and pivoted. Lester Lapp stood in the doorway, disapproval etched on his features. His dark eyes shadowed by the brim of his straw hat.

Hannah quickly stepped away from Spencer as if she had been doing something wrong. Then she glanced down at her jeans and sweatshirt. She crossed her arms over her middle, as if she could hide her wardrobe. She felt equal parts defiant and embarrassed.

"I was out in the barn this morning. I thought it was more practical to wear these clothes than a dress." The words poured from her mouth. She felt like she was thirteen again, defending herself to her father.

"It wonders me if it would have been simpler to go out in your undergarments to avoid soiling your English clothes."

Hannah gritted her teeth. Spencer moved next to her,

his shoulders squared as if to defend her. She discreetly let the back of her hand brush his thigh, a silent caution.

Lester's eyes went to her hand and an emotion—disgust, maybe?—registered on his face. The gooey-sweet voice of a woman unaccustomed to talking to children reached Hannah's ears. *Fannie Mae.*

Lester gave her a smarmy smile. "It's time Fannie Mae spent more time with the children. *Gut, yah.*"

"You haven't given me a chance to make a decision." Hannah stepped forward. "I am here for the girls."

Spencer rested his hand on the small of her back, a reassuring gesture.

Lester's brow creased. "*Yah*, well, you can't even wear appropriate clothing. Fannie Mae will raise the girls as Ruth and John would have done until my brother comes home."

The simple statement sent sharp pains jabbing into Hannah's heart. She cut a sideways glance to Spencer, whose expression was hard to read.

The strong-willed part of her wanted to tell Lester to take a flying leap. To tell him in no uncertain terms that *she* was going to care for her sister's children. The practical side of her—the wounded, grieving side of her—feared he was right. She had no business raising her sister's children. She knew nothing about being a mother. Nothing about managing a farm on her own.

And worst of all, she questioned the Amish way.

Ruthie had reached out to Hannah in the final months of her life. Yet Hannah had failed to realize the seriousness of her sister's concerns. *Had Ruthie feared for her life and Hannah hadn't been able to read between the lines?* A throbbing started behind her eyes. She had let her sister down.

Hannah couldn't fail her nieces.

"The *hurrieder* we take Sarah and Emma into our home, the hurrieder they'll adjust. A delay is only making it more difficult. More confusing."

Hannah fisted her hands by her sides. She felt Spencer's gentle fingers brush against the back of her hand. "Can we talk?" he asked.

She nodded.

Spencer led her outside, down the steps and across the front lawn. "You don't have to decide right this minute."

"Maybe Lester's right. Maybe the sooner I leave, the less painful it will be for the girls." This had been the back-and-forth argument weighing in her mind for days. *Stay. Go. Stay. Go. Go. Go.*

She rubbed her throbbing temple.

Spencer squared off with Hannah and angled his head to study her eyes. "Those girls love you. It doesn't have to be an all-or-nothing proposition. Considering everything that's been going on, maybe you and the girls should get away from here for a little while. Don't feel you have to hand your nieces over to Lester and Fannie Mae."

Hannah stared at him, disbelief making her breakfast roil in her stomach. "I can't leave with the girls. My sister wouldn't want that. And if I move back to Buffalo alone, Lester won't allow me to visit my nieces. They're afraid I'll be a bad influence." She shook her head. "If I decide to allow Lester and Fannie Mae to raise Sarah and Emma, I'm as good as saying goodbye. Forever."

She turned to face the road as a pickup truck zoomed by. "I'll never see them again."

"Would they really be that cruel?"

"They don't think of it as cruel. They're trying to

preserve the Amish way. They interact with the outside world when necessary, but weekend visits with the black-sheep aunt would not be deemed necessary." She drew in a deep breath and let it go. Indecision crowded in on her. "Maybe life with Lester and Fannie Mae would be for the best."

"You don't have to give Lester an answer now. Think about it." Something in Spencer's tone gave her pause. Her heart kicked up a notch. Would Spencer be disappointed if she left?

Hannah strolled toward the house.

"Wait," Spencer called.

Hannah turned back slowly.

"Mrs. Greene, my landlady, has an empty apartment in the building where I live. You could take the girls there. You'd be safer."

She narrowed her gaze at him, letting his words sink in. Her lips moved, but no words formed. Could she rip the girls away from everything they've ever known? She shook her head and continued toward the house. She reached the top step of the porch and heard Fannie Mae's stern voice pierce the county quiet. "When you come to my house, we'll get rid of these scruffy dolls, now once. You don't need silly toys."

Hannah heard a smacking sound. "Stop fussing with your dress," Fannie Mae scolded.

Hannah stormed into the house, dizzy with adrenaline. She was ready to let Fannie Mae have it when the sight of the two girls clutching hands, standing in the center of the room, destroyed her. The sadness and fear on their faces spoke volumes.

Hannah had felt that fear while on the receiving end

of one of her father's tirades. No one had come to her rescue.

Her heartbeat pulsing in her temples, Hannah glared at Fannie Mae then Lester. Lester stepped toward the girls and clutched Sarah's shoulder. "Stop this nonsense. It was just a small tap on your wrist. It couldn't have hurt that much. We're going to take you to your new home, now once."

Sarah pulled away from him and clutched her little sister's hand. "*Aenti* Hannah, don't leave."

The last shred of resistance around Hannah's heart shattered. She knelt in front of the girls and drew them into a hug. Not accustomed to physical displays of affection, they stiffened before melting into her embrace.

Hannah lifted her head. Lester and Fannie Mae seemed shell-shocked. "The girls *are* home."

"*Neh*, you cannot stay and live like you are." Lester's nostrils flared as he gave her jeans and sweatshirt a once-over.

"You have no authority over me. I plan to stay here to raise the girls."

"Don't you mean until their *dat* comes home?" Lester tipped his hat, more out of habit, than a genuine goodbye. He stormed out of the house, his wife, her gown licking at her legs, followed behind in a tizzy.

Hannah's entire body trembled. She sat in the sitting room rocker. She gestured to Emma and the doll in her hand. When Emma realized what her aunt wanted, she handed the doll over with a pinched expression on her face. "I'll give it right back, sweetie." Hannah traced the stitching on the plain dress. "Your *mem* made this doll."

Emma looked down at her doll, a small smile tugging on her pink lips.

Hannah lifted her gaze to Spencer, who had come back into the house. A shudder worked its way down her spine. Was Spencer right? Was she not safe here with the girls?

The thick vein pulsing in Lester's temple came to mind.

Her sister's murder.

Her missing brother-in-law.

Would Lester have left so easily if Spencer hadn't been here? If she and the girls had been alone?

Across the room, Hannah locked gazes with Spencer. She couldn't put a single name to the emotions rolling off him. Uncertainty? Fear? Doubt? Or was she transferring to him all the emotions tangling her insides into a painful knot?

Later that day, Spencer looked across the cab of his truck at Hannah on their way into town to pick up locks for her front and back doors, and for her mother's house. She wore her sister's plain black dress and had her hair neatly pulled up and tucked under a bonnet. From regular clothes this morning to Amish clothes by lunch was quite the transformation. A part of him felt like he was dealing with a different person.

Hannah's two nieces were fastened in with seat belts in the backseat of his truck. Nine-year-old Sarah put up a surprisingly adamant fuss about getting into Spencer's truck. Her father, she claimed, would be very mad if they rode in an English car. It took some persuasion on Hannah's part, but Sarah wasn't fully buying the theory that it was okay for the Amish to ride in a vehicle, they just couldn't own or drive one. Thankfully, Emma was eager for a new adventure.

Spencer turned onto the main road, and Hannah spoke for the first time. "I appreciate your driving me into town." Hannah glanced over her shoulder and gave her nieces a quick look. "I need to be careful how I act because Lester's going to be looking for any reason to force me out." She neglected to add, "And take the girls." But Spencer knew that was her first concern.

"Your mind is made up?" Spencer cut her a sideways glance. He shouldn't care so much about the answer. But he did. She had sounded very convincing when she lashed out at Lester and told him *she* was going to raise the girls. He assumed that meant as part of the Amish community.

Hannah tugged on her seat belt and shifted to look out the window. It wasn't a fair question to ask while her nieces were listening from the backseat. He thrummed his fingers on the steering wheel. "What do we need to pick up?" His cheery tone sounded a little forced.

"Locks and a few basic necessities." Out of the corner of his eye he could see she was facing him now. "I do appreciate your help, especially with the locks, but if I'm going to do this, I have to figure out a way to do it on my own." Hannah fidgeted with the strings of her bonnet. "I can't call you every time I need a loaf of bread."

"*Mem* made our bread. We never needed to go to the store for that," Sarah whined from the backseat.

Hannah twisted to face her niece. "Maybe we can make bread together. You can show me how you and your *mem* made bread."

Tense silence expanded and filled the cab of his truck.

If Hannah was frustrated, she didn't let on. "What do you have there?" She stretched her arm over the seat and retrieved her cell phone from Emma.

"I found it on the table in your room," Emma said with a hint of apology.

"That's okay. Do you want to see how it works?" Spencer imagined Emma nodded because Hannah stretched into the backseat to show her niece how to dial the phone. "Pretty cool, huh?"

"Can I play with it?" Emma asked with all the enthusiasm of a six-year-old.

"Sure."

"She shouldn't play with that," Sarah said, her tone filled with disgust. "You're bringing too many worldly things here."

"It's okay, your sister's curious."

"And you really need to stop wearing English clothes," Sarah added, heaping on her annoyance with her aunt.

Hannah plucked the fabric gathered around her thighs. "I suppose you're right. I can't slip into my jeans and sneakers anymore because I think they're more practical."

Spencer pulled his truck alongside the curb in front of the General Store in the center of Apple Creek. She had a look of expectation on her face. "What is it?" he asked.

"I hate to impose, but I was thinking we could drive to the next town to the superstore. I need so many things, and I'm on a tight budget."

"I'd be happy to…but—" he gestured with his chin toward the row of shops "—I was thinking you and the girls might like some ice cream."

A click and a whoosh of fabric sounded from the backseat. Little Emma placed her chubby hands on the back of the seat and poked her face over the leather. "Can we have ice cream?"

A smile tilted Hannah's lips.

"My treat." Spencer climbed out of the vehicle before Hannah had a chance to protest. He walked around and opened her door. Hannah climbed out, looking around as if she were a fugitive. He leaned in close. "A quick ice cream cone, and I'll take you shopping in the next town."

Spencer opened the back door, and Emma scampered out, and a reluctant Sarah followed. Hannah nudged the older girl's shoulder. "What kind of ice cream do you like?"

"*Dat* says ice cream is only for special occasions."

Hannah sucked in a breath. "Well, this is a special occasion. Sheriff Maxwell is going to treat us. That's special, right?"

Sarah's expression grew pinched. For the briefest of moments, Hannah saw Ruthie in her daughter's face. Serious little Ruthie. Nostalgia formed a thick knot in her throat.

Spencer pointed to the clapboard sign mounted on the side of the ice cream shop. "Go pick your favorite flavor."

Emma bolted ahead, her little legs pumping under her long dress. Hannah whispered to Sarah. "Go help your sister read the board."

Sarah turned up her nose. "She can read."

"Not as well as you, I imagine." Hannah's tone was calm and encouraging. Spencer figured she didn't give herself enough credit when it came to the girls.

Sarah squared her shoulders and marched after her sister as if selecting ice cream flavors was a royal hardship. The two little bonnets moved together as they studied the board.

An Amish woman walked toward them. She lifted her head and seemed to snort her disdain. After she passed, Hannah said, "See what I'm up against? How can I raise the grandchildren of the bishop without everyone thinking I'm not good enough? They'll be pressuring me to turn the girls over to Lester and Fannie Mae." Hannah sat at a nearby picnic table, a faraway expression in her eyes. "Maybe I'm doing what I'm accusing others of doing."

Spencer lowered his chin.

"Maybe I'm too judgmental. Lester's sternness and Fannie Mae's strictness are not unheard of in the Amish community. My own father was very strict, yet I want to believe deep down that he was a good man. I saw how good he could be to Ruthie. Maybe…" She traced a groove in the picnic table.

Spencer touched Hannah's hand and she froze. Looked up at him. "Lester might not be the best choice. I've heard stories about the Lapp family even before…" He was going to say your sister's murder, but he stopped himself.

Hannah's brows furrowed.

"John and Lester Lapp didn't get along." Spencer shot his gaze over to the ice cream stand. Emma and Sarah were still selecting flavors. "I was called to break up a fight between the brothers."

"A physical fight?"

Nodding, Spencer lifted a hold-on-a-minute finger.

Emma ran over to them. "May I please have a bubble gum ice cream cone with sprinkles?"

"Of course you can." Spencer dug out a twenty and handed it to Emma. "Would you like anything, Hannah?"

She shook her head. Spencer patted his belly. "I better not, either."

Emma ran back to her sister. Hannah and Spencer continued their conversation out of earshot, but close enough to keep an eye on the young girls.

"What were John and Lester fighting about?" Hannah asked, her tone chilly on the hot summer afternoon.

"They wouldn't tell me." Spencer sat across from Hannah at the picnic table, stuffing his legs under the table. "But I did some asking around. Isaac, an Amish man who works at the General Store, seems to think there was some discord between the men because the bishop was pressuring John to sell land to his brother."

"That land has been in my family..." Her words trailed off, as if realizing how much had changed since her family farmed the land.

"John had gotten away from farming, and the land was sitting idle. Lester wanted a sizable chunk to build a home and farm." Spencer leaned forward, resting his elbows on the table. "Good land. Cheap price."

Hannah's eyebrow twitched. "Perhaps that was the change Ruth feared. She never came out and said. Maybe she was afraid of losing our family's farm."

About ten feet away, Emma sat at a child's picnic bench, and her sister joined her.

"How was John in his faith?" Spencer asked, sliding over a fraction to get under the shade of the umbrella.

"Ruth had been convinced her husband was more committed than ever to the Amish faith, perhaps because of his experience in the outside world. She said he claimed he knew how bad things could be." She played with the string of her cap. "I told her things weren't all that bad in the outside world. I guess I felt a little defensive. But I didn't paint an overly glowing picture, either. I didn't want to be responsible for any unrest on her part."

"Would you say his commitment was fanatical?" Spencer studied her face, and something flashed across her eyes. Fear? Annoyance? Confusion?

"Fanatical." Hannah seemed to be trying the word on for size. "My sister and her husband were Amish. By many people's standards, they would be considered fanatical."

"Fanatical by Amish standards?"

"I didn't know John." Hannah stood and grabbed a few napkins from the holder and offered them to Emma and Sarah at the nearby table. Emma had a big glob of sprinkles stuck to her cheek. Sarah ate her ice cream neatly with her spoon, watching a boy on a skateboard jump the curb. "Is the ice cream good?" Hannah asked, forcing a smile that didn't reach her eyes.

Emma's eyes grew wide, and she nodded. Sarah smiled tightly. "Thank you, Sheriff Maxwell."

"You're welcome."

Spencer thought he noticed Hannah shiver.

Spencer reached out and touched her hand. "You okay?"

"Not really." She ran a hand across her brow. "Not long ago, I was thinking maybe it was time to get a haircut, maybe paint my nails pink. Now I'm wearing my dead sister's Amish gown and making plans for her daughters."

Chapter Six

Later that afternoon, Hannah got Emma and Sarah settled in with a book so she could meet the tow truck driver from AAA out by the barn. Spencer was supposed to arrive soon and install the locks on the doors. She was looking forward to the distractions because she had just called her supervisor at the bank and resigned her position. Her mouth had been so dry she wasn't sure she was going to get out the words. But she had. And it was done. She was still wavering about her long-term plans, but she couldn't abandon the girls now. And her job wouldn't keep.

Hannah gathered her skirt in her hand and crossed the yard to meet the tow truck driver who'd just arrived. The cab of his white truck had the letters *Apple Creek Towing* with a little Amish buggy on the side. She smiled at the irony of it. She figured it was all in the marketing.

The tow truck driver hopped out of the cab, a perplexed look on his face. Hannah forced a smile and shook her head. "It's a long story." She handed him her AAA membership card and smiled at him. While he was calling in her information, she grabbed her cell phone and charger from the car. She'd have to figure out another plan for charging it in the near future. The driver finished his call and connected her vehicle with chains and hoisted it up on the flatbed truck. When he was finished, she asked him to drop the car off at Al's Garage in town. Al was going to put on four new tires and nearly drain her savings. Such was the life of a single, bank-teller-turned-Amish mom. She hoped to sell the car and use the money to hold her over. That was, if there was money left over after she paid off her loan.

"Okay, ma'am." He tipped his baseball cap at her. He hesitated before getting back into the cab. "If you don't mind me asking, I thought your people didn't drive cars."

Hannah gave him a weary smile. "We don't." She lifted her hand in a wave. "Al's expecting my car. Thank you."

The driver gave her a sheepish nod and climbed into the truck. She stood in the driveway and watched as the truck bobbled over the wagon-wheel ruts. *Well, there goes another piece of my past.*

A rustling sounded from inside the barn. Narrowing her gaze, Hannah moved toward it. Another nudge of guilt pinged her insides. She had pretty much left Samuel to take care of the animals the past few days. Her sister wouldn't have been so lax.

The thought of her sister's body in the silo forced her to catch her breath. *Poor Ruthie.* Would Hannah ever be able to fill her sister's shoes?

Once she reached the doorway of the barn, she noticed a dusting of hay sprinkling down from the loft like snow. Perhaps a bird of some kind had found its way into the loft.

Then she heard it. A trill from a cell phone. From the hayloft. Her heartbeat kicked up a notch.

"Hello?" She stepped back and stretched onto her tiptoes to try to see into the loft, but she couldn't. The ringing stopped almost as soon as it started. "Who's up there?" she asked when no one answered.

More hay sprinkled down from the loft. Then the top half of a head with thick brown hair peered over the edge of the loft. Samuel, her farm hand and Willard's son. "It's me, Miss Hannah."

Hannah let out a relieved breath and pressed a hand to her chest. "What are you doing up there?"

He disappeared and for a minute, Hannah thought he was going to ignore her question. "Samuel Fisher, come down her this instant."

"Coming, Miss Hannah. I just have to…"

"Bring whatever it is you had with you down here." Hannah stood with her hands on her hips as the boy backed down the ladder, a burlap bag flung over his shoulder. When he reached the ground, he turned and strode toward the door, a determined expression on his face.

"Wait a minute." Hannah's pulse thumped in her ears. "What were you doing up there? Was that a cell phone I heard?"

Samuel looked down and dragged the toe of his boot across the hay. "I…um… I…" His cheeks grew bright red.

"Tell me right now, or I'll be forced to address this matter with your father." There was no way Samuel knew she was bluffing.

A scared expression haunted the teenager's eyes. "Oh, please don't. He'll be mad. He won't understand."

Sympathy blossomed in her chest, but she had to remain strong. "I'm not mad. I want to know what you were doing in the loft. You don't have any business up there at this time of day, do you?"

"*Neh*, ma'am."

"Then tell me."

Samuel yanked at the edge of his burlap bag and pulled out a book. It looked like a science-fiction title. Surprised, Hannah tipped her head and studied his face. "You were reading up there?"

The boy nodded. "My *dat* thinks it's a waste of time. He thinks I need to direct all my focus on farming." Samuel shrugged, making himself seem so much younger than his seventeen years. "Taking care of God's land."

"And you have a cell phone?"

Samuel nodded. "Some of *die Youngie* have cell phones. It's frowned upon, but it's overlooked during *Rumspringa*. A bunch of us got them at the superstore in the next town. I have enough odd jobs to pay for it." He dropped the book into the bag and twisted the burlap opening, a nervous gesture. "My *dat* wouldn't understand."

"I know all about struggling with a parent."

The boy looked up at her, hope glistening in his brown eyes. "Is that why you left the Amish?"

"Did your *mem* share my past with you?" He was way too young to remember the scandal when a young Amish girl named Hannah Wittmer jumped the fence.

"I overheard *Mem* and *Dat* talking about it."

"*Mem*? Rebecca, your stepmom?"

"She is my *mem* now." He fingered the strap of his burlap bag.

"What did you overhear?"

"*Mem* and you were good friends, and *Dat* thinks it's best if you didn't rekindle your friendship." The color rose in his cheeks, as if he realized he had said too much. "I don't mean to be rude, but I have to get home. *Dat* will be looking for me."

"I've had a few problems around here since my sister died. Do you know anything about that?"

Samuel unwound the bag. "What problems?" He poked at the hay with the toe of his boot. He had a tendency to do that.

She jerked her thumb toward the open barn door. "Someone slashed the tires on my car. Someone may have knocked over a lamp causing a small fire in the barn."

The boy shook his head, fear evident in his eyes. "*Neh*, it wasn't me."

"Have you brought any of your friends around here? Perhaps you mentioned that you were helping me out?"

"I didn't." Samuel shifted his feet. The set of his mouth was hard to read.

Hannah held up her hand. "You can go, Samuel."

"Are you going to tell my *dat*?"

"No, unless you think I have reason to."

He shook his head. "I'll be back in the morning to take care of the animals."

"Sounds good." Hannah watched as Samuel took a few steps toward the door. "Oh, and Samuel, you're welcome to read your book here anytime. Just knock on the door of the house and let me know you're here." She had gotten lost in the hayloft more than once herself as a young girl while reading Laura Ingalls Wilder.

An I-can't-believe-my-luck smile played across his lips. "Thanks, Miss Hannah."

"And one last thing."

"Yes?" Samuel's whole demeanor had brightened.

"If you ever need anything, just ask. I'm a pretty good ear."

Samuel lowered his gaze without saying anything.

"Have a good afternoon."

Samuel nodded and spun around. He broke into a jog, but the fear on his face when she mentioned telling his father was etched in her memory. What was the boy so afraid of?

"This isn't exactly in my job description." Spencer turned the last screw into the plate of the dead bolt on Hannah's front door. Locks had been installed on all the doors, including her mother's.

"Thank you." Hannah handed him a cold glass of lemonade.

Hannah sat on the rocker on the porch and gently rocked back and forth, pushing off the floor with her bare foot. A chip of pink nail polish clung to her big toenail.

"It's peaceful out here." Spencer placed the screwdriver into the toolbox and snapped the box shut. He crouched down and examined his work. Installing the locks had taken less time than he had anticipated.

"I suppose if I'm going to raise these girls, I need to expand my circle of friends. Make it a little less quiet for the girls. The neighbors came by with food after my sister died, but their visits stopped long before the last casserole was consumed."

Spencer glanced around. "Are the girls still at your mother's house?"

"She likes the company. She's all alone with her

thoughts." Hannah looked off in the distance, squinting against the sun low on the horizon. "That's what I miss about the outside world, all the distractions. Radio, TV, computer, you name it. A person can get lost for hours without once examining their thoughts."

"Do you think that's a good thing?"

"Sometimes I'd love to get lost in a game of Angry Birds."

Spencer tested the lock one last time and sat on the rocker next to Hannah. "Really? You don't strike me as an Angry Birds kind of person."

She laughed. "That game's addictive. Have you played it?" She stopped suddenly and looked at him. "Tell me something about you."

Spencer chuckled, surprised by the abrupt change of topics. "Didn't we already cover that topic? Change of pace. Small-town life appealed to me."

"I can't imagine a guy like you didn't leave someone brokenhearted back in Buffalo." Her cheeks flushed pink.

Spencer scrubbed a hand across his close-cropped hair. "Actually, someone I cared about broke my heart. Turns out her idea of a husband was a corporate lawyer, not a city cop."

Hannah stopped rocking. "Oh, I'm sorry. I didn't mean to pry. I was trying to be funny…"

Spencer nudged her bare foot with the tip of his boot. "And what pretty feet you have."

Hannah tipped her head, and he was left to inspect the top of her white bonnet. He reached out and traced the edge of her cap where it met her soft brown hair. Hannah lifted her head, and he dropped his hand. He couldn't quite read the expression on her face. Alarm? Annoyance? Horror?

Clearing his throat, he held up two shiny gold keys on a small wire loop. He knew he should apologize for being so bold, but he wasn't sorry. This young woman fascinated him, even if he had no business being fascinated by her. He had fallen for the wrong woman before. But Vicki and Hannah were different extremes. Vicki was about money and success. Hannah was…well, Hannah.

Spencer dropped the keys into her palm. "The keys are identical. Each works on the front and back doors. One key opens both the lock in the handle and the dead bolt. I left the key for the lock on your mother's door on her kitchen table."

Hannah closed her fingers around the keys. "Thank you. I'll sleep better tonight." She rearranged her dress over her legs. "I've been thinking about why John might be coming around to harass me."

Spencer studied her closely. "We don't know for sure it's him."

Hannah's lips twitched, as if she were holding back her emotions. "Hear me out. John's not in his right mind. Maybe he found out Ruthie was meeting with me. Maybe that's why he killed her. If he couldn't control her…" All the color drained from her already pale skin. "I blame myself. If she hadn't been meeting with me…"

Spencer reached out and touched her knee briefly. "The only one to blame for your sister's death is the person who—" he lowered his voice because it seemed to be the respectful thing to do "—who ended your sister's life. Don't you dare blame yourself."

Don't blame yourself?

How many times had his friends tried to convince *him* of that? Yet he did blame himself. If he had kept a closer eye on Daniel in Buffalo, the boy wouldn't have been murdered on a street corner.

"Hey…" Hannah's soft voice cut through his reverie. "Where did you go just now?"

"Nowhere. Just tired."

The look of skepticism in her eyes told him she wasn't buying it.

"I get it. I'm tired, too." She leaned back and rested her head on the back of the rocker.

Spencer gathered her hands into his. "You don't have to stay here. I can take you and the girls someplace safer."

She pulled her hands away. "No. I can't do that to Emma and Sarah or my mother." She uncurled her fingers and looked down at the keys for the newly installed locks. "We'll be safe."

He couldn't resist covering her hand again, dragging his thumb across the smooth skin on the back of her hand. "I'll make sure you and the girls are safe."

Hannah bowed her head and covered his hand with hers. "Why is it I finally meet a great guy now?"

Spencer couldn't stifle his smile. "You think I'm a great guy?"

Shaking her head, she leaned back and sat very still. "I'm embarrassed." She pushed to her feet and scooted past him. She braced her hands on the porch railing, her back to him

Spencer joined her. "I didn't mean to embarrass you."

She ripped her bonnet from her head. She smoothed a hand across the flyaways and tugged at the bun a bit, but left it in place. "When I was in Buffalo, the few relationships I had with guys ended because they thought I was too conservative." Hannah flicked him a sideways glance. "They made me feel so…awkward." She brushed her pinky against his on the railing. "You've always made me feel comfortable."

"I feel a but coming on…"

Hannah turned to him and gave him a sad smile.

"I'm trying to be a good parent to my nieces. And if that means being Amish, then so be it. And that means you can't keep hanging around."

Disappointment twisted his insides like a kick to the gut.

"My faith is important to me. I don't want to put words in your mouth, but I get a sense—" she searched his eyes for a moment "—I sense you lost your faith somewhere along the way."

Feeling exposed, Spencer turned away. God had let young Daniel down and in turn, Spencer *had* lost faith. But something about this woman and her devotion to doing what's right sparked the kindling to his renewed faith. Just maybe…

"I think we met for a reason," Hannah continued. "God wanted our paths to cross. Perhaps so you could be our protector." She ran the flat of her hand across the railing. "We live in different worlds." Hannah nodded slowly as if she had convinced herself of something.

Oh, if only circumstances could have been different.

He leaned in close and tipped her chin, forcing her to look at him. "Just because you're chasing me away, doesn't mean I'm not going to do my job. I'm the sheriff, and my job is to keep you safe."

Indecision darkened her eyes. He hoped maybe this meant he had a chance. Then his heart plummeted. How fair was that? The only way they could have a future was if she left the Amish once and for all. He learned a long time ago, you couldn't force someone to live a life they hadn't signed up for.

Vicki's harsh words scraped across his memory.

Cold, icy regret settled in his gut. He had a job to do. That was all.

Spencer missed seeing Hannah. He had hoped to run into her in town, but either he had the worst timing, or she hadn't been off the farm much since he last saw her several days ago.

Spencer's police cruiser found its way out to the Lapp farm. Something he did several times a shift while he was on patrol. The late-afternoon sun burned bright in the sky on the sweltering summer day.

Near the Lapp farm, a young man in a buggy tipped his hat at him as his horse galloped down the street. Spencer knew he wasn't the most welcomed guy in the Amish community, but if he could prove to them that he was on their side, he'd hoped to win them over. The Amish wanted to live apart, but sometimes the two worlds collided. And when a law was broken, Spencer knew they'd need him.

The Amish couldn't live completely separate.

Spencer parked and walked up to the house. He heard soft singing coming from inside. *Hannah.* He hated to knock, knowing it would halt her singing. He waited for a moment, listening, and laughed when he recognized the Top 40 pop tune. It wasn't a song the young Amish would sing at their Sunday gatherings.

He knocked and as expected, the singing ceased.

Hannah appeared at the door, drying her hands on a dish towel.

"Didn't mean to interrupt," Spencer said through the screen door, trying to subdue his smile.

"Oh, I didn't see you come up the driveway." Almost reflexively, she lifted her hand to her bonnet. Hannah glanced out the door and around him, a shy smile growing on her pretty lips.

"It's just me. Were you expecting someone?"

"No." She took a step back, yet seemed reluctant to invite him in.

"Is something wrong?" He flashed his best disarming smile. He knew exactly what was wrong. He wasn't holding up his side of the bargain to stay away. Let her settle into her new Amish life.

She mirrored his smile and dropped her shoulders. "Please come in. I was about to check on the girls. They've been playing outside, and I need to take the laundry off the line."

He detected a hint of fatigue in her tone. "Your job is never done."

"You're telling me." She lowered her voice. "I miss the days of a nine-to-five job and popping in a microwave dinner then plopping in front of the television. I didn't realize how good I had it." Then just like that, her cheeks turned pink, and she lifted her hands to them. "Listen to me. I'm being selfish…"

"You don't have to explain anything to me." He leaned in close and whispered, "I won't tell anyone."

Hannah glanced toward the kitchen. "I better go check on the little ones. Last I saw them, they were playing on the back porch. They promised me they'd be good." She rolled her eyes as if she wasn't sure she should believe them. "They've been fascinated with a stray cat they found yesterday."

She walked toward the back door, her bare toes against the hardwood floor. Her long dress flapping against her legs. Despite her Amish wardrobe, she had a modern air about her. Or maybe he thought that because he had caught a glimpse of the woman she was in her jeans, sweatshirt and ponytail.

One can't unsee who a person really was. He rubbed a hand across his jaw and followed her through the house and onto the back porch.

Sarah sat with her legs crossed, petting an orange tabby cat.

"The cat seems to be pretty domesticated. I wonder if someone is looking for it," Hannah said, her tone none too concerned.

"A neighbor's, maybe?" Spencer suggested.

Hannah shrugged, then a line deepened on her forehead. "Where's your little sister?"

Sarah looked up, a look of disinterest on her features. "She liked to help *Mem* with the laundry. I think she's in the yard."

Hannah locked eyes briefly with Spencer before snapping her attention to the yard. A laundry line was stretched between a pole and a tree around the far side of the house. She ran down the steps and around to the side of the house.

A row of dresses of various shades of blue and purple ended where an out of place sweatshirt, jeans and pj's clung to the line.

"Oh, my…" Hannah ran over to the clothesline. She touched the shredded fabric and turned to meet Spencer's gaze. Her sweatshirt had met a similar fate. All her

English clothes had been shredded and splattered with something black.

"Where's Emma?" she asked more urgently, fear straining her features. Sarah had strolled over with the cat in her arms. She shrugged again. Spencer scanned the yard, unease prickling the hairs on the back of his neck. Out of the corner of his eye, he noticed movement near the corner of the house.

Little Emma walked over with her black hands, palms up. "*Mem*'s laundry was never dirty." Her lower lip jutted out in a pout.

Hannah ran over and crouched in front of the child and pulled her into a fierce embrace without regard for her dirty hands. "Are you okay?" She pulled Emma out to arm's length and gave her a once-over. "Are you hurt?"

Emma shook her head. "My hands are sticky."

Spencer crouched next to both Hannah and Emma. "Where did you get your hands dirty?" A pungent odor, like tar, reached his nose.

The little girl pointed to the side of the house. Spencer stood and walked around to where she pointed. Next to the house was a bucket of what looked and smelled like tar. A few sets of footprints were in the muddy yard.

He glanced back at Hannah and the girls, all eyes watching him. "Did either of you see anyone out here?"

Emma glanced over at Sarah, and the two of them quickly shook their heads. Almost too quickly.

"Are you sure you didn't see anything?" Hannah asked.

"No, *Aenti* Hannah," Sarah said. Emma bowed her head and bit her lip.

Sarah buried her face in the cat's fur. Emma inspected her hands.

"Let's get you cleaned up." Hannah guided the child by the shoulder. "Spencer, would you mind watching Sarah until I get back?"

"Of course." He sat on one of the rockers on the back porch and Sarah settled down with the cat. His gaze drifted to the side yard, where the Amish clothes hung clean on the laundry line and Hannah's English clothes fluttered in the wind, tattered and stained. Destroyed.

Chapter Seven

Hannah grabbed the laundry basket and slipped outside to take her destroyed clothes off the line. Tears burned the backs of her eyes as she stretched to pinch the clothespins. Her favorite pair of jeans dropped into her arms.

She tapped her index finger gingerly over the black, tacky tar. She had purchased these jeans after she had saved enough money from her job as a bank teller. She sighed heavily, her lungs filling with the nasty scent of tar.

The designer jeans had symbolized her first success of sorts. She had, for the first time, felt like an official *Englischer*. She was proud of herself, a feeling so foreign to her Amish roots.

An emptiness expanded in her chest. She'd never be able to afford to replace them.

You don't need to replace them.

Hannah worried her bottom lip and dropped the jeans into the laundry basket.

"Are you okay, *Aenti* Hannah?" Hannah spun around

to find Emma staring up at her. "Are you sad because that man ruined your fancy clothes?"

"Did you see who did this?" Hannah struggled to keep the panic out of her voice.

Emma glanced down and played with the folds of her dress. "Um…"

Hannah knelt in front of her niece and forced a smile, even as her pulse whooshed in her ears. "It's okay. You can tell me."

Emma shrugged her thin shoulders. "I saw Samuel."

Hannah swallowed hard, and her ears burned hot. "You saw Samuel do this? Samuel, who helps around the farm?"

Emma nodded, her eyes wide.

"When did you see him?"

"A little while ago."

Hannah smoothed a hand over the cotton of her cap. "Did you see him throw this yucky tar on my clean laundry?"

Emma shook her head slowly. "No. He was running. Fast."

"Which way did he run?"

Hannah spun around to find Spencer standing behind her. She guessed he had heard the entire conversation.

"That way." Emma pointed toward the road, toward the Fisher's house.

"We should go talk to him," Hannah said then hesitated. "But I'm not sure it's a good idea to talk to him in front of his father. When I talked to him earlier, he seemed afraid of his father."

"I'll talk to him." Spencer crossed his arms over his broad chest, anger tightening his mouth.

Hannah grabbed his arm. "No. The sheriff showing

up will only make matters worse." A band of indecision tightened around her chest and made it hard to breathe. "I need to talk to him."

"I'm not letting you go alone." The determination in his eyes left no room for debate.

Hannah patted Emma's shoulder. "Want to visit Granny for a little bit while Sheriff Maxwell and I run an errand?"

Emma's eyes brightened. The child was so eager. A ray of sunshine.

Hannah held out her hand. "Let's get your sister and go see Granny."

After Hannah and Spencer got the girls settled, they took the short drive down the street. Spencer pulled up in front of Willard and Rebecca's house. He reached to open the door, and Hannah grabbed his arm. "Wait. We need to talk to Samuel without his father. You wait here. I'll knock on the door, pretend I need to talk to Samuel about his chores on the farm."

Spencer gave her a brief nod, indecision flickering in his eyes. "Okay. I'll be right here, watching."

Hannah mimicked his quick nod and pushed open the car door. She strode up the porch, her laced boots heavy on the wood planks. She closed her eyes and said a silent prayer that she'd know what to say if Willard answered the door. Lying wasn't in her makeup, but a little white one was warranted under the circumstance, if it meant protecting Samuel. She didn't want to accuse him of anything in case Emma was mistaken.

And if Samuel was pulling these destructive pranks in some misguided attempt to chase her away, she needed to get through to him. Yet she didn't want him to run away from Apple Creek if his stern father came down too hard on him.

Like she had run away from her stern father.

Hannah pressed her fingers to her temples. A headache threatened behind her eyes.

Rebecca appeared in the doorway with that wary expression she had come to wear. Hannah missed her bubbly friend. So much had changed since their youth. Rebecca angled her head to look around Hannah to the police cruiser parked on the street.

After a long hesitation, Rebecca pushed open the door, the dish towel pressed to her chest. "Is something wrong? Is Samuel…?"

Hannah took her friend's cool hand in hers. "No one is hurt." She lowered her voice. "I was hoping to talk to Samuel. Isn't he here?"

Rebecca narrowed her gaze. "I'm not sure where he is. I expected he'd be home for dinner by now."

"Is your husband home?"

"Willard's out in the barn." She lowered the dish towel to her side. Worry lined the corners of her eyes. "Do you want me to get him?"

"I'd like to talk to you alone first, if I may."

All the color drained from Rebecca's face. "I don't know…"

"You can have friends, right? I'm dressed appropriately." Hannah cocked her head and smiled. "We're friends. Remember?"

Rebecca shrugged. "I can talk for a minute. Out here on the porch."

Hannah nodded, studying her friend's face. "Is Samuel having trouble at home?"

Rebecca's expression grew shuttered. "Samuel's a *gut* boy."

Hannah weighed how much she should say. She didn't want to cause any more trouble for Samuel, but if he had destroyed her clothes on the wash line, he needed help. And he needed to be stopped.

"Can I share something with you, and can you promise me you won't get mad at Samuel?"

Rebecca's long pause gave Hannah all the permission she needed.

"I found Samuel in my barn reading a book his father wouldn't approve of." Hannah decided to ease into the conversation.

Rebecca's forehead twitched, but she immediately smoothed out her expression. The dish towel she twisted in her hands received the brunt of her emotions.

Hannah touched her friend's forearm. "It wasn't anything horrible. He was reading a novel that seems to be very popular today. I read it myself. Other than some fantasy themes that you might not like, it's rather a good book."

Rebecca's expression grew pinched, and her gaze flicked to the doorway.

"He was afraid his father wouldn't approve."

"No, Willard wouldn't," Rebecca muttered. "He likes to limit what Samuel reads." Her knuckles turned white around the twisted dish towel. "I'll make sure I tell Samuel to stick to his chore list when he comes over."

"No, that's not why I stopped by. I felt bad for him. I struggled myself when I was his age."

Anger flashed in her friend's eyes. "Don't fill his head with ideas." She pointed adamantly to the ground.

"Samuel belongs here in Apple Creek. With his family. He is my son. Don't…" Her voice wavered.

"I would never do that, Rebecca. I'm worried. If Samuel is afraid of his father, he might run away on his own. You don't want to lose him forever."

Rebecca met her friend's gaze and hiked her chin. "What did you need to speak to my son about? This book? I will talk to him about it." Something flitted across her dark eyes that unnerved Hannah.

"There's something else." Hannah watched Rebecca's face on the verge of crumbling. "Someone threw tar on my English clothes. I want to know if Samuel knows anything about it." Hannah made a spontaneous decision not to tell her friend that Emma had seen Samuel running away from her farm.

Rebecca's brow furrowed. "Of course he doesn't know anything about it. He's a *gut* boy." She started waving the dish towel at Hannah like she was a housefly she needed to shoo away from her freshly baked pies.

"Rebecca!" Willard's voice boomed from inside the house. He must have come in through the back door. Rebecca flinched, and Hannah immediately regretted any trouble her presence might cause her friend. Footsteps sounded through the house, and then Willard appeared at the screen door.

"I didn't realize we had company." Willard stepped outside, his gaze searing the length of Hannah before he turned his focus to Spencer's cruiser parked on the road. "Is something wrong?"

Hannah took a step back. "Spencer… Sheriff Maxwell stopped by the farm, and when I needed to talk to Samuel he offered to drive me over."

"You need to talk to Samuel? He's not home. Can I help you with something?"

"She wants Samuel to come fifteen minutes earlier in the morning because she has a few extra chores," Rebecca interrupted. "I told her that would be okay as long as he was home in time to do chores around here."

Willard studied his wife. He opened his mouth to say something then stopped. He nodded. "Samuel will come by earlier in the morning. Anything else?"

Hannah shook her head, feeling foolish. She waved and turned on her heel. *"Denki."* She hustled down the stairs toward Spencer, who had gotten out of the car. She caught his elbow and turned him around.

Spencer opened the door for her, and she climbed in. Her gaze drifted to the porch where Willard watched her. Spencer got in his side and slammed the door.

Her stomach dropped. "I'm worried Willard overheard Rebecca and me. I had no intention of getting Samuel into trouble with his father."

"Even if he destroyed your property?"

"What if Emma was mistaken? She's only a child. What if it was John as we've suspected all along? Maybe Samuel had witnessed something and ran away." A weight pressed heavily on Hannah's lungs. "And if Samuel did destroy my clothes, he's a troubled young man. I fear Willard's temper would only strike fear and resentment in his son and make Samuel lash out more."

After Hannah put her nieces to bed, she grabbed a plastic garbage bag and slipped outside to the back porch to where her ruined clothes sat in a laundry basket. She picked up her jeans and muttered, "Some nerve."

"We'll catch him."

Hannah spun around, her hand pressed to her beating chest. "You scared me." She had to stifle the urge to slug Spencer. The slow smile spreading across his face didn't help.

"Sorry," he said, his voice husky. "You left your cell phone charging in my car." He placed her phone and charger on the window ledge.

"Thanks."

"And I thought you could use some company."

"Hmm…" She was too much in a funk to admit that yes, she was happy for the company. "Keep hanging around here and people are going to talk."

"People talk anyway." Mischief danced in his eyes, which were partially shadowed by the gathering dusk.

She ignored his comment. With swift jerky motions, she stuffed the ruined clothes into the garbage bag. She dropped the bag, and it landed with a plop on the pine planks of the porch. Hannah leaned against the railing and tugged off her bonnet. Her tight bun was giving her a tension headache.

Hannah rolled her shoulders and sighed. "I don't believe Samuel did this."

Spencer sniffed. "Even though Emma saw him running across the yard?"

"Even though Emma saw him running across the yard." Hannah bit the inside of her lip. "He might have been running so I wouldn't see him coming out of the barn again. He's afraid his father will scold him for reading inappropriate books, or using a cell phone." She shrugged, considering another less likely scenario. "Or he might have seen who really ruined my clothes and ran away in fear."

Spencer made a sound from the back of his throat. "I

tried to track Samuel down after I dropped you off. No luck. I'll try again tomorrow."

"Yeah," Hannah said resigned. "I suppose we won't know more until we talk to him."

Leaning over the laundry basket, she grabbed her favorite pj bottoms, now pink with splatters of black tar. "You'd think a girl could wear whatever she wanted to bed without being harassed."

She dropped the pj bottoms into the garbage bag and wiped a splotch of black tar from her thumb onto the plastic. "Someone's determined to chase me away."

"Who has the most to gain if you leave?" Spencer's voice was calm, calculating as he was working the pieces of the case. She didn't understand the empty disappointment that suddenly expanded within her. She lowered her gaze, pretending to study the black plastic bag at her feet. This *was* just another case to him. It wasn't personal.

"Lester and Fannie Mae are determined to raise the children," Spencer added, still deep in thought. "And more important, if I leave, they can finally take over the land. They want to farm the land that is sitting idle."

Spencer let out a heavy sigh in the gathering darkness. He stood and joined her next to the railing.

Hannah closed her eyes briefly. "I didn't like Lester from the minute I met him, but would he really be this…underhanded? This destructive? I don't know him well enough."

"I'm going to ask you again, Hannah. Would you please consider leaving the farm with the girls? It would be safer." The concern in Spencer's voice made a tingling start in her fingers and shoot up her arms.

"I can't leave with the girls. Their grandparents and

aunt and uncle will argue the case that John will come back. He is still their rightful guardian."

She shook her head. How had she gotten into this mess?

"What's going on in your head?"

"This whole situation is so far out of my element. But there's one thing I learned all the years of living alone in Buffalo." She braced her hands on the railing and hung her head.

"Care to share?" The breeze kicked up. The overpowering smell of tar was replaced by grass and dirt and hay.

"It's cliché but true. The grass isn't always greener on the other side."

"You're telling me." Spencer turned and rested his hip on the railing.

"You?" She angled her head. "You wear your police uniform very well." She couldn't imagine him not being able to find his place in the world.

Spencer held out his hand and laughed. "You wear your Amish wardrobe with flair."

Hannah smiled demurely. "Flair. Hardly." She swept her hand across her long gown. "I feel like I've been asked to put on clothes that I never thought I'd have to wear again. But I need to search for happiness in here." She covered her heart with her hand. "I was miserable and terribly lonely in Buffalo. I never seemed to fit in. I refused to come back because I had made a mess of things when I left. Now—" she twisted her lips "—maybe this was all God's plans. Allowing me to return. With grace. And to do what my sister would have wanted me to do."

"I wish I had your faith."

Hannah studied his face closely. "Didn't you grow up going to church?"

Spencer frowned. "Oh, we went to church, all right. Sat in the front row. My mother forced us to go."

Hannah's heart sank.

"Once they left the sanctuary, my father went back on patrol, disillusioned with the things he saw every day on the streets. And my mother's only concern was praying my dad came home every night. She was the devout one." He drew in a deep breath and let it out slowly. "My father struggled with his faith. I suppose that's why I've struggled with mine. My father warned me not to become a police officer. He said the job stole part of his soul. I only understood that after I worked the streets of Buffalo."

Hannah covered his hand. "It's never too late…"

Spencer cocked his head and pulled his hand away. He pointed to the garbage bag. "Now about those clothes."

Hannah studied him for a moment. Now was not the time to push issues of faith. She cleared her throat. "Someone wanted to make a point." She nudged the bag with the toe of her boot. "Point taken. I want it to end here. I don't want any more trouble."

"It needs to be investigated. Someone was on your farm. Destroyed your property."

"I know." Her words came out clipped. Tired. "We need to be careful how we proceed. I don't want to get Samuel caught up in this if he's innocent."

"What if he's not innocent?" Spencer seemed to stare right through her, and a bundle of nerves tangled inside her.

A creak sounded by the door, and Hannah spun

around. She saw a flash of blond hair before it disappeared. "One of the girls is looking for me. I better go in."

Spencer nodded and strolled down the steps. "Night."

"Night." Hannah slipped inside and closed the door and turned the key in the lock, something she had never imagined doing as a young girl growing up on the farm. She moved to the window and watched Spencer's shadow disappear around the side of the house as he headed to his car.

Hannah found Sarah curled up in the rocker with the cat in her lap. The creature had made himself completely at home.

"Maybe the cat prefers to stay outdoors. We could make her a soft bed in the barn," Hannah suggested. Growing up, her family had never kept pets in the house. Cats were meant for chasing mice in the barn.

Sarah glared right through her aunt without saying anything.

"Come on." Hannah tapped her niece's shoulder. "It's time to get into bed." She strode toward the stairs, hoping her niece would follow.

"He's not a nice man."

Hannah turned around slowly to see Sarah stroking the kitten's head and staring at her. The girl's eyes were hardened and too cold for the sweet child her sister had raised.

Hannah checked her tone and carefully chose her words. "Sheriff Maxwell is a good man. He's helped me a few times since I returned to Apple Creek." She softened her tone. "And remember he got us ice cream?"

Sarah pinched her lips and shook her head. "*Dat* told me policemen are bad."

Hannah swallowed back her protest. Despite how

much she despised John Lapp for what she suspected he had done to her sister, she had to remember he was the girl's father.

"*Dat* wouldn't want him coming around here. When my *dat* gets back, he's going to be really mad."

Anger grew in Hannah's belly, but compassion ruled her brain.

"We need to consider each person for who they are, not their profession. Just because Sheriff Maxwell wears a uniform, doesn't make him bad. In the English world, people count on law enforcement to help them. Even though the Amish like to keep separate, law enforcement is also there to protect us."

"He's nosy." Sarah dragged her hand down the cat's tail.

Hannah sat in the rocker next to her niece and leaned forward, resting her elbows on her thighs. "According to your *dat*?"

Sarah nodded, some of the anger slipping away from her tight expression, perhaps at the mention of her father.

"Do you know why your *dat* would say that?" Hannah trod carefully, not wanting to upset the child. Her mother had died less than two weeks ago and her father had disappeared.

"*Dat* said Sheriff Maxwell knew nothing about the Amish way, and he should keep his nose out of our business."

Replaying her niece's words in her head, Hannah reached over and petted the cat. "Have you named him?"

Sarah's steely gaze faltered. "Pumpkin."

"That sounds like a lovely name."

Sarah scrunched up her face as if she were giving it some thought.

"Why didn't your father like the police? Did something happen?" Hannah was thinking about the fight John got into with his brother in town.

Sarah stroked the cat from head to tail and then again. Without looking up, she said, "My *dat* and Uncle Lester were talking really loud in town." *The fight.*

"Do you know why they were talking really loud?"

"Uncle Lester was mad at *Dat. Dat* claimed Uncle Lester didn't know how important it was to be Amish. My uncle laughed. He thought my *dat* should be farming, not working for someone else."

"Did you hear anything else?" Hannah kept stroking the cat, hoping to keep her niece talking.

"*Dat* said he'd never sell Uncle Lester the land." Sarah's thin shoulders crept up to her ears. "I don't know what he meant."

Hannah tucked a long blond hair behind Sarah's ear. Too much adult stuff for such a little peanut. Hannah leaned in close. "Do you like living here?"

Sarah looked up with a question in her eyes. "*Dat* should be home soon."

Tingles bit at Hannah's fingers and raced up her arms. What if her father was already home? Harassing *her*?

Sheriff Maxwell swung by the police station after stopping by the farm. He had let the pretty Miss Wittmer distract him long enough.

"You're here late." Deputy Sheriff Mark Reynolds sat at his desk with photos spread out in front of him.

Spencer leaned over and picked up a photo. It was of an Amish man with a fat lip, but more important, his beard was slashed at an angle. Spencer slowly lifted his eyes to meet Mark's. "Is this recent?"

Mark let out a long breath. "Yeah, the hospital called." Mark consulted the file in front of him. "Abram Leising was attacked while he slept last night. His beard was cut."

"Last night?" Spencer picked up another photo and studied the pained expression on the elderly man's face.

"Mr. Leising arrived at the hospital late this afternoon. The staff told me he was an unwilling patient. He's already back home."

"We haven't had a case like this in six months."

Mark nodded. "You think it's our missing guy, John Lapp?"

Spencer rubbed his hand across his jaw. "He was a person of interest in our last break-in and beard cutting."

"How much priority should we give this? I drove out to the Leising farm, but Abram was pretty tight-lipped."

"Did he see the guy who cut his beard?"

"No, claimed it was dark. When he woke up, the intruder punched him in the mouth, dazed him." Mark pushed the photos around with the eraser of a pencil. "I get the impression he wouldn't have come to the hospital except the guy lost a tooth, and his grandson made him come in."

"Maybe it's John…maybe it's a copycat." Spencer mentally ticked through all the events of late. An Amish man's beard was part of his identity. The perpetrator was lashing out against the Amish? Someone who has a grudge against the Amish? Did this sound like John Lapp?

Mark crossed his arms and leaned back in the chair. "How far do you want me to pursue this? The Amish like to live apart from us. Why should this be any different? Let them work it out for themselves. No one's getting hurt…" He hesitated for a fraction. "Not really."

From his perch on the corner of the desk, Spencer assessed his young deputy. "Why don't you tell me how you really feel?"

The deputy slouched, some of the bravado draining out of him. "You don't know what it was like to grow up in this town. The Amish can be a real pain sometimes. They need our help, but then refuse to press charges in court." He waved his hand. "The kidnapping and murder of Mary Miller had the whole town divided. Got my boss fired." He held out his hand. "But I guess that worked in your favor."

Spencer felt a muscle working in his jaw. "It's our job to bridge that gap. Make sure we have a good relationship with the Amish."

Mark stood and strolled toward the door. He turned around and casually crossed his arms. "That may be how things work in the big city, but you can't change people's hearts in a small town. They've already formed their opinions."

"If you really feel that way, you're going to have to look past it to do your job."

Mark slid a hand across his utility belt. "I'll do my job. I always do." He turned to walk away and tossed a "Night, boss" over his shoulder. The word *boss* was edged in a brittle tone.

Spencer dismissed it and glanced down at the photos his deputy had left on the desk. Had John Lapp been responsible for this and previous attacks? Had he been unstable long before he went after his wife? *If* he had gone after his wife…

Guilt wormed its way into his heart. If only Spencer

had caught the intruder the first time a church elder was attacked in his home, perhaps he could have prevented Ruth's murder.

The next morning, Hannah came downstairs in an Amish dress and started a breakfast of eggs and bacon. Any thoughts of resorting to her English wardrobe had gotten tarred and destroyed yesterday on the clothesline, save for a couple pairs of jeans and a few T-shirts. If she could just keep the girls on a regular routine, maybe the rest of the chaos in her life would settle down.

Wishful thinking?

She grabbed the kettle from the stove and went over to the sink to fill it. Through the window, she noticed a dark plume of smoke billowing up over the barn.

Frozen in place, her heart stopped. She spun around when she noticed Sarah's thin coat was missing from the hook. She ran into the sitting room and nearly tripped over Emma, who was stacking blocks in the middle of the floor.

Hannah crouched down and clutched Emma's shoulders, panic making it difficult to talk, to think. "Where's your sister?"

Emma's eyes flared wide. "She told me not to tell you."

Hannah swallowed her growing fear. "You must tell me where she is." She glanced out the window. The sky over the barn had turned black with smoke. "Did Sarah go out to the barn?"

Emma stared at her. Tears filled the little girl's eyes. It took all Hannah's energy not to shake the information out of her. "Emma, please tell me. Did she go to the barn?"

Hannah stood and ran to look out the window. Red and orange flames licked the roof. "You have to tell me."

Emma nodded. "It's a secret…" The little girl's voice trailed off. Hannah held her breath, waiting for her to reveal what she knew. "Sarah went looking for Pumpkin. She thought you made her sleep in the barn."

Hannah's heart plummeted. "Stay here. Do you understand? Stay here."

Hannah turned off the stove under the bubbling bacon. She grabbed a dish towel and ran it under water. She burst out the back door and bolted toward the barn barefoot. She rolled her ankle on a wagon-wheel rut. Pain shot up her leg, but she ignored it.

"Sarah! Sarah!" she screamed as she made her way to the barn. She scanned the yard. Adrenaline fueled her forward momentum and narrowed her vision.

Dear Lord, please let Sarah be okay. Please let her not be in the barn. Please Lord, let me find her now. Please, please, please…

She reached the barn with no sign of Sarah. The barn door was cracked open about a foot. Enough for a nine-year-old to easily slip through if she was looking for her kitty.

Hannah's stomach revolted.

Not wanting to feed the flames, she squeezed through the door. Black smoke swirled around her. Creaking wood and howling flames sent terror clawing at her heart.

"Sarah!" Smoke gagged her.

Covering her mouth with the damp dishcloth, she pushed forward. What she wouldn't do to not have this full, highly flammable skirt dangling around her legs.

She squinted and pushed farther into the barn. The

rough, dry hay felt brittle under her bare feet. Her throat narrowed. *No sign of Sarah.*

In his stall, Buttercup neighed wildly. Holding her breath and covering her mouth, Hannah ran to his stall and opened the gate. The sweet animal was too frightened to move.

Dear Lord, I don't have time for this frightened animal. Let me find Sarah.

She talked calmly to Buttercup and nudged him toward the door. Sensing freedom, he bolted outside to the open field.

Thank You, Lord.

Hannah sucked in a quick breath of fresh air at the door. "Sarah!" she yelled. "Sarah!" She covered her mouth with the damp cloth and slipped deeper into the barn.

Her lungs screamed for air. Stars danced in her line of vision. She opened the doors at the far end of the barn and shooed the cow out.

Panic and flames pushed in from all sides. "Sarah!"

A loud crack sounded. Terror squeezed the air from her lungs. She glanced up. A shadow descended on her.

Darkness.

Chapter Eight

Spencer had pulled onto the road and lifted Mrs. Greene's hot brew to his lips when his cell phone went off. He glanced down and smiled. *Hannah.* Surprised, he lifted the phone to his ear. "Morning."

Silence stretched across the line. His heartbeat kicked up a notch. His intuition told him something was wrong.

"Hannah? Are you there?" He waited what seemed like an eternity until he heard a little voice.

"My *aenti* needs help."

Spencer secured his coffee in the cup holder and pressed the phone tighter to his ear. "Emma?"

He did a quick check of traffic, made a U-turn and pushed the accelerator to the floor in the direction of the Lapps' farm. "What's going on, Emma?"

"There's a fire."

"Where?"

"The barn…" He strained to hear her soft voice above his thrumming heartbeat.

"Listen carefully, Emma. Stay away from the barn. I'm on my way."

"I'm scared."

"It's going to be okay. Where is your aunt?" He held his breath while waiting for the answer.

"The barn."

He swallowed around the lump of terror in his throat. "I'm on my way. Okay?"

Without waiting for an answer he ended the call and dialed dispatch. "Send a fire crew to the Lapp farm on County Route 77."

With his hot coffee roiling in his gut, he gripped the steering wheel tighter.

As he rounded the curve near the farm, he saw bright red flames shooting into the sky backed by ominous black clouds. Adrenaline surged through his veins. He slowed his vehicle and whipped into the driveway. His vehicle bobbed over the ruts in the driveway. He pushed open the door and ran to Emma crouched on the porch, her dress pooled around her legs. She held her faceless doll to her nose. Tears tracked down her cheeks.

Spencer clutched the little girl's arms. "Where's Hannah? Where's Sarah?" His words squeezed out from a too-tight throat.

Emma's watery eyes lifted to the barn.

"In the barn?"

Too frightened, Emma nodded.

"Okay." Spencer watched the black plume of smoke billowing up from the barn. The smell of charred wood made him cough. "Stay right here, Emma. The firemen will be here soon."

Sirens sounded in the distance. Spencer ran to his cruiser and popped the trunk. He grabbed a blanket and raced toward the fire.

A prayer came spontaneously to mind.

Dear Lord, please guide me. Let me find Sarah and Hannah safe.

When he reached the barn, the door yawned open. He pressed the blanket to his face and surged forward, holding his breath. Then his training kicked in. He dropped to all fours where the air wasn't so thick with smoke. He crawled into the barn, the rough feel of hay cutting into his hands.

Fear and panic like he'd never known propelled him forward. He didn't dare yell Sarah or Hannah's name for fear it would be his last breath.

Gloom and darkness pushed in on him from all sides. Heat and panic tightened the collar of his shirt.

Keep moving.

Something, a knowledge, a knowing, made him turn right. Splayed across the barn floor was Hannah. A beam blocked the view of her face. But it had to be Hannah.

He pushed forward and shoved the beam off Hannah's lifeless body. Terror seized his heart.

An image of Daniel flashed in his mind's eye. Too late; he was too late. Again.

He stared, frozen. Every mistake he had ever made in his past weighed down on him. Would this be the end?

In the flash of a moment, he thought of terrified Emma. Alone with her doll. Mustering a strength he didn't know he had, he drew in a shallow breath near the barn floor. It smelled of hay and charred wood and burning hair.

Spencer slid his hands under Hannah's body, one arm under her legs, the other around her shoulders. He plucked her off the ground and ran toward the exit holding his breath. When he was a safe distance from the barn, he laid Hannah on the grass.

He pushed Hannah's hair away from her face and leaned in close to listen for a breath. Over the roar of the fire and the cacophony of the rescue vehicles, he wondered if he imagined her breath. He pressed his fingers to the pulse point on her neck. *Thank You, Lord.* "Hannah, Hannah." He gently tapped her cheek.

Dear Lord, please let Hannah be okay.

He grabbed her arm and felt her pulse again.

The first hint of relief started pumping through his veins.

"Hannah," he said. "Hannah."

Hannah's eyelids fluttered. Hope blossomed in his chest.

A sputtering cough erupted from her throat. Spencer wrapped his arm around her shoulder and eased her to a seated position. Tears tracked down her dirty cheeks as she coughed and sucked in huge gulps of fresh air.

A firefighter ran to their side with his emergency kit. "Anyone else inside?"

Hannah's eyes grew wide. She struggled to stand, but Spencer made her stay on the ground. "You need to stay put."

"Sarah." She coughed again. "I can't find Sarah."

Hannah couldn't catch a breath. She coughed until tears streamed down her cheeks. Struggling against Spencer's firm hold, she tried to stand. She had to find Sarah.

The heat from the burning barn singed her cheeks. "I can't find Sarah." She covered her mouth with her hands, and grief nearly cut off what little breath she could draw into her lungs. "Sarah, she's nine…" She clawed at the firefighter's turnout gear. "You have to find her. She went into the barn looking for her cat. Please…"

The firefighter pulled away from her and patted Spencer on the shoulder. "Move her back." Then to Hannah, "We'll find your little girl."

"Please…"

The firefighter ran over to the other firefighters and gave them instructions she couldn't hear. But based on his urgent gesturing, it must have been that a child was trapped in the barn.

Spencer's hand felt heavy on her back. She wanted to fling it away and run into the barn herself. Find Sarah.

She'd die if something happened to Sarah. She had promised Ruthie she'd make sure her children were safe. An image of little Emma popped into her brain.

"Where's Emma?"

"She's fine." Spencer's voice was calm despite the chaos swirling around them. He pointed beyond the fire truck. A young female firefighter was crouched next to Emma. It looked like she was introducing a teddy bear to her doll.

A fist of grief tightened Hannah's throat. *"Mem…"*

"She's okay, too."

Hannah's gaze drifted to her mother standing in her doorway, clutching something to her chest.

Hannah bowed her head, feeling the weight of the world on her shoulders. She had let her sister down.

She had let poor, sweet Sarah down.

A firefighter came back over to them. He opened a huge medical kit, much like the toolbox her father used to have. "Ma'am, I'd like to look at that head injury."

Absentmindedly, Hannah touched her forehead and

pulled her hand away. Blood and soot marred her fingertips. "I'm fine."

Oh, she was far from fine. She lifted her arm; the effort sent a sharp pain through her upper arm. "Find my niece. Please. I'm fine."

The firefighter made eye contact with Spencer, who nodded. The firefighter walked away, but left his kit next to them.

Hannah struggled to her feet with Spencer's help. "I have to do something. I can't just stand here. Sarah's—" An explosive cracking sound filled the air. The roof of the barn collapsed into itself. A spray of sparks filled the air.

Terror pumped through her veins. Sarah had been her responsibility. Hers…

She pressed her palms together and touched her lips. *Please, Lord, bring Sarah safely back to me.*

The firefighters aimed their hoses at the fire. She turned toward Spencer, who gathered her into an embrace. She pulled away from him.

"Walk around that side of the barn."

Spencer narrowed his gaze at her.

"Please, I'll go around the other way. I have to do something."

Hannah strode around the barn. The acrid smell of burning wood filled her lungs. "Sarah!" she screamed. "Sarah!"

A quiet whimper caught her attention. She slowed her pace. The heat from the barn only ten feet away warmed her face. She stopped and strained her ears against the roaring fire, the fire hoses and the shouting of the firefighters.

"Sarah!"

Another whimper.

Hannah spun around and faced the trees. She ran to the edge. The fallen branches scraped her bare feet, her bare legs.

Hannah cupped her hands and shouted her niece's name again. She squinted into the dark shadows. Suddenly, a darker shadow rushed at her from the trees.

Sarah!

The child flung herself at Hannah, wrapping her arm around her waist and burying her head into her side. Tears blurred Hannah's vision as she smoothed the little girl's hair. She bent over and kissed Sarah's forehead. She smelled of fire and earth. And heaven. Pumpkin meowed in Sarah's other arm.

"Oh, sweetie," Hannah said into Sarah's hair, "are you okay?"

Sarah nodded.

A firm hand touched her shoulder. Hannah glanced up, and Spencer smiled down on her. "Is she okay?" he asked, his voice gruff.

"I think so."

Hannah reluctantly pried the little girl's arm from her waist and crouched to look at her. Flames danced in her terrified eyes. "I—" the little girl swallowed hard, her gaze drifting to the fire "—I wanted to see Pumpkin. I figured you made her go stay in the barn."

Hannah cupped Sarah's cheek. "Oh, sweetie. I didn't. She must have gotten out herself somehow. Did you go in the barn when it was on fire?" Scolding her now seemed ridiculous when everyone's emotions were running high.

Sarah shook her head. "The barn wasn't on fire. I found Pumpkin next to a hay bale. I started to get her when I heard a man yelling. Pumpkin ran past me and into the woods." She stroked the kitten's head. "I had to find her."

"You heard a man yelling?" Spencer asked.

Sarah nodded again.

"Did you see him?"

"No," Sarah said in a very soft voice. Her lips quivered.

Hannah rubbed her hand up and down her arm. "Did you hear what the man said?"

"He said, 'Get.'" Spencer and Hannah locked gazes. Tingles of fear rained down on her like hot sparks from the fire.

"Is that all?" Hannah forced a smile, trying to draw the child out.

"I don't know..." Sarah whispered. Hannah smoothed her hand over her niece's soft hair in much the same way as Sarah stroked her beloved kitten's head.

"It's okay, honey. It's okay."

Spencer wrapped his arm around Hannah's shoulder, and the three of them walked to the other side of the barn. Her mother stood on her porch with Emma.

Emma broke free and bolted toward them, her little arms pumping, a huge smile on her face. "You found Pumpkin!" Emma shoved her new bear in her big sister's face. "And I got a new toy."

Hannah cupped Emma's chin. Complete peace settled around her. She lifted up a silent prayer.

Thank You, Lord, for keeping my family safe.

The next morning, Spencer yawned and squinted against the rising sun as he drove out to check on Hannah. He grabbed his travel coffee mug from the cup holder and took a big swig. He was going to have to hook up an IV of caffeine to stay awake today.

Yesterday, once the fire was contained, Hannah had insisted she was fine and that Spencer leave.

He had questioned the neighbors, including the Fishers. No one had seen anything. Young Samuel claimed he had finished his chores and returned home before the fire started. He hadn't seen anything out of the ordinary and no, he hadn't seen Sarah out looking for her cat.

Twenty-four hours later, he had no evidence to prove differently.

When Spencer reached the farm, two buggies sat in the driveway. Apparently, word had gotten out about the barn fire. He stepped out of his pickup and strolled over to join Lester, the bishop, Willard and his son, Samuel. A regular party. But no sign of Hannah.

They were talking excitedly and pointing to the barn. They were probably planning a barn raising. He had watched the Amish with fascination gather for a weekend and construct a barn. Old-fashioned techniques did not mean inefficient.

"Officer Maxwell." Willard seemed to take in Spencer's casual clothes. "Any word on what caused this fire?"

Spencer crossed his arms and widened his stance. There was something about this guy that rubbed him the wrong way.

"It's still under investigation."

Willard lifted a skeptical eyebrow. "And you're working on your day off?"

Spencer didn't like the implication in his question, but he let it go.

Willard placed his hand on his son's shoulder. "My

son here saw something yesterday, and it's best if he tells you all at the same time."

Lester adjusted his hat back on his head and Bishop Lapp made a *hmm* sound.

Spencer's pulse whooshed in his ears. He shifted his gaze to Samuel. "Why didn't you tell me you saw something when I questioned you yesterday?"

Samuel kicked a clump of mud with his boot and shrugged. He cut a sideways glance to his father.

"The boy was afraid. That's all." Willard's authoritative tone left no room for discussion. "He's here now."

Samuel looked up, a hint of something indiscernible in his eyes. "I saw someone running out of the barn."

Spencer narrowed his gaze. He locked eyes with Willard then glanced back to his son.

"Go on." Willard nudged his son with his elbow. A flash of annoyance, and then fear crossed Samuel's features. The boy was seventeen, on the cusp of being a man. His father wasn't going to be able to bully him for much longer.

Samuel cleared his throat and looked Spencer in the eye. "I had finished cleaning Buttercup's stall when I heard heavy footsteps, too heavy to be Miss Wittmer's or one of the little girls…" Samuel seemed agitated as he plucked at his suspenders.

"I ducked behind some hay bales when I saw Mr. Lapp."

"Mr. Lapp?" An uneasy feeling settled in Spencer's gut.

"John Lapp," Willard added.

"You saw my son?" The pain and confusion in Bishop Lapp's tone was palpable.

"My boy," Willard continued, "saw John Lapp march

into his very own barn with a canister of gasoline. Only through *Gott*'s good will did my son escape."

"Are you saying Mr. Lapp started the fire and then ran out?" Spencer studied Samuel's face. Red blossomed on his cheeks. Willard never removed his hand from his son's shoulder.

Bishop Lapp bowed his head, his expression hidden by the broad brim of his hat.

"Why would my brother do such a thing?" Lester stepped closer to Samuel. "You have to be mistaken."

Samuel toed the hard-packed earth, freeing another clump of dirt. "He didn't see me. I ducked to the side and then when the flames started coming, I ran home."

"Why didn't you alert Hannah?" A mix of anger and disbelief hollowed out Spencer's gut.

Samuel swallowed hard. "*Yeh*, well, I was afraid. I heard the rumors…that he killed Mrs. Lapp. I wanted to get away. Far away."

Willard clapped his son's shoulder. "You did *gut*."

Lester let out a heavy sigh and ran his hand down his scraggly beard. A look of capitulation crossed the hard angles of his features. "I suppose John has been struggling. Only *Gott* knows what's in his heart. I fear I don't know my brother anymore."

"My son is alive." Bishop Lapp's shaky voice was almost inaudible, but Spencer caught the trace of hope in it. "John is alive."

Lester's brow furrowed. "*Dat*, this is not good news. John burned down his barn."

"My boy saw what he saw," Willard interrupted.

"My younger brother…" Lester pushed back his straw hat and shifted his feet, effectively blocking out Willard. The men obviously did not like each other.

"Would you like to talk in private?" Spencer offered.

Lester hesitated a minute. "*Neh*. My feelings in this community are no secret." He tugged on the brim of his hat. "My brother was not content to follow the *Ordnung*. He questioned the rules and our father all the time. My father is not a young man. He should have been respected. The rules of the *Ordnung* are agreed upon by the community. Yet John kept wanting to push his will on all of us."

"Were his ideas radical?" Spencer studied Samuel, who seemed fidgety.

"They were what you might call extreme," Lester said, somewhat apologetically. "He wanted the Amish of Apple Creek to stay separate from the rest of the world."

"I'm confused," Spencer said. "Aren't the Amish already separate?"

"We set ourselves apart. We are to follow Romans 12:2." Willard squared his shoulders and continued. "'Do not conform any longer to the pattern of this world, but be transformed by the renewing of your mind.'"

Lester held up his hand. "The sheriff didn't come here for us to preach at him. We all know how you feel about the Amish ways, Willard. If you and my brother had your way, we wouldn't interact at all with the English."

A muscle ticked in Willard's jaw. "The outside world is an evil place. We must protect our ways."

"We are both conservative and practical," Lester said, purposely not looking at Willard. "We know we can't completely isolate ourselves. We adapt as the world moves around us."

Willard seemed unusually quiet.

"What do you think, Mr. Fisher?"

"John and I were friends. But John deviated from the

path. He lost his way." Willard shook his head in obvious disgust, then he clapped his son on the shoulder. "Unless you need anything else from us, we have chores to do." He turned to Lester. "Let us know how we can help your family rebuild here."

Willard and Samuel climbed into their wagon and left.

"Mr. Lapp, you and your family need to be cautious until we take your brother into custody."

"I'd feel better if my nieces weren't staying here. My wife and I could keep them safe at our home now that it's obvious my brother is never going to be able to care for those girls."

"Sarah and Emma have their aunt." Spencer glanced toward the house. Still no sign of Hannah.

Shaking his head, Lester pursed his lips. "Those girls need to be in a stable family. With a proper *mem* and *dat*." He lifted his palm to the burned out remains of the barn. "Sarah could have been killed in that fire.

"I'm going to take the girls today. They've experienced enough tragedy in their short lives. The girls need to be raised in a proper Amish family." Lester fingered his beard.

"Perhaps the family can have a meeting and come to some sort of agreement." Spencer knew Hannah wasn't going to hand over her nieces.

"I will not agree to let my nieces stay under Miss Wittmer's care." Lester made a sound of disbelief.

The screen door creaked open, drawing Spencer, Lester and the bishop's attention. Hannah stepped onto the porch wearing jeans and a T-shirt. Her long brown hair flowed over her shoulders. She strode over to them, a determined look in her eyes.

"I'm done. I can't live like this anymore."

* * *

Hannah pushed open the door and stepped onto the porch. As if she had yelled, "Look at me," all eyes landed on her. But the face she focused on belonged to Sheriff Spencer Maxwell.

Why did she care so much about what he thought?

She pushed back her shoulders and a twinge of pain shot down her arm. Dismissing it, she strode across the yard, careful not to twist her ankle on one of the ruts. Her head pounded with each step. She planted her hands on her hips, trying to muster a confidence she didn't feel. "I'm done. I can't live like this anymore."

She ignored the smug look on Lester's face and instead focused on the hurt expression on Spencer's. "Can I talk to you in private?" she asked, trying to quell the tremble in her voice.

"Where are the girls? Fannie Mae and I will take them home right away."

Closing her eyes briefly, Hannah took a calming breath. "The girls are with their grandmother."

Lester strode toward the *dawdy haus*. Hannah ran after him and grabbed his arm. He stopped and looked down at her, then at her offending hand. She let go, but said in no uncertain terms, "Leave the girls, please. Give me a few minutes to talk to Spencer, then I'll explain everything."

Indecisiveness crossed Lester's face. He didn't say anything, but he didn't move, either.

Hannah held up her hand. "Give me a minute to talk to Spencer." She was surprised her words sounded so calm despite her dry mouth, her racing heart.

Lester cleared his throat. "I'm going to take some

measurements." He turned on his heel and walked toward the barn.

Hannah was too focused on her decision to register Lester's comment.

"Can I talk to you…on the porch?" Without waiting for an answer, Hannah stuffed her hands in her jeans pockets and walked toward the porch and hoped Spencer would follow. The calmness that had settled over her in the middle of the night—when she had made her decision to leave the farm—took flight and was replaced by a million butterflies flitting in her stomach. She hadn't planned on making the announcement to Lester and Bishop Lapp this soon.

She reached the porch and grabbed the railing. She lowered herself onto the second step, fearing her knees were going to give out.

Spencer sat next to her and patted her knee. "What's going on?"

Her gaze drifted to the burned-out barn. Willard had come by this morning with Samuel and had taken the animals over to his farm to care for them until her barn was rebuilt. She was sure she could talk Rebecca into keeping them long-term, unless… Her gaze drifted to Lester measuring up the barn.

Her focus faded. "I'm leaving the farm."

From the look on his face, Spencer seemed to be struggling with something. "You're going to let Fannie Mae and Lester raise the girls?"

Horror shot through her. "Oh, no. Absolutely not. I promised my sister I'd make sure they were taken care of. It was only after the fire that I realized I could take care of the girls much better if I…if I was living on my own terms."

"You've thought this through."

Hannah bowed her head and threaded her fingers through her hair. Had she thought this through? Or had she made a knee-jerk reaction to a near-death experience?

"Maybe it's for the best." Spencer gave her a boost of confidence.

"You're probably the only one who will agree."

Spencer shifted to look at her. Something in his expression made her blood pressure spike. "What is it?"

Spencer told her what Samuel had witnessed right before the fire. Hannah muttered, "I can't believe it…"

"I've notified dispatch. All patrols will keep an eye out for John."

Hannah pushed to her feet and swiped a hand across the seat of her pants. "Is that apartment in your building still available?"

"I'll call Mrs. Greene, my landlady."

"Thank you." She wrapped her hand around the railing. "I have to talk to my mother and the girls now."

Would she be able to talk her mother into moving with her?

Lester and Fannie Mae came to mind. If her mother wouldn't leave her residence, maybe she could get Lester to move into his brother's house. They could come to some agreement. They'd be close if her mother needed anything. And Hannah would still be in Apple Creek. They might treat her like an outsider, but there was no reason she had to be shunned.

Unease tickled the far reaches of her mind. Fannie Mae and Lester had always wanted the land to farm, didn't they? And Hannah was about to give them exactly what they wanted.

Chapter Nine

Instead of dragging the girls out of the only home they've ever known the exact day Hannah made her announcement, she decided to ease the girls into the transition. Now, a few days after she dropped the bomb in *typical* Hannah fashion—if she were to take Lester's mumblings to heart—she was still living in her sister's home. But not for long.

Hannah glanced out the window. She caught the tail end of a horse and buggy as it trotted down the street. She had a few more things she wanted to clean and tidy before Spencer arrived to drive them into town. His landlady, Mrs. Greene, was more than willing to rent the fully furnished apartment on a month-to-month basis.

Upstairs, Hannah found Emma stuffing her face-less doll into a suitcase Spencer had dropped off. Sarah sat stone-faced on the bed with her arms crossed over her middle. Hannah suspected she'd have to pack a few things for the older child.

Emma glanced up and smiled. "Do you think we could get one of those pretty dolls you mentioned? I'd like the dolly *Mem* made for me to have a friend."

"We'll have to buy a lot of things at first. Once we get settled, we can look into another doll." Thankfully, her car sold so she'd have a little extra money, but she'd have to be careful until she found a job. The apartment was located in the center of town, so she should be able to walk for necessities.

"Dolls are stupid." Sarah's harsh words snapped Hannah out of her musings.

"Sarah!" Hannah said, unable to keep the shock from her voice. *Lord, give me patience*, Hannah had prayed more than once.

She opened her mouth to offer some encouraging advice to her sullen preteen when she heard the door creak downstairs. She held up a finger. "Pack your things. We're moving to the apartment this afternoon. I don't want to keep Sheriff Maxwell waiting."

Sarah huffed.

"I know this is difficult, but things will get better. I promise." Hannah hustled down the stairs. She came up short in the kitchen when she found her mother sitting at the kitchen table. *"Mem."* She immediately ran a hand down her T-shirt and jeans.

"You're leaving today?" Her mother's voice had a faraway quality.

"I've delayed long enough." She pulled out the chair and sat across from her mother, guilt pinging her insides. "I'm worried about you out here."

Her mother waved a shaky hand in dismissal. *"Yah,* well. We've been over that. I must live in the Amish community."

Hannah had tried every argument to convince her mother to live with them in the apartment. But her mother was unwilling to walk away from her Amish faith, and that's what she was convinced she'd be doing if she left her home.

Hannah was deeply frustrated, sad, but she understood. Her mother was a humble Amish woman.

"Well… Rebecca's nearby if you need anything. And soon Lester and Fannie will be living in Ruthie's house."

The lines deepened around her mother's mouth. "I suppose it will be *gut* to have someone farming the land again."

"I'll work with a lawyer to make sure Lester pays you a fair price for the land."

"*Gott* will see me through."

"I'll only be a few miles away." The words did nothing to ease the guilt weighing heavily on her.

"You'll be further away in your heart." Her mother's gaze was unwavering.

"I want you to see your granddaughters as much as possible. I hope we can do that."

Her mother studied the table. She ran her gnarled hand along its edge. "It seems like only yesterday I was feeding you and your sister at this table."

Her mother drew in a deep breath, filling her lungs. Hannah stopped and watched her mother, a million conflicting emotions tugging at her heart. "*Mem*, I'm sorry I couldn't stay. I tried…" Her words rang hollow. How hard had she tried? She had only been here for a couple weeks.

But the fire. The fire had cemented her decision. A decision she had struggled with from the minute she slipped on her sister's black Amish dress and tried to pick up Ruthie's life where she had left off.

She couldn't do it. She had to live her life as best

she could given she now had two little girls who were counting on her.

Her mother reached out and pulled her hand into hers, something very uncharacteristic for her mother. "You were never happy here."

Time seemed to slow around them. *"Mem..."*

Her mother shook her head. "Your father was hard on you. Harder than he ever was on my Ruthie..."

A flush of warmth rolled over her. Something about the way her mother said *my Ruthie* made her both sad and jealous.

Hannah was about to protest when her mother squeezed her hand and said, "When I was eighteen, I left Apple Creek... I was a lot like you." She lifted her watery eyes.

A lump formed in Hannah's throat. Her mother had left Apple Creek?

"I met a nice man. An *Englischer*." Her lips flattened into a thin line. "I thought we were going to be married."

Hannah listened, fascinated, her heartbeat pulsing in her ears. She had never known this part of her mother's life.

Her mother's gaze dropped to the scarred pine table. "I got pregnant."

Hannah stifled a gasp, one of surprise, not of disapproval. The last thing she wanted was for her mother to think she disapproved or was being judgmental.

Emma ran into the kitchen, her loud footsteps snapping Hannah out of her intense focus.

"Sarah said she's staying here, but I want to go with you." The determined set of Emma's jaw reminded Hannah of Ruthie.

Hannah ran her shaky fingers over her niece's silky hair. The little girl had grown fond of leaving her hair down.

Eager to continue the conversation with her mother, Hannah swallowed hard. "Go upstairs with your sister. Tell her I'll be up in a minute to talk. Okay? Look around and make sure you have everything you might need. Hairbrush, your doll..." She'd have to buy new clothes for the girls once they started their new life, but for now, they had to gather what they could.

Emma nodded and spun around, the skirt of her dress flaring out. She watched her niece run away and thump up the stairs. Muffled complaints floated down the stairs.

Hannah shifted to face her mother and covered her mother's hands. "What happened?"

"We were supposed to get married. We were making plans. He was hit while riding his bike to class at the university..." Her mother got a faraway look, and she shook her head.

A ticking began in Hannah's head. A warm flush of realization washed over her. She swallowed around a knot of emotion. "I'm that baby."

Her mother set her jaw and closed her eyes briefly, her shame so deep she couldn't say the words.

Hannah jerked back and pulled her hands down into her lap. In one instant, she had learned her father wasn't her father, and her real father was dead. She blinked back dizziness.

Her mother folded her hands in front of her and hiked her chin. "I came back to Apple Creek, heartbroken. Ashamed."

Hannah fought back the tears. She wanted to ask her

mother a million questions but feared she'd stop sharing altogether.

"I married Eli Wittmer, a good Amish man. He had always been sweet on me before I got worldly ideas." She sniffed and closed her eyes. "He accepted the child I was carrying as his own. No one knew any differently."

Her mother closed her eyes and nodded. "Your father, the man who raised you, saved me from shame. He allowed me to be a respectable Amish woman."

Mesmerized by the in and out of her own breaths, Hannah reframed her entire life. It made sense, explaining why the only father she had known favored Ruthie, his true daughter, while coming down hard on her.

"Eli was a good man, but he looked at you and remembered what I had done." Her mother unthreaded her fingers and threaded them again. "I'm sorry. It wasn't your fault."

The walls pulsed, and a bead of sweat rolled down Hannah's back. "*Mem*, why are you telling me this now?"

Her mother's lips pursed then relaxed. "You need to follow your heart. You were never happy here. Go. I know Ruthie would want you to raise her daughters, even if it's not on this farm in the Amish community."

She squeezed her mother's hand. A tear trailed down Hannah's cheek, but she didn't bother to wipe it away. The information her mother had shared, although difficult for both of them, had been an amazing gift.

"Lester and Fannie Mae are going to fight me for the girls."

"Do what you have to do to keep them." Her mother put her palms on the table and stood. She cupped Hannah's cheek. "I was happy raising my family here, in the Amish community. But I can see in your eyes, this life is not for you." She coughed and put her fisted hand to her mouth. "Just promise me a few things."

Hannah waited.

"Make sure you visit me often. I can't bear to lose you and your sister *and* my granddaughters."

"Of course. I'm not leaving Apple Creek."

Her mother gave her a knowing look. "Oh, I fear you will. But wherever you go, make sure you keep *Gott* in your life. In all of your lives."

Hannah swiped a hand across her wet cheek. "I will, *Mem*. I will…"

"But why can't I keep the cat?" Sarah whined from the backseat of Spencer's truck. She had Pumpkin curled up in her lap. His heart went out to the little girl.

Hannah shifted in her seat, her features strained. "Sweetie, the apartment doesn't allow us to have animals. My friend Rebecca said she'd take good care of Pumpkin."

"What if she runs away? She ran away before."

Spencer cut a sideways glance to Hannah. She blinked slowly a few times, as if giving it some thought…or praying for strength. "Pumpkin found her way to us, right? God was looking out for her. We fed her and made sure she had someplace safe to sleep. She's a smart cat. She'll be fine."

In the rearview mirror, Spencer watched Sarah smoothing her hand down the kitten's head and back.

"God will make sure Pumpkin is cared for," Hannah reassured the child.

"Maybe God wants *us* to protect Pumpkin."

Hannah slumped into the seat and tugged on the seat belt, defeated.

When Spencer pulled in front of the Fishers' property, Sarah instinctively tucked Pumpkin under her chin.

"Come on, you can show Pumpkin her new home," Hannah said, forcing a cheery tone.

They all climbed out and headed toward the barn in back. "We can say hello to Buttercup, too," Hannah added. Rebecca's family had taken in all their animals displaced by the barn fire. Although tragic, the barn fire and the subsequent removal of the animals from the farm had allowed Hannah to make the choice to leave. A part of Spencer felt hopeful this meant a possible future for them.

Spencer resisted the urge to reach out and place a reassuring hand on Hannah's back. She looked as if she was ready to bolt, as if she expected Willard to storm out of the house and demand she get off his property now that she had fully embraced her English roots.

The door creaked open, and Rebecca hustled toward them, a look of worry on her face. "Samuel is gone. I've checked everywhere, and he's gone!"

Hannah clutched her friend's arm. "What do you mean?"

"He must not have come home last night." Her eyes blazed with fear.

"I'll have patrols keep an eye out for him, but boys his age do that on occasion."

"Oh, I don't know. Willard wouldn't like law enforcement to get involved."

"He doesn't have to know," Spencer reassured her.

"I shouldn't go against my husband. He's out looking for him." Rebecca dipped her head. "At least we know he's not hiding in your barn. The fire took care of that."

Resentment or something else flattened Rebecca's lips into a thin line.

"I never encouraged him to hang out in my barn to read." Hannah's tone was rightfully defensive.

"Perhaps you didn't discourage him enough."

Hannah opened her mouth then snapped it shut.

Spencer brushed his hand briefly across Hannah's back, a silent show of support.

"Why do you think he left?" Spencer considered a few scenarios. Could he have been responsible—perhaps accidentally—for the barn fire and run away in guilt? Perhaps he had lied about seeing John Lapp there to protect himself.

"Samuel's been hanging around the wrong people," Rebecca said quietly. "The stricter his father got with Samuel, the more he rebelled." She kept cutting her gaze toward the barn. When Willard strolled out, Spencer understood why.

"We came to drop off the cat," Hannah said.

Willard's hard gaze shifted to the cat in Sarah's arms. "Go on and put it down, child. That cat'll be fine. We'll see that it's fed. And we'll have a few less field mice around here for our troubles." He let out a gruff laugh.

Sarah buried her face in the kitten's fur before setting the cat down on the ground. If only Mrs. Greene wasn't allergic.

Willard cleared his throat. "My wife is sharing news of my Samuel. He'll be fine. He's doing what some young Amish boys do. He'll come home once he gets it out of his system. I did. He'll realize worldly ways are not for him."

Willard scrubbed a hand across his unkempt beard. "Now, about Sarah and Emma…"

Hannah reached out and clutched Emma's hand, tugging her closer. Sarah stood with her chin pressed to her chest, watching Pumpkin explore the long grass near the edge of the barn.

"The girls and I will be fine. Thank you for caring for the animals." Hannah seemed to be measuring each word. "Come on girls, let's go."

"There are plenty of Amish families that would willingly take in Sarah and Emma Lapp."

"They are my nieces." Hannah turned and strode toward the truck.

Emma skipped next to her, holding her hand, oblivious to the tension hanging in the air. Sarah followed, begrudgingly, unwilling to leave Pumpkin behind.

"They are meant to be raised Amish," Willard called out as Spencer helped the girls get into the truck. He opened the door for Hannah.

Spencer slammed the door. "Hannah will make sure her nieces are well cared for." He narrowed his gaze, cautioning Willard to back off, as he walked around to the driver's side.

Once inside the truck, Spencer turned to Hannah. "What do you make of Samuel taking off?"

"I'm not sure. He's afraid of Willard."

"Hmm… I remember being afraid of my father when I was a kid. I did some boneheaded things when I was young, and I knew my father was going to make sure I stayed on the straight and narrow." Spencer turned the key in the ignition. "That's what happens when your father's a cop. He understood what was at stake if I screwed up."

"My father was strict with me." There was a faraway quality to her voice. "And I ran away."

"That makes three of us." He thought of the girlfriend and law practice he had left behind. He tipped his head and unsuccessfully tried to coax a smile out of her.

"I fear there's a big difference here. Samuel has been at the center of some suspicious activities. Do you think this makes him look guilty?"

Spencer slipped the gear into Drive. "It doesn't scream innocent."

Emma sat on her new bed in the apartment and bounced. "I have my own bed? I don't have to share with my sister?" The awe and sincere excitement in her young niece's voice warmed Hannah's heart after a rough couple of weeks.

"You should find everything you need to get settled." Mrs. Greene ran her hand down the hand-stitched quilt, probably made by one of the Amish women looking to earn extra money. The irony wasn't lost on Hannah.

"Thank you so much, Mrs. Greene. I appreciate your letting us move in so quickly."

Mrs. Greene waved in dismissal. "It was sitting empty. And I like having it occupied. I don't feel quite so alone. Sheriff Maxwell has been busy lately and hasn't had time for our evening chats." Her blue eyes twinkled. "I guess now I understand where he's been."

Hannah opened her mouth to protest and settled on a smile instead.

Mrs. Greene walked toward the bedroom door and patted the door frame. "I'm right downstairs if you need anything."

"Thank you." Hannah turned to her older niece. "Do you think you'll like it here, Sarah?"

Sarah stuffed a dress into the drawer, shoved it closed with her hip and narrowed her eyes at her watchful aunt.

Hannah slipped out of the bedroom, letting the girls get used to their new surroundings. She found Spencer unloading groceries in the kitchen. "Thank you."

He turned around, a warm smile on his handsome face. "It's the least I can do."

Hannah slumped into the kitchen chair and rested her chin on the heel of her hand. "Do you think I'm doing the right thing?" Her head was swirling with all the changes.

With news of her biological father.

But she couldn't share any of that with Spencer for fear of betraying her mother. It was a heavy burden to bear.

Spencer placed the instant coffee on the shelf in the pantry and turned to face her. "You've made a lot of tough decisions in your life."

"Like leaving the Amish for the first time?"

He nodded. "That had to be the toughest decision."

She rubbed her forearms. "This is harder because now I'm making decisions for my nieces." She glanced toward the bedroom to make sure they couldn't hear them talk. "Emma seems up for the adventure. But I'm afraid Sarah will never forgive me. She thinks I'm going against everything her parents raised her to believe."

Wasn't she?

She looked up and found Spencer watching her, a look in his eyes that she couldn't quite define.

"How can I make such a huge decision for them? What if I'm wrong? What if they end up—" she shook her head "—I don't know on drugs or..."

Spencer slipped into the chair across from hers and covered her hand. "No parent knows for sure they're making the right decision. You'll have to have faith, right?"

A smile tugged on the corners of her mouth. "I'm surprised to hear you talking about faith." She narrowed her gaze. "Or are you humoring me?"

"I'm here for you. For whatever you need." They locked gazes. He leaned across the table, and her heartbeat kicked up a notch. He leaned and brushed his lips against hers. Warmth coiled around her heart.

She pulled back and pressed her fingers to her mouth.

A half smile quirked his lips. "I'm sorry."

She shook her head slowly. "No, don't be sorry." A new feeling, hope maybe, made her smile. "The kiss was nice, but I have so many things going on right now. I can't think straight."

Spencer pushed away from the table and stood. He brushed his hand across her shoulder. "I have to go, but you know how to reach me."

"Thank you." She had been saying that a lot lately. She sighed heavily and listened to his footsteps retreat across the hall to his apartment. From the girls' bedroom she heard arguing. Her shoulders slumped, and all the energy and determination that had driven her to march out of her sister's home in jeans and a T-shirt evaporated.

Since Hannah had sold her car, she was glad the apartment she rented was within walking distance from town.

In usual fashion, Emma skipped alongside Hannah and chatted while Sarah was her moody self. Hannah felt a little guilty for not giving the poor girl more slack, but Hannah was doing everything she could think of to bring the nine-year-old around. When they reached the thrift shop, Hannah decided to look for clothes for

Emma first, hoping Sarah would eventually warm up to the idea.

Hannah pulled out a few pretty tops and khaki pants for Emma. The little girl grabbed them excitedly. She was extra excited when her aunt added a bright pink skirt, so different than the plain clothes she was accustomed to.

As expected, Sarah was much harder to please. Everything she touched was in dull blues and browns. Hannah pulled out a bright purple skirt and a white blouse with blue and purple flowers on the collar. It wasn't exactly what nine-year-olds in the city would wear, but it seemed to be a nice compromise—a transition between her Amish clothes and the English world she was being forced to enter.

Hannah watched Sarah's tentative expression as she fingered the flowers on the collar. A faraway look descended into her eyes. After a moment, she looked up. "*Mem* liked pink roses." Her face grew flushed and her eyes shiny. "I miss *Mem*."

Hannah's heart crumbled. Deep inside this petulant child was a little girl who missed her mother. Holding back tears, Hannah reached out and pulled Sarah into an embrace. "I miss her, too." Hannah traced Sarah's long braid with a finger. "I know this is hard for you. I promised your mom I'd make sure you were well taken care of, and this is the only way I know how."

Sarah buried her head into Hannah's side and nodded. "I wasn't very good out on the farm."

"We'll do much better in town. And we'll be close to Granny and your other family."

Sarah stepped back and held the skirt. "I like this

one. Do you think I could get some of those shoes I saw over there?"

Hope blossomed in Hannah's chest. "Show me."

The three of them wound their way around the racks of clothes to a display of colorful sneakers.

"Of course." Hannah playfully tugged on a strand of Emma's hair. "Let's try on a pair for you, too."

Ten minutes later, they walked out of the store, the girls dressed in their new English clothes. Emma fit in quite nicely in her purple sweatpants and T-shirt with a kitty on it. Sarah looked cute, but a little dated in her long skirt and Peter-Pan-collar blouse.

Small steps.

Her heart burst with joy and hope.

A police cruiser pulled up alongside the curb, and Hannah squinted against the sun reflecting off the windshield. The door swung open, and Spencer climbed out. The serious expression on his face made her good mood evaporate. Something was wrong. Definitely wrong.

Hannah leaned over and said to the girls, "Go look at the cute things in that window." Emma ran ahead to peer into the boutique window. "Go on now." Hannah nudged Sarah when the girl didn't move. After the second prompt, Sarah did as she was told.

"What's wrong?" Hannah asked Spencer.

Spencer took off his hat and sunglasses. She didn't want to explore the look in his eyes. She wanted to hold on to the feeling of hope she had only moments ago.

"Is it my mother?" Terror seized her heart. She should have never left her mother alone on the farm. She should have forced her to come to the apartment with her.

"No," Spencer said, "it's John Lapp."

"You arrested him?" Panic seized her heart. Her eyes

drifted to her nieces. *He's going to claim he's innocent, and he's going to fight for custody of the girls.* The girls she was finally winning over.

"It's not what you think."

Hannah pressed a hand to her heart. The world narrowed to a small tunnel. "What happened?"

"Hikers found John Lapp's body in the woods. It looks like he killed himself."

Her heart dropped. She looked over at the girls. Emma was pointing out a stuffed kitten in the window to her sister. Sarah was only half paying attention, seemingly more interested in her and Spencer, but she was too far away to hear them.

Panic heated her cheeks. *Oh, what was she going to tell sweet Emma and Sarah?*

Another piece of her heart shattered for her nieces.

Emma and Sarah's father was dead. There would be no goodbyes. No tearful jailhouse visits.

Nothing.

Her brother-in-law had taken the coward's way out. He had killed himself. She plucked her T-shirt away from her heated skin. She couldn't think straight through the haze of anger.

"We'll never know what happened or why—" she lowered her voice even more "—with Ruthie."

Spencer cleared his throat. "John Lapp left a note."

Hannah's heart stuttered. *A note?*

Spencer seemed to be watching her warily, as if he feared she was going to pass out on the sidewalk. He touched her arm lightly. "It would be best if you and the girls came down to the station."

"Oh, okay." Hannah forced the words out. She didn't know how much more the girls could take.

A quiet calm descended over her.

Maybe with John gone, they could finally get on with their lives.

Maybe.

Chapter Ten

The sheriff's station was surprisingly busy for a small town. Spencer led Hannah and her nieces across the office. Seated in a far corner were Fannie Mae, Lester and Bishop Lapp. Hannah reflexively squeezed her nieces' hands. *She* was going to raise them. She had promised her sister.

"I didn't know everyone was going to be here," Hannah whispered, leaning forward so only Spencer could hear.

"We decided it best if everyone was here when we read John's letter." Spencer glanced down at the girls; a hesitant expression flashed across his face.

"What about Sarah and Emma? They shouldn't be here."

Spencer held out his palm. A young woman dressed in a uniform approached them. "Hello," the officer said, smiling brightly. "I'm Officer Pyne. Perhaps the girls would like to come with me and have some cookies and juice."

Hannah squeezed the girls' hands again. "It's okay.

Go with Officer Pyne. I'll be right over here talking with the grown-ups."

Emma went eagerly, but in usual form, Sarah seemed hesitant. She went along all the same. Hannah stood rooted in place as she watched the girls follow Officer Pyne into an adjacent room Hannah assumed was the break room.

Nerves tangling in her stomach, Hannah joined the small group clustered in a corner lined with uncomfortable-looking beige plastic chairs. Knees going weak, Hannah sat, leaving two open spaces between her and Fannie Mae. The Amish woman shifted her knees toward her husband, who sat on the far side of her as if Hannah had somehow offended her.

"Thank you all for coming here under short notice." Spencer walked around his desk and grabbed a folded piece of paper from the drawer. "I'm sorry for your loss."

John Lapp's father, the bishop, made a sound of discomfort and leaned on his cane heavily as he lowered himself into a chair. "My youngest son lost his way a long time ago."

Lester sat rigid. By his side, Fannie Mae fidgeted with her skirt. "Now that we know John's…" Fannie Mae couldn't get the word *dead* out of her mouth. "Lester and I should take the girls. They belong with us. They need to be raised in an Amish family." She held out her hand. "*She* has them dressed like *Englischers*. Their parents would be so disappointed."

Hannah scooted to the edge of her chair, her heart pounding in her ears. "Now, wait a minute…"

"We have a lot to sort out." Spencer held up his hand. "Let me read the letter John left. It was found next to his body."

Nausea clawed at Hannah's throat. How desperate John must have been to kill her sister and then kill himself. *Lord, give me strength to get through this day.*

The bishop crossed his wrists on his cane and bowed his head, as if bracing himself.

Hannah tucked her hands under her thighs and pulled her arms close to her body. Suddenly, she was very, very cold. The air-conditioning pumping out from the ceiling vent didn't help. She clenched her mouth to keep her teeth from chattering.

Spencer unfolded the letter. "This is a copy of the letter. The original is evidence." He lifted his eyes and locked gazes with Hannah before he started to read.

"Sorry. I hurt many people. I pray Gott forgives me. Sarah and Emma should be raised by my brother Lester Lapp. He and his wife have a gut home."

The chatter in the room swirled around Hannah's head. The voices sounded loud, garbled, unintelligible. The walls closed in on her. The papers on the bulletin board swirled and blended and loomed out, a moving 3-D collage. She blinked. Her palms grew moist. Panic made her want to flee. She closed her eyes and drew in a few deep breaths, trying to tamp down her emotions. She willed herself to focus.

Opening her eyes, she blinked back the sight of Spencer crouched in front of her, a look of concern on his handsome face.

"You okay?"

Hannah blinked a few more times. She looked up to find three more pairs of eyes on her. Lester offered her a cup of water. She took a sip and her light-headedness subsided.

Seeming satisfied that she was fine, Lester said to

Spencer, "So, it's settled then. We'll take Emma and Sarah home to live with us."

Alarm swept over Hannah. She jumped to her feet and felt the hard plastic of the chair pressing against the back of her knees. She swallowed hard and prayed for strength. "Nothing is settled. Not if you think you're going to take my nieces from me. My sister—" she lowered her voice for fear the girls might hear "—was killed by your brother. My sister asked that I make sure her children were cared for."

"Ruth would want her children to be raised Amish." Fannie Mae clasped her hands and pressed them to her chest. "You may think I'm stern, but I only want what's best for the girls. I would be a *gut mem*."

For the first time, Hannah noticed a softness, a sincerity, about the woman she had initially overlooked. Hannah bit the inside of her cheek then finally found the words, "I am going to raise the girls."

Lester threw up his hands. "My brother expressed his interests, too. Don't his wishes count?" His question was obviously directed to Spencer. "He specifically documented what he wanted."

"The note is not a legally binding document, if that's what you're asking. We don't even know if he wrote it."

Lester blinked rapidly under the brim of his straw hat. "Who would have written it? Are you suggesting he didn't kill himself?"

Hannah watched Spencer carefully. He kept a neutral expression that did nothing to calm her nerves.

"We have no reason to believe your brother's death is anything more than what it looks like on the surface." Spencer crossed his arms over his broad chest and stepped closer to Hannah. "This letter does not give Lester and Fannie Mae legal custody of Emma and Sarah."

Lester bristled. "We don't have to live within your legal system."

"What can I do, Spencer? Can I file for full custody of the girls now that we know their father isn't coming back?" Hannah hated the desperate tone of her voice.

"This isn't something we can resolve right now. I suggest you allow the girls to stay where they are and maybe the two families can come to some sort of agreement. A judge will have the final say."

The bishop, who had sat quietly all this time, pushed to his feet. "*Neh*, the children cannot spend part of the time in the outside world and the other part as Amish children. It would lead to much confusion."

"I am not going to hand them over." Hannah lifted a shaky hand to push back her hair.

"I did not suggest you turn them over," the bishop said. "I ask that everyone go home and pray. Pray that we make the right decision for these two orphans."

Hannah slowly shifted her attention toward the break room where her nieces were probably drinking soda and having a treat, blissfully unaware. They were the true victims.

A sharp pain jabbed her stomach. How was she going to tell her nieces their father was dead?

Spencer escorted the Lapps to the exit, then returned and found Hannah sitting where he had left her.

He sat. "You okay?"

She nodded but didn't say anything for a long time. When she finally looked up, her eyes shimmered with unshed tears. "John's really gone?"

"Yes."

She nodded again and swiped a tear. "How likely do you think it is that I'll get to keep the girls?"

He searched her eyes. "Is that what you want?"

She rubbed her forehead. "I believe it's best for the girls."

"Then I recommend you go through the legal system. I suspect Lester and Fannie Mae will fight it, but it's the only hope you have."

"Okay, okay..." Hannah seemed to come to some sort of conclusion. She pushed to her feet. "I need to get the girls. Get them home." She sucked in her lips. "I have to tell them about their father."

"I can come with you."

She nodded, a mournful expression on her face.

"Give me five minutes, and I'll take you home."

"I need to pull myself together before I face them."

Spencer squeezed her shoulder in a show of comfort then crossed the office space to a filing unit. His fellow officer, Mark Reynolds, approached. "Looks like you were right all along. That John Lapp was up to no good. He was the one who attacked the church elders and cut their beards in the middle of the night."

"We still have a lot of unanswered questions," Spencer said noncommittally, yanking open a file drawer.

Mark rested his beefy arm on the credenza. "Why defend him? The guy spelled it out in his suicide note. He was mad at the elders for not enforcing stricter rules." Mark rolled his eyes. "Who knew an Amish man would want stricter rules?"

"I didn't share that part of the note with the family."

"You can't tell me a guy who kills his wife and offs himself wasn't the guy who broke into the homes and whacked the beards off some old Amish guys. He was a loose cannon. You called it. Looks like we'll be able to close two cases."

"Show a little respect. We need to give the family time to grieve before we interview them about the beard-slashing case." His fellow officer's lack of sympathy bugged him. "The bishop lost his son."

Mark shrugged. "Do you think Ruth Lapp knew what her husband was up to?"

A familiar guilt nudged Spencer. If he had identified John as the perpetrator earlier, could he have saved Ruthie?

Unable to sleep, Hannah climbed out of bed and checked on Sarah and Emma. The girls both were sound asleep in their twin beds. Blessed sleep. Sarah had the sheet partially over her face, and Emma had her leg flung over the edge. Sleeping as she lived, with complete abandon. The poor sweet girls had been through more than most people had in a lifetime. When Hannah had broken the news of their father's death, Sarah cried quietly, and Emma appeared less affected, plucking at the hem of her doll's plain dress. It was almost as if Emma hadn't expected her father to come back anyway. Or maybe she was too young to fully understand.

Hannah walked through her upstairs apartment and double-checked the locks on the interior door and windows. She wished she had some sort of definitive answer from Spencer that John had been the one and only bad guy. With him dead, were she and the girls safe? Spencer had cautioned her that they still had to determine a time of death. The adrenaline pulsing through her veins made it difficult to think straight.

Emma had claimed she saw Samuel running away after her clothes were tarred. But that may have been a teen prank or again, maybe Emma was mistaken. Samuel had claimed he saw John and perhaps he had run away in fear.

Hannah plopped down on the couch and pulled back the sheer curtains and stared over the dark yard. She squinted. Was that a shadow lurking beyond the ring of light cast by the lone streetlight? She dropped the curtain and slumped into the couch. She couldn't shake the feeling someone was out there. Watching her apartment. Waiting for her.

You're safe. John's dead.

And Spencer lived right across the hall.

Footsteps sounded in the hallway. She crept to the door and peered through the peephole. Spencer was unlocking his apartment across the hall. Hannah finger-combed her hair and opened the door.

Spencer turned, a tired and surprised look on his face. "It's late."

"I couldn't sleep."

He slipped his hands into his pockets. "You've had a rough few weeks."

"I'm not worried about me." She drew in a breath and let it out. "I'm worried about the girls." She rested her hip against the door frame. "Did you see anyone outside when you were coming in?"

Spencer shook his head. "Was there someone out there?"

Hannah shook her head briskly, immediately doubting herself. "It was probably shadows. I'm on edge."

Spencer put his bag down. "I'll go check it out."

Hannah grabbed his hand as he passed. "No, don't. I'm sure it was nothing."

Spencer lowered his gaze to her hand touching his and smiled. She quickly clasped her hands behind her back.

"Have a seat." Spencer gestured to the top step.

Hannah sat and rested her shoulder against the wall and shifted to face him. He did the same, and their knees brushed. She wished life could be just this simple: two people sitting in the stairwell talking on a quiet summer evening.

"Do you think I'm doing the right thing?" Hannah hated the uncertainty in her voice.

"What does your heart say?"

She lowered her eyes and studied a chip in the pale blue paint near the pine molding on the stairs. "I can't live as an Amish person. It's not who I am. Not anymore. But what about Sarah and Emma?"

"Do you think they'd be happy with the Lapps?"

Memories of her father's stern rebukes flashed in her mind's eye. With the new information her mother had shared about her real father, Hannah was now reframing her childhood in a new light. It didn't justify her father's angry outbursts, but it explained why he favored Ruthie, his *real* daughter.

"What?" Spencer tapped her leg gently. "You seem a million miles away."

"Searching for happiness is an English convention. The Amish live God-fearing, humble lives. Community centered. What if…" A horrible idea came to mind. What if her bad decisions prevented Sarah and Emma from eternal life in heaven?

No…

That had been a threat the Amish held over the unbaptized to keep them in line, but even humble Amish didn't feel they were guaranteed heaven. It was a hope. And Hannah had hope in her Christian faith even if she decided not to be baptized Amish. Once her life settled down, she'd follow through with joining a local church with her nieces.

She looked up and locked eyes with him. "I believe that as long as you have faith and you're a Christian, and you live a good life, then it's okay." She tipped her head, and her hair fell in a curtain to cover her face. "Then I think about what a crazy world this is, and I wonder if the sheltered life of the Amish would be better for them."

"The world *is* a crazy place. I thought by coming to Apple Creek, I could escape some of the harshness of it." He sniffed and shifted on the stair, leaning his elbows on his knees. "As you know, before coming here, I worked in Buffalo." He turned his face away from her, but the pain was evident in his voice. "Through an outreach group, I befriended a high-risk boy. He was fourteen…"

Was fourteen…

"I thought I was making a difference. But I couldn't save him from the violence of drugs and gangs. He was shot and killed outside a convenience store running an errand for his mom. He was wearing the wrong colors that day, and a rival gang took him out. I should have been able to do more." He turned and looked at her. The pain in his eyes cut her to the core.

"Like what?"

"I had made a few phone calls about getting his family moved to subsidized housing in the suburbs, but I got distracted. Busy with the job."

Hannah's heart broke for him.

"Is that why you left Buffalo?"

"Let's just say I had reached my breaking point." He gave her a sad smile. "My fiancée…well, my ex-fiancée had been on me. We met in law school. She had dreams of a nice life in the suburbs, big house, kids."

Hannah tipped her head. "What's wrong with that?"

"Nothing. But she didn't count on her lawyer boyfriend going into law enforcement."

"Why did you? I mean, when you could have made more money as a lawyer."

"I wasn't happy practicing law. I wanted to get out there and do something directly to help people. As much as my dad grumbled about his job as a cop, I admired him. I know some lawyers find a way to help people, but I wanted to be a cop since I was a kid. My father pushed me to be a lawyer. Then my girlfriend pushed me to stay a lawyer. When I passed the officer exam and entered the police academy, she thought it was a phase. Our relationship didn't survive my new career."

"I'm sorry."

His smile made her forget her troubles. "I'm not. All our choices send us down a path. The road might be littered with obstacles, but if things came too easily, we might not appreciate them." He lifted an eyebrow. "God has a plan."

"God has a plan," she repeated. "You seem to have had a change of heart yourself." Warmth blossomed in Hannah's heart.

"You've been a positive influence on me. I never knew someone with such strong faith in times of adversity. You made me reexamine my own faith."

She tilted her head and smiled. "That's probably the nicest thing anyone has ever said to me."

Half of Spencer's mouth quirked into a smile. He

leaned in and pressed a warm kiss to her lips. She reached up and cupped his cheek, scratchy from his five o'clock shadow. She pulled back and smiled. "Why does everything have to be so complicated?"

A twinkle lit his eyes in the dim light. "Want the absolute truth?"

Her heart beat loudly in her ears. "Can I handle the truth?" She laughed, an awkward squeak.

"I have never met anyone quite like you, and I need to open my heart to you."

Hannah's mouth went dry.

"I don't want you to be baptized Amish. I don't want you to leave Apple Creek. I want to see if this—" he waved his hand between them "—is going anywhere."

"I…" Hannah couldn't think straight.

Spencer held up his hand. "But in the end, you have to make the best decision for you."

Her heart beat wildly. "And the girls," she whispered.

"And the girls," he repeated, a look of hope in his eyes. "No one can define you. Only you should be able to define you. If it's in God's plans, I want to be part of your life."

Chapter Eleven

On his morning off, Spencer ran over to the bakery and picked up cinnamon rolls for Hannah and the girls. He also grabbed coffee.

He whistled as he strolled up the walk. Mrs. Greene was sitting on the porch knitting. "You seem very chipper today."

"If I had known you'd be up so early, I would have bought you a coffee."

She tapped the handle of her teacup. "I'm having a spot of tea."

Spencer put down the bag and cup holder and sat across from Mrs. Greene. "How are you today?"

"I didn't sleep well last night. I heard you and Hannah talking in the stairwell."

"I'm sorry."

She waved him off. "No worries. I'm an old lady. We don't sleep well anyway." She tucked in her chin and studied him for a minute. "Oh, don't worry, I wasn't listening. I heard your voices, not the details of your conversation. I had to make sure no one was up to no good."

He smiled.

"You and the Amish girl are getting close." It was more a statement than a question.

"Hannah's not Amish."

"She grew up Amish, she'll always be Amish in her heart."

"Why do you say that?"

"Oh, I've seen plenty of young Amish people get caught up with *Englischers*. That's what they call us. They always go back to their community."

"Always?"

"From what I can see from my corner of the world." She took a long sip of her tea.

Hannah stepped onto the porch with her nieces. Hannah and Spencer locked gazes, and something zinged his heart. Oh, he was in deep. Mrs. Greene cleared her throat. He shifted his gaze to hers. "But what do I know. My corner of the world is pretty small."

He felt himself smile. Then he remembered the cinnamon buns and coffee. He got to his feet. "I brought you breakfast."

Hannah rested her hands on the backs of each girl's head. Emma smiled brightly whereas Sarah seemed shy, but not quite so angry anymore. "How nice of you. We were going into town. It's a beautiful morning."

Mrs. Greene stood and gathered her teacup and breakfast dish. "Please, all of you, sit and enjoy the porch. I have some chores to do."

"Don't let us chase you away," Hannah said.

Mrs. Greene waved as she was inclined to do. "I'll enjoy relaxing out here once I know my chores are done." Spencer held the screen door open for her.

He pulled out the napkins and put them in front of two spots at the small table tucked in the corner. Hannah took the coffee from him and inhaled deeply. "This is wonderful." He pulled out a roll with a napkin and handed it to her. "Thanks so much."

As they enjoyed their breakfast, a man dressed in a suit walked up the pathway. Everyone stopped eating and watched him. Spencer met him at the bottom of the steps.

Spencer crossed his arms and widened his stance. "Can I help you?"

The man's gaze shifted toward Hannah. "I'm looking for Miss Wittmer."

Hannah stood. "I'm Miss Wittmer."

The man stepped forward, his hand outstretched, then seemed to think better of it. "I'm Frank Jones, a lawyer with Jones and Jones." He tipped his head. "My father," he added, clarifying the second Jones, a question he must have been asked a lot.

"How can we help you, Mr. Jones?" Spencer shifted his stance to block Jones from advancing on Hannah.

"I have been retained by the Lapp family."

Hannah swiped the back of her hand across her forehead. "I don't understand. Why?"

"They plan to gain custody of their nieces." He reached into his pocket and consulted a piece of paper. "A Sarah and Emma Lapp."

Spencer felt a muscle working in his jaw. "Mr. Jones, as you can see, we're enjoying breakfast. Perhaps you can speak to Miss Wittmer—" he tipped his head toward the little girls "—at a more appropriate time."

"When would be a more…ah…appropriate time?"

Spencer dug into his back pocket and opened his wallet. He extracted a business card and handed it to Mr. Jones. "Contact me at this number, and we'll arrange an appointment."

A smug look settled on Mr. Jones's features. "Can't Miss Wittmer speak for herself?"

"You heard the sheriff. You need to go through him to get to me." Hannah stepped down onto the walkway. "And you can tell the Lapps that I will never hand over these girls. I'm surprised they would even employ a lawyer."

Mr. Jones straightened his tie and seemed to stand a little straighter. "I offered to represent them pro bono."

Spencer's eyebrows shot up. "You approached them?"

"Their ignorance of the law makes them ripe targets to be taken advantage of."

"By you?" Spencer couldn't hold back his retort. "No sense wasting an opportunity to get your name in the paper," he mumbled.

Mr. Jones lifted a thin eyebrow, never taking his gaze from Hannah's face. Spencer fisted his hand. "Here's my card." The lawyer reached into the inner pocket of his suit coat and offered her his card. "I'll be filing the paperwork this afternoon. I expect the judge to order you and the children not to leave town."

Hannah felt dizzy and her vision narrowed on the man's cheap suit and bad comb-over as he sauntered down the walkway.

"Can he do that?"

Spencer turned to the girls. "Emma and Sarah, Mrs. Greene has a great tree for climbing over there." He pointed to a low tree with thick branches sprouting from the earth like an octopus's tentacles. "Why don't you check it out?"

Emma bolted down the porch steps. Spencer turned to

Sarah. "Would you mind making sure your sister doesn't fall out of the tree?"

Sarah rolled her eyes. "You're sending us away so you can talk in private."

"You're right. We have grown-up things to figure out. Now go watch Emma. Thank you."

Sarah stuck out her lower lip. Her shoulders slumped and she stomped across the porch. Hannah let out a long sigh as she settled down on the wicker couch. "Ah… she'll fit into the English world, yet. And to think she's just a preteen." She shook her head.

Spencer sat across from her. Hannah watched Emma straddle a branch only five feet off the ground. Sarah leaned against the trunk and crossed her arms.

"I know nothing about raising kids in the Amish world, or in this one."

Spencer gave her a look of approval. "You didn't do too badly just now."

"What am I going to do?"

"You knew eventually the courts would have to get involved to decide guardianship for the girls…now that John's body has been found."

"I didn't think the Lapps would use the court system against me. They're going to fight me on this. It's not the Amish way." She placed her palms together and tucked them between her knees. "You were a lawyer once. How likely are they to gain custody?"

"I didn't practice family law. But I can contact someone in Buffalo who can help you." He reached over and patted her knee. "This Jones guy probably read about your brother-in-law's death in the paper and the circumstances surrounding your sister's death and thought he'd make a name for himself."

"I'm going to have to get a job and get the girls enrolled in school if I hope to stand a chance of gaining permanent custody. Classes start in a few days."

Spencer met her gaze. "Are you sure you want to do this?"

"Raise my sister's daughters?"

"Yes."

"Of course." She couldn't understand why Spencer was asking her this.

"You could give them to the Lapps. I'm sure they'd do well by them."

"My sister wanted me to make sure they were cared for."

"What if making sure they were cared for meant giving them to another family? An Amish family."

Hannah pressed the tips of her fingers to her lips. "I've thought a lot about it. The girls would be better off with me than with the Lapps." She thought back to how stern Fannie Mae had been with the girls. How rigid Lester seemed. Was there anything wrong with being strict? Good parents were strict.

"Sometimes when you do something because you think it's the right thing, you become resentful," he said.

"You know this from experience?"

"Exactly. I had so many people around me, demanding things from me. It was only after I took this job in Apple Creek that I finally felt like I was doing what I was meant to do."

"You are blessed." She closed her eyes briefly, then looked at Spencer. "Growing up Amish, you don't think as a kid about what you're supposed to do in life. You're expected to toe the line. Live life much as your parents did. You generally don't walk around wondering what you should do with your life to make you happy."

Spencer laughed. "Cuts down on a lot of the teenage angst."

Hannah couldn't help but laugh in response. "Not exactly. My father was always hard on me. Harder than he was on Ruthie. My mother recently told me why." She shrugged. "I don't want to betray my *mem*'s confidence, but growing up, feeling like I could do no right, makes me want to do the right thing for my nieces. I need to raise them." She threaded her fingers and squeezed. "I know with certainty that I need to raise these girls. I pray God gives me the wisdom to help them through the transition from farm life to—" she held up her hands "—to this life."

Spencer smiled brightly. "Looks like you have your answer."

Her eyes narrowed. "You baited me. You wanted to force me to realize what I wanted to do."

Smiling, he lifted his hands. "You got me. Now you can stop questioning yourself."

"Yes, it's time I stopped waffling."

"Will you stay in Apple Creek?" She thought she noticed a bit of eager anticipation in his voice.

"I want to be here for *Mem*. I can't leave her." Indecision weighed on her. "As it is, I feel horrible about leaving her alone on the farm." She rubbed her hand along the back of her neck. "My *mem* is a much stronger woman than I ever gave her credit for. She made sacrifices in the hopes of giving me a better life. Besides, I have to stay until Emma and Sarah's guardianship is resolved."

Spencer stood and leaned over, brushing a kiss on her warm forehead.

A little girl's laugh made her look up. Emma was covering her mouth, stifling a giggle. Spencer strolled over and ruffled Emma's hair. "What's so funny, little one?"

Emma spun around, her skirt billowing in a colorful cloud and she raced away from Spencer and joined her sister by the tree.

Later that day, Spencer drove Hannah and her nieces to the Lapp farm to visit Mrs. Wittmer. He had to go to the farm anyway to meet a fire investigator.

"I'll be out back." Spencer tipped his head toward the charred structure that once was the Lapps' barn. Chief Fire Investigator Carl Owen's truck was already parked alongside the barn. Spencer had called his old friend from Buffalo to help him pin down the cause of the fire.

"Okay." A faint smile played on Hannah's lips. "I'll take the girls in to see their granny."

Spencer cupped her elbow. "I can take you guys home whenever you want."

"Thank you." Hannah stretched and brushed a kiss on his cheek. "I don't know what I'd do without you."

Spencer was about to say something witty when Sarah called out impatiently, "Come on, Aunt Hannah." Emma ran ahead to her grandmother's door.

Hannah shrugged, a hint of embarrassment glistened in her eyes. She turned and followed her nieces inside.

Spencer strode across the yard to the barn. He stopped at the edge of the structure, not trusting that it would be sound. The smell of charred wood hung in the air.

"Ah, you made it." Carl came around the corner, a clipboard in his hand.

Spencer extended his hand. "Thanks for driving in from Buffalo. I appreciate it."

"What's all the fuss about a barn fire?" Carl gave him a who's-the-girl smile. "Don't tell me you've fallen for a nice Amish girl?"

Spencer laughed. "Does she look Amish?" He decided to be purposely vague. Most of his friends from Buffalo had razzed him when he told them he was moving to Apple Creek. Amish country.

"Not exactly," Carl had to admit.

Spencer tipped his chin toward the barn. "What did you find?"

"Patterns of an accelerant on the wood. The fire was set intentionally."

Spencer's shoulders tensed. "Not a case of someone tipping over a kerosene lamp?"

"Not unless the person shook the kerosene lamp before dropping it." Carl stepped inside the footprint of the barn and pointed to darker marks on the partial walls. "See, that's where the accelerant raced across the walls. Look around. A barn is ripe for a devastating fire." Carl tucked his pen in his shirt pocket. "Got some leads on this one?"

"Maybe." Samuel had claimed he saw John Lapp at the barn shortly before it went up in flames. However, a dead man wasn't able to give up secrets.

"The owner of the house had been out here asking questions. Before you got here."

Spencer narrowed his gaze.

Carl consulted something on his clipboard. "A guy named Lester Lapp."

"Hmm… He didn't take long to claim ownership."

"Claimed he was moving in and had stopped by to make a few repairs."

Spencer ran a hand along his jaw, considering something. "Want to take a ride with me? Give me fresh eyes on something?"

"Sure. I'll follow you in my truck."

Spencer drove over to the Fisher's home and parked along the road. The two men climbed the porch steps, their boots creaking on the planks. Through the screen door Rebecca could be heard pleading with someone.

He held up his hand to silence Carl who looked like he was about to make a crack about the Amish.

"Neh, neh…" Rebecca pleaded. "You cannot…"

Alarmed that a domestic situation was getting out of control, Spencer knocked loudly on the door. It grew quiet inside.

Too quiet.

"Mrs. Fisher, it's Sheriff Maxwell."

"Go away," she hollered.

"Is everything okay in there?"

A rustling sounded from inside the log home. He could hear hushed whispers from deep in the house. All his senses went on high alert.

"Mrs. Fisher, I need you to come to the door. *Now.*" Spencer pointed to the side of the house. Carl nodded and backed off the porch.

A second later, Rebecca appeared at the door, smoothing her hand along her bonnet. The panic and worry in her eyes had him searching the entryway behind her.

"Who were you talking to?"

Rebecca studied the hardwood floor at her feet.

"Is your husband home?"

The young woman's head snapped up, her eyes wide

with fear, definitely fear. "Oh, no. Willard's not home."
She glanced around Spencer, and her eyes landed on
Carl standing in the front yard. "My husband should be
home soon. You're only making things worse. Please
leave, he doesn't like to deal with outsiders."

"Why is that?" Spencer searched her face. "I find
most Amish to be quite chatty in town. Why is Willard
Fisher against fraternizing with his non-Amish neighbors?"

She stepped onto the porch, her eagerness to have
them gone radiating off her. "My husband will be home
soon."

"Then we'll wait." Spencer could feel his friend Carl
watching them.

"I'm going to take a walk around back," Carl said.

Spencer nodded briefly but didn't say anything.

"Sheriff Maxwell. You have only been kind to me
and my son, but I need you to leave. Willard—" she
shook her head "—Willard won't like that you're here."

"We can protect you if you're afraid of your husband."

Rebecca's lower lip began to quiver. "I don't need protection from my husband." Her tone was not convincing. Behind her in the house, her two younger children
watched with wide eyes.

Spencer lowered his voice so as not to scare the children. "Have you heard about a few of the elders having
their beards cut off in break-ins?"

Rebecca's eyes widened. "Of course. This is a small
town. Such a terrible thing." She made a tsking noise
with her mouth.

"Do you know anything about it?"

A deep line marred her forehead. *"Neh. Neh."* She
nudged his forearm directing him toward the steps.

Anger with a hint of apology flashed in her eyes. "You must go, *please*."

Spencer descended the steps. Carl appeared at the side of the house holding an angry Samuel by the forearm. "Is this who you were looking for?"

"Yeah." Spencer shot a sideways glance at Rebecca.

"He has done nothing wrong. *Please*."

"I only want to talk to him. Find out what he knows about the fire in the Lapps' barn."

Samuel's eyes grew bright. "I didn't..."

Rebecca ran down the steps, the fabric of her skirt flapping around her legs. "Samuel is a *gut* boy. He told you he saw John Lapp there. He knows nothing else."

"Let the boy talk," Spencer said, watching Samuel carefully. "You and your *mem* were arguing when we arrived. What about?"

"I'm leaving." Samuel pushed the dirt around with the toe of his boot, like he always seemed to do when confronted with authority.

"You can't leave." Rebecca's tone bordered on hysteria.

"I can't stay."

"Why not?" Spencer gestured to Carl to let the boy go.

Samuel yanked his arm away and narrowed his gaze at Carl. "I'm sick of this town."

"Samuel! You cannot leave the Amish faith."

"Why not? *Dat* did."

"He came back. He made a mistake. The world is filled with wicked things. You cannot ignore everything we've taught you."

Feeling the situation escalating, Spencer decided to take it down a notch. "Samuel, if you love your mother, you'll stay put. At least tonight. The morning often brings a brighter outlook."

Samuel twisted his mouth in indecision.

"How about this," Spencer reasoned. "Give it seven days. If you still want to leave, I'll drive you wherever you want to go."

Rebecca gasped.

"Would you rather he ran away on foot tonight? It will be dark soon."

Rebecca lifted a shaky hand to her mouth. "I don't want him to leave. Ever."

"You can't tell *Dat*. I can't stay if you're going to tell *Dat*."

Spencer turned to Rebecca. She bowed her head, but didn't say anything.

"I will keep your secret, Samuel, if you promise not to run away in the middle of the night."

Samuel adjusted his hat low on his forehead to hide his eyes. Something in Spencer's gut told him Samuel Fisher harbored more than one secret.

Chapter Twelve

"Mem, are you sure you're feeling okay? You look a little pale." Hannah's mother's seemingly frail health had her visiting again the next afternoon. Spencer had dropped her off and promised to return in an hour. Hannah plucked at her T-shirt as she sat in the rocker next to her mother near a woodstove pumping out excessive heat on the warm summer afternoon.

"I'm a little chilled, that's all." Her mother ran her hands up and down her thin arms.

"I feel bad leaving you here."

"It's a little quiet. But I understand Fannie Mae and Lester will be moving in soon." A look Hannah couldn't quite decipher swept across her features.

"I registered the girls for school this morning," Hannah said, eager to change the topic.

Her mother stared straight ahead. "At the public school in town?"

"Yes, and their new teachers gave them a few books to read. They're excited. They decided to stay home and read. Our landlady, Mrs. Greene, is keeping them company." Hannah omitted that she wanted to talk to her mother in private.

"I should be the one spending time with my granddaughters." Her mother pressed her fingers to her temple and winced.

"You could return to the wild days of your youth and move into the apartment with me." Hannah tried to lighten the mood.

Her mother raised her hands. "I wasn't baptized then. If I left now, I'd be shunned. As it is, I'm not sure the bishop will like you visiting me so often now that you've taken the girls away."

Anger warmed Hannah's cheeks, reminiscent of the days she'd been fuming over her father's strict discipline. "How many of your neighbors have stopped by since the fire? Since you've been left alone out here? The bishop has to understand I need to look in on you."

Her mother lifted her face, a look of surprise on her pale features. "Several of the neighbors have stopped by." She reached over and picked up her knitting project from the table next to her rocker.

Embarrassment replaced Hannah's anger. "I just assumed…"

"Have you forgotten what a tight-knit community Apple Creek is? My friends have been checking in on me." Her knitting needles clicked as her hands deftly worked the yarn. "They didn't come around as much when you were here, because they knew you were here."

"I should have known."

Her mother tipped her head, observing her as if for the first time since she arrived. "You have a lightness to your hair."

Hannah grabbed her ponytail and inspected it. "Oh, I

had highlights put in a while ago. They're mostly washed out."

"Is that expensive?"

Hannah laughed. "Probably more than I should have spent on a bank teller's salary."

Her mother smiled. "There is a big world out there, isn't there?"

"I wouldn't really know. Mine wasn't too big."

"When I met your father, your biological father, I imagined a world outside the farm for the first time. It was an exciting, heady time." A hint of a smile touched her lips. "Your father had a lot of dreams. He was in college studying to be an accountant. I thought it was interesting you had a job at a bank."

"I'm sorry I never met him."

Her mother fidgeted with the string of yarn, but stopped working the needles. "If he hadn't died, our life would have been completely different." Her mother's lips pressed into a thin line. "God works in mysterious ways. You were a blessing. I learned to be content with my life here. Eli spared me a life of shame." She put the knitting aside. "I hope you've had time to forgive Eli for being stern with you. Without him, I would have been lost. *We* would have been lost. I can't imagine my life as a single mom in a world that was mostly foreign to me."

"I do forgive him." The words sprang from Hannah's mouth. Yes, she did forgive him. It was rather freeing. How could she not forgive the man for allowing her sweet mother to return to the life she cherished?

"I hope you can forgive me, too."

"You've done nothing wrong, *Mem*."

"I should have intervened when it came to your father."

"*Mem*, that is not the Amish way. A wife defers to her husband."

Her mother bit her lower lip but didn't say anything.

Realizing her mother felt uncomfortable, Hannah smiled and asked, "Can I do anything for you while I'm here?"

"I ran out of strawberry jam. Can you get a jar out of the basement?"

"Absolutely." Hannah got to her feet.

She walked through the kitchen and opened the basement door. She descended the wood steps, remembering how terrified she was of these steps and the gaps between them when she was a kid. She hadn't even seen the horror movies that she had as an adult to instill such irrational fear.

She crossed the dirt floor of the basement to get to her mother's stored collection of jams and vegetables. For some inexplicable reason, the tiny hairs on her arms prickled to life. Dark shadows crept out from every corner and underneath the stairs. The two windows were mud caked, blocking natural light.

Hannah sucked in a deep breath and immediately regretted it when the musty scent filled her lungs. She grabbed a jar of jelly and ran up the stairs, taking them two at a time. She slammed the basement door shut, feeling a little silly for letting a few shadows get the best of her.

In the light of day, she looked at the label. Grape. "*Mem*, is grape okay?"

"I prefer strawberry. Am I out of strawberry?"

Hannah pushed back her shoulders. A little voice said, *The least you can do is get your mother some strawberry jam.*

"I'll check. I grabbed the wrong one."

"Take the flashlight from the kitchen drawer."

Hannah rustled through the drawer and found a flashlight. Feeling its heftiness in her hand, she opened the door and descended the stairs. She wasn't sure if the flashlight was a good or a bad thing. It illuminated only what was in its beam, leaving the rest of the basement in darker shadows as her eyes strained to adjust.

She found her mother's storage closet and pointed the flashlight at the line of jars. She found the strawberry jam.

Something tugged on her hair. Terror clawed at her throat. She couldn't move her head. Someone had her ponytail in his grasp. A scream died in her throat. She fought against his hold and brought up the flashlight to hit him. Metal crashed on bone. A deep groan whispered across her cheek. A ripping sound tore through the confined space. She was suddenly free. She pushed back and spun around. Dark shadows dipped and dodged. She stumbled forward and landed hard on one knee. The flashlight rolled out of her grip and the beam of light swept across a cobwebbed corner.

Her hair was gone.

"Who's there?" A knot formed in her throat. She slowly lifted the beam of her flashlight. Every nerve ending fired to life.

Footsteps pounded up the stairs. A door slammed.

Heart in her throat, Hannah scrambled to her feet and bolted up the stairs.

Her mother.

She turned the door handle, but it didn't budge. Her pulse whooshed in her ears. Hannah slammed her shoulder against the door and was rewarded with splintering pain that radiated through her shoulder and neck.

She pounded on the door, frantic. *"Mem! Mem!"*

Terror narrowed her throat. She closed her eyes briefly and sent up a silent prayer to protect her mother. Her poor, defenseless mother.

From somewhere in Hannah's mother's house Spencer heard a pounding. Without knocking, he rushed into the house. Mrs. Wittmer was moving things around, looking in drawers, in baskets, and on every flat surface. She was shaking, frail.

"What's going on?" The door at the end of the kitchen vibrated from pounding.

"Hannah's stuck in the basement. I can't imagine what happened to the key or how she got stuck down there."

"Are you okay?" Spencer hollered through the door, flattening his palm against the surface as if he could better connect with her.

"Yes. Yes. Open the door, please." Hannah's tone was desperate, panicked. She stopped pounding.

"Hold on." He jiggled the handle.

Mrs. Wittmer grew more agitated the longer she searched for the key.

"Do you have a screwdriver?"

"Mr. Wittmer has a toolbox—" she looked up slowly "—in the barn."

"It's okay." Spencer placed a reassuring hand on Mrs. Wittmer's shoulder. "I have a toolbox in my truck." He pulled out a chair at the table and encouraged Mrs. Wittmer to sit.

He tapped the door with his palm. "Hannah, I'll be right back. I need to get tools from the truck."

"Hurry, *please.*"

Was she crying? Maybe she was claustrophobic and overreacting to being trapped.

Spencer hustled out the door and returned a few minutes later with his toolbox. When he finally tapped out the bolt from the hinges, he pried the door open and leaned it against the wall. Hannah practically fell up the last stair. She dipped her head, resting her forehead on his broad chest. He gave her back a gentle rub. "Are you…?" The last word died on his lips. He threaded his fingers through her shorn locks. Anger burned his gut. Someone had cut off her ponytail.

He gripped her forearms and placed her at arm's length. "Who did this to you?"

"I don't know." She tugged the elastic out of her hair and it fell in uneven layers. "I slugged him with the flashlight."

He couldn't help but smile. "Good for you."

Spencer inspected the door frame. On the floor he noticed a narrow piece of wood. "He must have stuffed this piece of wood in the door frame to jam the door closed."

"Your hair?" her mother whispered. "Maybe it's the same man who's been attacking the elders. Cutting their beards."

John Lapp had been their primary focus in those cases.

But John was dead.

Maybe John hadn't been responsible for terrorizing Hannah.

Or maybe John hadn't worked alone.

"I didn't see his face." Hannah let out a long breath

between tight lips. "I need air." She pushed past Spencer and ran out the back door onto the porch. Spencer followed. She braced her arms on the railing and peered into the yard. "Where did he go?" she asked in a faraway voice. "Where did he go?"

"How do you know he went outside? I need to check the house."

"Go, check the house, but I heard the back door slam. My guess is he's long gone."

After checking the entire house and the house next door, Spencer returned and gave them the all clear. Hannah's mother had joined her on the porch.

"*Mem*, you can't stay here."

Hannah's mother shook her head. "This is my home."

Hannah held up a shorn lock. "Look what he did to me."

"God will protect me. I cannot live in your world."

Spencer felt like he was intruding on their conversation. He touched Hannah's shoulder. "Your mother is probably right. If the person you encountered in the basement wanted to hurt your mother, he could have done it at any time. *You* are the person he's targeting."

Chapter Thirteen

Emma raced up the stairs to the second-floor apartment ahead of Hannah. Emma bounced on the balls of her feet with impatience at the door, waiting for her aunt to unlock it.

"You had a good first day of school, huh?"

"It was awesome," Emma said, shifting from foot to foot. "They have a library, and I can take books home anytime I want. I have to remember to bring them back. I can't keep them forever."

Hannah slipped the key into the lock and heard the dead bolt click. "You know they have bathrooms at school?" She smiled at her niece.

"I was so excited to get on the bus to come home, I forgot." Emma shot past Hannah and disappeared into the apartment.

Hannah paused at the door, waiting for Sarah to climb the steps. Her older niece was harder to read. "How was your day?"

She shrugged.

"So, it wasn't so bad?"

"A girl told me I looked plain."

Hannah angled her head to study her niece. She reached out and dragged a strand of her niece's long hair through her fingers. "You are a beautiful girl."

Sarah scrunched her nose. Either her niece didn't believe her aunt, or she had been offended. The Amish were a humble people. Just because Hannah had moved Sarah out of Amish country didn't mean Sarah relinquished her modest sensibilities.

Sarah followed Hannah to the kitchen and tossed her backpack down on one of the stools.

"Do you think you could grow to like living here?" Hannah desperately wanted her niece to say, "Yes." Instead, all she got was another shrug.

Emma raced into the kitchen and hopped up on a stool.

"Did you wash your hands?"

Emma rolled her eyes. "Of course. I love the strawberry soap." She took a deep whiff of her hands. "Can I have a snack now?"

Hannah was grateful at least one of her nieces had adjusted readily. She grabbed a bag of baby carrots from the fridge and filled a small bowl. Emma happily chomped on a carrot, and Sarah picked one up and inspected it. Hannah leaned her elbows on the counter. "I love you guys."

Emma slipped off the stool and ran over to Hannah, wrapping an arm around her waist. "Love you, too, Aunt Hannah. And I really like your haircut." Hannah had had to go into town and get her hair cut and styled after the ponytail incident in her mother's basement.

"Thank you." She dragged her fingers through her hair, still unaccustomed to the short bob, but it felt freeing.

"Can I get one?" Emma smoothed her long ponytail over her shoulder and inspected the ends with crossed eyes.

Hannah laughed. "Sure, if you'd like." Her gaze drifted to Sarah. "Maybe we can take a few inches from your hair, too, Sarah."

Alarm flitted across Sarah's bright blue eyes.

"We don't have to," Hannah reassured her.

Sarah pressed her lips together, and her nose twitched. She sniffed. "I miss *Mem*."

"I miss her terribly, too. She was my little sister."

"Like me. I'm the little sister," Emma said, jubilantly.

"And your big sister will keep an eye on you."

"Yeah, if it wasn't for me—" Sarah sniffed a few times "— Emma would have left her backpack on the playground when it came time to board the bus."

"I left it by the school door. I wouldn't have left it behind," Emma said in a petulant tone.

"That's not where I found it. It was behind the tree near the front walk. You're not supposed to leave the playground."

"I didn't." Emma flared her nose and shook her head at her big sister.

"Stop arguing. Emma, you have to make sure you don't lose your things." Hannah couldn't afford to replace backpacks. She had a job interview with the credit union in town tomorrow. Hopefully her finances would turn around then. The few thousand dollars from the sale of her car wouldn't hold out forever.

Hannah scooped up the floral backpack Emma had picked out. She gravitated toward an explosion of colors now that she wasn't restricted to her plain clothing. Sarah's navy backpack sat next to her little sister's. Obviously, Sarah was going to take more time.

Hannah planted the bag on the stool and unzipped it. She pulled out Emma's take-home folder with its glossy cover of cute kittens, a staple of the elementary school set. She opened the folder, and her heart stuttered. An envelope with Hannah's name scratched in bold letters poked out from one of the pockets.

Relax. Perhaps the teacher had sent home a note.

Her pulse thumped in her ears. The jagged writing didn't resemble the neat, cursive handwriting of the teacher who had given Hannah a school-supply list last week.

Mouth growing dry, Hannah turned her back to the girls and slipped her finger under the flap of the envelope. Brown hair poked out of it. Nausea clawed at her throat. Emma was talking, but her voice sounded as if it were coming through a tunnel.

"One minute," Hannah said absentmindedly as she moved toward the window for better lighting. She pulled out a square piece of yellow paper with the words, "Go Home, *Englischer.*"

Hannah stuffed the paper back into the envelope with the hair—*her hair.* She cleared her throat and tried to keep her tone calm. "Sarah, help your sister get another snack. There's milk in the fridge and cookies in the pantry. I have to make a phone call." The walls of the small apartment grew closer, and a sheen of sweat slicked her palms as she fumbled for her cell phone in her purse.

Hannah was only vaguely aware of Sarah's complaining. Hannah stepped into the stairwell and dialed Spencer's cell phone. She knew he wasn't home.

He answered on one ring.

"The person who attacked me on the farm is at it again." She fingered the soft strands of hair. "He is not going to stop until I'm gone."

* * *

Happy to be home, Spencer strolled up the walkway and found Hannah standing behind the screen door.

"Hey."

"Hey."

"This creep is never going to stop, is he? I thought our problems were over when John died." Hannah's voice trembled. "Maybe I'm doing the wrong thing. Maybe I should let Lester and Fannie Mae raise the girls. Maybe then all this would stop. The girls would be safe."

Spencer climbed the porch steps, watching Hannah carefully. Fear radiated from her eyes. He opened the screen door and cupped Hannah's elbow. "You are not going to let this person chase you away."

For selfish reasons, he didn't want her to leave. But was the choice his?

With a shaky hand she offered him an envelope. He opened it and read the note and cursed under his breath. "Let me lock this in my truck."

When he returned to the porch, Hannah was sitting on the top step, slumped against the post. Her new short bob hung forward, hiding her face. He brushed his fingers across her knee and sat next to her.

Hannah looked up. Her eyes glistened in the late-afternoon sun. "I'm afraid."

A memory slammed into him. Another mom. Another time. Another family in jeopardy.

"I'm going to make sure nothing happens to you and the girls."

Spencer had made that promise before. He had promised fourteen-year-old Daniel's mother he would make sure the boy was safe. And he mistakenly thought that keeping him out of gangs would protect him. He hadn't counted on finding Daniel dead on the sidewalk outside the corner store. The milk he had purchased for his little brother slung in a plastic bag, its handles twisted around his wrist. All because he had worn the wrong color that day.

Some things were out of his control.

"How are you going to do that? You can't be with me and the girls all the time," she said, as if she were reading his mind.

No, no, he couldn't. Spencer wanted to stand and punch the post, but instead he drew in a deep breath through his nose.

Think rationally.

"Whoever is doing this wants you to leave Apple Creek. Who has a motive?"

Hannah flicked the ends of her hair. "Someone who is willing to lurk in my mother's basement and cut off my ponytail isn't exactly dealing with a full deck." She tucked her hands under her thighs and shuddered.

"Who would want you to leave?" Spencer repeated.

Hannah slowly lifted her eyes. "Fannie Mae and Lester Lapp?"

"You've all but given them the farm and the land they wanted," Spencer said, thinking out loud.

"They want the girls." All the blood rushed out of her face, leaving her deathly white. "But doesn't this seem too radical? It made more sense—if you can call it that—when we thought John was harassing me. Could both brothers be equally ruthless?"

Spencer rubbed the back of his neck. "I'll talk to Lester again."

Sitting on the porch step, Hannah leaned forward and covered her face with her hands. "I don't know how much more of this I can take." Her shoulders shook, then she stilled. She pulled her hands away and stared at him. "The person who chopped my hair is probably one of the men who cut the elders' beards. I can't see Lester being part of that group."

"Do we ever truly know what's in someone's heart?"

"What have you uncovered about this radical group?" Hannah stretched her legs in front of her and crossed her ankles.

"They left notes in the Amish homes where they cut the beards." Spencer shifted toward her, icy dread flowing through her veins.

Hannah drew her legs in and hugged her knees. "Notes?"

"The notes were cryptic. One in particular read, 'remove a wicked person from our midst.'" Spencer scratched his arm. "The Amish men who were attacked didn't want to talk, and other Amish men claimed the note might refer to the Amish custom of staying separate or apart from outsiders." He shrugged. "John Lapp had been one of our suspects, but he's dead."

Hannah let out a heavy sigh. "I called the school. No one saw anyone hanging around the playground at dismissal." She scratched the top of her head. "Perhaps whoever did this blended in."

"I'll look into it further." Careful to keep his expression void of emotion, Spencer said, "I have friends and family in Buffalo you and the girls can stay with until we catch this guy."

Spencer followed Hannah's gaze as she scanned the neighborhood. Across the street, an older gentleman took his garbage out and dumped it in a trash can at the side of his house. A few doors down a thin, wiry man cut the grass with a plug-in lawn mower.

Hannah met his gaze. "My harasser could be anyone, couldn't it?"

Spencer shook his head. "Not anyone. We have to look for someone who has a reason to want you to leave."

Hannah bit her lower lip. "What if it's Samuel, angry at me for getting him in trouble with his father?"

Spencer had considered Samuel, but ranked him low on the suspect list. "The tire-slashing incident occurred before you caught Samuel reading in the barn."

"What if my brother-in-law started to harass me and Samuel continued it?"

"He doesn't strike me as that kind of kid. But we should consider all possibilities."

"I like Samuel." She laughed, a mirthless sound. "I might be too naive, but I hate to think a nice young Amish boy would be set on revenge. That's not something I've seen a lot in the Amish community. They foster forgiveness."

"The Amish are human. They aren't perfect."

She threaded her fingers through her hair. "Tell me about it."

"What about his father, Willard Fisher?"

"He's strict, but again, that's not unusual in an Amish home." She lifted her eyes heavenward.

"I'll reach out to Rebecca, again." Spencer ran a few scenarios through his head.

"No, you can't put her in jeopardy. If Willard gets wind of this…"

Hannah's phone rang. Her brow creased. She reached into her pocket and pulled it out. "Hello." Her expression grew startled. "Yes. Okay. I'll be right there."

She ended the call and jumped to her feet.

"What's wrong?"

"*Mem.* She's in the hospital."

The hospital doors whirred open. "Are you sure Mrs. Greene doesn't mind keeping the girls again?" Hannah asked as they strode toward the hospital information desk. Her nerves were fried, and she was grateful Spencer was at her side when she had received the phone call from the hospital.

"Mrs. Greene loves the company. Don't worry, I told her to stay inside behind locked doors. I'll have a patrol drive by every thirty minutes." Spencer slowed, and Hannah glanced over at him; the compassion in his eyes touched her heart. "The girls will be safe. No one knows they are in Mrs. Greene's apartment."

A shudder skittered through her. *Please Lord, let them be safe.*

Spencer asked for her mother's hospital room information, and the volunteer at the information desk handed them two purple visitor passes, which they slapped on their T-shirts.

Hannah led the way into her mother's room. She came up short when she found Rebecca sitting in the corner of the room. Her bonnet and gown seemed in stark contrast to the modern room with the TV on the wall and the monitor mounted on a mobile stand next to her mother's bed.

Hannah's gaze shifted to her mother. Her eyes were closed, and her head hung at an awkward angle on the raised head of the hospital bed.

"Is she...?"

"She's sleeping. I don't know any more. The doctor was waiting for family to arrive."

"Did you find her?"

Rebecca nodded. "I brought her an apple pie. When no one answered, I went in. She was unconscious on the kitchen floor."

"She should have never been alone. I should have been there." Panic made her nauseous.

What was she going to do?

"I ran across to the English neighbors. They called an ambulance. I didn't know what else to do." A mix of fear and relief played across Rebecca's face. Hannah's poor, sweet friend.

Hannah touched her friend's arm. *"Denki."*

"You're welcome." Rebecca drew in a deep breath and let it out. "I should get home. Willard will be looking for his dinner. *Mem*'s minding the little ones." Rebecca gave Hannah a watery smile. "Please give your *mem* my best."

Rebecca stiffened when she hugged her. "Thank you again." Hannah gestured to Spencer. "Spencer could drive you home."

"I'd be happy to," Spencer said.

Rebecca shook her head. "I'll call a cab." She walked toward the door, her footsteps quiet on the tile floor. She slowed in the doorway and turned around. "I miss you. I wish you'd come home."

"I can't." The words got lodged in Hannah's throat. "Please forgive me, Rebecca, but I have to lead my own life. I'll make sure Sarah and Emma are raised in faith."

Rebecca's features grew pinched. "You have your *mem* to consider now."

The walls began to sway, and the room seemed suddenly very hot. "I have a lot to figure out." Hannah watched as Rebecca left the room.

Hannah pulled up a chair next to the bed and grabbed her mother's cold hand. She rubbed her thumb across the back of it. Forgetting Spencer was there, she closed her eyes and said a silent prayer.

Thank You for sending Rebecca to look in on Mem. Please make her well. She opened her eyes and found Spencer watching her. Fidgeting with the folds of the blankets, she lowered her gaze. *Please help me do what's best for my family. My entire family.*

The sound of the door opening drew her attention. A woman in a white lab coat with a stethoscope draped around her neck walked into the room. If Hannah hadn't been studying the woman's face, she might have missed the fleeting look of confusion.

Hannah pushed to her feet and extended her hand. "I'm Hannah Wittmer. This is my mother." Hannah gently squeezed her mother's hand, trying to explain the familial relationship.

"I'm Dr. Jennings." The slow cadence of her voice left a question floating in the air-conditioned room.

"I'm not Amish. My mother is."

The physician seemed to mentally shake herself. "Your mother's fortunate."

"Oh?"

"She had a grand-mal seizure. Well…she could have suffered more serious consequences if she had been driving a car or…" The doctor's voice trailed off. "I'm sorry. I realize the Amish don't drive cars. It's a good thing she wasn't alone."

Insert knife. Twist.

Hannah let out a shaky breath, not sure what to say.

"We're going to have to run more tests."

Hannah nodded. The tips of her fingers felt numb.

"When are you going to run the tests?" Spencer stepped forward.

"Tomorrow morning. I've scheduled a CT scan."

Hannah felt Spencer's firm hand on the small of her back as if to say, "I'm here. I'm not going to leave you."

Her mother squeezed her hand. Hannah leaned in. Her mother was awake. "How do you feel, *Mem*?"

"Gut." She struggled with the blankets and the IV in the back of her hand.

"Leave it be. You're in the hospital. Do you remember anything that happened?"

"One side of my mouth was droopy this morning." Her mother's words were garbled a bit, as if she were struggling to enunciate.

Hannah glanced at the physician, looking for reassurance. But her serious gaze made Hannah's heart stop. She didn't want to say any more for fear of scaring her mother.

"Mrs. Wittmer, I'm your physician. You had a seizure, and we'd like to do more tests in the morning to see what caused it."

Her mother swiped at the wires running into the back of her hand. *"Neh*, I want to go home."

Hannah placed a reassuring hand on her mother's arm. "Please, *Mem*." She searched her mother's eyes. "Consider it an adventure." She gave her mother a knowing smile.

Her mother gave her a tepid smile in return. "Some adventure." She relaxed into the pillow and closed her eyes.

"I've scheduled the CT scan for 8:00 a.m.," the physician said. "We'll know more then."

A knot tightened in Hannah's gut. Tomorrow they would know more.

Tomorrow.

Hannah couldn't shake the dread buzzing her nerve endings. She reached up and covered Spencer's hand on her shoulder. Without Spencer, she would have surely folded under the pressure.

Chapter Fourteen

The next morning, Emma held Spencer's hand. She was such an easygoing little kid. Meanwhile, Sarah lagged behind as they meandered the halls of the hospital from the cafeteria to the main lobby. Hannah sat in the corner, her head bowed and her cell phone pressed to her ear. Apparently sensing them, she glanced up and pulled the phone away from her ear. "Hey, there."

"You missed it." Spencer smiled, trying to lighten the mood. "They have the best French toast ever."

"Hmm…" Hannah said, a million miles away. He had seen that look before, the look of a woman trying to make a huge decision. He had seen it in Vicki's eyes before she told him she hadn't signed up to be the girl-friend of a cop.

Spencer shook away the thought. Now was not the time to be selfish. Mrs. Wittmer was currently having a CT scan, and Hannah was nervously awaiting the results. One of the nurses promised she'd come find them in the lobby after Hannah's mother returned from her scan.

Spencer plopped down in the chair next to Hannah

and covered her hand with his. "No matter what happens, I'll help you through this."

Hannah slowly shifted in her seat. Her knee brushed his. She scooted back; a weary smile crossed her lips. "Thanks for taking the girls to breakfast."

"My pleasure."

Hannah opened the bag next to her and pulled out a Laura Ingalls Wilder book. She stretched across and handed it to Sarah. "I think you'd enjoy this book. I picked it up in the hospital gift shop."

"*Dat* doesn't like us to read things without his approval." Sarah froze, and her eyes locked on her aunt's as if she had just realized what she said.

"Your mother and I loved this book when we were kids. Since you're missing school today, I think you should at least read." In light of the threatening note found in Emma's backpack, Spencer wanted to keep the girls close.

Sarah took the book and turned it over. She pushed back in her seat and opened the cover. The hope on Hannah's face pierced Spencer's heart. He had never met a stronger woman in his life.

He quietly said a prayer to give her continued strength to deal with whatever was about to unfold with her mother. The idea of praying caught him off guard.

Emma ran over to Hannah. "Do you have a book for me?"

"Of course." From her tote, Hannah produced an early reader with Cinderella on the front. Emma skipped over and plopped down next to her sister.

"Cinderella?" Spencer asked, a smirk tilting his lips.

"Too English?" She laughed. He loved the sound. "I didn't experience the world of Disney princesses until

after I left Apple Creek. My favorite was Cinderella."
She twisted her thin lips, and something flickered briefly
in her eyes. "But we all know fairy tales are just stories."

Spencer leaned in close and couldn't resist kissing
her soft cheek. Her shampoo smelled of strawberries.
"Maybe I have your glass slipper."

Hannah pulled back, a sad smile on her face. "There
are plenty of women who would be a better fit for the
slipper. For you."

Something twisted in his gut. He could feel her pulling away. Erecting a wall between them.

"Excuse me, Miss Wittmer." A woman dressed in
pale blue scrubs entered the waiting room.

Hannah's eyes radiated fear.

The young nurse clasped her hands and lifted them
to her chest. "Your mother is done with her CT scan."

Hannah slowly stood, clutching her hands in front of
her much like the nurse had done. "Is my mother okay?"

The nurse lowered her gaze, as if the diamond pattern on the worn blue carpet had suddenly become very
fascinating. Spencer's heart broke for Hannah.

"Dr. Jennings would like to talk with you in your
mother's hospital room."

Hannah turned slowly, her hand extended to her
nieces. "The girls."

"I'm sorry," the nurse said. "No one under sixteen is
allowed on the patient floors."

Spencer touched her back. "I'll stay with the girls."
He hated that he couldn't go upstairs with her.

Hannah nodded slowly. She kissed Sarah and Emma
on top of their heads, the action so deliberate, he sensed
she was savoring each moment, as if she knew her world
was about to be turned upside down.

* * *

Hannah was quiet on the drive to the apartment. It had taken all of her energy to collect the girls from the lobby and make it home without crumbling. Even now that she was home, she was struggling to stay composed.

Thankfully, Spencer read the situation and didn't ask her any questions. Before he disappeared into his apartment across the hall, she had asked him to come back after she had put the girls to bed. She needed to talk to someone, to figure things out, or she feared she'd explode.

As she made mac and cheese for the girls, she forced herself to focus on the moment. Boil water, pour in noodles, stir.

Don't think about Mem.

"Is dinner almost ready? I'm hungry." Emma climbed up on the stool and rested her elbows on the counter.

Hannah reached across and squeezed her small hand. "Almost."

Across the small apartment, Sarah was curled up in the corner chair with her nose in her *Little House on the Prairie* book. Maybe Sarah was more like Hannah than she had thought.

A knock on the door brought Sarah's head up. Hannah smiled. "Let me get that." She crossed the room and rose onto her tiptoes and looked through the peephole.

Spencer.

Hannah unlocked the door and opened it. "Hey, there." His friendly smile was like a warm embrace. He was light to her darkness.

"You're early."

"Looks like I'm just in time."

Hannah glanced over her shoulder at the steam rising over the small pot on the stove. "It's only mac and cheese."

"Sounds good."

Hannah laughed. "Whatever floats your boat. I'll put out another plate."

The four of them enjoyed a quiet dinner. Afterward, the girls retired to their rooms to read. When Hannah came back out, Spencer had already cleared the dinner dishes.

"You're a keeper." As soon as the words came out of her mouth she wished she could call them back. She blinked a few times and took a step back.

He tipped his head but didn't say anything. He had an unnerving way of studying her. He led her to the couch and pulled her down next to him. "Tell me about your mom."

Immediately, tears burned the backs of her eyes, and a thick knot lodged in her throat. She let out a long, slow breath. Spencer ran his thumb across the back of her hand.

She pressed her lips together as if that would stop the tears. One escaped and trailed down her cheek. Spencer cupped her cheek and wiped the tear with his thumb. She leaned into his palm, reveling in its warmth. Comfort.

She reached up and wrapped her fingers around his wrist. "You really are a good guy."

"What's on your mind?" His voice was low and husky.

She bowed her head and studied her lap. She couldn't keep it together and look him in the eyes. "The CT scan revealed—" she cleared her throat "—my *mem* has a brain tumor."

Spencer brushed a kiss across her forehead and pulled her head against his chest. "I'm sorry."

She drew in a deep breath. He smelled clean, a mixture of soap and a subtle aftershave. She tried to clear her mind, her panic.

After taking a minute to pull herself together, she straightened her back. "They're going to release *Mem* tomorrow. She refuses additional treatment."

Spencer's brow furrowed. "What did the physician say?"

"Dr. Jennings said she wanted to refer my mother to a specialist. She figured they'd want to operate and then follow it up with radiation and chemotherapy. She couldn't say for sure until the specialist reviewed my *mem*'s case."

"Your mother refused?"

"She wants to go home and live in peace."

"What about the seizures?"

"The doctor said she could manage the seizures and pain with medication." Hannah traced a seam in the couch cushion and when she looked up, she met a look of sympathy in Spencer's eyes that was nearly her undoing. "I can't force her to have surgery and undergo radiation. I can't."

"Maybe she'll change her mind."

"I don't think she will."

Spencer rubbed her forearm. "What does this mean?"

"I have to go back. For my mother."

"You're going back? What do you mean?" Spencer was unable to hide the disappointment from his tone.

Hannah tipped her head, purposely avoiding his eyes. "I have to take care of my mother."

"Bring your mother here." His plea was more out of selfishness than practicality.

"I need to do everything I can to make her feel comfortable. If she came here, I'm afraid she'd be shunned." She shrugged and tucked a strand of hair behind her ear. "She's a good Amish woman. I don't want to cause her any more undue stress at this time."

"How…?" He wanted to ask her how she planned to return to the Amish community after her grand exit, but he could see from the look on her face that she had no idea. Yet she was determined to do it.

After sitting for a few minutes with her head in her hands, she stood and paced. "I can't force Lester and Fannie Mae to leave the house." She rubbed her forehead unable to smooth the worry lines. "Maybe…" She fidgeted with the ends of her new short, *English* haircut. It was hard to imagine her as the Amish woman he had greeted on the porch of her childhood home not that long ago. So different than the woman standing in front of him.

He stood and pulled her hand in his. "How can I help?"

"You don't think I'm crazy?" The pain in her eyes pierced his heart.

He dragged his knuckles across her cheek. "You wouldn't be the woman I've come to know, if you didn't take care of your mother when she needed you."

Hannah fell into his embrace and stayed there, longer than he expected. He memorized every detail of the fleeting moment.

Hannah pulled back and looked him in the eye. "What about the girls? I can't confuse them like this. One minute they're Amish, then English, then Amish again." She held him tighter. The frustration rolled off her in waves.

He wanted to ask, *What about me? What about us?* That wasn't important now.

"I'll have to make sure you're secure on the farm." The horrible memory of burning wood filled his nose. "Do you think my moving in with you and your mom would be frowned upon?" Humor tilted his lips.

Hannah patted his arm. "I'm sorry, Spencer. I haven't been fair to you. You're a really good guy."

"I feel a but coming on." He let out a long breath.

Hannah sat on the arm of the couch. "My mother gave up her dreams for me." The intensity in her expression told Spencer there was more to that comment than she was letting on.

Spencer sat on the corner of the coffee table and waited for her to continue her story.

"I don't want to betray my mother's confidence, but I know I can trust you." Hannah relayed the story of how her mother had run away with her English boyfriend and returned to the Amish community after she found herself pregnant and alone. "My *mem* was afraid, but she firmly believed she was doing the best thing for me. She had no way of knowing what waited for her in the outside world once my father died, so she retreated to the familiarity of the Amish. She did that for me."

"But your Amish father didn't treat you well."

"My mother had no way of knowing that would be the case. Her decisions were made with my best interests at heart." Hannah slid off the arm of the couch and slouched into the deep cushions. "I owe my mother this much. I need to let her live the last days of her life in her home."

"I'll go back."

Spencer pivoted around the corner of the coffee table.

Sarah stood in her pink pj's looking very much like any other nine-year-old girl. The only thing that hinted at her Amish-ness was her hair, tightly pleated in a braid down her back.

Hannah scooted to the edge of the cushion, but didn't stand, perhaps afraid of spooking Sarah. "I thought you were starting to like school."

Sarah's lips twitched. "I want to be with Granny."

"Did you hear us talking…about Grandma?"

Sarah's face crumbled. She rushed over to Hannah and fell into her arms. Hannah closed her eyes, and a tear slipped down her cheek. Spencer looked away.

"Do you think Emma will be okay with going back?"

Sarah nodded without lifting her head. "She's little. She'll be okay as long as she's with you."

"Thank you, sweetie." Hannah patted Sarah's back. "Thank you." On the second thank-you she met and locked eyes with Spencer. He knew how much Sarah's words of support meant to Hannah. And just how much he'd miss living across the hall from this little family.

Chapter Fifteen

Hannah grabbed her mother's elbow, bony under her touch. It seemed she had lost a few pounds since going into the hospital three days ago. Dr. Jennings had worked wonders in allowing her mother to stay in the hospital long enough to work out her prescription doses. Hannah glanced over her shoulder while Sarah and Emma scooted out of Spencer's truck dressed in their bright-colored skirts and graphic T-shirts.

Butterflies flitted in her stomach. It was a surreal feeling, almost like she was sneaking back into her childhood home, much as she had sneaked out all those years ago.

"Girls, I'm going to get Granny settled, then we'll change our clothes. The bishop is going to stop by." Hannah glanced toward the main house, wondering if Fannie Mae or Lester had moved in yet. An empty space of charred earth marked the spot where the barn had stood. She had heard rumors in town that they were going to have a barn raising in a few weeks, well before the bad weather rolled in.

"Watch the step, *Mem*." Hannah tightened her grip

on her mother's arm, stretching out to open the door. A staleness from being closed up for a few days rolled out and greeted them.

Spencer and the girls followed them into the home. She wondered how they'd all live in the small space. Urgency made her mind race. The bishop was supposed to be here before sundown, and she didn't want to cause her mother any more stress. Her Amish clothes were stored away in a chest in the main house. Her mother's discharge had taken longer than expected, and it was late.

Hannah guided her mother to a rocking chair. "How do you feel, *Mem*?"

Her mother's stiff carriage relaxed. "I'm home."

"Maybe you should lie down."

Her mother made a face. "I'm not going to crawl into bed and wait to die."

A crushing weight pressed on Hannah's chest. The walls closed in on her. She opened a window and breathed in the fresh country air. She grabbed a pink bandanna out of her back pocket and wrapped it around her head, holding her hair off her face. Could she do this? Could she return to her Amish roots, for her mother this time?

A knocking sounded on the door. Hannah's heartbeat thudded in her ears. Reflexively she tugged at the hem of her T-shirt. She hadn't had time to change yet.

She watched in slow motion as Spencer opened the door. Lester and Fannie Mae Lapp entered the small space, followed by the bishop. Fannie Mae had an almost hopeful expression on her face.

"You're here already," Hannah said, unable to hide her annoyance.

"We said we'd stop by," Lester said, his steely gaze

firmly locked on Hannah. "Fannie Mae and I are living next door now, and my father came by to wish your mother well."

"*Gut* to see you're home, Mrs. Wittmer." The bishop ignored the terse exchange and limped into the small space, leaning heavily on his cane. "How are you feeling?"

"No more fuss. I'm fine." Her mother reached over to grab her knitting, but left it sitting on the table as if even that took too much effort.

Emma and Sarah hung back in the doorway between the sitting room and kitchen. Perhaps they were hiding their English wardrobe from the bishop. Perhaps Hannah should have changed the girls into their dresses before they left the apartment.

Perhaps she'd been trying to delay the inevitable.

Fannie Mae silently gestured to her husband with her eyes. Lester tipped his head toward Hannah. "You've decided to stay?"

Hannah nodded curtly. "We just arrived. We haven't had time to change our clothing."

"Returning to the Amish community means more than wearing plain clothing." The bishop stared at her, his expression hard to read.

"Can we talk outside?" Hannah asked.

The group filed outside. The girls stayed inside to keep their grandmother company.

Hannah was keenly aware of Spencer's presence. She wondered how long he could hang around before he drew the ire of the Amish community.

Hannah took a deep breath and sent up a quick prayer, seeking guidance. "I'll be honest. I *am* struggling with my decision."

"It's not fair to drag my brother's daughters back and forth. They need stability." A muscle ticked in Lester's jaw.

"I'm stuck in a very difficult situation." She swallowed hard as a tingling bit at her fingertips. "My mother is very ill." The words, *She's dying* froze on her lips.

"I need to be here for her."

A very calm expression came over the bishop's face. "*Gott* works in amazing ways. This is what needed to happen to bring you home."

"I pray I'm doing the best thing for my sister's daughters." Hannah shot a sideways look at Lester. Had God truly intended her mother's illness to be the inciting event to force her back to the ways of the Amish for good? Her heart was conflicted. God had a plan, but could she claim to know it? She had to trust Him.

"The *dawdy haus* is small. The girls can sleep in their old bedroom." Fannie Mae spoke for the first time.

"That's a great idea," Lester agreed.

A nervous knot twisted in Hannah's stomach. The girls were slipping out of her grasp.

"That might be best," the bishop added. "And you'll stay close to your *mem*."

Hannah felt like she had no choice. She'd have to make some concessions if they'd allow her to live among the Amish and care for her mother.

The bishop turned to leave. "Hannah, slow down and be in the moment. I think *Gott* brought you back here for a reason." He took a few more steps and turned back around. "We'll see you at service next week."

Hannah nodded, relieved to have that confrontation behind her. The bishop climbed into the wagon and flicked the reins. The horse took off at an easy trot.

Aware of Lester and Fannie Mae's gazes, Hannah pushed open the door to her mother's home. "Emma, Sarah, come here, please."

The girls appeared in the doorway. Emma smiled and greeted her aunt and uncle. Sarah, as always, was more reserved. Hannah placed her hands on the girls' backs. "How would you two like to sleep in your old bed?"

"I don't want to go to bed yet," Emma complained.

Hannah tapped her back. "Not yet. Later."

Sarah looked up, worry in her eyes, a look that threw Hannah off balance. "Where will you sleep?"

Hannah raised her palm to the room where her mother sat. "Here with Granny. I'll be right here," she added for reassurance.

Fannie Mae held out her arms and each girl took a hand. "Come now. Let's get some proper clothes on and fix your hair." She tugged at one of Emma's curls, a playful tug.

Hannah watched the girls walk away, and her heart broke into a million pieces.

Lester followed his wife, leaving only Spencer and Hannah to watch the last bit of sun dip below the horizon. "Are you okay?" Spencer asked, his voice smooth and comforting.

"I'm grateful I'm here for my mom. Please thank Mrs. Greene again for being so understanding that we broke our lease."

"Don't worry. Focus on your mother."

Hannah nodded, exhaustion making her eyelids scratchy.

"Go. Rest. I'll make sure I have patrols check the property every hour."

"Isn't that overkill?" A chill skittered up her spine.

Who was she kidding? All indications were that someone was still after her.

Hannah and Spencer stood looking at one another.
The setting sun cast his handsome face in a beautiful
glow. Something she didn't dare explore squeezed her
heart. Shaking her head to break the spell, she stepped
back and looked down and waved her hand up and down
her jean-and-T-shirt-clad body. "I'd better change into
Amish Hannah."

He smiled. A sad smile. "Hey, Hannah."

She turned back around slowly. "Yeah."

"I don't know if you can trust Lester. Please be careful."

Hannah's eyes grew wide. "Do you think the girls
are in danger?"

Spencer shook his head. "You seem to be the primary target."

Target.

She hated the harsh sound of that word. She let out a
long sigh. "I have to be here for my mother."

"I know." He sounded resigned.

"For my mother's benefit and out of respect for the
Amish community, I have to put my heart into this."

"Your mother needs you." What he didn't say lingered between them.

"Yes, she does." It was time for her to be selfless for
her mother, like her mother had been for her.

"I'll make sure you're safe." Something in his eyes
told her he needed to keep her safe for reasons all his
own.

Spencer climbed the steps of Mrs. Greene's porch,
tired, hungry and ready to flop on his couch and forget

about the past few days. He had asked the two officers on duty tonight to alternate checking on Hannah at the Lapp farm every hour. He had also convinced Hannah to keep her cell phone close by.

She promised she'd secure the locks at night.

He opened the door and stepped inside the foyer. It smelled like garlic. *At least some things go on as normal.* Mrs. Greene had dinner on the stove.

He smiled when he heard her shuffling footsteps, then the rattling of the doorknob. He suspected she watched all the comings and goings from the recliner positioned near the large window overlooking the yard.

The door opened slowly, and Mrs. Greene peered up at him, her eyes wise from years of experience. "I half expected her to be with you. Didn't think she'd really do it." There was no need to clarify who *she* was.

"Her mother's sick." His heart was heavy, far heavier than it should have been for a woman he had met on the job. Who was he kidding? It had become far more than just a job.

"She's a good daughter, then." Mrs. Greene let her comment hang out there. She was good at eliciting conversation from him even when he didn't feel like talking.

"She's doing what she feels is right."

"And you?" Despite her five-foot stature, she leveled a gaze at him that commanded his attention.

"I liked it better when she was here so I could keep an eye on her."

Mrs. Greene lifted a suspicious eyebrow. "Is that the only reason?"

"I'm afraid you've gotten to know me well, Mrs. Greene." He mirrored her raised eyebrows.

"I raised three sons."

Spencer let out a long breath. "I don't begrudge Hannah for being there for her mother." Even if it meant they couldn't be together.

And his conscience couldn't have him hoping her mother would die soon.

As if reading her mind, Mrs. Greene asked, "How is Mrs. Wittmer?"

"As well as can be expected. She's refusing any major medical intervention. She only agreed to drugs to control the seizures and the pain."

Mrs. Greene patted his cheek. "You'll be fine, my dear boy. You'll be fine. A handsome man like you will meet some nice young woman." She pressed her index finger to her mouth. "My friend Mildred has a granddaughter..."

Spencer waved her off and laughed. "Cut a guy a break."

"Cut yourself one, too."

"Night, Mrs. Greene."

Mrs. Greene held up a hang-on-a-minute finger. She pivoted in her slippers, her colorful housecoat a sight to see, and scooted into her apartment. She returned a minute later with a covered dish. "I figured you didn't have a chance to eat dinner. I made you my meat loaf."

He smiled. "I love your meat loaf."

"I know." She crossed her arms, a smug expression on her face.

That night, Hannah made sure her mother was comfortable with tea and her knitting next to her rocker. Her mother wasn't quite ready for bed and wanted to sit up for a bit.

Hannah, still dressed in her English clothes, planned

to collect some of Ruthie's Amish clothes from the main house and while there, check on Emma and Sarah. Hannah hated to let the girls out of her sight, but it only made sense to allow them to sleep in their old house.

Hannah stepped outside, and the sound of crickets filled the night air. The rich smell of earth reached her nose. There was something very comforting, soothing, nostalgic about the country life. A comfort she had never found in the city.

Most of her life, Hannah felt like she had been caught between two worlds. Never quite fitting in either.

Out by the street, a police cruiser slowed down. She knew it wasn't Spencer's. He had told her he had the rest of the night off. She waved, and the officer flicked his headlights in acknowledgement.

Hope pushed out her anxiety. Maybe whoever was so determined to bother her would back off once he thought she had committed to returning to the Amish faith. Unless, of course, his motive was to have her gone. *Period.* She stifled a shiver.

Hannah raced up the few steps to her sister's home, now Fannie Mae and Lester's. She knocked, feeling a little foolish since this has been her home not long ago. Lester pulled open the door as if he had been waiting for her. His mouth compressed, and his eyes narrowed just a fraction.

"I need to get clothes." Hannah wanted to diffuse the situation before it got volatile.

He stepped away from the door and kept on walking. Hannah didn't see Fannie Mae, so she entered the house and went directly upstairs. In her sister's old room, Hannah grabbed a few dresses from the trunk where she had stored them. For half a minute, she considered changing into the dress, then realized that would be silly. It was almost time to get ready for bed. She didn't want to create more laundry for herself. She swiped at her jeans and decided she wouldn't risk hanging them out on the line. She couldn't afford to replace more clothes.

But you won't need your English clothes anymore.

She rubbed the back of her neck, praying God would guide her toward the right path.

Hannah hustled out of her sister's old bedroom, feeling like an interloper now that Lester and Fannie Mae were living there. Sleeping there. Across the hall she found Sarah reading to Emma. Hannah's heart expanded when she realized it was the *Little House on the Prairie* book she had given Sarah. She stood in the doorway for a few minutes, taking in the scene, not wanting to disturb them. They both had long pajama dresses on, reminiscent of those she had seen the actress Melissa Gilbert wearing in the old TV show adapted from the books.

The thought that she'd have to show the girls that program left as quickly as it came. Sarah and Emma wouldn't be watching TV anytime soon, if ever.

Was that such a bad thing?

Emma was the first to notice her aunt standing in the doorway. She scooted off the bed and ran over to Hannah and wrapped her arms around her aunt's waist. "Are you going to stay here?"

Hannah placed the clothes down on the chair near the door. Tears pricked the back of her eyes. She flicked her thumb toward the *dawdy haus.* "I'll stay with Granny."

"I'm glad she's not sick anymore." Clearly, Emma assumed her grandmother's homecoming meant she was all better. She gave Emma a little squeeze. Sarah looked up from her book for the first time.

"Everything okay?" Hannah asked.

Sarah shrugged.

Hannah guided Emma over to the bed. Hannah sat next to Sarah and pulled Emma onto her lap. "Are you not happy here?"

Sarah scratched her hair, where her bun met the back of her neck. "I liked school."

"You can go to school."

Sarah shyly shook her head. "I liked my new school."

Hannah's heart thundered in her ears. She suddenly felt guilty. Poor Sarah and Emma were unwitting pawns in her indecisive life.

Hannah cleared her throat. "Right now, you can't go to Apple Creek Elementary." She bit her bottom lip, wondering if there was any way she could make arrangements. It was impossible, given the circumstances.

Sarah slumped into her pillow. "Mrs. Gallivan said I'm good at math."

"I have an idea. Why don't I talk to your old teacher and get the assignments and we can work at home together."

"Really?"

"Really."

Sarah's entire face transformed from glum to hopeful with one little word.

"I like math, too," Emma said, resting her head on Hannah's shoulder.

"I can help you with math, too."

"Girls, I think it's time for bed." Lester appeared in the doorway, looking stern. Hannah almost jumped out of her skin. How long had he been standing there?

"Did you brush your teeth?" Hannah forced a smile, trying to ease the nerves clawing at her throat.

Both girls nodded.

"Then I guess you're ready for bed." Hannah took the book from Sarah's lap and set it on the nightstand. She stood, and Emma climbed into the warm spot next to her sister. "Night girls. See you in the morning."

"Night, Aunt Hannah," they said in unison, using the English word *aunt* and not *aenti* as they had when she first arrived.

Hannah gave them one last tuck and a kiss on the forehead. She scooped the dresses up from the chair and brushed past Lester, whose anger was rolling off him in waves.

Smiling smugly, as if she had won a small battle today, Hannah descended the steps. As she was coming down, Fannie Mae hustled up. "Are you ready for bed, girls?"

Hannah stopped on the steps. "They're all set."

Fannie Mae gave her a sidelong glance and kept climbing the stairs. Hannah reached the door and stepped outside onto the porch. The cool air felt good on her fiery cheeks. Gloating from her one small win had been fleeting.

Hannah drew in and released several deep breaths, hoping to calm her emotions. She felt like she was losing everything that was important to her. The door opened behind her. Hannah swiped away at her tears and squared her shoulders. The heavy footsteps told her it was Lester. Her heart dropped. He approached and eyed her English clothes and the bundle of Amish clothing in her arms.

He took off his straw hat and rubbed his head. "Fannie Mae and I would love those girls as our own."

"I… I…" Hannah's mouth went dry, and she couldn't form the words.

"My father believes your mother's illness has brought you back again. To fully commit to the Amish way." He leaned in close. He smelled of hay and horse and apple butter. "*Yah*, well, I don't think that's your plan."

Their gazes locked. She made a conscious decision not to lie to him.

She had done enough lying to herself.

Hannah rolled over for what seemed to be the hundredth time on the tiny cot she had set up in the sitting room of her mother's small home. She tugged on the quilt and covered her shoulder, unable to get comfortable. She held her breath and listened intently for any sign her mother was in distress. She resisted the urge to get up and go into her room. Last time she had, her mother said, "I'm not dead. Yet." The droll tone was very uncharacteristic of her mother.

The physician had rattled off all the potential effects of a growing tumor as it pressed on the brain. Hannah suspected she was trying to frighten her mother into agreeing to treatment. But you can't frighten a woman who has her faith, and a woman who is more afraid of the treatment than the effects of not treating it.

Resigned that sleep wasn't coming anytime soon, Hannah swung her feet over the edge of the cot and sat up. The cool evening air touched her skin, sending a chill skittering down her spine. Wrapping the quilt around her shoulders, she stood. As if lured by worry, she found herself lurking in her mother's doorway. Her mother rolled over and tugged at her sheet.

Regret for all the years she had been estranged from

her family weighed heavily on her. All the years she had missed.

A creak on the front porch made her breath hitch in her throat.

Creak.

Hot tingles swept across her scalp. Clutching the quilt closer to her shoulders, she moved silently through the small home. She slid open the drawer in the hutch and pulled out her cell phone. The reality of how vulnerable she was out here on the farm struck her. Even if she dialed Spencer's number, how fast could he get here?

She heard a quiet knock and a voice, "Aunt Hannah?"

Hannah dropped the phone on the doily her grandmother had made and ran to the door. She undid the bolt and flung the door open.

"Sarah?" Confusion swirled in her head. Deep in the house, she heard her mother cough then grow quiet. Hannah stepped out onto the porch and pulled the door over, leaving it ajar so she could hear her mother.

"It's late. What are you doing here?"

Sarah lifted and dropped her shoulders. Perhaps she had lost her nerve for whatever had brought her out into the night.

Hannah guided Sarah to the steps and they sat. Staring into the dark yard, Hannah waited. Out by the street, a lamppost lit a small sphere of country road. Finally, Sarah shifted to face her. "I'm sorry for being grumpy."

Hannah smiled. She remembered her mother using that expression anytime Hannah or her sister Ruthie was in a bad mood. It was such a pleasant way of saying they had been downright intolerable. Ruthie must have repeated the expression to her daughters.

Hannah took a chance and reached out and wrapped

her arm around her niece's shoulder. Sarah leaned her head on Hannah's shoulder, and Hannah's heart expanded. "You've lost a lot, sweetie. You don't have to apologize to me."

Sarah looked up. Tears glistened under the moonlight. "I don't want to lose you, Aunt Hannah."

"Oh, sweetie, you're not going to lose me."

"*Mem* always told me what a great sister you were. She told me and Emma we needed to always look out for each other."

A band tightened around Hannah's lungs making it hard to catch a breath. Had she been there for her sister?

"I wasn't always the best big sister. I wish I could have been there for your *mem* when she really needed me."

Sarah swiped at a tear. "*Mem* always spoke fondly of you."

"You seem wise for a little girl."

"I'm not so little."

"You're young enough that you shouldn't have had to deal with so many adult problems."

"I promise I'll be nicer to Emma."

Hannah swatted at a mosquito. "Are your worries keeping you awake?"

Sarah's voice got very tiny. "I thought if I was nice to you it meant finally accepting that *Mem* was…" She bowed her head and her shoulders shook.

Hannah pulled her closer. "I'll never replace your *mem*. No one can. But I'll try to be the best aunt ever."

Sarah sucked in a shaky breath. "When you leave, I want to go with you."

Hannah pulled back to look into Sarah's eyes. "Why do you think I'm going to leave?"

"I heard Uncle Lester talking to Aunt Fannie Mae. He said that Emma and me would be staying with them."

Hot anger pulsed through Hannah's veins. Footsteps crunched on the dried bent grass. Pinpricks of apprehension coursed across Hannah's skin. She reached up and grabbed the handrail, rising to her feet even as her knees felt weak. She scanned the yard.

Maybe it was an animal.

Hannah was about to urge Sarah to go inside, when a deep voice boomed from the shadows.

"What are you doing out of bed, Sarah?"

The anger in Lester's voice vibrated through Hannah. It slammed her back to another time. Her father's harsh reprimand. Followed by his firm hand. Hannah squared her shoulders. "Sarah was feeling unsettled—"

"Of course she feels unsettled. You've pulled her away from the only home she's ever known. She should have stayed here. Where she belongs."

Sweat slicked her palms. Suddenly, she felt very exposed. Alone. Defenseless.

Her phone was inside the house on the hutch.

Hannah leaned down and whispered into Sarah's ear, "Go inside. Lock the door. My cell phone is on the table. Call Spencer."

The word *why* formed on Sarah's lips when Lester exploded. "Stop corrupting the child."

Sarah got to her feet and sprinted inside, but the door yawned open. She willed the child to close and lock it.

Hannah's raspy breaths sounded in her ears.

She moved behind the railing on the porch, and thankfully, Lester didn't advance on her.

He lifted his beefy hand and pointed at the door. "Sarah needs to come home with me where she belongs."

Hannah shook her head. "She belongs with me."

A second man emerged from the shadows. Hannah froze, wide-eyed. The man's arms came around fast and furious. He brought a board down on Lester's head before Hannah could get a scream across her dry lips.

Lester went down in a silent heap, not knowing what hit him.

"She belongs among us." Willard Fisher's angry snarl registered under the moonlight. Fear rained down on her, hot and tingly. Hannah spun around to get inside. Lock the door.

Willard dove, and his hand wrapped around her ankles and she landed with an *oomph* on the porch, the air rushing out of her lungs. She opened her mouth to warn Sarah, to tell her to close the door, lock the door, but she couldn't catch a breath.

Willard yanked her by the ankles. Her body thumped down the stairs. Her ribs. Her elbow. Her hip.

Hannah violently shook and twisted her body, trying to free her ankles from Willard's brutal grasp. She thought she heard a mischievous laugh as he dragged her around the side of the house into the darkness.

Chapter Sixteen

Spencer pulled into the Lapps' dirt driveway, his head-lights arcing across the darkened home. The memory of Sarah's frantic sobs over the phone rang in his ears. *Hannah's in trouble.* A trail of sweat ran between his shoulder blades. He pushed open his door and aimed the flashlight around the yard. The beam of light hit on a prone form.

For an instant, his heart stuttered, then his brain kicked in. It wasn't Hannah. It was a man, an Amish man. Walking toward the body, he swept the flashlight around the yard.

No one else in sight.

Aware of his surroundings, he crouched. Lester Lapp lay unconscious with his nose mashed into the dirt. Spencer pressed his fingers to Lester's neck. His pulse was steady.

Had Hannah knocked out Lester? His pulse ticked up a notch. What if she hadn't?

He strained to listen for sounds of distress. Nothing but crickets.

The headlights from his vehicle stretched to the front

porch. The front door was open, and a little girl stepped out. He had to squint to realize it was Sarah.

"Stay on the porch." He held up his hand and scanned the area. The adrenaline surge heightened all his senses. The scene was different, but the feelings were the same. Little Daniel had died under his watch. Someone had called dispatch from the convenience store. Gangs had gathered in front of the store. By the time he got there, Daniel was dead. An innocent victim.

Spencer blinked back his mounting anxiety. He wasn't going to let anyone else die.

Spencer moved to the porch and ushered Sarah inside and locked the door behind them. He canvassed the small space. Empty save for Mrs. Wittmer sleeping in her bed.

Back in the sitting area, he crouched in front of Sarah. "Where's Hannah?"

Every inch of her small frame trembled.

"You're safe now. Tell me what happened."

Sarah relayed a story about missing Hannah and then her uncle yelling at her and Hannah got afraid and told her to call him.

That didn't explain Lester unconscious on the lawn. "Did Hannah and Lester fight?"

Spencer's nerves hummed as he pried answers out of the frightened girl.

"I heard angry voices. I didn't see. I hid inside. I'm sorry." Sarah buried her face in her hands and sobbed.

Spencer nodded, trying to maintain his composure. "I'm going to find Hannah. I want you to lock this door behind me. Do you know how to do that?"

Sarah shook her head. Spencer took pains to show Sarah how to work the lock. He stepped onto the porch and listened to Sarah fasten the lock. He tested the door.

"Stay inside until I come get you. Don't open this door for anyone except me."

Sarah didn't answer, but he was sure she heard him through the thin door. A thin door that wouldn't hold back anyone determined to get in. But he feared the person who had been here already had the person he wanted.

Spencer cast the beam of the flashlight around the yard, and that's when he saw it: a pink bandanna had been discarded at the corner of the house. Heart beating loudly in his ears, he strode toward the bandanna. Hannah had had one in her hair earlier.

When he reached the corner of the house, he saw nothing but grass stretching toward the neighbor's cornfields. His heart sank.

Hannah could be anywhere.

"If you scream, I'll make it worse. I'll go back into that house and make that disobedient child remember the rules," Willard growled as he lumbered across the yard, dragging Hannah by one ankle.

Hannah bit back a gasp. Willard's strong fingers dug into her flesh. The more she fought and thrashed about, the more pain shot up her legs and thighs.

Panic and fear clouded her brain. Her back and arms bounced off the uneven earth. Her body flipped and she braced her fists against the earth to protect her head, her face.

Dear Lord, help me. Help me...

Tears burned the backs of her eyes, and she drew in a deep breath. Willard dragged her into the cornfields. Stalks whacked her arms, and she squeezed her eyes shut against the assault.

No one will find me out here. Please Lord, spare me. Don't take me away from Sarah and Emma. Please...

Willard stopped and in one quick swoop, pressed his knee into her back, crushing the air from her lungs. He leaned in close and whispered in her ear, "You couldn't just leave. *Neh*, you had to force your worldly ways on all of us. You are no better than your sister."

Hannah briefly closed her eyes and fought the wave of grief that washed over her. She focused instead on the pain radiating out from where his knee pressed into her spine, channeling it into survival mode.

Willard forced her cheek into the earth. The smell of dried corn and manure plugged her nose. She bit back nausea.

"John couldn't control her. Ruth needed to be obedient to him."

Hannah strained to watch Willard out of the corner of her eye. He was watching something, searching. Was someone coming?

"So you killed them? You killed Ruthie...and John?"

Willard pushed her head deeper into the damp earth. Something in her neck cracked. "I did what was necessary to preserve the Amish way. I've lived in the outside world. It's an evil place. The Amish must be ruthless in preserving their quality of life. They must be separate. John had been on my side, but when Ruthie started questioning him, John was weak. He softened his stance. I couldn't allow her to destroy our plans. To destroy the Amish way of life."

Willard's weight and her panic pressed on her chest. "Is murder the Amish way?"

"Shut up."

"You wrote the note making it look like John had committed suicide?" She spit out a chunk of dirt.

"*Yah*. Yet you still wouldn't leave. I thought once you knew John wasn't coming back, you'd hand the children over to a good Amish home." Willard roughly dragged his fingers through her short hair. "A woman's hair is her glory. You…" He seemed to lose his train of thought, pushing harder on her back. Hannah sucked in shallow breaths as tiny stars danced in her line of vision.

"You corrupted my son. You corrupted your nieces. Your death is one small sacrifice to make things right."

"No…no." Hannah's brain whirled, but she couldn't form the words, the words to plead for her life.

"But Lester…" She couldn't think straight.

"Lester never saw what hit him. Even he couldn't make his brother see the light." He laughed, a mirthless sound. "The brothers came to blows in town when John got the foolish idea to leave the farm for other work. What fools."

"The sheriff—"

"The sheriff's office is incompetent. It took them ten years to solve Mary Miller's disappearance, remember that?"

The delight in his words made her blood run cold. "Don't underestimate Sheriff Maxwell. He'll find you."

Willard leaned in close. "Some things are worth the sacrifice." Stale breath washed over her and made her gag.

Willard shifted his weight, and Hannah rolled, just far enough to fall out of the cornfield and onto the open field. She filled her lungs with fresh air.

Willard lunged for her, his features contorted in anger. She rolled again and scrambled to her feet. He grabbed her by her hair and yanked. "You're not getting away."

"No!" The word ripped from her throat.

The beam of Spencer's flashlight landed on Hannah as she furiously tried to wiggle free from Willard Fisher's grasp.

Tightening his hold on his gun, Spencer bolted across the yard. Willard spun Hannah around and wrapped an arm around her neck. "Easy, *Englischer*."

Spencer leveled his gun at Willard's head. "Let her go." Spencer bit out the words, his breath coming in jagged rasps.

"You wouldn't shoot an Amish man, would you? Think of all your hard work to mend bridges between law enforcement and the Amish."

Hannah yanked on Willard's arm stretched across her chest. Willard flipped out a pocketknife and pressed it against her neck.

"Drop it."

"I'll stick her like a pig." Willard's gleeful expression twisted Spencer's gut. His finger twitched on the trigger.

"Dat, neh!" Samuel ran up to Spencer. "Stop!"

"Get back, son," Spencer said, not taking his eyes from Willard.

Samuel stood his ground. "No. Stop."

The lines around Willard's lips grew pinched, agitated. "Go home."

"No. I will not let you hurt Hannah. She's done nothing wrong."

"Her ways are poison. Poison to the Amish ways. Poison to *you*."

Samuel shook his head, a maturity about him Spencer had never noticed before. "You have become poison."

Willard's face twitched, a mix of grief and rage. His hand loosened around the knife. Spencer took the opening and slammed Willard's shoulder, knocking him away from Hannah. The knife flew from his grip and landed in the field.

Spencer pushed Willard facedown into the earth and handcuffed him. Spencer dragged him to his feet. Willard rearranged his features into one of smugness.

Hannah stood apart from them, rubbing her neck. Spencer wanted to do nothing more than take her into his arms. Thank God she was safe. But for now, he had to take Willard in to the station.

"He killed Ruth and John." Hannah's tone was one of anger and grief.

"No one will believe you." Willard narrowed his gaze.

"He made me destroy your clothes on the line," Samuel said, pacing pack and forth. "He made me give Emma and Sarah the cat." He drew in a ragged breath and glared at his father. "He *made me* tell them bad things would happen to their kitty if they said anything—" his voice grew quiet "—but he...he burned down the barn. He wanted to punish me for reading in the loft. To punish you, Miss Wittmer. I don't know what else he's done. But he's been obsessed with running you out of town, and he tried to force me to help him. He made me lie and tell you I saw John Lapp out by the barn before it went up in flames." Samuel bowed his head briefly. "After I ruined your clothes, the guilt was terrible." The young man sniffed, and his shoulders shook.

"Shut up," Willard spat out. "You're a fence jumper, just like the worthless rest of them."

"Like you, *Dat*. You left…" Samuel's stern tone belied his trembling lips. "I wish you never came back."

A siren grew closer. Spencer pushed Willard in handcuffs toward the driveway. Willard's chest heaved from unspent anger.

Hannah brushed her hand across Spencer's forearm. "I'll go check on Sarah and my mom." Spencer nodded.

Deputy Sheriff Mark Reynolds's cruiser bounced up the driveway. Spencer squinted against the glare of the headlights. Mark climbed out, a smirk on his lips. "Looks like you got this one all wrapped up yourself."

Spencer handed off Willard. "Take care of him. And make sure Lester Lapp receives medical attention."

"Stupid fool got in my way. He can't have much more than a big lump and a headache." Willard shook his head, a look of disgust on his face. "I couldn't let Lester see what I was about to do. Wrong place, wrong time."

"Thanks," Spencer said wryly. "We can add additional assault charges to the long list. Take him," he said to the officer. "I've got something else to handle."

Mark pushed Willard roughly toward the cruiser. "Wait," Spencer called out. "How did you get the note in Emma's backpack?"

Willard narrowed his gaze. "Don't you want to know if I chopped off her hair first?"

"No, I know you did that because you put the lock of hair with the note in Emma's bag." Spencer studied the man's face in the moonlight. Willard seemed more angry than anything else.

"It wasn't hard to grab her backpack after she tossed it down when she ran off to the playground. It took two seconds to stuff the envelope in her bag then drop it behind a tree as I strolled away. No one seemed to notice me. Even if they had, they'd only remember seeing an Amish man, not me specifically." Willard blinked slowly.

Spencer gestured with his chin toward the car. "Now you can take him away." Spencer watched as Mark stuffed Willard into the backseat of the cruiser. All the tough guy seemed to have drained out of him.

Spencer turned around and cupped Samuel's shoulder. "You did well, kid."

Hannah came back outside and made her way across the lawn holding Sarah's hand. "My mother's still sleeping," she said. "The EMT is tending to Lester. He's conscious, but he's got a wallop of a headache. He's refusing to go to the hospital."

"I'll make sure he goes," Spencer said.

Hannah nodded.

Samuel's features grew pinched, a faraway look in his eyes. "I hate my *dat*. I hate everything he represents." He lifted his gaze to Hannah. "I'm sorry." He held out his hand to Sarah. The young girl leaned her head against Hannah's side. "I'm sorry I scared you. I would never hurt you or your cat."

"It's okay," Sarah said in a soft voice. "I never saw anyone do anything bad. I never had to keep a secret."

"Eventually, you will have to find a way to forgive yourself. To forgive your father. To free yourself from the burden." Hannah's tone was full of understanding.

Samuel nodded, clearly not convinced.

"I can drive you home, Samuel," Spencer offered. "Your statement can wait until tomorrow.

"I need to clear my head. I'll walk home."

"I'd feel better if I drove you."

Samuel shook his head. "The evil is gone. I'll be fine."

Spencer and Hannah stood in silence as Samuel walked across the field, his shoulders slumped with a burden no son should carry.

Sarah looked up. "May I go inside with Granny?"

"Of course." Hannah kissed her niece's forehead, and they watched her run into the house.

Spencer pulled Hannah into an embrace. "I don't ever want to lose you again." She pulled back and looked up at him; something flashed across her eyes. A band around his heart squeezed. "I suppose we'll have to figure out this Amish thing."

Hannah laughed, a beautiful sound. "I don't suppose you'll be converting anytime soon." She patted his cheek and laughed even louder. "Oh, you should see the look on your face." She rested her forehead against his shoulder.

"I love you, Hannah Wittmer."

He held his breath as the silence stretched between them.

Finally, finally, Hannah lifted her head. A slow smile spread across her face. "I love you, too."

Epilogue

Four months later...

Hannah wrapped the scarf around her neck and hustled down the porch steps to wait for the school bus. Winter had hunkered down for the long haul in sleepy little Apple Creek, New York.

The squealing of the bus brakes signaled its approach before she saw its big yellow body rounding the corner. She waved at the bus driver, indicating the new stop. It was the girls' first day back at the public school.

The bus doors slid open with a whoosh, and Emma appeared in the doorway, looking happy and cute as pie in her matching Hello Kitty hat, scarf and gloves. She hopped off the bus and Hannah planted a kiss on her niece's cool cheek.

"How was your first day back?"

"My teacher told me I knew just as much as the other kids." Emma dropped her backpack on the snowy walkway, and Hannah picked it up. "You did a good job teaching us at home."

Hannah's heart expanded at Emma's cheery report.

She shifted her gaze toward the bus. Sarah was chatting animatedly to a girl in the front seat. Then she bounded down the stairs. "I met a friend who lives down the street. Do you think we can have a playdate?"

Tears burned the back of Hannah's eyes. Happy tears. "Of course." She didn't bother asking her older niece if she had a good day. It was abundantly clear that she had.

A gust of snow whipped up and drifted under Hannah's collar. "Let's get inside. I'll make us some hot chocolate."

The girls ran ahead and greeted Mrs. Greene in the foyer as they passed.

"Take your boots off," Hannah hollered up the stairs as she closed the door behind her.

Mrs. Greene held out a plate. "Here are some chocolate chip cookies to go with that hot chocolate."

"You're spoiling us," Hannah said, gratitude filling her heart.

"I can't take credit. Your friend Rebecca dropped them off."

Hannah tugged at her scarf. "Rebecca?" Hannah hadn't spoken with her friend since the day after her husband, Willard, was arrested. Back then, Rebecca had been hurt and angry and had turned her childhood friend away.

"Your friend has such beautiful skin." Mrs. Greene lifted her hand to her wrinkled cheek and then seemed to mentally shake herself. "She said she was sorry and she hoped to see you soon. She seems like such a dear girl."

Hannah drew in a deep breath and smiled. "That's very good news. I'll have to take a drive to visit her." Through the Apple Creek grapevine, she had heard Rebecca was faring surprisingly well. Perhaps she found peace in being out from under Willard's oppressive thumb now that he was in jail, most likely for the rest of his life.

Mrs. Greene looked at Hannah thoughtfully. "I'm *so* happy to have you back. The girls fill my quiet home with laughter. It's a blessing." Mrs. Greene fidgeted with the edge of her apron. "I'm sorry I wasn't able to do more for you and your mother when she was ill."

"My mother and I had plenty of support from her Amish friends." Hannah smiled at the bittersweet memory of her mother's last days. Although the brain tumor had zapped her strength, it hadn't diminished her faith. And mother and daughter had grown especially close in those last few months.

Hannah hesitated a minute then glanced up the stairs. "Would you like to join us for our afternoon snack?"

"Oh, no." Mrs. Greene waved in dismissal. "You're busy."

A stomping sounded on the porch. Through the sheers on the door, she saw Spencer in his sheriff's uniform. She pulled open the door, a wide smile on her face. "Fancy meeting you here."

He kissed her on the forehead with cold lips, warming her heart. "I wanted to see how the girls made out their first day back at school."

"Great! Come on up, I promised them hot chocolate." Hannah turned to go upstairs while Spencer closed the door behind him. "Can I talk to you first?"

Mrs. Greene's eyebrows shot up. "Why don't I keep the girls company while you chat?"

Hannah smiled, pleased Mrs. Greene had gotten over her reluctance to join them. "That would be wonderful." Hannah handed over the chocolate chip cookies.

After Mrs. Greene went into Hannah's apartment, Hannah turned to Spencer. "It's really snowy out there."

He tipped his head and gave her a look, a look that said, *We're not going to talk about the weather, are we?*

"How are you doing?" The sincerity in Spencer's voice warmed her heart.

"Better. I miss my mom, but I know she's in a better place."

Spencer nodded. He reached out and held her hand. "She was blessed to have you."

"And I was blessed to have her." She bowed her head; a tear fell unbidden down her cheek.

He dragged his knuckles tenderly across her cheek. "I hope your mother didn't mind my visits. I did the best to respect the Amish ways."

"My mom really liked you. I'm glad she got to know you." She leaned into his hand.

"What's not to like?" A light twinkled in his eyes.

"We never spoke of it, but my mother and I came to an understanding. She's at peace with my decision to leave the Amish. She knows my faith is strong. She knows I'll do what's best for the girls."

"I'm happy for you." He paused long enough for her to wonder what was on his mind. "I have good news."

Hannah's heart raced. She swallowed hard. "About the girls?"

"Yes." Half his mouth quirked into a grin. "I ran into that lawyer Jones in town. He told me the Lapps weren't going to fight for custody of Emma and Sarah."

"Really?" she said on a huge breath of relief.

"That's what he said. I'm sure you'll have to sign a few legal forms. The lawyer seemed surprised the Amish don't like to deal with the court system. I suppose if

Jones knew that, he would have never approached them in the first place."

"I'm sure that was part of it," Hannah said, brushing a dusting of snow from Spencer's shoulder, "but I also want to believe the Lapps came to realize over the past few months how much I love the girls. And that they're happy with me."

"I'm happy with you." The intensity in his gaze tangled nerves in her belly. "You have brought so much into my life. I finally feel I have found my purpose. God's purpose for my life. I can't thank you enough."

Hannah drew in a shaky breath and watched him through blurry eyes. "Thank *you* for being patient with me."

"You're worth the wait." Spencer leaned in and pressed his lips to hers. He deepened the kiss, sending tingles of awareness coursing through her body.

"Are you going to be my new dad?" Emma appeared at the top of the stairs. She had already dropped the Amish *dat* for dad.

Hannah and Spencer pulled away. Embarrassment added to the heat of the kiss.

Sarah appeared and put her hands on her little sister's shoulders. "*Are* you going to be our new dad?"

Kids adjust easily, her mother had said during the final days of her life. Her mother had given her lots of pearls of wisdom that kept popping into her head now that she was gone.

"Girls!" Hannah playfully scolded.

"Would you like that?" Spencer asked the girls and squeezed Hannah's hand.

They both nodded eagerly.

Hannah turned to look at Spencer. Hesitation flashed

across his features, and for one horrifying moment, Hannah thought Spencer looked like a deer caught in the headlights. A slow smile transformed his face. He unzipped his coat and reached into his inside coat pocket. Her pulse thrummed in her ears.

Spencer pulled out a small black box, and Hannah almost passed out with surprise. Her vision tunneled onto his handsome face.

He dropped to one knee right there on the slushy-wet foyer carpet. He popped open the box, revealing a solitaire diamond engagement ring.

"Will you marry me, Hannah Wittmer?"

Lifting her free hand to her mouth, she nodded. Tears flooded her eyes.

"What did she say?" Mrs. Greene asked from the top landing.

Hannah and Spencer laughed in unison.

"Yes," Hannah said while he pulled himself to his feet. "Yes, yes, yes… I'll marry you."

Spencer slipped the ring onto her finger and lifted her hand to his lips. "I love you."

The thudding of little feet racing down the stairs broke the trance. Hannah and Spencer held out their arms and pulled the girls into their embrace.

"Well, if this ain't better than the afternoon soaps, I don't know what is." Mrs. Greene held up a finger. "I hear the kettle. Time to celebrate with some hot chocolate."

Spencer and Hannah climbed the stairs to her upstairs apartment, his arm wrapped around her. The little girls ran ahead.

"I never thought I could be this happy," Hannah said, thinking about all the failed attempts to fit in throughout her life.

"I know what you mean."

When they entered her apartment, Hannah stopped and turned to face him. "Where will we live once we get married? Your apartment or mine?"

Without a moment's hesitation, as if he had been considering this a long time already, he said, "I had my eye on a little hobby farm in Apple Creek. If you want, we can take a drive out tomorrow to look at it."

Excitement bubbled in her chest. "You've given this some thought."

"Yes, and I've also given something else some thought."

Hannah jerked back her head, confused.

Spencer dramatically placed an index finger on his lips. "I bet two little girls would like a kitty for our new home."

Emma's eyes grew wide. "Yes!" She hugged him around the waist.

Spencer placed his hand on Emma's back. "I talked to Rebecca yesterday. She told me Pumpkin would be much happier with you and Sarah."

Sarah dropped the cookie she had picked up and ran over and hugged both Emma and Spencer. Hannah's heart melted all over again.

"Thank you," Hannah mouthed to her future husband.

A warm smile played on his lips.

Hannah approached her little family and placed her arm around her future husband.

"Now, who am I going to fuss over if you four move out?" Mrs. Greene's lips twisted into an I-don't-know-what-I'll-do smirk.

"Why do we think you'll be just fine?" Spencer

winked at the older woman who had become like a grandmother to him. "Besides, we're not moving far."

Mrs. Greene blushed and a mischievous grin lit her face. "You got a good one here, Hannah. Good thing I'm not a few years younger." She hustled to the stove and lifted the kettle from the burner. "Who wants whipped cream in their hot chocolate?"

Emma and Sarah ran over to the island and sat down. Spencer wrapped his arm around Hannah's shoulders. A feeling of contentedness settled over her like a warm shawl on a snowy afternoon. She turned and whispered to Spencer, "I finally feel like I belong."

"Me, too," Spencer said. "Me, too."

* * * * *

Love Inspired®

Save $1.00

off the purchase of any
**Love Inspired®,
Love Inspired® Suspense** or
Love Inspired® Historical book.

Available wherever books are sold, including
most bookstores, supermarkets, drugstores
and discount stores.

Save $1.00

on the purchase of any Love Inspired®, Love Inspired® Suspense
or Love Inspired® Historical book.

Coupon valid until May 31, 2016. Redeemable at participating retail outlets in the
U.S. and Canada only. Limit one coupon per customer.

52613513

Canadian Retailers: Harlequin Enterprises Limited will pay the face value of
this coupon plus 10.25¢ if submitted by customer for this product only. Any
other use constitutes fraud. Coupon is nonassignable. Void if taxed, prohibited
or restricted by law. Consumer must pay any government taxes. Void if copied.
Inmar Promotional Services ("IPS") customers submit coupons and proof of
sales to Harlequin Enterprises Limited, P.O. Box 3000, Saint John, NB E2L 4L3,
Canada. Non-IPS retailer—for reimbursement submit coupons and proof of
sales directly to Harlequin Enterprises Limited, Retail Marketing Department,
225 Duncan Mill Rd., Don Mills, ON M3B 3K9, Canada.

5 65373 00076 2   (8100)0 12144

U.S. Retailers: Harlequin Enterprises
Limited will pay the face value of
this coupon plus 8¢ if submitted by
customer for this product only. Any
other use constitutes fraud. Coupon is
nonassignable. Void if taxed, prohibited
or restricted by law. Consumer must pay
any government taxes. Void if copied.
For reimbursement submit coupons
and proof of sales directly to Harlequin
Enterprises Limited, P.O. Box 880478,
El Paso, TX 88588-0478, U.S.A. Cash
value 1/100 cents.

® and ™ are trademarks owned and used by the trademark owner and/or its licensee.

© 2016 Harlequin Enterprises Limited

LIINCICOUP2

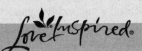
"It looks delicious," a male voice murmured in her ear.

"Eli!" she gasped and turned, her heart beating wildly. "You startled me."

His eyes twinkled. "I couldn't resist taking a look."

"And now you want a piece," she guessed.

His handsome mouth curved into a grin. *"Ja."*

"I shouldn't give you one, but…" She sighed dramatically, but she was pleased that he was eager to try it.

Eli looked delighted. "Then I may have a piece now?"

Martha chuckled as she picked up the cake and carried it into the other room. "One. You may have one slice." She sliced a piece, set it on a plate and gave it to him.

"Danki," he whispered, beaming. He dipped his fork into the cake, brought it to his lips.

Martha couldn't seem to take her eyes off him. "I should have brought two cakes."

"Eli? Are you coming outside?" a young voice called into the house.

Eli continued to eat his cake. "That was delicious," he declared after he'd eaten his last bite.

LIEXP0316

"I'm glad you enjoyed it," she said.

"I wouldn't mind a second helping, but I won't ask," he added quickly when he saw her disapproval.

"*Gut*," she replied, trying hard not to be charmed by his smile.

"I should go." He paused to study her a long moment. "*Danki* for the cake."

"You're welcome."

Martha continued to feel his gaze on her as she crossed the yard to join the other women who had gathered on the back lawn.

She knew the exact moment when Eli had rejoined his friends. The girlish laughter grated in her ears. Martha frowned. Why would she care who he spent his time with?

Suddenly, Eli locked gazes with her. A small teasing smile played about his lips, making her heart race.

You can bring chocolate cake anytime, he mouthed. Martha looked away.

She had to admit that Eli was both handsome and kind, and if she'd been younger, never married and had never suffered a broken heart, she might have felt differently. Like the giggling girls, she might have welcomed the man's attention. But she wasn't young and she wasn't looking for another husband.

Twice men had disappointed her. She wouldn't allow one to disappoint her a third time. Especially a man like Elijah Lapp.

Don't miss
ELIJAH AND THE WIDOW by Rebecca Kertz,
available April 2016 wherever
Love Inspired® books and ebooks are sold.

www.LoveInspired.com